Josephine Moon

The Jam Queens

MICHAEL JOSEPH
an imprint of
PENGUIN BOOKS

MICHAEL JOSEPH

UK | USA | Canada | Ireland | Australia
India | New Zealand | South Africa | China

Michael Joseph is part of the Penguin Random House group of companies whose addresses can be found at global.penguinrandomhouse.com

Penguin Random House Australia

First published by Michael Joseph in 2021

Cover photography by Shaiith/Shutterstock (biscuits), Nataša Mandić/Stocksy (jam), Tegan T/Shutterstock (flowers)
Cover design by Louisa Maggio © Penguin Random House Australia Pty Ltd
Author photograph by Anastasia Kariofyllidis
Typeset in 12/16.5 pt Minion Pro by Midland Typesetters, Australia

Printed and bound in Australia by Griffin Press, part of Ovato, an accredited ISO AS/NZS 14001 Environmental Management Systems printer

NATIONAL LIBRARY OF AUSTRALIA

A catalogue record for this book is available from the National Library of Australia

ISBN 978 0 14379 203 1

penguin.com.au

FSC www.fsc.org MIX Paper from responsible sources FSC® C009448

For Clara, at last,
for the words, the humour,
and all-round ninja brilliance

1

Aggie unfolded the piece of paper and lifted it onto the tip of her forefinger. She balanced it there, marvelling that something lighter than a tiny finch could carry such a heavy burden. For all the pain the words on the page inflicted, they may as well have been carved into steel bars and chained to her body.

Five choices, one impossible decision.

In a sudden burst of anger, she screwed up the paper into a ball and threw it across her small kitchen, where it bounced off the freestanding stove and fell to the floorboards. There it paused, stretching its wings and growing in size once more, refusing to be silenced.

She would have to speak to Gideon.

She retrieved the letter and flattened it to check the details. They still had time, about a month, which wasn't much, but enough that right now she could pretend this moment hadn't arrived.

Shoving it into her colourfully embroidered leather handbag, she returned to the task at hand, which was to make a new batch of strawberry jam, preparing as she was for the Royal Adelaide Show in a couple of months' time. The berries were out of season here in the valley, where the best local strawberries wouldn't be ready until November at least. These ones had been sourced from Queensland, which provided strawberries for the southern states over winter.

She had just pulled out her digital scales to weigh the fruit as she washed, dried and hulled them, when her mobile phone rang.

She checked the screen. It wasn't Holly, as she thought it might have been, and nor was it Savannah, calling from the cafe with some sort of business issue Aggie would need to sort out. It wasn't a number she recognised but it was local, so she answered it.

'Is this Agatha Hermann?' a woman asked, gravely enough to indicate that she was not an enthusiastic telemarketer. This woman had something important to say.

Aggie's gaze flicked to her handbag, in which today's surprise letter was buried, wondering if this call was connected. 'Yes,' she replied, automatically moving to a seat. A cold winter's draught slipped around the side of the kitchen door and she pulled her indigo cardigan tighter at her waist.

'My name is Ingrid, I'm a senior nurse at Angaston Hospital.'

'Is it Holly? Is she hurt?' Aggie had visions of her daughter being struck down by a car on a desolate road while out walking.

'Holly?' The woman was momentarily thrown. 'No. It's Valeria.'

'*Mum?*'

'Yes. She has you listed as her next of kin.'

This was surprising. At a frantic pace, Aggie's mind sought to pull these pieces together. Her mother was turning seventy this year, so a call from a hospital wasn't implausible. The part that was surprising was that her mother had asked for Aggie.

'But we haven't spoken in three months,' Aggie blurted.

Ingrid paused, then cleared her throat. 'Well, she's called for you now. Your mother has had a TIA.'

'What's that?'

'A transient ischaemic attack, otherwise known as a ministroke.'

Aggie felt herself draw in a puff of air that didn't make it all the way down into her lungs. 'Is she . . . okay?'

'She is stable for now, though during the event she also broke her wrist. Look, are you able to come in? She'll need someone to take her home and stay with her overnight.'

'Yes, of course,' Aggie said, observing the tremor that had begun in her hands.

'Excellent. We'll see you soon.'

The first thing Aggie thought when she saw her mother was that Valeria looked exceptionally well for someone who'd just had a stroke. Her mother peered from the bed where she was propped up by many pillows. A curtain divided her bed from whoever was on the other side. Her broken wrist was in a splint, elevated on yet another pillow beside her.

'You seem disappointed,' Valeria said, and returned her gaze to the open magazine on her lap.

'No . . . I . . . it's just, I thought you might be dying,' Aggie said in a rush, her hand at her throat. It was deeply unnerving to see her mother like this. She realised with a jolt that she'd never seen her mother in a hospital bed at all. Somehow in her mind she had blended together all the times they'd spent at her father's bedside as he died. But Valeria had never been the one in the bed before, only sitting beside it.

'So, you *are* disappointed,' her mother said, wryly.

'No, of course not.' Aggie rubbed at her brow now, clamping down on a rush of anger that turned her stomach to acid. 'You called for me, as your next of kin.' She said the words cautiously. 'It sounded bad.'

'A stroke is not bad enough for you?'

'Mum, please. I'm trying here,' Aggie said, calmly. Despite her mother's apparent stoicism and still-sharp tongue, she'd undoubtedly had an awful scare today and was probably in shock, not thinking straight.

Valeria sighed and slid the magazine off her lap. She couldn't quite reach the bed tray next to her, so Aggie took the opportunity to approach her and help.

'Thank you.'

Aggie pulled up a chair and sat down, straight-backed. 'What happened?'

Valeria made a disgusted noise and cast her eyes to the ceiling where a small television hung, the blank screen reflecting a miniature version of themselves. 'I was in church this morning, as usual . . . and I simply came over all funny.'

'Funny how?'

'Things went black,' her mother said, quietly now, her fingers picking at a loose thread on the hospital's cotton blanket. 'I tried to speak to Elca next to me but I couldn't get the words out.' For a moment, her mother's face reddened and her eyes brightened with tears. 'I tried to stand, but I fell. That's when this happened,' she said, nodding to her left arm.

'Oh, Mum,' Aggie said, reaching out a hand to place on top of her mother's unbroken one. 'That must have been frightening.'

Valeria didn't answer but chewed her lip. Then she laughed, emptily, and withdrew her hand from Aggie's, running it through her short hair, the curls flattened on one side. She tried to fluff it up. 'I must look a state.'

'You really don't,' Aggie said. 'You look amazing. Strong as ever.'

'Yes, well, that's how it is with these *transient things*,' Valeria said, grinding her teeth over the last two words with distaste. 'They come on and then they're gone.'

Aggie waited a moment. 'I spoke to the doctor before I came in.' Her mother glanced at her, suspicious. 'She said the CT scan showed you were okay for now, but that these types of things are warning signs of what might still be coming.'

A stroke – that was what might still be coming. A full-on, life-altering stroke. It was deeply sobering. Valeria set her jaw but said nothing.

'Did she talk to you about all this? About where to go from here?' Aggie pressed her.

'Yes.'

Aggie spied a pile of information leaflets on the over-bed table and nodded, but said no more about it. Her mother obviously wasn't ready to talk about it, and clearly not with Aggie. 'I thought you might have called Myrtle,' Aggie said, then regretted it the moment her mother's glare landed on her. No, Valeria wouldn't want to call Myrtle either. She wouldn't have wanted to call anyone.

'Anyway,' Aggie said, heartily, 'I'm here now and happy to help.'

Her mother swallowed tightly and nodded.

'I've got an overnight bag with me in the car,' she went on, 'so I can stay in my old room tonight to be on hand if you need me.'

'Honestly, that's not necessary . . .'

'They won't let you leave without a plan for support for the next twenty-four hours,' Aggie said, ignoring the stab of emotion that her mother didn't want her in the house.

'What about the cafe?' Valeria said. 'Surely you're needed there.'

'Savannah can handle it. Trade has slowed now that winter's here.'

Aggie felt her shoulders tense slightly as she spoke Savannah's name. A teenage mother was not Valeria's idea of a suitable second-in-command.

A teenage mother was not Valeria's idea of *suitable*, full stop.

With irritation flaring under her skin, Aggie almost opened her mouth to volunteer Holly instead, which she knew Valeria would prefer, but she held back the offer and ploughed on. 'Come on. Let's get you out of here.'

Aggie's mother still lived in the house in which Aggie had grown up. It was a rendered stone home, built at the turn of the nineteenth century, set on forty hectares of farmland on the outskirts of town. It had once been a hundred hectares but after Aggie's father had died, her mother had sold off sixty hectares and the sheep, and leased out the rest of the land. Today, the land ran sheep once more, which were visible in the distance and dirty grey from the drizzling winter rain.

'I think I might go and rest,' Valeria said not long after their arrival at the house.

'Of course,' Aggie said, bright on the surface but deeply uneasy beneath. She made Valeria a cup of tea and some toast, then turned on the heater in her mother's room, and made sure she had her medications and water near her bed.

After closing the bedroom door softly behind her, Aggie wandered through the house, feeling like a stranger. The home was solid and worth good money, but definitely in need of a style update. It was stuck in the era of florals, lace, brocades and wood veneers, with at least five different types of floor covering throughout. It was cold, and damp hung in the air, so she set the dial on the heater in the living room too, then ventured to her old bedroom.

She hadn't slept in this room since she was sixteen years old.

Gone were her posters of Michael Hutchence and *Beverly Hills, 90210*. Gone were her boxes of mixtapes recorded off the radio top forty countdown each week. Gone were her high school textbooks, the biology book almost too heavy to carry home each day in her bag, and the modern history book – the subject she had tried so hard in because her father taught it at university. He could bring history to life, igniting her mind, but she mused now that she could remember very little of it, and much less of her father than she would have liked, too.

She ran her hand along the brown desk in the corner of the room, then ducked down to see where she'd scratched *Mal* into the side of the drawers with the tip of a protractor. She ran her fingers over it, wondering if her mother had ever found it. She doubted it. She imagined Valeria would have burnt the desk if she had.

She sat on the edge of her single bed, the springs squeaky under her weight, and surveyed the boxes of random items that had been stored in this room over the years. Old exercise equipment, tax files, bags of clothes and bedding. Aggie wondered how many of her father's clothes her mother had kept, if any. She sneezed as swirling dust particles reached her nostrils. She'd have to give everything a good wipe down in order to sleep here tonight.

She pulled her legs up onto the bed and leant against the wall, remembering the tears, the endless tears that had soaked through her pillow on her last night in this room. The shame, the guilt, the fear, the confusion. Her mother had been firm, and her father had done nothing to stop it.

Her mobile phone sprang to life, jolting her from the memory. *Gideon.*

Her heart rocketed to her throat, and her hand hovered over the phone as she deliberated whether or not to answer it. Eventually, she sent his call to voicemail.

2

The next day, Aggie watched Myrtle's pink Mini Cooper purr to a halt outside the cafe. She raced out to meet her, hopping over the water sloshing through the gutters and holding an umbrella above her great-aunt's head as Myrtle levered herself from the car.

'Lovely day for it,' Myrtle said in greeting.

'The ducks agree,' Aggie replied, nodding towards a grassed laneway across the road, where two brown wood ducks were flapping their wings with glee.

'Lucky ducks,' Myrtle said, and they hurried inside Strawberry Sonnet. 'It's raining cats and dogs out there,' she remarked, cheerily, taking off her pink puffer jacket and hanging it on the rack as the door closed behind them. Aggie smiled. Myrtle's presence always seemed to herald an uplifting of spirits. For the millionth time, she wondered what would have become of her if her great-aunt hadn't stepped in and done what her own mother wouldn't do when Aggie was sixteen.

'How are you?' Aggie asked, hugging her.

'Chipper, thank you.' Myrtle was the same height as Aggie, the former stooped with age, the latter naturally petite. Aggie released Myrtle and fluffed the woman's hair where raindrops had flattened it. Her great-aunt had the most adorable grey and white curls, twisting gently away from her face. Holly had loved grabbing at those curls when she was a baby, and no matter how many times Aggie suggested that Myrtle tie them back to stop them from being yanked, she wouldn't do it. *It's worth the pain to see that adorable smile*, she would say. Curls ran in the family: Valeria, Aggie and Holly were all blessed with them, or afflicted with them, depending on the day. Aggie was the only one who kept her hair long, letting the weight drag the curls down into looser waves.

'Thanks for coming over. Pull up a chair.' Aggie guided her to one of the smaller tables set for four, with wooden chairs and cushions for comfort, rather than one of the long tables with backless bench seats.

'How's Valeria?' Myrtle asked, taking her time to settle herself in.

'I think the shock's worn off,' Aggie said, darkly. 'She was pointedly wiping up my crumbs from the bench with her good arm before I'd even finished cutting the toast.'

'Is she allowed to be home alone now?'

'From today, yes, but I asked Holly to go over and stay with her for the day anyway to make sure she can cope okay.' She paused, wondering how Holly was getting on.

Myrtle looked as if she was about to speak but was interrupted by the bell chiming above the cafe door. 'Hi, Myrtle,' Savannah called, flapping an umbrella and shrugging out of a windcheater. Aggie was struck by how vibrant Savannah looked, despite the fact that she would have had broken sleep last night with her baby. Aggie had slept badly in the small bed in her old room, with dusty surroundings and a mind full of bad memories, and knew the bags under her eyes reflected that. Savannah, on the other hand, was clear-eyed, with smooth, neat hair – the luck of the young.

'Good morning, Savannah, dear.' Myrtle beamed at her.

'Would you like a coffee?' Savannah called, already moving towards the grinder.

'That would be lovely, thank you.'

'You too, Aggie?' Savannah lifted her blue denim apron over her head and tied the straps behind her. Tin watering cans holding bunches of flowers stretched along the tables in the cafe, and Savannah looked as though she could be a florist, here to pluck and arrange beautiful blooms.

'Most definitely, thank you,' Aggie said.

Aggie studied her great-aunt. Myrtle wore a lifetime of facial expressions easily, each line telling a story, and her eyes might well have belonged to someone much younger than eighty-four. The colour of autumn leaves, deep brown with flecks of orange, they seemed bigger, rounder and brighter every year.

'So, Captain Aggie, what's going on?'

'A couple of things . . .' Aggie began, smiling.

Savannah swooped in with their coffees and the women thanked her, pausing their conversation till they were alone once more, then Aggie continued.

'I didn't sleep much last night so I had a lot of time to think.'

Myrtle blew on her black brew and said, 'That's not surprising, but I'm sure Valeria appreciates it, deep down. It was generous of you to help her.'

Aggie waved her praise away. 'No, it's not. It's just what family does, isn't it?'

'Not all families,' Myrtle replied, and arched a grey eyebrow.

'True,' she conceded. 'Anyway, you know that these past two years I've been at a bit of a loss with, well, everything . . .'

At that, Myrtle gave a sympathetic cluck and waited for her to continue.

'So, at around three o'clock this morning, I made a decision.'

'Go on.'

'Enough is enough. I need to fix things.'

'What things?'

'*All* the things.'

Myrtle straightened, as best she could, her eyes alight. 'Everything?'

'Yep, everything, and for some of them, I need your help.'

Now Myrtle grinned, revealing perfectly polished dentures. 'Count me in. You know how much I love to see a woman look at a mountain and declare she'll conquer it.'

A gulp of coffee lingered in Aggie's mouth for several moments while she gathered her reply. 'I have four things on my list and the first two involve you,' Aggie began. 'Mum's accident yesterday . . . The stroke and the fracture, well, these are *big* things.'

Myrtle nodded her agreement. 'Wake-up calls.'

'Exactly.' Aggie inhaled deeply. 'You know better than anyone that Mum and I have a difficult relationship, and I understand now that it will never be what I want it to be. But, at the same time, I hope it could improve. I want whatever time we have left together to be better than the way things have been up till now. She could have another stroke at any moment. Next time, she could die.'

The words were weighty and hung in the air like mist on a cold morning.

'How can I help?' Myrtle asked, patting her lips with a serviette.

'I want to do something really special for Mum's seventieth next month. I'm hoping you can help me come up with an idea.'

'Hmm.' Myrtle drummed her fingers on the tabletop, enticed by the challenge.

'I want it to be something she'll really appreciate,' Aggie continued. 'Something that shows we've thought about her and what she would really love to do.'

Aggie was not the only one who was at odds with Valeria – Myrtle was too. A perfect birthday surprise from the both of them would surely go a long way to softening her heart towards them.

'Holly will still be here for a few weeks, so it's a good opportunity for this to be a real celebration of family, and something she'll remember forever. If Mum is . . . deteriorating, at all, it might be our last chance to do it.'

They sat in silent rumination for a few moments and Aggie finished her coffee, relieved to feel the caffeine beginning to hum through her veins. She signalled to Savannah for another round of coffees.

'I'll mull it over and get back to you,' Myrtle said.

'I'll think about it too.'

'Good. Now, what's next on your list?'

Aggie straightened her shoulders, took a deep breath and lifted her chin. 'I want to take you up on your offer.'

Myrtle frowned for a moment, clearly trying to pinpoint what Aggie was talking about. In fairness, it had been months since they'd spoken about it. Then her eyes widened and a smile crept across her face. She twirled a finger in the air. 'About the cafe?'

'Yes.'

'Oh, my darling girl, well done.'

Aggie swallowed her rising nerves.

'Stop thinking about Valeria,' Myrtle said, accepting the second steaming coffee from Savannah with a nod of thanks.

'I can't help it. This decision affects her too.'

'It's my house, it's my money, it's my last will and testament, not hers, and not yours either.'

'Still. Shouldn't we at least talk it through with her?'

'I don't really think now is a good time to raise her blood pressure, do you?'

Aggie blanched. 'No, I suppose not.'

'I want to sell this shop. You want to buy this shop. A few years ago you would have had the money, but since you lost it—'

'I didn't *lose* it,' Aggie muttered.

Myrtle held up a hand. 'Apologies. Poor choice of words.' She sipped her coffee slowly. 'I'm only trying to say that life can be cruel and unexpected. Circumstances change. Right now, I can offer my house as guarantee for this loan. It's really very simple. Take the chance while it's there.'

'I do need to get in control of my future,' Aggie conceded. She'd spent two years living in a sort of limbo, not knowing how to go back or forward. The letter that arrived yesterday had triggered something in her, a need to take a step, in any direction. The chance to buy Strawberry Sonnet was in front of Aggie right now. She was months late in claiming that chance, and it was still intimidating, but it was time.

Her cafe was positioned on Murray Street, between the Barossa Valley Cheese Company and the Italian wine bar Casa Carboni. Aggie's sophisticated black and white colour scheme fitted in nicely next to the cheese company, which also used black and white, and the Italian enoteca, the facade of which was a golden cream, with a stylish striped awning. All three shops had greenery planted in heavy terracotta pots at the front, though Strawberry Sonnet had no awning. It was one of the things she planned to do after buying the shop: it would improve the look and shelter customers from the rain, and it would also let her put her own stamp on the place.

Myrtle always said she'd chosen to buy that particular shop when it came on the market because it was at the foodie end of the street, away from the likes of the auto body repair shop and the blacksmith museum up the hill. It was also not far from a large parkland with a playground, which would attract families, and was on the way out of Angaston heading towards the larger town of Nuriootpa, famous for Maggie Beer's farm shop and restaurant, which attracted a steady stream of visitors looking for gastronomic delights.

Aggie was grateful for Myrtle's smart investment all those years ago. It had meant she'd had a space in a good location to build her business of artisan strawberry feasts. From the start, she'd shied away from anything too over the top or childish, like strawberry shortcake or garish pink icing. She'd avoided clichéd red and white bunting and polka-dot tablecloths, instead favouring a more natural aesthetic. Her shop featured framed sepia-toned and hand-drawn botanical illustrations of strawberry plants and framed excerpts of poetry, including Shakespeare's famous *Sonnet 116*. When strawberries were in season, glass jars on the cafe tables were filled with cuttings of green leaves and tiny white strawberry flowers with yellow centres. She'd created and nurtured every inch of this space and now was the time to officially make it hers.

Despite the competing emotions she was feeling, despite the pain that the mention of the lost money brought up, Aggie found herself smiling at Myrtle. 'You're pretty amazing, you know?'

'Tell that to Valeria once she realises I transferred everything in my will to you and not her.'

Aggie squirmed, still uncomfortable with that knowledge. It was her main concern about this transaction, despite the fact that the idea had come from Myrtle and, as she said, it was her house and her money.

'Come on, then,' Myrtle said. 'What else is on your fix-it list?'

'Holly,' Aggie said, and closed her eyes. 'There's something going on with her. She's not herself.'

'Have you asked her what's wrong?'

'She keeps saying it's jet lag.'

Myrtle considered this. 'It could be. I've had some horrendous jet lag in my time.'

'I suppose. It's just a nagging feeling, though. I think there's more going on.'

'Mother's instinct?'

'Yes.'

'You'll work it out.'

Aggie wished she was as certain. Holly's reluctance to tell her what was really going on struck at Aggie's guilt that she'd not been there enough for her daughter in the past two years – that she'd given all her mothering away and had not left enough for Holly.

'Now, what's the last thing on your list?' Myrtle prompted.

Aggie stared at Myrtle, suddenly unable to say it aloud. The last thing was the biggest and she had no idea where to begin.

'That one's . . . complicated,' she said, cringing at how weak her words sounded. 'I might need to think about that one for a bit longer.'

'Is it about the jam?'

'What? Oh . . . no.'

'It's your turn to be the jam queen this year,' Myrtle went on. 'And what a year to win.' She winked proudly.

'There's no guarantee I'll win, though,' Aggie said, reining in her hopes and her ego. Just because she'd won first place nearly every time she'd entered, and never not placed, didn't mean she'd win this year. She cast her eyes over to the counter, adorned with strings of colourful award ribbons. 'Anything can happen.'

'If you hadn't declared this year, I'd be entering.'

'That was a stroke of luck.' With so many jam queens in their family – including Dolce, who was an honorary family member – an unspoken rule had emerged over the years. Immediately following the Royal Adelaide Show, after the winners had been announced, the jam maker who wanted to enter the following year made her declaration and everyone else stood aside. By chance, Aggie had declared before the announcement of this year's special award – a sponsored cash prize of two thousand dollars and the chance to appear on Maggie Beer's cooking show.

She grimaced. 'Mum will be seething that she didn't declare. You know how much she worships Maggie Beer.'

Myrtle puckered her lips in agreement.

'But the money would certainly help,' Aggie said, hopefully. 'I'm about to sign my life away to the bank for a mortgage to buy this shop.'

'You'll need the publicity from winning, too,' Myrtle agreed, taking another sip of her coffee. 'Luckily, you and jam making are like ducks and water.'

'I'm macerating today, actually.' She tipped her head in the direction of the strawberries that had been abandoned after yesterday's phone call, which she'd brought in to the kitchen to work with today.

'Perfect. Prize-winning jam will be bottled by tomorrow.' Myrtle checked the time on her silver watch. 'I'll head over to the solicitor's today and start the paperwork to sell this old girl to you, and then you'll be able to check off one thing from your list. Then I'm going to have lunch with Dolce, and by this afternoon I'm sure we'll have come up with the perfect plan for Valeria's birthday. As for Holly, if anyone can help her, it's you.'

'Thank you, that means a lot.'

'And as for the fourth thing on your list . . . I'm here when you want to talk about it.'

Two customers entered at that moment, flicking water from their hair and coats, and Savannah greeted them, guiding them to the long bench. Aggie hugged Myrtle, helped her back to her car, then headed to the kitchen to prepare the strawberries and cover them with sugar to macerate until tomorrow. She was wiping the stainless-steel bench in order to begin her work when her phone rang. She pulled it from her apron pocket.

Gideon, again.

The fourth thing on her list.

She froze. She had no idea what she wanted to say to him, and was equally clueless about what he might want to say to her. She would have to talk to him, she supposed . . . but did it have to be today? She was so tired after last night that she couldn't trust herself right now. The phone stopped ringing but he didn't leave a message, and she breathed a sigh of relief.

3

It was the boozy lunch with Dolce that gave Myrtle the great idea.

They were lunching at one of the Barossa's many vineyards, about twenty minutes out of Angaston. They'd caught a cab there and they were catching one home again, so they could both indulge in the eight-glass wine flight that accompanied their three-course meal.

They'd asked to be seated at the furthest end of the restaurant in the converted stone stables, so their hearing aids were less bothered by the sound system at the front. So far they had enjoyed more crumbed asparagus spears, prawn cocktails and arancini balls than they could count. They were at least one too many glasses ahead of their planned drinking schedule, but everything had looked and smelt so wonderful that they couldn't resist. Myrtle had now cracked open her free gift – a small jar of prosecco and strawberry jam – and had taken the tip of her knife to it, carving out slices of jam straight from the jar and enthusiastically consuming them alongside wines and cheeses.

Dolce, meanwhile, was preoccupied. Somewhere in their conversation – Myrtle couldn't quite remember how it had come up – they'd got onto wondering about a long-lost friend named Margaret. It had taken them a few moments to agree on which friend they were discussing, because Margaret had been a consistently popular girl's name during the 1930s – Myrtle had googled it, and it featured in the top ten for each year – and therefore they did know quite a lot of them. Myrtle had been pleased to discover that her own name did not rate in the top one hundred, which made her feel distinguished, until she found that it had rated highly in the late 1800s, which briefly made her feel old-fashioned, until she remembered that she didn't actually care what other people thought.

She took another slice of the prosecco jam and sucked it slowly, feeling the warm buzz of the wine she had consumed so far. She swallowed hard, blinking at the many glowing lights of the room, which had gone a little blurry. 'What are we talking about again?'

'Margaret,' Dolce said, possibly a bit too loudly.

'The one we played tennis with?'

'Yes!'

'Okay, I'm with you. Where did she go?'

'Tasmania,' Dolce said.

'Because of her husband?'

'Yes.' Her friend frowned. 'What was his name?'

'Dennis.'

'No, that was the second husband,' Dolce said.

'How many husbands were there?'

'Three, I think. Or maybe only two.'

Myrtle felt herself sway towards the edge of the table and quickly righted herself. A waitress appeared with a jug of water and poured them both tall glasses before slinking away. Dolce squinted at Myrtle, raising her hand to shield her vision, and Myrtle realised with a start that her friend was quite drunk. She should watch out for her.

'I think the man she's with now might be just a lover,' Myrtle continued.

'Huh.' Dolce considered this a moment, as if it was a fanciful idea. As Dolce had married three and a half times in her long life before calling it quits (the half was a non-legal, whisky-fuelled declaration on a boat in Kakadu), Myrtle thought it possible her friend had never considered simply sleeping with people rather than marrying them first. She'd never thought to ask her.

Myrtle looked at her best friend of more decades than she cared to count. They were shrunken women now. Dolce had two new hips. Their noses were bigger these days than when they'd first met. Dolce leaked a bit. Myrtle passed wind more than she'd like. They had glasses, dentures, hearing aids and walking sticks. They also had mobile phones, the internet, money and a mutual love of travel. It was *their thing*, the adhesive that glued them together, their never-ending adventure.

That was when genius struck.

'I've got it,' Myrtle said, waving her knife in the air at Dolce.

'What?'

'What we need to do for Valeria. We must take her on a trip for her seventieth.'

Dolce narrowed her eyes. 'A trip?'

'Yes! She's always wanted to go on the Ghan.'

Dolce lifted her chin, a corner of her mouth twitching, and Myrtle knew she had her hooked. A few weeks ago, Dolce had made murmurs about being 'done' with travel, but Myrtle hadn't taken her at her word. Dolce had had pneumonia at the time, not bad enough for hospitalisation, but enough to give her a fright. She couldn't have been serious. The two of them had travelled all over the planet and now was the time to get in more travel, not less, to seize the day and enjoy every last minute they could.

'I'm amazed we haven't done it ourselves yet,' Myrtle said, taking a sip of one of the champagnes. She didn't care what the rules said, she refused to call them 'sparkling wines'; it was such a pedestrian term. Myrtle had completely forgotten which wine was which and couldn't be bothered checking the menu. Dolce was nodding slowly, sipping a rosé.

'I *have* always been interested in that trip. I do love train travel.'

'The Canadian trip was incredible,' Myrtle reminded her, encouragingly. 'And the Scottish one.'

Dolce grunted in agreement.

'So, how about it? Shall we do it?'

'Well . . .' Dolce was wavering, and also leaning slightly to the side.

No, wait, *Myrtle* was leaning to the side. She carefully corrected her centre of gravity. 'It might be the last time we get to do something like this for Valeria,' Myrtle said, which was true, but also deliberately coercive. 'And also Holly. Who knows if she'll ever come back from America for good?'

'Aggie can't afford it, and neither can Holly, I expect, even with the US dollars.'

Myrtle waved an unconcerned hand. 'I'll pay for them. My treat. It will be worth it to get this trip right, for Aggie's sake as much as Valeria's.'

Dolce pondered this and Myrtle waited, knowing well enough at their age that Dolce didn't respond well to being pushed. At last she was rewarded.

'All right.'

'Excellent,' Myrtle said, raising her glass to Dolce. 'I'll book it tonight.'

'Wait until you're sober,' Dolce instructed, holding up a warning finger. 'We don't want another misadventure like the ferry to Greece.'

'No,' Myrtle agreed. That time, she'd booked the tickets from Italy to Greece after a few too many sherries and they'd found themselves without a sleeping berth and only spots in deckchairs overnight. In winter. 'I promise to wait until I'm completely sober.' She tried to suppress her joy that Dolce was reneging on her previous threat to quit travelling, but was unable to hide it.

Dolce held up the stern finger again. 'But, Myrtle, this is absolutely the last trip.'

'Okay.'

'I mean it.'

'I believe you.'

But she didn't.

•

Valeria stood in front of the framed photo in the hallway. Holly handed her a mug of hot chocolate and Valeria swallowed a mouthful. It was overly sweet but today she didn't mind.

'Thank you.'

'Easy,' Holly said, then opened the front door and stepped out into the rain. She opened a large rainbow-striped umbrella above her head, her spine straight as a pillar, and set out to walk.

'Be careful out there,' Valeria said, though she didn't know why. This was the Barossa Valley, not Los Angeles. But Holly didn't answer her, just waved long fingers and strode off as if she had an important mission to complete.

The abrupt stillness of the house unnerved her. Her wrist was aching and all of a sudden she felt afraid of the blood pumping through her veins, of the vessels in her brain that might see fit at this very moment to bulge or split. An enemy lurked inside her.

She studied her late husband's face in the frame on the wall, struggling to remember how many years he'd been gone. She frowned, recalling the current year, working out how old he'd been when he died, the difference of years, reminding herself that he was the same age as her . . .

Good gracious! He'd been gone twenty-three years.

Forty-seven was a cruel age for a man to die. She touched the glass covering his image, taking in the redness across his nose and cheeks, the blown capillaries. There were the eyebrows, so thin and fair they may as well not have been there. And there was his toothy smile and the way his eyes lit up like a twenty-year-old's when he really laughed at something she said. It was his laughter she missed most. She and Bertie had appreciated each other's wry sense of humour like no one else ever had. She missed it sharply, more than she missed the feel of his soft academic's hand in hers, or the feel of his thick, curly chest hair against her cheek.

Unbidden, his image was replaced by another man's.

She withdrew her fingers from the glass as though they'd been burnt. The features of the Englishman came into sharp, technicolour focus. His clear, pale-blue eyes. His smooth scalp with white hair at the sides and back, clipped like a friar's might be. His clean white goatee and moustache and that smooth, pink lower lip. His ears, absolutely not cauliflowered or hairy or blemished, as if they'd never seen a lick of sun.

Sometimes she wondered if she'd dreamt it all.

4

Aggie padded along the wooden floor of the hallway towards the kitchenette, which had been a later addition to the postwar brick house she'd been renting now for twenty years. Holly was already up and Aggie checked the time. It was only six-thirty.

'Good morning. Why are you up so early?' She squeezed Holly's shoulder as she passed, noting the boniness of her upper arm. 'You're on holiday, you know.'

Holly tapped her finger against her coffee mug absent-mindedly, staring out the window at the pouring rain. 'Jet lag,' she said, and shrugged.

Aggie refrained from challenging that and instead brewed more coffee, rubbing her hands together against the chill. Wet winters were typical of the Barossa Valley, and the weather tended to keep the tourists away. She couldn't blame them. Her cafe's trade was now falling into the slow season, and she could plod along with just her and Savannah. By September, though, the bare, twisted grapevines would burst into greenery, the sun

I are planning on taking Mum away on a trip for her seventieth,' she said. 'It would be great if you could come too.'

Holly focused her eyes. 'Oh, sure, that's a great idea,' she said, though her tone lacked true enthusiasm. 'Let me know.' Then she slid her arm out from under Aggie's hand and stood. 'I'm going for a walk.'

'Okay,' Aggie said, trying not to sound disappointed at her abrupt departure. 'Take my windcheater and the umbrella by the door, if you like.'

'Nah, I'll walk in the rain. If I can't swim, I might as well use what I've got. Water is falling from the sky – I'll just pretend I'm swimming.' Then she was gone.

Aggie's day at the cafe sped by, with a surprising number of customers arriving over the course of the day, perhaps looking to get out of the awful weather and into somewhere cosy. She'd obtained a liquor licence as soon as she could raise the cash and now sold mason jars of vodka with strawberries soaking inside, which were snatched up today by two separate lots of customers. A family group ordered long boards piled high with fat strawberries alongside dishes of dipping sauces, from balsamic vinaigrette to melted dark chocolate and lemon and cream cheese frosting. A local book club ordered handmade strawberry pies with lattices of golden pastry on top, served on black stone plates with dishes of Maggie Beer's ice cream on the side.

Savannah was consistently effective, friendly and eagle-eyed. She might have been young but she was mature and confident. She didn't need a job in order to pay for clothes and nightclub adventures, or even drugs or midnight runs to McDonald's; she needed to provide for her child, and that made her the most committed, loyal and hardworking employee Aggie could have hoped for. It made Aggie proud to employ her, and others like her over the years. Often, it felt like paying it forward – taking the help and support she'd received from Myrtle and replicating it for other teenage mothers. Sometimes it felt like going back in time and helping herself, showing teenage Aggie that she would be okay, that she'd make it. That she could do more than just get by, that she could even make something of herself, build something that would last.

At the end of the busy day, Aggie waved Savannah off early to go spend time with her daughter, then shut up shop and took home the strawberries she'd started macerating yesterday, setting them on the stovetop to make jam. She was a slow jammer by nature, preferring to take her time over two days, sometimes even three. Her mother, on the other hand, liked to get a batch done all at once, blocking out the rest of the world until it was finished, overseeing its every moment of transformation. Clearly neither method was superior, given how many ribbons they'd both won. Rather, it reflected their personalities – Valeria approaching her jam with science and technique while Aggie preferred to approach it as artistry, allowing the end result to take its time to emerge out of the raw ingredients in a unique way, rather than dictating how it should be.

In her view, jam making could take as long as one wanted it to. Far better to amble along like the tortoise than rush through like the hare and burn it, or lose concentration and miss the chance to scoop the frothy pink scum from the top. You could stop and start jam as many times as you liked. She had a theory that the jam liked it that way, giving it a chance to adjust to its transformation.

Aggie's favourite jam-making pot was a heavy, cast-iron one that had worked terrifically so many times she was now afraid to use anything else, especially this year with the special prizes attached to the competition. She stood at her small stove, stirring the strawberries and the now-liquefied pink sugar over a medium heat. She was playing Pachelbel's *Canon in D*, the famous piece to which brides often walked down the aisle. On one occasion when she'd taken out first place at the Adelaide Show, a newspaper reporter had asked what her secret was and she'd confessed, 'I play music to my jam.' He hadn't believed her, or perhaps thought it too kooky, and didn't print it. More fool him.

The strawberries were just starting to soften, though still holding their shape, when Holly came home.

'Hello?' she sang down the hall, shutting the front door behind her.

'Hi! I'm making jam.'

'I've brought takeaway,' Holly said, depositing the food on the kitchen table. 'I'll just have a shower first.'

'Okay.' Aggie smiled, pleased that Holly sounded upbeat after her day of wandering in the rain. In the back pocket of her jeans, her phone buzzed. She wondered if it was Gideon and was almost afraid to check, but breathed a sigh of relief when she saw that it was Myrtle.

I'm on my way over. Be there soon.

She pocketed her phone and resumed her stirring of the berries, enjoying their intense aroma, but after a minute she realised she was distracted and turned the flame off again. Instead, she dished out the Chinese food, making a plate for Myrtle as well. By the time Holly finished showering, her wet hair wrapped in a green towel, Myrtle had arrived and they all sat down at the little table in the kitchen to eat.

'Jam smells good,' Myrtle said, sniffing the air appreciatively. 'Smells like a winner to me.'

'I hope so,' Aggie said, pouring her a red wine.

'Thank you,' Myrtle said, *oomph*ing into her seat and taking up the glass.

Aggie watched with pleasure as Holly tucked in to a large bowl of Mongolian beef and sweet and sour pork with rice, her cheeks full of colour. Maybe her day out and about had done her good.

'Now, I know exactly what we should do for Valeria's birthday,' Myrtle said, smiling triumphantly. 'We're all going on the Ghan – including you, Holly.'

Holly stopped chewing and slid her eyes sideways to meet Aggie's, raising her eyebrows.

'The Ghan?' Aggie said. 'That sounds amazing, Myrtle, but there's no way I can afford that, I'm sorry.'

'Neither can I,' Holly mumbled through a mouthful of food.

Myrtle was already waving away their objections. 'No arguments. I'm paying for you all, except Dolce, who's well able to pay for herself.'

Holly swallowed quickly. 'What?'

'No, it's too much,' Aggie protested.

'Phooey. It's my money and I get to decide what to do with it, just as I have for my entire life. Besides, I ran it past Dolce yesterday and she's agreed. Given how cagey she's been about travelling lately, I'm not going to change the plans now.'

'When?' Holly asked. 'I've got to be back in the States to start school at the beginning of September.'

Myrtle grinned wickedly. 'I know. Lucky for you, there's a trip the week of Valeria's birthday that still has tickets available. It leaves in a month, on the twenty-sixth of August, from Darwin. I figure we can head up there to explore Darwin a couple of days before, then you'll be back here on the twenty-ninth, and if you get on the next flight you'll be back in California to start the school year in the nick of time.' Myrtle sighed, obviously pleased with herself. 'You'll be jet-lagged, of course, but you're young. You'll cope,' she said with a smile.

Aggie sat in shocked silence, taking all this in. On the one hand, she didn't feel in the least bit comfortable having Myrtle pay for both her and Holly. A trip on the Ghan was pricey, and Myrtle was already helping her so much with the sale of the cafe, acting as guarantor, not to mention changing her will to leave her house to Aggie. She'd never be able to repay Myrtle in her great-aunt's lifetime. On the other hand, she knew what Myrtle was like. The woman had lived a life of freedom, never having to answer to anyone for anything, and once she decided to do something, there really was no stopping her. Aggie peered at Holly, who seemed equally lost for words, and the thought of taking such an iconic journey with her daughter, her mother and Myrtle – her second mother – was an overwhelmingly seductive notion.

'Are we really doing this?' she asked.

Myrtle took a gulp of wine and smacked her lips. 'You bet we are.'

Aggie smiled at her daughter. 'Holly? What do you think?'

Holly wrinkled her nose for a moment, thinking.

'Let me remind you, Holly, that I am eighty-four years old and could drop dead at any moment,' Myrtle said. 'It would be unthinkably cruel of you to refuse me this wish and break my heart, thereby expediting my journey to the grave.'

Holly snorted and rolled her eyes at Myrtle, then the corners of her mouth twitched upwards into a smile. She hadn't been able to resist Myrtle when she was a baby and she couldn't resist her now. 'Fine, you win.'

'I always do.'

Aggie and Holly shared a look, then turned to Myrtle and said 'Thank you, Myrtle' in unison.

Myrtle held up her glass in a toast, and the three of them drank to their coming adventure. 'Now, eat up, Holly. You look like a half-starved, drowned rat.'

5

The following week, Myrtle called a family meeting at Strawberry Sonnet for 9 am, before the cafe got too busy. She and Aggie agreed to meet half an hour earlier to go through the official paperwork to seal the deal on the loan guarantee and the transfer papers for Strawberry Sonnet. It had stopped raining, finally, and dog walkers were out in force, passing by the cafe's front windows where she and Aggie sat, making the most of the sunshine while they could.

Aggie extricated a pen from somewhere inside her hair bun as she read through the paperwork, hovering the nib over the lines of text as she digested it all. They were alone, the room silent. Myrtle waited patiently, knowing this was a big moment for Aggie, a serious commitment to this building and her business.

'I can't remember,' Aggie said, worrying at the edge of a fingernail. 'Are we telling Mum about this?'

'Eventually, of course,' Myrtle said. 'But I think it best we wait until some time has passed after the Ghan, don't you?'

Aggie nodded. 'I suppose so. That trip is for her. I'd hate for things . . . well, you know how she is.'

'I do.'

'I want this trip to go well.'

'Agreed.'

Aggie took her pen to the pages that were marked with a sticky tab and signed with a flourish on every dotted line, then she passed the paperwork to Myrtle, who did the same.

'Congratulations, Aggie,' Myrtle said, holding her arm out towards the centre of the cafe as if she were a game show host indicating a prize pool. 'You're the new owner of Strawberry Sonnet. Her future is in your hands.' She beamed with pride.

Aggie grinned, relief washing over her face. 'Thank you so much. It's scary, but exciting, and you know I'll take good care of her.'

'I do.'

'I'm so grateful to have had you in my corner all these years,' Aggie said, her eyes gleaming. 'I can never thank you enough.'

Myrtle's heart swelled in her chest. Aggie was the daughter she'd never had. It made her deliriously happy to be able to make her life better. She had been the unexpected gift that brightened up Myrtle's life, along with her fierce, wild little daughter who'd kept her on her toes and kept her younger than her years.

'So now you've checked off one thing on your fix-it list,' Myrtle said. 'Two are in progress – Holly and your mother – so that just leaves . . . the mystery box.'

Aggie closed her eyes for a moment and took a deep breath.

'Would you like to talk about it?' Myrtle pressed.

Aggie placed her elbows on the tabletop, threaded her fingers together one by one, then rested her forehead on her knuckles. 'It's the embryos,' she said.

Myrtle tilted her head, puzzled. 'The embryos?'

'Yes.' Aggie raised her eyes and crossed her arms over her body, hugging herself. 'Time's running out, and Gideon and I—'

The bell chimed over the door and Valeria entered, gazing around cautiously. Aggie shoved the papers at Myrtle, who scooped them up as quickly and innocently as possible, shoving them into her bag.

'Morning, Mum,' Aggie said, getting to her feet and plastering a smile on her face. She lifted her arms as though to hug Valeria but the older woman's shoulders stiffened and Aggie quickly adjusted her plan, laying an arm around her shoulders, squeezing her awkwardly instead. 'Would you like a coffee?'

'No, thank you, I just had one.'

'Come and sit,' Myrtle called, waving Valeria over.

Holly was next to arrive, her hair blow-dried into lovely ringlets that fell to her jawline, a thicker, dark-brown version of Myrtle's fine grey ones. She was smiling, the first genuine smile Myrtle had seen on her face since she'd arrived three weeks ago. Perhaps jet lag had been the problem after all.

'Grandma, how is your wrist?' Holly asked, touching the brace on Valeria's arm.

'It's fine. I'm lucky it wasn't my right hand,' Valeria said mildly.

'Well,' Myrtle interjected, bringing the attention to her. 'Let's get down to why we're here.' Three pairs of eyes turned to Valeria.

'What?' she said, straightening her back, suspicious.

'We have a surprise for you,' Myrtle said, reaching into her bag to retrieve five gold envelopes. She began to hand them out. 'Dolce couldn't be here this morning as she had an appointment, but one of these belongs to her.'

'What is it?' Valeria asked.

'Open it,' Myrtle instructed her.

Aggie and Holly held onto theirs without opening them, instead watching Valeria, who looked at them all, confused, and lifted the flap of the envelope. She pulled out a gold ticket. It wasn't a real ticket but one that Aggie and Holly had created and printed out for Myrtle, who then added in flight details and the Ghan itinerary by hand.

'We are taking you on the Ghan to celebrate your seventieth birthday,' Myrtle said, happily, grinning with the joy that came from delivering a wonderful surprise.

Valeria frowned. 'What?'

'We're all going with you,' Aggie said, indicating the four of them.

'Plus Dolce,' Myrtle added.

'I can fit it in right before I have to go back to the States,' Holly said, and if Myrtle wasn't mistaken, her voice pinched in sadness on that last word. Perhaps Holly was beginning to miss Australia and would return home again soon. She hoped so. It was agony for Aggie for her to be so far away. She could see Aggie watching her daughter carefully, and Myrtle guessed she was working hard not to beg Holly to stay. Myrtle offered her a sympathetic wink.

'I don't know what to say,' Valeria said, staring at the golden ticket, then pulling out more paperwork from the envelope and flicking through it.

Aggie piped up. 'We fly up to Darwin, spend two nights there, then ride the Ghan through the centre of Australia and finish in Adelaide. You, Holly and I will have single cabins . . .'

'And Dolce and I will share a twin cabin,' Myrtle finished.

Valeria's bottom lip wobbled. 'But it's so expensive,' she said, looking stricken.

'Forget about the money,' Myrtle said. 'It's all done and paid for, and there are no refunds, so now there is nothing left to do but celebrate you and your birthday.'

Valeria tucked the paperwork back into her envelope and arranged her features in a polite smile. 'Thank you,' she said, then cleared her throat. 'Lucky me.' But her tone lacked conviction.

A collective sense of disappointment drifted around the table, followed by an awkward stall in the conversation. Aggie jumped to her feet. 'Coffee, anyone?' she asked, to break the mood.

Receiving three enthusiastic yeses, she scuttled off to hide behind the barista bar, while Myrtle mused that containing all of them in such a small space on the train with no escape would be interesting, to say the least.

•

Just before lunchtime, while Savannah prepared the cafe for mid-day diners, Aggie slid on her wool coat and headed out into the sunny but cold and blustery day, crossing the street and heading for the playground. She sat on a wooden bench and pulled out her phone. She'd put off this call for too long.

He answered on the third ring. 'Hello?' There was a query in his voice, as though he wasn't sure it would be her.

'Hi. Are you busy? Can you talk?'

'I can. I just came home for lunch,' Gideon said, and she heard him drop his keys onto a bench or table.

There was a lingering pause and she scrambled for something to fill the gap. 'How's Banjo?' Her heart squeezed as she said the dog's name. She still regretted that she and Gideon hadn't agreed on some sort of dog-share arrangement. She'd lost so much – did she have to lose her dog too? Even one year on from their separation, some days she still expected Banjo to be standing beside the bed first thing in the morning, staring at her, willing her to wake. The second her eyes fluttered open, he'd spin delightedly in a circle, his claws clicking on the floorboards, his breaths short, excited huffs.

'Happier now the rain has stopped. You know what he's like,' Gideon said.

'Yeah, I do.' She swallowed a sudden lump in her throat, longing to run her fingers through Banjo's long red coat. In the past couple of weeks of rain, Banjo would have been lying by the door, his nose pressed to the wood, waiting for the moment the deluge ended so he could run through the vineyards again. That had been the clincher in the decision about who would keep Banjo. Aggie spent too much time indoors in the cafe, while the Irish setter was born for life at the vineyard, sitting up on the tractor, throwing himself in the lake whenever he could and chasing away any birds that dared to land on the grapes. Health and safety laws dictated that she couldn't take him to work with her, and she knew he'd miss being outdoors with Gideon too much. It wasn't fair to have him locked inside her small house all day, waiting for her to return.

'Listen,' she said, mustering her *we need to talk* voice. 'I got a letter.'

'I know. So did I,' he said, quickly, slightly defensively. 'I've been calling you . . .'

'I'm sorry about that. I just couldn't face it.'

She heard him swallow and, because she knew him so very well, she could tell it was a mouthful of wine, probably from a bottle he'd plucked from the racks at the vineyard to take home and test over lunch. That was one of the perks of being a winemaker – drinking wine was a bona fide part of the job.

'Do you know what you want to do?' he asked.

She watched a small child climbing up a slide, his mother hovering nearby, ready to catch him if he fell. She shook her head for several seconds without saying anything, then whispered, 'No.' She had many, many thoughts about all of it, many opinions on every option, but they were too vast, too confusing, too loaded. 'Do you?'

He swallowed again, more of a gulp this time, speaking on a sigh. 'No.'

She loved him for that – for being as clueless as her, for none of it being black and white. 'We have a little more time before we have to make a decision,' she began.

'There are a lot of options there,' he said. She heard him flick a piece of paper and assumed it was the letter outlining their choices.

'I'm not ready to go through each option yet. I just wanted to let you know that I got the letter, that I'm thinking about it, and that I know this is hard . . . for both of us.'

This was the last thing connecting them. What they decided to do with the embryos would alter their lives forever – push them together, or sever the tie between them.

'I'm glad you called,' he said, softly. 'We'll speak again soon, hey?'

'Okay.' She ended the call and sat for a long while, watching birds flitting in the treetops and a toddler wrapped so tightly in puffy winter clothing she could barely waddle around, her little arms and legs stuck out at angles, like a hot-pink starfish.

If things had gone differently two years ago, Aggie would have had a toddler around that age beside her right now. She lay her hand on the empty space of the bench next to her and felt the absence, the ghost child who drifted beside her.

6

Valeria had found herself knocking about the house all morning, not quite knowing what to do. With a broken wrist, she was certainly constrained from lifting anything, gardening or even cleaning beyond using her good hand to wipe down the bench. Aggie had been bringing her shopping, even though Valeria had insisted she could get it delivered. Aggie had also organised for a cleaner to visit once a week for the next two months, covering the time Valeria would be in a cast as well as a bit more, when her arm would be weak from lack of use.

Holly had been popping over twice a week to do Valeria's washing and change the sheets. Elca had driven her to the GP several times, where she'd been lectured about cholesterols, fats, salt, alcohol and exercise, then handed fistfuls of leaflets about lifestyle and warning signs. Myrtle had even showed up a couple of times for a cup of tea, brandishing board games, and Valeria had found it all excruciating. She did not like this version of herself or her life, not one bit, and she didn't believe for a moment that any of these people actually *wanted* to help her, but were rather performing duties they felt they should do.

Her shoulder ached from holding her body in awkward new positions, and she had spent the past week trying to be happy about taking a trip on the Ghan, for which they were leaving in just a few days. She'd wanted to take the trip for many years now but had always felt she didn't want to go on her own. The train would undoubtedly be full of retired married couples, enjoying their twilight years. She would never have dared to ask Myrtle to go with her. Dolce was Myrtle's travelling companion and considerably more fun than Valeria. If they went as a trio, she'd be the awkward third wheel.

She had to confess that their birthday surprise was an inspired choice. It was just that it was difficult to be thoroughly enthusiastic about it when the people involved were clearly motivated by the idea that a blood vessel could snap in her head and kill her at any moment. Their need to get in 'one last special trip' – something to prove their love for her – was palpable. Tired of restlessly pacing the house, she sat down at her laptop. Perhaps a spot of online shopping would relieve her agitated state. She could do with a new fedora to wear in the outback. She could go into town to look, but preferred not to deal with people's anxiety about the state of her health and bones.

As soon as the machine booted up, it pinged to alert her to a new email. She clicked it open, read it and wondered if she should reply. It wasn't the first time a journalist had contacted her asking for quotes for a story about the jam queens of the past five decades. Valeria was champion of them all, but was only ahead of her own daughter by a single purple ribbon. She wondered if the journalist knew this. If she didn't, Valeria would be doing the young woman a favour by filling in the missing gaps in her knowledge. She assumed this Cassandra person was a young woman from the exclamation marks and emojis she'd used in her email. Her chirpy, irreverent tone made Valeria grimace, anticipating more emojis or perhaps even kisses to sign off the email. Since when had it become so common to put kisses on everything? Social media was flooded with them. Sighing, she scanned her eyes down the list of questions.

Do you have any tips you can share?
What important lessons have you learnt through competition?
How has the jam scene changed over the years? Modernised at all?
Was there one win in particular that was extra sweet? (Pardon the pun! ☺)
Will you be retiring anytime soon or will you keep going?

Would she . . . would she be . . . *retiring*? What an insolent, preposterous question! Why on earth would she be retiring? Did this Cassandra think that just because she was turning seventy she was due to be sent out to pasture? That she should step aside and let the young ones have a chance? That she might be satisfied with having won before and therefore didn't need to continue, as if there was no joy in it anymore? The *cheek* of her. And this year, of all years, when there was two thousand dollars and a spot on Maggie Beer's show up for grabs. Well!

Once her indignation subsided, a warm wash of guilt moved slowly up her body from her toes. She might not be about to retire, but she was supposed to be standing aside this year. Agatha had declared last year, straight after Valeria won the strawberry jam blue ribbon and then the overall preserves championship ribbon. It was her daughter's turn.

But three months ago, the deadline had rolled around for competitors to lodge their entry forms and Valeria had put hers in too. Just quietly, of course – no point upsetting the coop. The truth was she always did, even when others had declared. She did it as an insurance policy. Having to submit entry forms so far in advance meant anything could go wrong between then and the day entries were to be delivered. She always put in the forms, paid her fees, and made her jam. If by chance someone fell over, was sick, or suddenly decided to escape winter and head to Fiji for a bit, she'd be ready to step in. This year was no different.

Except that this year Maggie Beer had put herself forward, shining like the gourmet queen she was, offering a chance to cook with her in her gorgeous kitchen, with all her glamorous appliances, with all her wit and charm and humour . . . on television.

Valeria owned every single one of Maggie's books. Had watched every single episode of *The Cook and the Chef*, and owned them on DVD too. Her pantry was full of Maggie's quince paste, verjuice, sparkling cabernet, pear cider, burnt fig jam, vegetable stock and linseed crackers. No one could possibly expect Valeria *not* to enter, could they? She knew it would ruffle some feathers, but in this case her age *did* matter. She had just had a ministroke. She had just broken her wrist. Who knew how much longer she had on earth? Who could deny her the chance to cook with Maggie Beer? No one who truly loved her, that was for sure.

She began to type her responses to Cassandra, starting with the last question.

I have absolutely no intention to retire.

Satisfied with her plan to go ahead and enter her preserves in the Royal Adelaide Show this year, Valeria made herself a hot chocolate and added a splash of whisky and a dollop of thickened cream. She calculated the days between now and the show and knew she wouldn't be able to make new jams in time. The cast wasn't due to come off until just after the show started. She wouldn't be able to manoeuvre her heavy pot, to lift the cutting boards and scrape the fruit into the pot, sterilise glass jars and handle them hot, in oven mitts, with only one hand. But there was nothing she could do. Fortunately, she already had a number of jars made up from the bountiful autumn produce in the valley that she could use. She'd find enough winners in there, for sure.

She eased herself onto the lounge to drink her hot chocolate and watch *The Crown* again. She'd just pulled up her blue and white rug, one she'd crocheted herself, when her phone lit up on the coffee table. She inched forward on the sofa to see who it was, carefully balancing her mug, and then nearly dropped the hot contents in her lap when she saw the name. She stared at her phone, frozen, until it stopped ringing and the Englishman was sent to voicemail.

•

Aggie paused mid stir of her mandarin marmalade. It was still too watery, bubbling gently, taking its time to reduce and thicken, the golden orange slowly turning amber. The aroma was intoxicating – so fresh, so joyful. Mandarins always made her feel like a happy child. She let her silicone spoon rest on the edge of the pot, her ears pricked. Holly was on the phone in her room talking to her best friend, Nala, a fellow teacher from California, and her voice was suddenly raised.

'I don't want to talk about it.'

Aggie silenced the jazz music she was playing to this marmalade and inched closer to the kitchen doorway, standing sideways, as if having her ear facing the hallway would make that much difference.

'That's great for you but I don't need help,' Holly said. 'I'm fine.'

Aggie stared at the floor, wondering if she could take a step out of the kitchen towards Holly's room in order to hear better, if her boots would be quiet enough on the wooden boards. The last thing she needed was for Holly to burst out of her room and catch her eavesdropping. It was so enticing, though. This was the first solid evidence that Holly's mercurial moods were the result of something more than jet lag. Aggie's mind raced to a thousand scenarios – a broken love affair, a falling out with Nala, drug use, alcoholism, an eating disorder . . . an assault? A stone dropped in her belly. Surely Holly would tell her about something that awful, wouldn't she? She wanted to ask her directly, but Holly had always been the type to withdraw from interrogation, shutting down instead of opening up, and Aggie knew that for now she would have to wait.

There came a thump from Holly's room.

Aggie sprang back towards the stove like a startled cat and picked up her spoon, her heart striking hard against her ribs. Holly emerged a second later and went straight to the fridge.

'Is there any cake left?' Holly muttered, her head inside the fridge while she shifted things around.

'No, sorry. I finished it when I got home from work,' Aggie said, lightly. She was about to offer to make another when Holly shut the fridge door and rubbed her eyes.

'I'm going for a walk.'

'Holly, wait,' Aggie said, holding up her hands as if to soothe an agitated horse. 'What's going on?'

'Nothing.'

'I've noticed you've seemed unhappy since you've been home, not your usual self. Is there anything I can do to help?'

'No, I'm fine,' Holly insisted, arranging her features into a placating smile.

'Did something happen back in California before you came home?'

'No, of course not,' she said, and Aggie knew she wasn't telling the truth because Holly stared her straight in the eye, defiantly, lifting her chin a fraction the way she'd always done when she was little and Aggie had caught her in a lie. 'I'll be back soon.' Holly left, closing the front door behind her.

Aggie looked to the ceiling and sighed. She didn't want to argue with Holly during the small window of time she was in the country before she left again for who knows how long, but she couldn't ignore the signs that something was not right in Holly's world.

Having lost her mojo for the marmalade, she turned off the heat to let it rest. An Adelaide Show batch needed to be its best, and that meant she would only work with it when she was in good spirits herself. Instead, she flopped onto the couch and took out her phone, opening Instagram.

Since their family meeting, she'd been following the hashtag #theghan, which allowed any photos posted with that tag to turn up in her feed. Her excitement had been building with every picture of food-laden tables in the dining car, with deep-red earth or a violet sky glittering with white stars visible through the train's window.

Now she scrolled through the latest tagged photos, allowing herself to be seduced by the romance of it all, then paused at one photo of a big black sky with a candle in the foreground. The caption read: *Next week I'll be leaving Darwin on #theghan and looking at this same sky but with a totally different view from the centre of this big country of ours. Reminds me that we are never the same person twice.*

She clicked on the profile attached to it: Harry Lyon. If he was leaving Darwin next week, that meant he would be on the same train as her. She read his profile bio.

I loved fiercely, I let go disgracefully, now walking soberly.

She didn't know if she was intrigued or annoyed by that. Was he a poet? A melodramatic millennial? A recovering alcoholic? Maybe an annoying life-coach type?

His profile photo only showed half his face, some of his scruffy sandy brown hair, and a snippet of some sort of beads around his neck. *Hippie* was her first thought. The eye she could see looked kind – blue or green or hazel, she wasn't sure which – and he had a deep tan, with a striking resemblance to a young Harrison Ford, even from only half a face. An unexpected zing of interest made her scoff at herself. Nevertheless, she scrolled down through the other photos on his grid.

There was a photo of an elderly woman in a wheelchair, laughing. The caption read *My favourite girl.* A golden sunrise over the water. *Every day, begin again.* A bare maple tree, its brown and red leaves covering the ground below. *Release to renew.* A baby possum swaddled in a blanket. *My couch surfer, bunking for the night till I find a carer tomorrow.*

She scrolled back to the top of his profile. He only had a hundred or so followers, and no website or any kind of sales pitch or link to an online shop. No photos of himself, other than his profile picture. She concluded that he used Instagram as a personal journal of sorts. He seemed . . . nice. Then again, he could be a total fraud, and this was a completely fake display of things he thought women might want. But then, wouldn't he have more photos of himself, or whoever the attractive man in the profile picture was, if he was trying to hook women?

She dropped her phone onto the couch beside her thigh, chastising herself for getting sucked in to a perfect stranger's curated life. She returned to the marmalade, reigniting the gas, placing the washed jars and lids on a tray to go into the oven to be sterilised, then started the music again, this time something upbeat and cheerful, something she could wiggle her hips to and sing aloud. She didn't want her jam to be maudlin. It needed to be bright and cheerful and stand out to those judges. She needed to get all her entries finished before the trip on the Ghan.

There was still time for her to live her best life, even if it wasn't the one she'd imagined it would be, and this marmalade was a part of it: the chance to win the championship ribbon with her many entries, claim fantastic publicity, take command of her business and steer it into new waters. With every new preserve she made and bottled, she was taking another step towards that life. Of all the things to fix on her list, her business plan should be the easiest to deal with.

'Come on then, marmalade,' she said, encouragingly. 'Let's win this thing.' She would finish the rest of her entries over the next few days, mark the day of Cora's anniversary just as she had last year – alone, with tears, wine and chocolate cake – then pick herself up again, and they'd be on their way to Darwin.

7

Myrtle gazed out the window at the land below. They were somewhere over the Northern Territory, and it wasn't too long before they would land in Darwin. Below them, red earth moulded itself into tight mounds and escarpments, occasionally pierced by snaking black rivers so shiny they looked like giant oil slicks.

Myrtle always took the window seat on the plane, while Dolce preferred the aisle, never wanting to be trapped if she needed to use the bathroom, and because she was slightly less steady on her feet than Myrtle. They flew business class, as a rule. They agreed that, at their age, it was not the time to be miserly, especially as this was their last trip together (according to Dolce). Myrtle hadn't been quite so generous in booking the tickets for Valeria, Aggie and Holly, who were sitting in economy; however, she had been considerate in separating Valeria and Aggie by placing Holly between them.

The young, handsome flight attendant, who had immaculate

eyebrows and wore a smart, pressed vest, returned. 'Would you ladies like one more mojito?' he asked, smiling.

Myrtle smiled at Dolce. 'Shall we?'

Dolce nodded, knitting her fingers together and resting them on her doughy abdomen. 'Indeed.'

The attendant returned with glasses full of ice, mint leaves, lime wedges, sugar and white rum, with a swizzle stick to stir the concoction.

'Here you are, ladies,' he announced, holding out the tray for first Myrtle and then Dolce to take their drinks. 'You enjoy those,' he said with a wink and disappeared into the galley.

It was a reasonably long flight, more than four hours including boarding and disembarking time. They'd flicked through the in-flight magazines, which usually brought considerable inspiration for their next adventure, but today as they'd each perused the colourful pictures, neither had dared to speak of the many places they could still go.

Myrtle's mood had faltered then, absorbing the idea that Dolce truly believed this was the last adventure outside of the Barossa that she would take before she died; therefore, it would be Myrtle's too, unless she found herself a new travel companion, or convinced Dolce to change her mind.

By the time she'd finished sipping on her mojito, the turquoise sea had appeared, having forced its way over the land in wide waterways that curled in smooth loops before straightening then splitting into jagged lightning strikes across the rusty soil.

Dolce leant across her to look through the window too. 'It's so different up this end of the country, isn't it?'

Myrtle nodded her agreement, always amazed at the diversity of Australia's landscapes. She knew then with a sharp certainty that she never wanted to stop travelling. She had to find a way to keep going, with or without Dolce, though if she had anything to do with it, she'd turn Dolce's mind around. They weren't done yet, not by a long shot.

•

The five of them collected their bags and made their way out of the small Darwin airport beneath large corrugated arches colourfully painted with Aboriginal artworks. It was beautifully warm, sunny and dry here at the top end of Australia – exactly double the maximum temperature forecast for Adelaide today – and Aggie loved it. The pouring rains had begun again last week in the Barossa and showed no sign of stopping. This bright, hot sun in winter was a delicious treat. As she removed the cotton scarf she wore around her neck, she spotted a maxi taxi and held up her hand to get the driver's attention. They piled in and Myrtle, sitting in the front, gave him the address of the accommodation she'd booked online.

It was about a twenty-minute drive through the flat landscape before they reached their unit block in the south of Darwin, a cluster of neat three-storey buildings tucked behind a flaccid chain-link fence and graffitied corrugated iron. Aggie rushed to pay the taxi fare, determined not to let Myrtle shoulder all the costs, and they clambered out, dragging their suitcases to the door of the ground-floor unit.

Once inside, Myrtle instructed them, 'Valeria, you take the one closest to the bathroom, Aggie, you take the one with the door to the patio, Holly in the next room – a single bed in that one, I'm sorry to say – and Dolce and I will share the last one.' Dolce moved off with her suitcases towards the room her friend had allocated them.

'But you're paying,' Aggie protested. 'You and Dolce should have your own rooms.'

'Nonsense,' Myrtle said. 'Dolce and I haven't spent decades travelling the world without having to share a bed along the way. We're quite good at it now.'

'As long as I have earplugs to muffle the sound of your snoring,' Dolce called from inside the room.

'And as long as you haven't been eating curry,' Myrtle retorted.

'Really, it's no problem,' Aggie tried again. 'I can sleep on the couch and one of you can have my room. I don't mind.' She did mind, quite a lot, but it was the least she could do to show Myrtle some gratitude for selling her the shop and paying for this trip. 'After everything you've done for me lately . . .'

Myrtle flicked an alarmed gaze towards Valeria, who was adding nothing to this conversation, standing with her good hand supporting her broken wrist.

'It's not just you,' Myrtle interrupted, giving Aggie a meaningful *stop talking now* look. 'Everyone's got a ticket on the Ghan, just the same. Stop fussing, please.'

Aggie closed her mouth and nodded. 'Okay, thank you.' She dragged her suitcase to her room and pulled back the heavy curtains just as her phone rang. It was Savannah, who was in charge of the cafe while Aggie was away. Aggie had run through everything with her yesterday, checking and double-checking deliveries coming in, and rostering on some additional casual staff to assist.

'I'm sorry to call you so soon,' Savannah said, her words pinched tight with worry.

'It's fine, I told you to call if you needed anything. What's happened?'

'A guy from the council came around this morning. He handed me a notice to give you. I'll photograph it and send it to you.'

'What was it?'

'He said the council's been auditing commercial properties and Strawberry Sonnet infringes something or other about signage.'

Aggie's mind ticked over, imagining the front of her shop. She didn't use sandwich boards, so it couldn't be that. She only had the shop facade sign and some tasteful window writing.

'All our signage is regulation,' she said, confused. 'It's been there for five years.'

'He says it's not anymore.'

She felt her shoulders rise. 'What do you mean "anymore"?'

'Like, they passed changes or whatever, bylaws or something, a couple of years ago. I can't remember the exact details. But the big sign, the one hanging below the roof, isn't the right size.'

Aggie sat on the side of the bed. This was ringing a very small, very faint bell. Two years ago, Cora had shifted the landscape from beneath her feet. She had fuzzy, untethered memories of reading something from the council around that time, something about commercial buildings and signage, and burying the piece of paper to be dealt with at another time. She cursed herself. 'Okay, send me the notice and I'll have a read.'

'Problem is,' Savannah said, 'they want it fixed by the end of this week.'

Aggie rocketed to her feet. 'What? They can't do that. That's unreasonable.'

'What do you want me to do?'

'Leave it with me. I'll call them and let you know.'

'Sweet,' Savannah said, sounding much relieved. 'I'll send you this document now.'

The image arrived quickly and Aggie zoomed in on her phone to review it. It indeed said she had until Friday to take the sign down or she'd be fined one thousand dollars. 'Bloody madness,' she mumbled. She called the council. Adopting her most polite voice, she explained who she was and asked to talk to someone who might be able to help her with the problem.

Luke Wellington sounded surprisingly young, a lot younger than Aggie.

'Hi, Luke,' she said, warmly, and then went on to explain her situation. 'Of course, I absolutely want to do the right thing by the council, and I will do as soon as I can, but as I'm on the other side of the country till the end of this week, I'm wondering if you might be able to extend this deadline for a bit, even just another week?'

'Can't do it,' Luke said, shocking Aggie with his abruptness. She could hear him tapping on his keyboard and wondered if he was making notes on their conversation or whether he was uninterested and working on something else entirely.

'May I ask why not?'

'The council isn't in the business of providing extensions.'

'I understand that, but, again, I want to assure you that I am happy to comply one hundred per cent with the regulations, but given the short notice—'

'You've had two years,' he interrupted. 'That's a long time, wouldn't you say?'

'Look, Luke. I've been in business in Angaston for the past twenty years and have been nothing but a good citizen, both as a business owner – supporting the very important tourist trade through the Barossa Valley – and as a resident.'

'You don't own property here, though,' he said.

'What?'

'I'm looking at your data on our system. You don't have property, so you don't pay rates. You don't even own the shop you're working from—'

'Excuse me?' She couldn't suppress her outrage and was about to inform him that, as a matter of fact, she was now the owner of the shop and his records needed updating, but he got in first.

'—so I'm not sure how your claim to be a good citizen is relevant as far as council is concerned.'

She gasped audibly, stunned by his rudeness. 'Can I speak to your supervisor, please?'

'Don't have one.'

'Of course you do. You're not the mayor, so you have a supervisor.' She was on her feet, pacing, and noticed that Myrtle, Dolce, Holly and Valeria were all hovering outside the doorway, drawn by the sound of her raised voice.

'I have to go now,' Luke said. 'The ruling stands, and you have until Friday close of business to fix your signage to meet with the regulations, which, again, you were notified about two years ago.'

'How do you know I even got the letter?' she said.

He snorted spitefully. 'I never said it was a letter.'

'I never got a reminder.'

'The council doesn't issue reminders.'

Regrettably, she knew that to be true. A few years back, she'd received an email notice for the renewal of Banjo's dog registration and forgotten to pay it. They sent no reminder, simply a fine for one hundred and eighty dollars six weeks later.

Luke hadn't finished yet. 'The council assumes its residents are responsible adults, not recalcitrant children.'

She was about to argue that his pompous use of the word 'recalcitrant' was incorrect – she wasn't obstinately defying authority, she'd simply had a brain fail – but he spoke again before she could get the words out.

'Friday, close of business, or it's a fine of one thousand dollars. Thanks for your call.' With that he was gone, leaving Aggie burning with rage.

It was only a couple of kilometres to the city mall, but that was too far for the seniors in their company to walk so they ordered a maxi taxi for the short distance and stepped out near the tourist information centre at the top of the mall.

'Oh, look, it's one of those red buses that takes you around the city,' Holly said, pointing across the road, where a man sat beneath a pop-up tent selling tickets for the Big Bus Darwin Explorer hop-on, hop-off tour. They headed over to join the next tour and the man handed them all maps just as the double-decker bus rumbled into a stop, disgorging tourists all similarly dressed in hats and sunglasses, shorts and shirts.

Dolce, Myrtle and Valeria opted to take seats on the lower level rather than climb the steep stairs to the top. 'It's not getting up that's the worry,' Dolce said, swaying from side to side as she moved towards the back of the bus. 'It's the getting down again. One false move and you end up with a broken tailbone, spending your holiday wearing an unflattering hospital gown.'

The change of scenery had helped boost Aggie's mood and she felt a surge of, if not excitement, then joyful anticipation of what they'd see on the tour. She still needed to send an email to the council but she could do that from her phone.

'Want to come up top?' Aggie asked Holly.

'Yes, it's a little stuffy down here,' she said.

They trooped up the stairs. The top floor had a roof to keep the sun off but open sides for airflow, and Holly and Aggie moved to sit down. Just as Aggie was taking her place, she noticed a man sitting on his own in the seat behind them. He was next to the open window, gazing outside, but looked up as she made to sit down in front of him.

It was young Harrison Ford.

Her heart gave a hard thump. He smiled easily at her, just one traveller greeting another, yet the warmth in it made her stop. She was stuck for a moment, wanting to blurt out to him that she knew him, that he was the poet/alcoholic/melodramatic millennial/life coach she'd seen online. Her mind raced to remember his name. It was a bit like Harrison. It came to her a split second later.

Harry, that was it. Harry Lyon.

His lips rose slightly on one side, a small, crooked, questioning smile.

'Hi,' she said quickly, trying to cover up her obvious reaction to his heart-stoppingly gorgeous face. Though it wasn't just his face, it was his . . . his . . . bloody hell, it was his *aura*, or some such crap. But it was true. His whole presence was so much bigger than him and it felt generous and kind. Magnetic. Definitely seductive.

She'd not been able to tell from his half-face photo if his eyes were blue or green but she could see now that they were neither. They were teal. *Teal.* Who had teal eyes?

She stumbled into her seat and turned to face the front of the bus, imagining his eyes on the back of her neck, which was exposed due to the heat, her long hair piled in a loose bun on the top of her head. The bus lurched into the road and the recorded voice narrating the guided tour broke out over the rumble of the engine. The sudden flush of attraction Aggie had felt to this man was ridiculous, and she fanned herself with the map in her hand. Harry was clearly much younger than her, for a start. Then there was the whole long drama of her repeatedly failed love life.

The new vision she'd forged for herself was modelled on Myrtle – a happy, independent woman who'd enjoyed a long career doing what she loved, growing her financial portfolio and travelling the world. There was nothing wrong with that. Myrtle had seen her future clearly from a young age, never wanted to marry, and armed with that insight, she'd crafted a great life for herself. It wasn't too late for Aggie. Her previous vision was gone, turned to ashes, along with Cora. She knew that there was still time for her to find joy in the world again, but that vision most certainly did not include the young man sitting behind her . . . regardless of how gorgeous his eyes might be.

8

The bus lumbered its way into Cullen Bay, a stylish resort area designed to be a haven against cyclones, according to the recorded tour guide. A large model of a saltwater crocodile sat on the wharf, its mouth open to the sky. Valeria had taken a photo of it on her phone, and was studying it when a message flashed up on her screen.

Two more sleeps. X

The Englishman.

She cast her eyes over at Dolce and Myrtle, who were sitting companionably across the aisle, staring out the window as the bus left the bay, heading towards its next stop at the casino. She covered the phone with her hand, as if they might accidentally read it. *What was he thinking?* But the only person she could blame here was herself.

After his first phone call, which she'd ignored, he'd continued to call her. He wanted a second chance, an opportunity to make it up to her. He hadn't meant to simply walk out and not return. Things were complicated. She still meant the world to him.

'Prove it, then,' she'd challenged him. 'Meet me on the Ghan.'

'All right,' he'd said in his refined but warm tone. 'I mean it, Val. I said I'd come back for you and that's what I intend to do.'

Now here he was, counting down the days till they met again. She might have issued the dare in a flash of impertinence, but she'd never truly believed he'd come. Now it looked as though he might really be meeting her on Wednesday, at the platform. If that was true, was he merely there to see her on the platform, or did he actually have a ticket for the train? She hadn't considered that before now, only believing he might be there to see her off, if he was there at all. She didn't know if she could trust him. She'd looked him up on Facebook a few times in the past two years. They weren't Facebook friends, neither having much to do with social media. They'd laughed at how it had seemed such a strange thing, this endless oversharing of everything, from what one's eggs looked like at breakfast to the most intimate and shocking details of one's life. When he'd left the Barossa two years ago to go back to north Queensland, he'd given little explanation. Then, earlier this year, she'd opened Facebook and entered his name out of curiosity, and there on his timeline was a photo. It had been posted by someone else but it had been tagged with his name, meaning it was visible on his profile page.

In the image, he was with a woman. She was tall and glamorous and younger than him, which piqued Valeria's anger. It was so infuriatingly typical, this older man – younger woman scenario. Granted, at least the woman wasn't in her twenties. She'd read a few comments, sentimental ones like *Look at you two!* and *Congratulations to you both*, and emojis with smiling faces and love hearts for eyes.

She'd closed the page quickly, her chest tight with jealousy and embarrassment. She'd really believed they'd had something.

For months they'd been inseparable, though keeping it quiet. With everything Agatha and Gideon had going on, it never seemed the right time to announce happy news. Then he was gone, saying he had to go back home.

Was he playing her now? Even if he turned up on Wednesday, which she had to admit was seeming more and more likely, she had no idea what his motivation was.

•

At the Darwin Military Museum, they got off the bus (leaving Harry behind, to Aggie's disappointment) to take in some of Darwin's World War II history, in the 'Defence of Darwin Experience'. The short film and interactive display about the bombing of Darwin by Japanese forces for nearly two years, starting in February 1942, had deeply shocked Aggie. The grainy black-and-white footage of naval ships, gunfire and bombs had seemed utterly surreal.

At the end of the day, the five of them trundled back to the unit carrying takeaway hamburgers and a bottle of vodka to make jamtinis. They were all tired from the early start, the flight, and the long bus tour. In the kitchen, Aggie poured two shots of vodka into five large tumblers. Holly dropped a tablespoon of jam – Myrtle, Dolce and Aggie having brought a selection with them – into each, followed by handfuls of ice, while Aggie squeezed lemons for juice. After some rapid whizzing with forks, topping up the glasses with fizzy water and floating garnishes of cut strawberries, the cocktails were ready.

Holly sucked a droplet of jamtini from her finger, then said, 'I still can't believe all that stuff about the war.'

'It's shocking, I agree,' Aggie said.

'And then Cyclone Tracy happened and the whole city was destroyed again,' Holly said, her deep brown eyes wide. 'Why would anyone live here?' She seemed genuinely baffled.

'Well, they said that after Tracy they rebuilt the city with cyclone standards in mind.'

'Yeah, but still, after all that, I think I would have left and never come back.' Holly carried the colourful cocktails over to the table, where Myrtle had laid out plates and Valeria distributed burgers, tight-lipped. Her mother was definitely distracted by something. The war, perhaps. Both Valeria's parents had served in the war, and both had held a lifelong distrust of the Japanese. Aggie could clearly remember her pop going on about 'the Japs', and after a few drinks would take verbal shots at anyone or anything connected to Japan. He couldn't understand how people could so quickly forget their prison camps, the horrendous cruelty; couldn't understand how the children and grandchildren of those who'd served in that terrible war could willingly travel to Japan, love their technology, eat their food. 'People have bloody short memories,' he'd say. 'Too quick to forgive. Not me.' He'd tap the side of his head, his eyes distant and glassy.

Aggie joined them at the table and tore open the paper of her barbecue chicken burger. It smelt amazing and she realised she was quite hungry. Chewing on a delicious mouthful, she thought about Holly's words: that she'd leave and never come back after losing everything. Aggie understood that sentiment. How often she'd wanted to run from her own life, her own body, her pain . . . and from Gideon, the memories of their losses hovering between them like sticky, invisible spider webs, impossible to disentangle.

Eventually, she'd pushed him away, leaving him no choice.

At the same time, she could appreciate why Darwin would rebuild itself, not just once but twice. It was hope, that stubborn human trait of believing in better days. That was why she and Gideon had tried again and again. They'd honestly believed each time that life would prevail. But they were wrong.

'I wonder if Darwin truly is cyclone-proof now,' she said, quietly, to no one in particular.

'It's a city built on trauma,' Dolce said, wiping tomato sauce from her chin.

'The resilience of its people is remarkable,' Myrtle said, smacking her lips appreciatively after a mouthful of apricot jamtini. She gave Aggie a meaningful stare. 'It's incredible what the human soul can endure.'

A general silence settled around the table.

The letter from the IVF clinic waiting at home was once more fresh in Aggie's mind. She wondered if she might gain some clarity about the decision she and Gideon needed to make, maybe by seeking advice from the wise women in her life. She put down her hamburger and wiped her hands. 'I received a letter last month,' she said, and waited a beat while the others turned their attention to her. 'Gideon got the same one.'

Valeria swallowed quickly before speaking. 'What was it?'

'It was from the clinic. The storage of our frozen embryos are due for renewal, or . . .'

'Or what?' Valeria prompted.

Aggie shrugged. 'We haven't decided.'

'What are the options?' Holly asked, carefully.

Aggie studied Holly's face. Since landing in sunny Darwin, Holly had been visibly relieved of whatever mental burden she was carrying; she seemed to be more present now that they were out of the Barossa. Aggie hoped this holiday would let her shake off whatever had been getting her down, once and for all. Still, the distance she'd been feeling between them, the sense that Holly was keeping something or someone from her, gave her pause.

Holly had been overseas through all the years of IVF. Aggie had talked about everything with her, of course, and Holly had been a compassionate listening ear, but she'd never truly been involved in the process, the losses, the emotional toll it had taken on Aggie and Gideon. More than anything, Aggie didn't ever want Holly to feel that the baby she didn't get to take home meant more to her than her firstborn. She never wanted Holly to feel as if she was 'the mistake' and that Cora had been the chosen one. She never wanted Holly to feel that she hadn't been enough. None of those things were true, but she knew how easily feelings of displacement could grow into lifelong resentments. She only had to look around the table at Valeria and Myrtle to see that.

Aggie took a sip of her strong, sweet raspberry jamtini and swallowed. 'Well, we can use them and try again for a baby. Or we can keep them on ice, we can donate them to another couple who are trying to conceive, we can donate them to science . . . or we can destroy them.'

There were several moments of silence and Aggie looked to Holly beside her, who frowned and clicked her tongue in commiseration but didn't offer an opinion.

'What did Gideon say?' Valeria asked.

'He doesn't know what he thinks just yet, either. We decided to wait till after this trip to make a decision.'

Valeria's jaw muscles flicked. 'Would he . . . do you think he'd go for it again, have one last try?'

Aggie felt her jaw unhinge, and words fought to erupt from her chest, but she took a breath to soothe them and choose her words carefully. 'As I said, we haven't discussed it, but I'm fairly certain neither of us wants that. We've been through too much.' Even as she said it, though, there was a tiny ember somewhere inside her: *Maybe this time it would be different.* Holly nodded and smiled sympathetically, as did Dolce. 'Besides, we're not even together anymore.'

'But that didn't stop you having a baby before,' Valeria said, and the tone of her voice made Aggie flinch. She quickly shot Holly a look but, thankfully, Holly raised a stoic eyebrow, seeming to weather that statement with equanimity. Never in a million years would Valeria let Aggie forget that she'd been a reckless, embarrassing teenage mother. 'You can't let them go to waste. You've been a single mother before, you could do it again.'

This time, Holly inhaled deliberately and reached for her jamtini too.

'It's not that simple,' Aggie said through gritted teeth. 'Even if I was okay to be, as you say, a single mother again, if Gideon doesn't want me to have *our* baby that way, I won't be able to. We both have to agree on what to do with the embryos.'

'But surely they're your embryos,' Valeria countered. 'He can't use them.'

'When you do IVF there's a whole lot of paperwork that is signed. As he fertilised the eggs, he is legally the father and therefore has a financial responsibility at the very least. Because of that, he would also have to agree for me to use them.'

'But Gideon's lovely,' Valeria went on. Myrtle glared at her, trying to get Valeria's attention, anticipating the awfulness of this conversation.

A loud, exasperated sigh escaped Aggie's mouth before she could stop it. *Gideon's lovely.* As if Aggie was not. 'I know you love Gideon, Mum – you've made that very clear.' She rankled at the memory of their argument several months ago, which had led to the prolonged period of non-communication that had only ended thanks to Valeria's recent hospitalisation. 'But we have broken up. These embryos are . . . they're just . . .'

What were they, exactly? Property to be decided upon? Legally, yes, that was exactly what they were.

'But you can't let them die,' Valeria said, shock evident across her face.

'They're not alive,' Aggie countered, pushing her chair back from the table, suddenly needing more space between her and Valeria.

'They're your babies. You can't abandon them.'

'They're not babies, though,' Holly said, reasonably. 'They're just a few cells at this stage, barely visible to the human eye.'

'But they could *become* babies,' Valeria went on. 'If these really are the last potential children you could ever have, then surely you want to give it one last try, don't you? Talk to him, Agatha. He'll understand, I'm sure.'

'Why aren't you listening to me?' Aggie said.

'I am listening. That's all I ever get to do.'

Aggie paused, confused, then said in a measured tone, 'I don't even know what that means.'

Valeria ignored that and continued. 'What would you do, donate them to someone else and have someone else raise your child – or children, if it's a multiple birth? Donate them to science and have them do goodness knows what to them? Keep freezing them until you're too old to have them anyway and only have to make this decision all over again? Or . . . destroy them? That sounds horrible.'

'Yes, Mum, it does sound horrible. It's agony, if you must know. Complete and utter agony. It's as if they are ghosts, floating around me, waiting for me to take them out of limbo and save them from their uncertain future.' Aggie felt tears welling then, and knew she couldn't stay. She held up her hands to signal that this conversation was over. She wished she'd never brought it up, and left the table, closing her bedroom door behind her.

9

'Here,' Dolce said, handing Myrtle her phone. 'Get a photo of me feeding the crocs and I'll send it to the kids.' She trailed the piece of meat hanging at the end of the bamboo pole over the crowded pool of juvenile crocodiles.

Myrtle held up the phone, ready to get a good picture, marvelling that they were still finding new things to do on their travels even at their age. The two of them had covered a lot of ground together. They'd been brave adventurers, something she was proud of, but there remained so much to do.

They'd first met back when Myrtle was a thirty-year-old teacher at a small school in the valley. Dolce had brought her eldest, Michael, to the classroom door on his first day of school. She and Myrtle were clearly around the same age, Myrtle discovering not long afterwards that Dolce was two years her junior, and they hit it off immediately. It was 1967, and it seemed the country was in constant flux. Harold Holt was prime minister, and the social fabric of the nation was changing. Myrtle and Dolce were like representatives from two different societies: Dolce, a wife and mother, Myrtle, progressive and independent. She'd never wanted to marry, having followed the sage advice bestowed upon her by her older sister, Dorothy – Valeria's mother.

Dorothy had been a little girl when World War II began, and her father was away in service for many years, leaving Dorothy as the only child at home. Many years later, after Dorothy was married with children she would warn her younger sister, Myrtle, never to marry. In hindsight, Dorothy could see that their father's absence during the war had left their mother with an unprecedented amount of domestic and personal freedom she'd come to relish. But after he returned, the light in her mother's eyes was extinguished as baby after baby came, the nappies endlessly flapping on the line, the relentless requirement to cook, clean and serve taking away the mother Dorothy had so loved as a young child. She saw firsthand what marriage could do to a woman and yet she herself had followed that same path, believing she'd had no choice.

'Promise me, Myrtle, promise me you won't get married,' she would hiss into Myrtle's ear as they stood in the kitchen, Dorothy stirring soup while rocking a baby on her hip.

'But what will I do?' the teenage Myrtle had asked. What else *did* women do?

'Listen to me. A career as a teacher won't pay you much but it is a reliable, respectable path to follow and will save you from the babies,' Dorothy said, her eyes close to spilling tears.

Myrtle looked at the grumpy, red-faced baby on her sister's hip and listened.

It was a choice Myrtle never once regretted. As luck would have it, she happened to love teaching, and it also offered her the opportunity to travel during school holidays.

Dolce, on the other hand, did what so many before her had done – marriage, children, homemaking, church attendance, and tennis once a week. But she had a cheeky smile, a glint in her eye and a willingness to ignore the rules, which Myrtle thoroughly appreciated. Plus, they made each other laugh, and when Dolce laughed her whole body shook with mirth. She had that rare quality of an effortlessly sunny, happy disposition. She was an easygoing soul who sailed smoothly through life no matter what else was going on.

Now Dolce's crocodile threw itself out of the pool, almost standing on its tail in its drive to snatch the meat. She whipped her pole back like a big-game fisherman, and there was a second's tussle before the string snapped and the croc disappeared below the surface again. Dolce turned around, beaming.

'Did you get it?' she asked. 'Did you get the photo?'

Myrtle laughed. 'I got several.'

'Oh, goodie,' Dolce said, shimmying her shoulders and handing the pole back to the attendant. 'I'll be the coolest granny around.'

'You always are,' Myrtle said, yet again wondering why on earth Dolce would want to stop finding new adventures to enjoy.

'Come on, I saw a cafeteria downstairs,' Dolce said. 'I could use a cuppa.'

They headed down the stairs, Myrtle walking in front of Dolce, just a little ahead.

'I know why you do that,' Dolce said, puffing slightly.

'What?'

'Walk in front of me when we're going down the stairs and behind me going up the stairs. You're worried I'll fall.'

Myrtle didn't say anything, but a small smile came to her lips. 'Oh yes?'

'You're not that much stronger than me, you know. What if I did have a fall and took you with me?'

'Then we'd go down together, just as we should.'

•

Aggie waved to Myrtle and Dolce as they came down the stairs while the phone was jammed to her ear. Not far away, Valeria and Holly were sitting on a bench seat while a reptile handler extracted snakes and lizards from bags and boxes to show to the tourists.

Aggie continued her conversation with Savannah. 'I haven't got a response from the council yet.'

'What should we do now?' Savannah asked, sounding confident and capable on her second day in charge.

Aggie liked the way her employee said *we*; it was a small but telling indication of her commitment to the cafe. 'They've backed me into a bit of a corner, unfortunately. It's impossible to get a new sign complying with the required dimensions in such a short time frame, so I'm going to ring around and see if I can find someone to come and take down the old sign. That will remove the problem of the current sign being an infringement.'

Having a denuded cafe frontage was not helpful in the slightest, but money was tight and it looked as though it was either that or pay the fine to the council, which she couldn't afford.

'Unfortunately, it's all I can do right now. Leave it with me and I'll let you know how I get on finding a sign writer or handyman at least.'

'I can do it,' Savannah said. 'That's what I'm here for, to give you a break.'

'That's a kind offer,' Aggie said, eyeing a particularly long python that the handler had just placed around Holly's neck, sending Valeria scuttling in the opposite direction. Holly's bravery made Aggie smile. 'But I think it's best if I deal with this one. Thank you, though.' She said goodbye to Savannah, then began searching the internet to find someone to help.

'Council still giving you trouble?' Myrtle asked, taking a seat at her table and unwrapping a chocolate-covered ice cream.

'Mm,' she muttered, sucking in her cheeks while scanning listings of signage professionals in the Barossa. There were a handful, so she started at the top and began making calls. The first two said they were booked up for the next month, the third said he'd see what he could do, and the fourth had a recorded message saying he was on holidays and wouldn't be back till late September.

'Damn, damn, damn,' she said, then, brightening her tone, 'Oh, thanks,' as Dolce slid a coffee across the table to her. 'Just what I need.' She took several big gulps, eager for the caffeine. Her night had been largely sleepless, the discussion about what to do with her embryos having opened old wounds so deep that on occasion she'd found herself holding her breath against the pain. She was still feeling choppy today, like water that had been stirred up by a big storm, taking its time to settle. As for her and her mother, they'd carried on as if last night's conversation had never happened, which was Valeria's preferred way.

She noticed that both Dolce and Myrtle looked thoughtful. 'What?' she said, smiling at them.

'Well, I was thinking about your embryos,' Dolce said, her eyes kind.

'Me too,' agreed Myrtle.

'That old chestnut,' Aggie said, tearing open two packets of sugar and tipping them into her bitter – possibly burnt – coffee. 'What do *you* think I should do?' She addressed Dolce first, having always appreciated the woman's maternal nature. She was a mother hen, the type that would adopt kittens or chicks of other species and tuck them under her wing.

'It's an impossible decision, of course,' she said, shaking her head sadly. 'Except that you do have to choose to do something.'

'The tricky thing is that you both need to agree,' Myrtle said. 'I mean, what if you simply don't? What do you do then?'

Aggie shook her head. 'No idea.'

'What happens if you do nothing?' Dolce wondered. 'If you just never responded to the letter, what would the clinic do?'

Aggie hadn't considered that this might be an option and was momentarily buoyed by the idea that there was an escape route, a blissful way to avoid making a decision at all.

'Surely the clinic would take legal action,' Myrtle suggested, licking ice cream from her lips. 'There must be a law to cover that.'

'I'm guessing they'd destroy them, by default,' Aggie said. After a split second of madness, wondering if she could simply do nothing, she knew she couldn't walk away from her embryos. They were her responsibility – hers and Gideon's. She was sure he wouldn't do that either. He had more integrity than that. As hard as it might be, they did need to make a decision. 'So if nothing's not an option, what would you do then?' she asked Dolce.

Dolce tapped her knobbly knuckles on the plastic tabletop, thinking. 'I think I would donate them to another couple who were trying to have a baby,' she said.

Aggie nodded and smiled at her. Yes, that was exactly what Dolce would do, sharing the babies with the flock. But for Aggie, knowing there might be children out in the world who were hers would be too much to bear. She couldn't begin to imagine strangers raising her babies. It was selfish, yes, but it was also self-preservation. 'Thanks,' she said.

'But it's not my body and they're not my embryos,' Dolce was quick to add. 'Only you and Gideon will know what's right.'

After they'd finished at the crocodile house and Dolce had bought trinkets and toys for her many grandchildren from the gift shop, they boarded the hop-on, hop-off tourist bus once more, making the most of their twenty-four-hour ticket. They disembarked at the museum and art gallery.

Aggie was distracted, wandering past the artworks and through the museum while searching the internet on her phone, continuing to try to find a handyman who could take down the offending signage at the cafe. She'd just secured one who would go out and take a look this afternoon, and was texting Savannah to let her know, when someone spoke to her.

'That's a happy smile,' he said.

She looked up into teal eyes.

Now that he was standing in front of her, rather than seated on a bus, she could see how tall he was. He wore a white T-shirt and loose khaki pants, with a woven satchel of sorts over his shoulder, and his smile stretched for days.

'Oh . . . yes,' she said, taken aback.

'I saw you on the bus yesterday,' he said. 'I'm assuming you're a tourist, like me, taking advantage of the last few hours of our bus tickets.'

'Yes,' she said again, willing her brain to come up with something more interesting to say.

'Are you by any chance boarding the Ghan tomorrow?'

'I am. It's a family trip. We're celebrating my mum's seventieth,' she said, scanning the room, looking for one of her family members. She guessed they might be viewing a museum display about Cyclone Tracy, as a soundtrack of screaming winds and the destruction of buildings emanated from a darkened room nearby.

'Nice.' He appeared to be in no hurry to move on – one of those unnerving people who was comfortable simply to stand still in their own skin. He thrust out his hand. 'I'm Harry.'

'I know,' she said, taking his hand, then blushing a split second later at his confused look. She laughed. 'I was searching the hashtag *theghan* on Instagram before I left, admiring photos of what was to come, and one of your photos came up, the one of the sky and the candle, where you said you couldn't wait to see it from a different perspective, or something like that.' She finished speaking in a rush.

He let go of her hand and studied her, a look of bemusement on his face. 'Right. Wow, that's a coincidence.'

'Crazy, hey? The modern world we live in.'

'Definitely.'

'I'm Aggie, by the way.'

'Great name.'

'My mum loved Agatha Christie novels so she named me Agatha, but she's the only one who calls me that. Everyone else calls me Aggie, or Ags, or if there's been enough alcohol or merriment, then it's Agadoo-doo-doo . . . It's my party trick.'

'It's a cult classic. Can you do all the actions?'

'Of course,' she said, and laughed.

'You're going to have to show me.'

'What? Here?'

'No, not here. You might cause a security alert or something. On the train seems like a perfectly logical place to dance to eighties kitschy novelty pop.'

She laughed again as she imagined this, and it was the kind of effortless laugh that left her feeling light and free. She needed that. 'My mother would have a fit. Not my Great-Aunt Myrtle, though – she'd join in for sure. She'd probably kick it off.'

'Can't wait to meet her,' he said. 'I work as a carer in aged-care homes. Seniors are my people.'

'My favourite girl,' she said.

He tilted his head, questioningly.

'In your photos, you had one of your residents, I guess. You said she was your favourite girl. It was very sweet.'

'You looked at my photos?'

'Just a few. I'm not a mad stalker, I promise. I didn't, like, set up this meeting or anything,' she said, her high-pitched laugh betraying how awkward she now felt. 'You know how you can get sucked into following threads on social media? It was just that – that's all.'

His face had changed, though, and he nodded, this time not enthusiastically but analytically. His lips twitched, as though he was wrestling with words. His mind was working, trying to figure something out.

'Anyway,' she said, trying to regain the light banter they'd just enjoyed, 'Myrtle is far from being in an aged-care home. She and Dolce are still happily travelling the world. I expect they'll keep doing it till the day they die.'

His shoulders had stiffened. While he smiled at her words, he was clearly distracted now.

With another effort to relocate the warm, open guy he had been a few moments ago, she said, 'I was just about to head down to the gift shop to have a look, if you'd like to come down too, maybe find something for yourself to take home?'

'Actually, I can't, sorry.'

'Okay, no worries,' she said, forcefully bright.

'Myrtle sounds fantastic, though,' he said, softening slightly. 'I'll be sure to look out for her. Thanks for the chat, Aggie.'

'Of course,' she said, trying not to let her disappointment radiate through her words.

'Enjoy the rest of your day.' He turned and walked away, and didn't look back.

She stared at his retreating figure, wondering what on earth had just happened.

10

Valeria took her seat opposite Agatha at the table for two. Her daughter placed Valeria's orange juice down carefully for her. She fleetingly eyed Valeria's plate of hot breakfast buffet portions, and Valeria was certain she was biting her tongue with unsolicited advice about foods appropriate to eat after one has had a TIA.

'Thank you,' she said to Agatha, grateful for the juice-carrying but furious she couldn't carry it herself. She detested being reliant on others and the tortuous way she had to lumber through everything with her broken wrist. Still, it wasn't long until she would be out of the cast, a couple of weeks at most. Then she would have to undergo hand therapy and rehabilitation.

They'd made an early start for the hotel that acted as the pick-up point for the Ghan departure buses, skipping breakfast at the unit and agreeing to eat here instead. There wasn't a table big enough to fit the five of them, and she'd been relieved that Agatha had readily followed her to a table after their bickering the other day. Despite what her daughter seemed intent on believing, she really did want them to have a harmonious relationship.

She lifted her knife, attempting to cut into a sausage, but it sprang towards her, scooting across the plate and only narrowly avoiding landing in her lap.

Agatha smiled indulgently and stabbed the sausage with her fork. 'This side of the city is definitely the nicest,' she remarked, when she had finished cutting up the sausage. She reached for her cup of tea.

Agatha looked lovely today, her long hair brushed and pinned to the side, something she only seemed to do when she was trying to make real effort, as opposed to just letting it hang free, or tied back if she was at the cafe. 'The esplanade is really pretty.'

'Yes, it is. It's a pity we missed market day. I keep reading about how good it is in the guides,' Valeria said.

'Yes.'

Okay, so they were being polite but that was better than sniping at each other. From inside her bag, Valeria's phone tinged. Her eyes darted to the handbag sitting on the floor.

Agatha noticed. 'Do you want me to pass you the phone?'

Valeria was sure it would be from Rupert, but before she could tell Agatha not to worry about it, her daughter had leant over and plucked the phone from her bag and, without looking at the screen – thankfully – handed it over.

'Thanks.' Valeria held it for a moment, her heart bouncing in her chest, not wanting to look at it with Agatha so close but also desperate to know what it said.

Agatha chewed a mouthful of toast and gave her a puzzled look, so Valeria glanced at the screen.

Can't wait to see you.

She blinked a few times, processing this information, which was simultaneously relieving and frightening. Was Rupert really travelling on the Ghan too? Her hand rose to her forehead and pressed there.

'What's wrong?' Agatha asked.

'Oh.'

'Mum, what is it?' The note of concern in her daughter's voice both touched and irritated her. This was how everyone would look at her now, like someone on the verge of collapse.

'It's . . . nothing, really.' She could see Agatha's shoulders droop, not from relief but from something more like resignation that her mother had closed down on her, was withholding something, didn't trust her. Valeria knew she should confide in Agatha and take this opportunity to strengthen their relationship, but she was feeling a whirl of confusion and hope; if something went wrong, if Rupert didn't turn up, she'd be humiliated.

Instead, she changed the topic. 'Did you find someone to go and look at the sign at the cafe?'

'I had a guy set to go out yesterday but then something came up and he didn't make it. I'm hoping he will have time this morning.'

'Such a shame the council is being so difficult. I've always thought good citizens should get some sort of reward points for time well served, something you can draw on in the future if you need to.'

'I think that's a great idea,' Agatha said. 'I can't afford the fine, even if I do win the jam competition.'

Valeria's fork hovered in space. Why couldn't Agatha afford the fine? She thought the business was doing well, and Myrtle hadn't raised the rent on the shop in years, as far as she knew. Was Myrtle getting tougher in her old age? Agatha wouldn't have a leg to stand on if Myrtle had prioritised money over family, given how much support she'd provided Agatha over the years. She wouldn't put it past Myrtle to be tightening the purse strings to boost her world travel goals. Maybe she should have a quiet word to Myrtle about it. Mind you, her aunt was also funding this whole trip, so anything Valeria said to her now would seem ungrateful in the extreme.

It wouldn't be wise to bring it up with Agatha, either. Myrtle and Agatha's relationship was one she'd had no say in from the moment Agatha was pregnant with Holly and Valeria asked her to find her own place to live. Instead of Agatha taking the opportunity to grow up and take responsibility for her life, as Valeria had intended, Myrtle had swooped in and overridden Valeria's efforts, taking Agatha and Holly into her own home, from that day forward becoming the one they saw as the mother and grandmother figure, inserting a wedge between her and Agatha. Valeria had been losing ground with her daughter ever since – usurped, replaced, diminished.

Maybe, then, Valeria should pull out of the competition. She thought about her jars of jam in the pantry back home. The thought of not presenting them at the Adelaide Show next month made her sad. But wouldn't a good mother step aside and allow Agatha to win, claim the cash prize to help her with whatever was going on with Myrtle and money, and take the spot with Maggie Beer?

But . . . Maggie Beer! The thought of losing her chance to meet her idol made her stomach clench painfully. Then again, if Aggie did get the spot on Maggie's show, surely she'd allow Valeria to accompany her to the set and to meet Maggie too? It wouldn't be the same, though. Valeria was the reigning jam queen. It was her place to stand there beside Maggie, shoulder to shoulder with her hero.

Perhaps, then, she *could* still enter the competition, and when she won she could give the money to Agatha, which would still allow her to keep her spot on the show.

Yes, that would work perfectly.

•

'You're all invited to the wedding!' the Ghan steward said into the microphone on the bus.

Aggie turned to Holly, sitting beside her, who grinned back, further buoying Aggie's spirits. Valeria was sitting across the aisle and leant forward to catch her eye too. No one had been expecting a wedding on the platform before their journey began.

'The life of an influencer, hey?' Holly said, widening her eyes. 'Why weren't these jobs on offer when I was at school?'

'They probably didn't exist then. The *internet* didn't even exist when I was at school. I don't understand how people can do things and use stuff, eat things and wear clothes, and get paid big bucks just to post photos about it.'

Holly looked thoughtful. 'I guess it's just the new world of marketing and PR, and influencers are the ones at the top of their game,' she said. 'They're basically the cool chicks at school, who now get paid for it.' She sighed. 'I was going to say maybe it's not too late for me to change careers and become an influencer, but I'm nowhere near cool enough.'

'Are you thinking of changing careers?' This was the first Aggie had heard of this.

Holly shrugged and popped a piece of chewing gum into her mouth. 'Maybe.'

Aggie tried to suppress her hope that this was true. A career change would save her from the ever-present threat of a school shooting. 'Are you not enjoying teaching anymore?'

Holly chewed her gum for a few moments before answering. 'I love working with students, but – I don't know . . .' She shook her head. 'The system is intense.'

'Do you think if you left teaching that you'd come back to Australia, or would you stay in America?'

Holly stared straight ahead. 'I'd come back home,' she said, though her tone conveyed no joy about that. Still, Aggie felt a quiver of excitement.

If Holly's moroseness had been due to a career crisis, a sense of feeling stuck, then she might be able to get her settled here in Australia with something new to look forward to. She mentally added that to her to-do list. Her job as a mother wasn't over yet.

The bus swung around a corner and the Ghan steward got to her feet once again. 'Now's the time to check your boarding card to see which end of the train you need to head to,' she said. 'Carriage A is at the front of the train and they go backwards from there.' There was a bustle as bags were opened and pockets checked for tickets. 'The bus driver will take you to the carriages at the furthest end after we make the first stop at the station. The train's nearly a kilometre long, and you don't want to be dragging your suitcases all that way. And remember, you are all invited to the wedding! It's happening outside the platinum carriages, which will be a short walk to the right after you enter the platform.'

'The influencers get platinum!' Holly cooed, envious, and Aggie could practically hear her trying to calculate how to launch this enviable new career. 'They're nearly twice the price of the gold-class carriages, but they get a queen-sized bed rather than the double bunks in the twin carriages.'

Aggie snorted. 'Or the tiny beds in the single cabins.'

Theirs was not the first bus to arrive and a large crowd had already gathered at the site of the wedding, which was cordoned off by a thin white rope to hold the guests back and make space for the two photographers, a cinematographer and a woman with a clipboard who appeared to be the director. The other guests for this trip were almost all seniors. Aggie spotted the occasional couple who looked to be in their fifties but none who were more youthful than that.

The couple getting married were as she'd expected – thin, gorgeous, with perfect hair, enormous smiles and glowing, dewy skin. The bride's dress was simple but elegant, and on her feet she wore R. M. Williams Chelsea boots. Her bouquet was a neat arrangement of desert-red roses, perfectly suited to promoting the Ghan. Aggie assumed their entire trip had been funded by the rail company, which would get significant social media traffic from this handsome couple. Another Ghan steward, in jeans, work shirt and Akubra, was handing out trays of petals to the gathered guests, for them to throw into the air upon command, while yet more stewards stood waiting with trays of sparkling wine in hand, ready for the celebration after the ceremony.

Aggie had to admit, the whole thing was captivating.

It made her wonder about her and Gideon, why they'd never got married. She'd once thought that she'd never married because she'd done all the significant life events in the wrong order – having a baby before graduating from high school had skewed that trajectory well and truly – and it had seemed too late to start again. But she and Gideon had been planning on having a baby, maybe two. Not just planning it, but investing eye-watering amounts of money and subjecting themselves to incredible stress and heartbreak to do it. Why on earth hadn't they married as well?

She tried to remember their conversations about it. They'd talked about the fact that a piece of paper changed nothing, that they'd rather invest the wedding funds into IVF cycles, that they were modern people and didn't see the need to conform to what was in essence an archaic arrangement that, until very recent times, had never had anything to do with love at all and everything about merging properties, finances or country alliances. Legally speaking, that was still pretty much what it was all about. Not love. Love was too big to be contained in a document anyway.

Now, though, she wondered if they still would have given up on each other if they had been married – if that one extra step, that added layer of commitment, the greater difficulty in separation would have forced them to try that little bit harder or longer. And, if they *were* still married, would their conversations now about what to do with the embryos be different? Would the criteria for when to quit have changed?

Or maybe it wouldn't have mattered at all.

A cheer went up around her, bringing her attention back, and she threw her dusky red petals into the air, letting them mingle with the others, as the groom dipped his bride back for a romantic, and somewhat gymnastic, kiss. They hovered there as long as they could while the professional photographers got many shots from many angles. They were still there, kissing, as the champagne flutes were passed around and the crowd applauded. Aggie felt herself smile and wished them well.

When the guests began to dissipate, Myrtle called their little group to order, checking everyone's carriage numbers. 'Let's walk to the end of the platform and get photos of us in front of the engine first,' she said.

At the front of the train, they passed their phones to some helpful fellow travellers who agreed to take photos of the five of them standing next to the red engine, with its large white circular logo of a camel being ridden by a cameleer. Then they took many more of each other in endless combinations of twos and threes, before heading back to where they'd left their luggage on the platform and making their way to their carriages, roughly in the centre of the train.

Dolce and Myrtle were sharing a twin room in one carriage, which left Aggie, Holly and Valeria in single cabins in the next carriage. They waved goodbye before heading in opposite directions, Aggie, Holly and Valeria to the right, the others to the left. They were greeted by yet more stewards in the vestibule of the carriage, who checked off their names and led them to their assigned rooms. Aggie and Valeria were side by side, both facing in the direction the train would travel, while Holly was on the other side of the aisle, opposite Valeria, facing the other way. After exclaiming at the compactness of the room, they each took some time to settle, delighting at the amazing view and how wonderful it would be to watch the night sky and then the break of dawn from their cosy beds.

Aggie worked out how to lower the small table that poked out from under the window, laying it flat against the wall, which instantly gave her some more space, and checked out the many hidden narrow cupboards and the drawer under the seat where she could store a few things.

'What a great exercise in tiny-house living,' she mused to herself aloud, which was one of her habits – one Gideon had found a little unnerving, though she'd tried to explain that it was regarded as a sign of intelligence.

'It helps if you're short,' a voice said from behind her.

She spun around, the hairs on her arms tingling.

'H-hi,' she stammered, partly excited to see Harry standing there, partly still embarrassed that he'd felt the need to flee from her yesterday.

He smiled and nodded to the room directly opposite hers. 'This is me.'

'Right. Well, that's a coincidence,' she said.

He shrugged. 'I guess there's only so many places to put the single travellers.' He stepped inside, easing his duffel bag through the narrow doorway. He held out his arms and touched both walls easily. 'I hope these magically open up to accommodate any size, Harry Potter–style.'

She couldn't answer. She was too stunned to see that the man she'd found online and had bumped into twice would now be sleeping an arm's length away from her. The man who made her palms sweat. The man who'd walked away from her yesterday as if he couldn't escape fast enough. For the next three nights he would be right here.

It had to be a cosmic joke.

The train's horn sounded, long and loud. The exterior doors of the locomotive slammed shut. A voice came over the loudspeaker, welcoming them on board, effectively cutting off any continued conversation with Harry, and they retreated into their rooms, she facing forward, he backward. She couldn't see his face through the open doors, but she could see his legs extended across the small space beneath his small table.

The conductor went on to inform them that the train would soon be departing and that lunch would be served in an hour's time. When he'd finished, Aggie heard her mother's phone ting from the cabin next to hers and wondered who she was texting.

She spent the next minutes pulling a few items from her suitcase before shoving it under the seat opposite, where it fit snugly and was out of the way. Feeling less claustrophobic now, she raised the blinds that sat between the two panes of glass and readied herself to watch the view roll by. She opened her journey companion booklet to read about the train. After a few minutes, something large and heavy clunked in the undercarriage beneath her feet and the engine began to haul its enormous load.

She gazed out the window at the greenery, which was soon to disappear into changing landscape, she knew, and for just a moment, she forgot all about the embryos, Gideon, her worries about Holly, the problems at the cafe, and whatever weird attraction to Harry she was feeling, and let herself be an adventurer, free from her daily life. The journey from the top to the bottom of Australia, following in the steps of the cameleers from long ago, had begun.

11

Valeria scuttled past Agatha's room on her way to the next carriage, which was one closer to the front of the train. Rupert was in room eight, which was not her favourite number. Eight was Agatha's favourite number. Valeria's was seven. If Rupert had been in number seven, Valeria might have seen it as some sort of sign. Once, while waiting for her colour to set at the hairdresser's, she'd flicked through the tattered women's magazine in her hand to find a frothy article on the meaning of numbers. Despite its likely fictional content, she'd been chuffed to read that seven was a powerful number, one that was both mystical and practical. That suited her to a tee, she'd thought, an avid churchgoer who loved to hear the mystical stories of the past, yet was a down-to-earth hard worker. She was also a Taurean, and according to the magazine that meant she was fixed and stubborn as much as loyal and protective. No one liked to be considered stubborn, though. That wasn't a generous term. She'd far rather think of herself as *consistent*.

With a slightly shaking hand, she pushed the button to open the double doors between her carriage and Rupert's. They sprang apart, revealing a thick rubber mat that covered the moving parts beneath her feet as she negotiated her passage through. She passed the tearoom, the cups and saucers rattling in their shelving, and made her way along the blue-and-cream-patterned carpet of the serpentine hallway. Some solo travellers had their doors open, a few playing music, while other doors were shut. The door of number eight was open.

She slowed as she approached, touching her short curly hair, straightening her cream blouse over her navy pants, wishing she'd worn something more flattering, like the bright shirt of swirling blues and greens she'd bought recently, an addition to the collection of clothes she was sourcing in preparation for her appearance with Maggie Beer. The camera added weight; everyone said so. Maggie was faultlessly stylish, a fashion inspiration for women of a certain age, and Valeria would have to match her standard.

With a deep breath, she poked her head into Rupert's room, half expecting it to be a mistake, that he wasn't here at all, that she'd got it all wrong. But he *was* there. He looked up immediately from his phone and smiled. She exhaled, relieved.

'Val,' he said, warmly, getting to his feet. 'Come in, come in.' She manoeuvred in and, by sheer virtue of their tight proximity, she brushed against him. She apologised and he laughed, and then held her arm and didn't let go until she looked into his glacier-blue eyes. 'It's so good to see you,' he said, his English accent a sense memory, igniting a storm of feeling inside her.

'You too,' she said.

He opened his arms, inviting her into a hug, and although she'd promised herself she wouldn't be jumping into anything again with this man anytime soon, she found herself willingly reciprocating. He was not a tall man, but she was not a tall woman, and their heads fitted neatly over each other's shoulders.

'You smell good,' he said.

She laughed. 'Well, that's a relief.'

He let her go and held her at arm's length. 'I mean, you smell the same as I remember.'

'I promise you I have showered between then and now.'

'Glad to hear it,' he said, returning her smile and indicating for her to take the seat opposite his. Their knees were close to touching across the space and Valeria suddenly wished for longer legs so that they'd be forced to do so. 'What's happened to your wrist?' he asked, his eyes narrowing with concern.

'Oh, nothing. I had a fall. It will be out of the cast in a couple of weeks.' She brushed over the event as quickly as possible. The last thing she wanted to get into with him now was the small matter of a *stroke*.

'I can't believe you're here,' she said.

'You invited me.'

'I didn't . . . that wasn't quite . . .'

'No, you're right. You didn't invite me. You dared me.'

Valeria felt the blush seep up her neck. Oh, the shame of it. As if she was a twelve-year-old playing a game of spin the bottle or something. Not that she ever did that as a kid. Maybe that was why she'd done it.

'I'm sorry about that,' she said.

Rupert cocked his head. 'Sorry that you dared me, or sorry that I'm here now?'

She searched her feelings. It was definitely the former, but also some of the latter. This was a family vacation and she'd gone and invited a stranger into it; a stranger who she clearly still had strong feelings for, even though she wasn't sure she should have. 'The former.'

He smiled, and rubbed at his snow-white beard. 'I'm pleased to hear it.'

They held each other's gaze for a moment while the train rocked from side to side. Valeria turned to the window. The landscape outside was changing from taller, broad-leafed greenery to short, scrubby bushes with cattle grazing between them. She wondered if it would be possible to completely avoid Rupert for the rest of the week, for her family to continue to know nothing about him, if she could even have him agree to this arrangement, and if they could perhaps start this over again once they'd reached Adelaide.

'What are you thinking?' he asked, squinting slightly as he tried to figure out the expressions crossing her face.

She swallowed. 'I'm here with my family.'

'For your seventieth.'

'Yes.' She chewed her top lip for a second before catching herself. It was an awful lifelong habit, one as unsightly as chewing fingernails or twirling hair, and she'd tried to break it many times in her life. Her mother had tried to stop her too, with no success, despite the punishments.

Rupert waited through the silence but his face had set. Not angry, but saddened, perhaps even gutted. 'You wish I hadn't come,' he said flatly.

'No,' she said, rushing to reassure him.

He tilted his head towards her, disbelieving.

'No,' she said again, firmly. 'I think it's incredible that you're here. It's such a . . . such a *grand* gesture, I couldn't possibly be anything other than flattered.'

'Then what is it?'

She knitted her fingers together around her knee. 'They don't know anything about you.'

'Ah, I see.'

'Does your family know anything about me?' she blurted.

After a beat, he said, 'Yes, they do.'

Valeria couldn't disguise her surprise. 'Really?'

'Yes.'

She experienced great pleasure at this, before irritation and confusion knocked it out of the way. 'And what about the young woman?'

Now his eyes hardened, defensive. 'Young woman?'

'The one I saw you with in a photo on Facebook.'

'I might need a bit more information.'

'Oh, really? Are there that many of them?' she snorted.

He took a breath, as though about to speak, then let it go. Finally, he said, 'I didn't know you and I were friends on Facebook.'

Her skin ran hot once more. 'We're not. I confess I searched for you a while back and, while your own profile is scant of posts, there was one in which you'd been tagged, standing beside a woman, your arm around her, with comments of joy and congratulations below it.'

He swallowed, shifted in his seat, and she felt a bolt of triumph.

'I don't think . . . I mean . . . how young are you talking?' he said.

'Are there many young women in your life? Have you lost count?'

'Of course not,' he replied, and there was a snap in his voice she felt sure he'd refined during his years as a headmaster in England before moving to Australia; if pushed to confess, she'd have to admit she rather liked it. 'If you mean who I think you do . . . well, it's complicated.'

'Oh, it's always complicated. Who is she?'

Rupert appeared positively grumpy now. She'd clearly hit a nerve, and was even more determined to get an answer from him before this could possibly go any further. 'It's part of the reason – *she's* part of the reason – I had to go home so abruptly. When you and I were seeing each other—'

His words were interrupted by the train conductor's voice over the loudspeaker, cutting clearly into the small room, drowning out any possibility of continuing the conversation. They were being called to the dining carriage for the first sitting of lunch, followed by a lengthy description of what would happen when they arrived in the town of Katherine after their meal.

Valeria and Rupert sat in strained silence, waiting for the voice to finish, occasionally catching each other's eye, then looking out the window at the bright blue sky and the towering desert termite mounds, which Valeria guessed to be two metres tall. When at last the microphone clicked off, Rupert spoke. 'Which lunch service are you in?'

'The first. You?'

'The second.'

'Right.' She was relieved not to be seated with him for this first meal aboard the train.

'Can we talk again? Maybe later today? I'd like to explain.'

Valeria sighed. 'I suppose so.'

He raised his eyes at that, possibly underwhelmed by her acceptance. 'Good.'

She nodded her farewell and left his room, making her way back to her own carriage, biting her top lip the whole way.

•

Aggie's boots trod softly on the carpet, passing through the narrow hall of the twin-share carriages, which differed in layout from the single-berth carriages. No zigzagging hall through the centre here, this one instead having a straight hallway positioned beside the windows of one side of the carriage, the sleeping rooms lined up along the other side. She hoped she didn't meet someone coming the other way, as she wasn't confident the passage was wide enough for two at once. She'd been trying to send messages to Savannah to check on the progress with the handyman, but the phone reception was becoming scarce and the messages were taking an age to send. She wasn't sure if Savannah had replied or not and her belly was alight with anxiety. Still, she should have some coverage in the town of Katherine this afternoon.

She pushed the button of the doors to the Explorer Lounge and stepped inside. The bar was themed gold and maroon, with guests occupying most of the seating options, already settled in with dishes of nibbles and drinks. Merriment was high, judging from the bursts of laughter that erupted around the place, temporarily drowning out the easy-listening music.

'Hey, Aggie. Join me?'

She startled, pausing mid stride, turning to her left where the voice had come from. 'Me?' she questioned, pointing to her chest.

Harry smiled, bemused, and craned his neck to look behind her. 'Is there another Aggie shadowing you I should know about?'

She felt the corner of her top lip reach for a smile but tempered it. 'You never know. Agatha is a vintage name and we are certainly surrounded by the right demographic for a team of Agathas and/or Aggies.'

'True. We could organise a scavenger hunt, with one of the tasks being to find an Agatha.'

'Could I capture myself?' she bantered.

'Sure, but only if I can do the same.'

A harried, perhaps ravenous couple, who seemed eager to get to the food, stepped around Aggie and she inched closer towards Harry to get out of their way, so close to him now that she could feel the heat from his bare arm next to hers. The Ghan was still travelling through the warm end of the country, though that would have changed entirely by tomorrow when they reached Alice Springs, with a predicted morning temperature of just two degrees. The couple passed and she released the breath she'd been holding.

'This seat is still free,' Harry said, lifting his glass from the small table in front of him. He took a sip of the clear, bubbly liquid and she guessed it was either sparkling water with lime wedges, or perhaps a vodka, lime and soda. With all food and drinks included in the ticket price, she knew many guests – including Myrtle and Dolce – would be keen to get their money's worth of booze.

Her gaze moved to the free seat. She wanted to sit down, wanted to spend more time talking to him, despite the way he'd brushed her off yesterday. There was something mysterious about a young man travelling on the Ghan on his own. By now she'd spotted one other guest who appeared to be around her age, but no one else as young as Harry or Holly, or the influencers with the staged wedding. The vast majority were clearly much older. As for herself, she definitely had more crow's-feet and sunspots than Harry had, more skin beginning to soften, definitely more grey hair, not to mention infertility.

She cast her gaze over to the curved booth seat tucked into the bar at the other end of the carriage, around which her travelling companions were seated, sharing drinks and snacks of some kind. Holly spotted the flirty exchange going on between her and handsome Harry and alerted Myrtle next to her, and the notification spread like electricity to everyone else so that all four sets of eyes were now looking her way. Myrtle smiled her approval and nodded slightly to indicate that Aggie should indeed sit down with Harry. Nudging and whispering began. Aggie wanted to roll her eyes at them. Still, shouldn't she join them? She was here on a family trip, and Myrtle was paying for her. It didn't feel right to abandon her.

She realised she'd been silent for too long in response to Harry's invitation. 'Sorry, I was just . . . that's my family over there.' Since they'd all spotted him she thought it only fair to give him some sort of notice in case one of them took it upon herself to meddle. Myrtle, most likely.

Harry turned, smiled and waved, easy as pie. He received a range of responses, from confused and wary (Valeria), to astute appraisal (Myrtle and Dolce), to giggly high spirits (Holly, who looked as if she'd already drunk too much on an empty stomach).

'They're great,' he said, returning to face her.

Aggie scoffed good-naturedly. 'You don't even know them. They could be serial killers.'

'Are they? We are heading into the remote heart of the country. It would be good to have some warning if our trip is going to turn into a live-action Agatha Christie novel.' He beamed, seemingly proud of himself for connecting her name with *Murder on the Orient Express*.

'Not that I know of, though with Myrtle you can never truly be sure of anything.'

'I'll take my chances.'

She was still standing, having no idea where to shelve the various emotions swirling through her right now – frustration over the lack of communication with Savannah, the ever-present sadness and confusion about the embryos, and unbidden attraction to this man, which was likely nothing more than her hormones reacting to his obvious virility, her uterus screaming that maybe this specimen could save her, that she had never been the problem after all, it was simply that she'd needed a Much Younger Man!

She shook herself firmly, used to wild fantasies of how things could be springing up out of nowhere, and knowing none of them were real. Still, they threw her. The fantasies had been silent for some time now but the letter had reignited them, reignited that tiny last glowing ember of hope that refused to be doused. The fertility journey was, she'd found, as much a mental battle as a physical one. Even more so.

As for Harry, he seemed completely at ease with her indecision, waiting patiently. Maybe it was a skill he'd developed in his time in nursing homes, conversing with those who no longer lived their days at a great pace.

'Why did you run away from me yesterday?' she asked. It came out blunter than she'd intended. 'At the gallery. We were having a good chat, at least I thought so, and then you just shut me down and left.'

The smile faded. He picked up his drink and sipped thoughtfully before replacing it on the cameleer-logo-stamped coaster. She noticed a muscle flicker in his forearm and had the distracting thought that he had a surfer's physique.

'That's a fair question,' he said. 'My apologies. I was enjoying our chat. Then I remembered something I had to do. It threw me off course and I had to go deal with it. But it was abrupt. Not my best exit.'

She waited a beat, expecting him to elaborate. When he didn't, it both irked and inspired her. Imagine not feeling as though you had to explain yourself all the time. She'd love to be more like that, and on a whim, she sat down.

12

'So, neighbour, what's your story? Where are you from and what brings you to the Ghan?' she asked, settling into her seat.

'I'm from Byron Bay.'

She grinned and snapped her fingers. 'Surfer, right?'

'You can tell?' He seemed pleased by this.

She lifted a shoulder. 'I had a hunch. We don't see many surfers in the Barossa, but I've been on holidays to Byron and Noosa. There's something ocean-y about you.'

'That's encouraging. I haven't always surfed. I've only been in the Bay a couple of years now. The true surfers still think I'm a wannabe, which is fair enough given how often I'm dumped.' He pointed to a scar above his left eye.

She grimaced. 'Tough crowd.'

'It's okay. It's good for my ego.' He chuckled. 'I think everyone should do something they're not good at. It helps if you love it, but you don't have to be good at it. It keeps it real, you know, up here.' He tapped the side of his head. 'It gets you out of your head and into your body. And every time you get dumped, you get back up again and you get stronger. It requires some bravery to do something you'll probably fail at, and fail in front of loads of onlookers too,' he said.

His tone was lighthearted but his words had touched something in her, stirring her feelings of failure over her fertility, or lack thereof, and the collective disappointment of everyone around her each time it all fell apart.

'It makes me get out of bed in the morning, forces me to show up, and keeps me sane. Riding a wave is the most powerful and vulnerable I can feel in a single moment.'

'I like that.'

'So, what's your thing?' he asked. 'What gets you out of bed in the morning? What makes you face your fears?'

She paused, then said, 'I think I need a drink first.'

Harry jumped to his feet. 'I'll get it. What would you like?'

'I'd love a vodka, lime and soda,' she said, and nodded towards his glass. 'Same as you?'

'Mine's just soda,' he said, easily.

Possibly a recovering alcoholic, then?

'Be right back.' He moved to the bar with long, purposeful strides. Four sets of eyes in Aggie's family watched him move, Holly smiling so widely her cheeks, which had mostly been drawn since her arrival in Australia, now bunched up like a chipmunk's. Aggie shot her a warning glare. It was great to see Holly enjoying herself but she hoped her daughter wasn't becoming too invested in a single conversation or, yes, even a moment of attraction, thinking it might mean *forever*.

There was no such thing. She knew that better than most.

Also, couldn't people just talk to people because they were interesting and different? Couldn't she simply make a new friend?

Harry had ordered her drink and was chatting to the restaurant manager, who threw her head back and laughed loudly. She looked over at Aggie and then nodded to Harry and went back to her dining list.

Aggie took the opportunity to shoot Holly, Myrtle and Dolce a warning glare, to which they simply gave amused looks in return. Valeria tapped her fingers on the table the way an irritated cat swished its tail.

Harry returned with her drink and she took a grateful sip.

'Right, you were about to tell me what gets you out of bed in the morning,' he said, scrunching his body into the narrow chair, ensconcing himself to listen to her story.

'It's a great question,' she said. *Maybe he's a life coach.* It was so rare to jump into meaningful discussion with someone so quickly after meeting them, of not having to struggle to find words to fill the silence. 'When I was younger, it was my daughter Holly.' She nodded in Holly's direction and he turned to follow her gaze, then quickly refocused on her.

She couldn't read what was behind his eyes, whether he was perhaps calculating their age difference or making snap judgements. Since she had nothing to lose with this guy, and since she was not looking for a romantic entanglement, and they were only going to be in each other's lives for four days, she saw no real reason not to divulge it all.

'I fell pregnant with Holly when I was sixteen. She's twenty-eight now.' Her eyes widened like an owl's every time she thought of Holly's age. It felt completely impossible that she was a grown woman, living her own adult life.

'Was it tough, having her so young?' he asked.

She loved that he asked her *if* it was tough, rather than simply assuming it was, as everyone usually did. 'Sure, it was tough. Some days it's still tough,' she said, laughing, thinking about how many hours she'd lain awake since Holly arrived home, wondering what she was hiding. 'It's true what they say, that having a child means living with your heart outside of your body forever more.'

Something crossed his face then, something she couldn't quite interpret, though she was sure he understood at least a little of what she was saying. Maybe he had a child too? Or maybe he'd lost one. He gave a small smile, and this time she was certain there was sadness behind it. She stopped herself from asking him more, naturally curious, but all too familiar with the pain of loss and the intrusion of constant questions.

'The thing is, though, over the years I've seen many women around me have babies, some of them when they're a teenager like I was, some of them in their twenties or thirties or forties, and it's *always* tough, no matter how old you are. It's tough for different reasons at every age, at every stage of life. I deliberately hire young mothers if I can, and it's the one piece of experience I like to impress upon them. It helps them shift their ideas about themselves, especially if everyone else around them is being fearful and negative.'

'That's wise.'

'It's true.'

'And what about now? What's the thing that you keep turning up for?'

There was a time when the thing that kept her going was hope. Hope that another round of IVF would work and she would once again have the chance to be a mum, but in a totally different way this time around – doing it *the proper way*, with a planned pregnancy, a stable life and a partner by her side. With that gone, there was really only one other thing, and that was why now was the time to invest in it and make it bigger than ever.

'I have a cafe in Angaston in the Barossa Valley. It's called Strawberry Sonnet. Operating a business is a lot like raising a small child. It needs your attention all the time until it's up on its feet and fending for itself, but even then you have to keep stepping in to help guide it in the right direction. Having a small business can be a truly terrifying experience but it's so rewarding. Also like raising a child.'

'And it keeps you sane?'

'Some days not so much,' she confessed, grimacing, reminded of the shop's sign she still had to sort out. 'But yes, I think it fits the same analogy – powerful and vulnerable.'

'That's cool,' he said. 'I like that.'

After a beat, she shifted the focus back to him. 'So, you're a surfer from Byron Bay and you work in aged care. What brings you onto the Ghan?' She also wanted to ask why he was alone but hastened herself to mind her manners.

'Ah.' He smiled again. 'The short answer is that it's a bucket list item.'

'And the long answer?'

'For the past couple of years I've been focused on living more simply, making more space in my life.'

'Space?'

'Yeah.'

'Marie Kondo–style?'

'Who?'

'She's the guru of minimalism. She wrote a book called *The Life-Changing Magic of Tidying Up* and has a show on Netflix. She's all about decluttering and making space – finding what brings you joy and removing anything that doesn't.'

He nodded, enthused. 'I'll have to look her up.'

'Is this trip a bit of a spiritual journey, then?'

'It's the physical space I'm interested in – the desert, the sky, the quiet. The inner world meeting the outer world.' He pulled a face to show her he wasn't taking himself too seriously, but just seriously enough. She was fascinated, hanging on his every word. But just as he opened his mouth to share more, the restaurant manager arrived at their side. Aggie caught sight of her name badge a second before she spoke. 'Right, Harry and Agatha. We're ready,' Christie said.

Aggie started. 'Oh, I'm with my . . .'

'I'm sorry,' Harry said, interrupting. 'I meant to tell you that I asked if it was possible for us to sit together, but then I was enjoying our conversation so much that I totally forgot to mention it and actually *ask* you if you wanted to. I didn't mean to spring it on you or assume anything.'

'Oh, right.' She was flattered but also thrown. She looked over at the gathering of her family, who were all looking their way, wondering what she was doing. 'I think maybe . . .'

'To be honest,' Christie said, 'you'd be doing me a favour.' She grimaced. 'I have a lot of people to get through the lunch service in time for arrival into Katherine and right now I have a spot for two people.'

'I see. Well . . . let me just . . .' she tilted her head to peer past Christie's hip in order to spy her family. Several hands were waving at her in a *go on, go on* motion. Aggie swallowed. 'Okay, then, let's go eat.'

Harry grinned at her, looking shockingly youthful – surely he wasn't in his twenties, was he? – and jumped to his feet. They followed Christie through the bar carriage towards the engraved doors of the Queen Adelaide Restaurant dining carriage. Aggie wagged an admonishing finger at Myrtle and Holly as she passed by, but the two of them simply laughed with glee, their cocktail glasses empty in front of them. Myrtle and Holly had always been a devilish duo.

What was she doing? Lunching with this handsome stranger was not in the plan. And yet, here she was.

•

Myrtle and Dolce's dining companions had been married for forty-nine years and, delightfully, still seemed to enjoy each other very much. Taking it in turns, their companions had explained that the husband had had a large section of his bowel removed. Myrtle and Dolce nodded in sympathy. Apparently, it had been a long recovery and now they were building up their travelling miles in Australia before testing themselves overseas.

'We aren't sure where to go, though,' the woman confessed, gazing at her balding, spotty husband with great care and concern. Myrtle and Dolce sat opposite each other, at the window seats on either side of the table, while their companions were seated in the aisle seats. It was obviously one of the things the restaurant manager did, allotting people to tables in a way that allowed them to meet other travellers and, she assumed, making sure everyone got a window seat at some point. 'We thought we'd start with New Zealand, perhaps.'

Myrtle nodded encouragingly. 'If it's your first trip overseas and you're a little unsure of your capabilities, or the potential need for medical care, then New Zealand is a wonderful choice.' She and Dolce were well past such a modest trip but that didn't mean she was insensitive to tentative beginnings. Not that she'd started her own travels that way. Her first trip overseas, in the mid-1950s, had been to Japan, much to her family's horror.

Dolce spoke. 'Once, when Myrtle and I were in Istanbul, we went to a hammam, a Turkish bath, and we sat in steam rooms made of marble that were four hundred years old. And then a burly man—'

'Like a bouncer,' Myrtle added.

'—moved us to a bigger room with a big round marble slab—'

'Like a crypt,' Myrtle recalled.

'—and he pointed to the slab for us to lie down, then tossed metal bowls of water over us before scrubbing us with mitts.'

'Like rough oven mitts,' Myrtle again assisted.

'Like loofahs,' Dolce agreed.

'And they went everywhere, you know, your legs . . .'

'Your stomach . . .'

'Even our chests, didn't they, Dolce?'

'Even our chests, then turned us over like sausages on a barbecue and did our backs.'

'Did they do our buttocks?' Myrtle wondered.

'I can't remember,' Dolce said, 'but it wouldn't surprise me. They were quite handsy, if I recall.'

'They were,' Myrtle agreed, arching a brow. Their companions were transfixed by their story, a mixture of shock and awe on their faces. 'Then they took us to another room and doused us with bowls of cold water. That was quite unpleasant, wasn't it?'

'Oh, yes, quite,' Dolce agreed, and laughed. 'Then we were back on the hot slab to be soaped up with bubbles that came from a cotton sack, inflated by the man's breath, the bubbles billowing out like snow foam.'

Their companions' eyes widened. 'By the man?' the woman asked, her hand at her throat.

'Yes,' both Dolce and Myrtle intoned.

'All over us, he was, till we were so soapy he could spin us around on the marble top like a record on a turntable.' Myrtle was pleased with this conversation. It was exactly what Dolce needed to remember and enthuse about if she was to change her mind about this being their last trip.

A couple of hours later, Myrtle shifted in her plastic seat to get a better view of the action taking place in the indoor arena of the working cattle station. A man in dark jeans with a shiny belt buckle cracked a whip above his wide-brimmed Akubra hat and the audience applauded.

She and Dolce had opted for the Katherine Outback Experience as their excursion this afternoon, while the others had gone for the boat trip down Katherine Gorge – or Nitmiluk Gorge, as it was now more frequently called, acknowledging the traditional owners' name for it. She wasn't sure why they'd come on this excursion, though, other than she'd let Dolce choose what they'd do this afternoon. But in all their travelling, they'd not ever been down the gorge before and if Dolce's determination held for this trip to be the last, she'd never get another chance. They'd been warned there was some walking to do along tracks over uneven ground, sure, but the passengers included scores of individuals with walking sticks and shaky legs and they'd still felt confident to go along. Why hadn't Dolce?

A second man in a dazzling blue shirt burst into the arena on horseback and the audience cheered. He was in the saddle on top of a shiny chestnut-coloured horse, but the horse was not controlled by a bridle or reins. Amazingly, the man was also carrying a guitar and singing a country song into a microphone headset as he rode the horse, using only his body to communicate with the majestic animal. It was, she had to admit, significantly impressive. They'd also seen working dogs rounding up cattle and ducks and geese and they'd met a pack of young blue cattle dog puppies, cuddling them to their chests, appreciating their sweet puppy breath, but this display between a man and his horse was deeply stirring. It was such a beautiful thing when humans learnt to work with animals rather than dominate them, a philosophy she'd fought hard to share with many school principals over her working life, encouraging the same attitude for engaging children.

'That's marvellous, isn't it?' Dolce said, smiling in wonder.

'It is.'

'I hope I always remember seeing this,' Dolce said, her voice suddenly tinged with sadness.

Myrtle turned in her seat to study her friend, just as the audience erupted in a round of applause. She recalled what Dolce had said about the reasons behind this being her last trip, that it was because she didn't want to be one of those old fools who didn't know when enough was enough, that she didn't want to collapse somewhere in a foreign country or wander off and get lost and cause a lot of fuss and trouble for everyone around her, that she wanted to end on a high, not a disaster.

To begin with, Myrtle had laughed it off, then when she'd realised Dolce was serious, she decided to wait it out. She'd learnt over the years not to take Dolce head on. She was a strong-minded woman – one of the many things she admired about her – and her mind was never changed simply because Myrtle could argue it should be. She'd come to her senses, that was what she'd believed. But now, hearing Dolce say something so out of character, she wondered. Was Dolce dying? And why on earth hadn't it occurred to Myrtle before now?

13

As they approached the town of Katherine, Aggie pulled out her phone to make the most of the reception to call Savannah, while Holly used hers to check social media. Aggie could see her feed full of photos from Californian friends out in the sun, swimming in lakes, canoeing, drinking cocktails and dancing. She cast a look at Holly, who smiled wanly as she added a comment here and there. She felt her brows pinch together.

'Are you regretting sitting on a bus here now with a bunch of seniors rather than dancing with your mates in a club somewhere?' she asked Holly, as casually as she could.

Holly didn't look up, just kept scrolling down the images. 'Nah. I'm over clubs.'

Aggie thought that was odd coming from Holly, who never looked happier than when she was dancing, but her thoughts were interrupted by Savannah, who answered the phone after a few rings. 'Hi.'

'Hey, how's it going? Did the handyman turn up?'

'He did,' Savannah said, but didn't sound happy about it. 'Unfortunately, he couldn't help.'

'Why not?'

'It's raining heavily here and he said it was too dangerous to get up on a ladder in this weather.'

Aggie muttered to herself a moment, knowing that it was understandable but still cranky it hadn't been fixed. She felt so useless up here, so far away, completely unable to solve this situation. 'Is he coming back? Tomorrow maybe?'

'I did ask him,' Savannah said. Aggie could hear her clunking the coffee basket into place on the machine and, if she listened carefully, she could also hear the rain hammering down on the roof.

'What did he say?'

'He didn't commit.'

Aggie stared out the window at the olive-green leaves of native trees set against an expansive blue sky above and red, ruffled earth below, the scenery rushing past as the bus rumbled its way towards Katherine. 'Okay.' She took a deep breath.

'I feel bad,' her assistant said.

'It's not your fault.'

'It feels like it, though. Like, if you were here, this would be sorted by now.'

'No, I'm sure that's not true,' Aggie assured her, though there was a small part of her that felt the same, while simultaneously knowing it was unreasonable. She tended to believe that if she just wanted something badly enough, and tried hard enough, she could fix any problem. Though clearly, as Cora had shown her, that simply wasn't true.

•

She hadn't felt Cora move today and she couldn't remember if she'd felt her yesterday either. But she was only twenty-eight weeks along and not sure if that was normal or not. Still, it was always better to be safe than sorry, so she drove herself to the hospital.

The admissions nurse placed Aggie in a bed and recorded her details, infuriatingly slowly, while Aggie told herself again and again, *It's okay, it's okay, it's okay.* The nurse instructed her to change into a gown, and took her blood pressure and temperature, writing on a chart. Finally, she got around to finding a Doppler to listen for the heartbeat. She frowned, biting her lip, and that was the moment Aggie knew that it was not okay.

Her baby had died.

•

As though summoned by her memories, Gideon's name arrived in her text messages. She smiled, slightly comforted to know they were still connected by invisible strings, as they always would be. She opened his message.

> I know we said we'd talk about this properly after the trip but I was awake most of the night. I can't stop thinking about the embryos. I don't want to donate them to another couple. Just thought I'd pass it on in case it was keeping you up at night too.

She replied immediately.

> Same here. Don't worry. We'll work it out together.

So that was that. Their list of options was down to four – donate to science, renew the clinic fees, implant the embryos in the hope one took, or destroy them. She sighed, suddenly weary, this day feeling huge already. Her emotions had swung in all directions and they still had their cruise down the gorge to go before heading back to the train for dinner and the overnight travel to Alice Springs.

Beside her, Holly finished typing a message and put her phone back in her bag.

'Is all well in the world?' Aggie asked.

'Yeah, just Mal checking in.'

'What?' This took Aggie completely off guard. Although Holly had moved to the United States on account of her father's American citizenship, and to California specifically, where he was a Mendocino County winemaker like his dad, they weren't close. It had been a great disappointment to Holly in the beginning but then she'd rallied, found a job, made new friends, built a life. To Aggie's knowledge, they only had infrequent conversations. She wondered why he would be contacting her now.

'I didn't know you two caught up that often,' she ventured.

Holly shrugged. 'It's a recent thing. No biggie.' She rested back on the headrest and closed her eyes, signalling the end of that conversation.

Aggie was confused, and felt shut out of Holly's thoughts yet again. She registered an immediate spike in anxiety that Mal might lure Holly back overseas again, right when Aggie had a chance of convincing her to stay here in Australia. The anxiety of being a parent was worse now, so much worse since losing Cora. She told herself that it was okay to feel anxious, that feeling that way didn't mean anything bad would actually happen to Holly. But it was there, always, simmering away. She'd lost Cora. She could easily lose Holly too.

The town of Katherine was small, sparsely populated and flat. Fibro houses sat high on stumps, with four-metre flood markers erected at intervals for the yearly wet season.

'The kids still have to go to school, though,' the bus driver said. 'They go by boat.'

They passed industrial lots with rusted machinery, a petrol station, a hotel and ubiquitous fast food chain outlets. The driver pointed out the large supermarket, which was apparently the site of some excitement in the last wet season when the town flooded up to the top of the building and a saltwater crocodile was discovered on the roof, not far from the meat section, taking advantage of the bounty of fresh produce floating by. They passed the School of the Air building, with a small patch of green irrigated lawn, and quickly motored through the outskirts of town on the way to the gorge.

'What did you learn about Harry over lunch?' Holly asked, suddenly, a bemused smile tugging at the corners of her mouth.

'Not much. The couple we were seated with were very chatty and it was really all about them. They only asked me where I was from but nothing else. Harry didn't seem to mind.'

'So what was the point of him asking you to have lunch with him, then?' she asked, slightly disgusted and disappointed.

Aggie shrugged, perplexed. 'No idea. But it doesn't really matter to me. Maybe he's lonely. He's travelling by himself.'

'That's seems a little unusual,' Holly said. 'Has he said why?'

'Just that he likes the idea of space.'

'Sounds like a commitment-phobe,' her daughter said with authority, which made Aggie laugh.

'That's probably not a bad thing. Romance isn't on my list of priorities right now.'

'Odd, though. Just by body language, he seemed to be really into you,' Holly said, narrowing her dark eyes, disapproving.

'He does seem to blow hot and cold,' Aggie agreed.

'Are you disappointed?'

'We've only just met,' she said, dismissing that quickly.

'You *are* disappointed,' Holly said, always able to read her far too well.

Fortunately, Aggie was excused from rebutting that idea as the bus driver spoke into his microphone once more to announce that they'd reached Nitmiluk Gorge. He instructed them to disembark here and follow the path down to the dock where the boats awaited, and to help themselves to a bottle of water and an apple from the basket on the way. And if Aggie's mind wanted to turn over the idea of Harry like a terrier with a bone, it didn't get the chance because it was distracted by the sight of her mother and a well-dressed gentleman standing close together and talking. She nudged Holly with her elbow and nodded towards them. It was clear by the proximity of their bodies that they were exchanging hushed words. The intimacy of their connection was surprising and fascinating.

'Who's he?' Holly whispered, captivated.

Her words carried on the light breeze to where Valeria stood, her back to them. Her shoulders stiffened instantly, her head snapped around to see their eyes trained on the two of them, and she quickly moved away, stalking alone down the hill to where the boat drivers waited. The man with the white sides of hair and goatee gave them a polite nod of recognition before also beginning the walk down the hill, though content at his own pace, not trying to catch the woman who'd just deserted him.

'Shit,' Holly said. 'Did you see that?'

'I did,' Aggie breathed.

'Who is he?'

'I have no idea,' Aggie said, feeling the great distance of non-communication between her and her mother stretch that bit further.

'This trip just got a whole lot more interesting,' Holly said.

'You can say that again,' agreed Aggie, and shot her a look of complete bewilderment before they began the descent down the hill, following Valeria and the mystery man.

•

Valeria collected her apple and bottle of water on her way down the footbridge to the boat, which was steadily filling with Ghan passengers taking their seats, and kept her eyes focused straight ahead, mentally willing Agatha not to ask questions. It was inevitable, she knew, but if she could hold her off for a little longer she'd have time to work out what to say. She should never have let Rupert try to speak to her here, out in the open, but she'd succumbed to the plea in his eyes.

'When can we talk? There's so much I need to tell you,' he'd begged her.

And now they'd been seen.

She took her place on a seat at the back of the boat, near the tour guide and his driving controls. It was a floating platform, really, with rows of bucket seats bolted to the floor, open sides and a metal roof to shelter them from the sun and rain. It rocked gently on the water's surface as passengers climbed aboard. She was deeply relieved to see Rupert choose to board a different boat.

'Mum, who is he?' Agatha asked, seating herself beside her, rolling her apple around in the palm of her hand. Holly sat down too, her face piqued with curiosity.

Valeria was irritated by the question – in fact, irritated that her daughter was sitting there beside her at all, because the only reason Agatha was there at this moment was because she wanted information. 'It doesn't matter.'

Agatha scoffed. 'It clearly does, or you wouldn't be so rankled. Do you know him?'

Valeria blinked, watching Rupert begin a congenial conversation with the people seated near him on the other boat.

Did she know him? She'd thought she had, once.

'Mum?'

She shook her head. It wasn't an answer but rather a dismissal. *Not now.*

To her great relief, the tour guide behind her started the engine of the boat and began speaking into his microphone. Agatha turned away, sighing in frustration, Holly shrugged, and the tour guide welcomed everyone on board, running through the safety information and giving a brief explanation of the Aboriginal connection to the area. A moment later, their vessel reversed across the reflective surface of the Katherine River and puttered on its way.

Despite her roiling emotions, the calm water and the stunning scenery did soothe her. Their guide pointed out a freshwater crocodile basking on an ochre-coloured sandy inlet, its mouth open as they tended to do. Signs warned of crocodile nesting sites.

'That's for the crocs' protection, not the people,' their guide said. He was tall and bronzed, with a dry sense of humour and an obvious respect for the land. 'Only about one in every thousand crocodile eggs survives through to become a young adult croc, and females don't reach sexual maturity until they're twelve years of age, so the stats are against them.'

He stalled the boat for several minutes so they could take photos of the crocodile sunning itself at the base of a huge cliff. The cliffs themselves were awe-inspiring and outlandishly beautiful, composed of blocks and layers of sandstone in colours ranging from dark grey to paler ochre and deeper orange, towering above them on either side of the gorge. Trees grew stubbornly from tiny cracks, offering bursts of greenery that jutted upwards or drifted downwards like a hanging garden. The river had worn its path through the gorge over tens of millions of years.

'We're just a blip to this earth,' Agatha said beside her. 'Humans have been here for such a short time.'

She was right. Life was fleeting, both for individuals and for our species.

It was quiet on the river, save for the boat motor and an occasional helicopter or light plane taking tourists on scenic flights above. As it was dry season and the river was low, they had to leave the boat between the first and second of the thirteen gorges in order to walk around the base of the cliffs to reach the second set of boats waiting in the next gorge.

The first thing they saw when they disembarked and climbed the steps to the pathway was the enormous Aboriginal artwork on the side of the cliff, several metres tall and many heads higher than ground level. The three women stood at its base and stared up.

'It was painted during the Ice Age,' their tour guide said, making them jump and turn around to see he was standing behind them, also gazing at it in appreciation.

'It's so big,' Valeria said, taking a photo on her phone. The artwork included several images of people and animals in a darker rusty red on a whitish background.

Agatha turned and smiled at her.

Valeria felt herself soften. 'It's incredible.'

They continued on their way, lifting their feet carefully over slippery rocks and stones, avoiding crevasses and puddles of water, to then descend and board the next boat.

'Grandma, who was that man you were talking to?' Holly ventured as they took their seats once more, the faintest wisp of an American accent touching occasional words.

'Leave it,' Agatha said, surprising Valeria with her defence. 'She doesn't owe us an explanation.'

Valeria turned away to gaze out at the view, embarrassed by Agatha's words of solidarity, but also grateful.

The boat began to reverse and their guide once more began to talk about the cultural heritage and significance of the area. They rumbled down the second gorge, the water rhythmically slapping the sides of the barge. She soaked in the sights, in awe of the place. It wasn't only the sheer size of the cliffs on either side of them that made it impressive. It was . . . well, *majestic* was the only word Valeria could think to adequately describe it. Its presence, its ancient history and its power were tangible.

She put thoughts of Rupert aside, enjoying the trip. She'd never be here again, of that she was sure. She knew she would have to tell the others about him and she'd do it soon, at least with Agatha. For now, though, she just wanted to breathe it all in. Tomorrow she turned seventy. Life was more uncertain than ever before.

A second boat in their tour group approached, travelling slightly faster than their own. The newlywed influencers were standing at the front of the boat, both dressed in neutral, earthy tones, desert flowers in the woman's hair, their arms wrapped around each other as they posed for yet more photos, with the glorious colours of the gorge's cliffs in the background.

Valeria felt Agatha stiffen beside her. She glanced at her quickly before following her gaze to the handsome young man she'd had lunch with today. She prickled. Surely Agatha couldn't be interested in that man. He was far too young for her, for a start, not to mention the fact that they'd only just met. But more importantly, Agatha needed to work things out with Gideon if they were to make the most of those embryos. Instantly, the sense of peace that she'd absorbed from being here in the gorge, and her feelings of ease with Agatha, slipped away, replaced by biting frustration. Why was her daughter so determined to ruin all her chances in life, particularly when this was her last one?

14

Back in her cabin, Aggie flicked through the in-room radio stations and stopped at Cole Porter's 'Night and Day', humming along as she ferreted through her things, not able to remember where she'd stashed everything in the many tiny compartments around the cabin. She was starving. Outside her window, darkness encroached on the flat, silent world, gathering in close and tucking itself around rocks and mounds and trees. It was only five-thirty and their dinner service wasn't for another two hours. Her belly growled loudly as she foraged for any food that she might have lurking in her bags. Coming up empty-handed, she pushed back her wood-panelled concertina door to check if Holly had anything, passing Harry's partially open door as she went, spying his long jeans-clad legs stretched out, a book in his lap.

She wondered what he was reading and was reminded of the Instagram account Hot Dudes Reading. As its name suggested, it featured photos taken – presumably surreptitiously – of men reading books. Usually, they were on trains or buses, or waiting in airports, or lying on the grass in parks, and occasionally in cafes or bars. She'd sneaked a peek at the feed once or twice and had to admit it had raw appeal. She wondered if she could capture a photo of Harry doing the same. She was still smiling when she reached Holly's open door.

Holly was sitting in her seat, travelling backwards, one leg crossed over the other, busily texting.

'Hey,' Aggie said.

Holly looked up, frowning. 'Hey, yourself. Hold on a sec, I'm just finishing a message to Nala. I've only got one bar and I know we're about to lose all reception until we hit Alice Springs tomorrow morning.' Her fingers stabbed urgently at the screen.

Aggie waited a few beats, wondering yet again what was going on with Nala and Holly that seemed to make Holly so tetchy.

'Right.' Holly tossed her phone onto the seat next to her as if shaking off a fly, took a deep breath and put her hands on her belly. 'I'm starving.'

'Me too. Have you got any food? I thought I had a stash of caramel butter lollies in my bag but I can't find them.'

Holly began opening little drawers and doors, then pulled out her suitcase, having to back out of the doorway of her cabin in order to open it and rummage through it properly. She flicked through shirts, thermal underwear, bras and creams and lotions but found nothing edible. 'Let's make a cuppa,' she said, standing once more. 'They've got biscuits in the tearoom.'

'Good idea.'

Aggie turned around to face Valeria's cabin and ask her mother if she wanted a cuppa too, but the room was empty. She paused.

'Do you think she's with him?' Holly whispered.

'I have no idea.'

'I love this. Such a mystery,' Holly said, running her hands through her curls. 'Who do you think he is? A billionaire lover? A debt collector?'

'From one extreme to the other,' Aggie said, grinning.

'Ooh, ooh, maybe a jam coach?'

'Don't think so. She'd never believe she needed any coaching with all the ribbons she's won. Besides, it's not her year this year.'

'Hmm, an investor?' Holly wondered.

'Do you think he's a con man? Someone she met on the internet? You hear of that sort of thing happening to lonely women all the time.'

'If he says he's a doctor, surgeon or army general I'd be very suspicious,' Holly agreed.

'Suspicious of what?' Valeria said, returning from the tearoom holding a cup of milky brew on a saucer, the teabag still steeping, and a packet of biscuits clutched in her other hand. She looked from Aggie's face to Holly's.

'Ah . . .' Aggie cursed herself for not being better at subterfuge.

'Me.'

Aggie and Holly whipped around to see Harry standing tall behind them, smiling easily at Valeria. He held out his hand to her. 'I don't think we've been properly introduced. I'm Harry, number six.' He indicated over his shoulder. 'Nice to meet you.'

Aggie watched a number of expressions cross her mother's face before it finally settled on something she would call *unamused*. Still, Valeria did take his hand. 'Nice to meet you, Harry. I'm Valeria, Agatha's mother.' She slid her gaze between Harry and Aggie and twitched her nose, a sign of judgement, Aggie knew, and wondered which part of her life her mother was currently disapproving of now.

'I see you've beaten us to the tearoom,' he said, nodding towards her cup of tea. 'The three of us were just about to go and find something to fill the gap before dinner.'

'Yes,' Aggie said, joining in. 'We came to see if we could get you anything.'

'I'm fine for now, thank you,' Valeria said and moved into her cabin, half closing the concertina doors and setting her cup and saucer down on her window table.

Aggie led the way to the tearoom, where the cups and saucers jangled loudly in their metal shelves. The three of them could only just squeeze in at the same time and Aggie bumped into Harry – which was not unpleasant, she thought, hiding a blush – as they perused the tea, coffee and hot chocolate options.

'Thanks for that,' Aggie said. 'I'd hate her to think we were gossiping about her. I was worried, that's all.'

'We have no idea who the man is that she ran away from at the gorge today,' Holly added, helpfully.

'Have you asked her?' Harry said, tearing open two packets of hot chocolate powder and pouring both into a small mug.

'That would be too easy,' Aggie said, wryly.

'Usually works, though,' he said, and his tone was supportive.

'I will ask her soon,' Aggie said, tipping out the tea she'd just made, in order to follow Harry's lead and make a hot chocolate instead, to try to quell the angry growling in her belly.

'Here, take extra biscuits with you,' Holly said, thrusting handfuls of packets at both of them. 'I'm going to swill this and then head for a shower. Bye,' she mumbled through a mouthful of biscuit and disappeared out the door.

Aggie sipped her drink and wondered about this guy next to her, who seemed to like her but also seemed to turn it on and off. She narrowed her eyes at him. Was he a player? Wasn't that what they did, love-bomb you then withdraw their attention, leaving you confused? Was *he* the con man and she the lonely woman, not her mother?

No, that was crazy. What had the world come to when people couldn't simply be nice to other people without their motives being questioned? She scoffed at herself for her paranoia and momentarily choked on her hot chocolate, spluttering until her eyes watered.

'Are you okay?' He patted her on the back, between her shoulder-blades.

'Fine,' she gasped, holding up a hand to indicate he could stop patting her.

He was gazing at her and she took in the features of his face. His youth was there, though now she looked more closely, she could see it was weathered too, and not just from sun, sand and surf, but from hard, grinding pain. She'd recognise it anywhere. It winded her, seeing herself in another, and made her suck in a sharp breath.

The corner of his lip curled up, questioning, slightly amused, but also a little concerned. 'What?'

'How old are you?' she blurted.

'Thirty-five. You?'

'Forty-five.'

He didn't flinch. He didn't make a joke. He didn't rush to assure her she didn't look a day over thirty or forty or twenty or something equally trite or reductionist. He didn't give her any kind of philosophy about age being meaningless, or talk about the wisdom he found in his aged-care clients, or his preference for older women, or let out a low whistle of shock, or make a hasty retreat, or . . . anything. He didn't react in any way at all. Instead, he continued to steadily hold her gaze and it was the sexiest response she could possibly imagine.

Her age meant absolutely nothing to him.

She saw him swallow, saw his gaze drop to her lips and quickly back to her eyes. A question. A searching. An invitation?

The train blew its horn, long and loud, and rapidly braked, tipping them forward towards the sink as it fought to stop its nearly eighteen hundred tonnes of weight from galloping along its tracks.

'Steady,' Harry said, his hand on her upper arm.

Her hot chocolate had spilt down her purple shirt, and he reached for paper towels for her. 'Thanks.' She took them and dabbed ineffectually at her shirt, embarrassed, the stain significantly covering one breast.

Harry was polite enough not to stare. 'I wonder what's happened.'

The conductor's voice came over the audio system. 'Ladies and gentlemen, you may have noticed that the train has come to a complete standstill. This is unfortunately due to three large buffalo wandering onto the tracks.'

'Oh no.' Aggie grimaced.

The manager continued. 'In situations such as these, it is protocol for our engineers to walk the length of the train on both sides, checking the undercarriage for any damage, as they are sizeable beasts. Given the length of the train is almost a kilometre long, I'm sure you'll appreciate that it will take a little time, but we'll have you on your way again as soon as possible.' The audio clicked off once more.

'Poor things,' Harry said, frowning.

'I hope it was quick for them,' Aggie agreed. They stood in silence for a moment before she rushed to speak. 'I'd better go and get changed. I'll take the time now to have a shower before dinner.' She paused in her retreat. 'Will you join me?'

'Sorry?' He looked startled.

'For dinner, not the shower,' she said, holding up her hands.

He grinned, revealing a depression in his right cheek that might once have been a dimple on a chubby child. 'Sure. See you there.'

'Great.' She made a hasty exit before she said anything else that might get her into trouble.

The shower at the end of Aggie's carriage was better than she'd expected, the bathroom being bigger than her own little cabin and the water nice and hot. With washed hair still hanging damply on her neck, she dropped her things back to her cabin then stepped next door to see her mother. Valeria was sitting on her day seat, the now-empty cup on the saucer on the little drop-down table. She was staring out the window at the dark surroundings.

'Hey,' Aggie said, pausing in the doorway.

Her mother turned, blinking as though her thoughts had been far away. 'I can see torchlight out there, moving around,' she said, nodding to the window. Her own image was reflected in the glass, superimposed on the nightscape beyond.

'They'll be checking the train,' Aggie said, feeling a pinch of pain for the buffalo. 'Can I come in?'

'Of course.' Valeria sat up straighter, tucking her legs back towards herself to give Aggie more room to move. 'Your hair's wet,' she observed, frowning.

'There wasn't a hair dryer in the bathroom.'

'You'll catch your death.' Valeria *tsk*ed.

Aggie scoffed. 'Unlikely, but I'll go look for a steward soon and see if they have one stashed somewhere.' She waited a beat, hoping her mother would take the lead. When she didn't, she took the initiative. 'I'm wondering about the man at the gorge.' She offered a supportive smile. If her mother was caught up in something, Aggie wanted her to know Valeria could trust her, that she wouldn't judge her.

Valeria tossed her head, slightly, a gesture Aggie recognised as one of annoyance. She felt herself bristle instantly in response. How would she and her mother ever improve their relationship if Valeria insisted on pushing her away? But she bit down on a snippy retort and waited instead.

And waited.

Tchaikovsky was playing quietly on Valeria's radio. A hint of her mother's sickly sweet perfume drifted to Aggie's nose, and she was surprised by the notion that Valeria's feelings for this mystery man might be more complex than she'd imagined. 'Are you in love with him?'

15

Valeria had met Rupert at the Royal Adelaide Show on delivery day two years ago. He stood out like the proverbial thumb, the only jam man in the line, carrying a shoebox of his jars tucked under his left arm. Around her, the queue of jam hopefuls tittered and whispered, sizing him up. Was he much of a threat? Was it really his jam, or was he delivering it for his wife? He wasn't from around these parts, was he? He must be new to the area or, worse, a professional from another state, come to claim the top prize here too. That would be just like a man, not content to conquer his own land but pillaging someone else's. Thick clouds of disapproval floated his way.

Then Margaret Beetle broke ranks and approached him, her own jam in a basket covered with a lace cloth. 'Hello, what have we here?' she sang, peering into his shoebox. 'Strawberry, is it?' She fluttered her eyes at him and touched her hair.

Gracious! Margaret was far too old for him. He would only have been seventy, surely, while she was pushing eighty, at a minimum, though word was she'd stopped ageing years ago.

He smiled and greeted her, and that was when Valeria heard his enchanting voice. 'Strawberry, raspberry and marmalade,' he said. He didn't proffer the box, though, didn't give her a chance to see them or touch them. Valeria was certain his arm clenched the box that bit tighter towards his ribs.

'Been jamming long?' Margaret Beetle went on.

'A few years,' he said amiably, but there was an assuredness in those words that made Valeria believe it had been much more than a few. There was also the straightness of his back, the confident set of his shoulders. This was not his first rodeo, as the saying went.

As Valeria watched Margaret press him for details and he deftly deflected, she found herself staring at the nape of his neck, where his snow-white hair was trimmed to perfection above his collar. It was the first time since Bertie died that she'd felt even the tiniest of stirrings, the most tentative flicker of interest in another man.

He inched to the front of the line. Not even pretending to be anything other than nosy, Margaret Beetle hovered at his side as he submitted his jars to the official behind the desk. He received his confirmation of entry and nodded his thanks before turning away.

'Good luck!' Margaret Beetle trilled as he walked past.

He nodded politely, chin held high as he left. But nearing Valeria, he caught her eye and his steps faltered, bringing him to a standstill beside her.

'Excuse me, are you Valeria Hermann?'

The line of hopefuls fell silent and Valeria felt the weight of their gazes on her.

'Yes,' she said, slightly wary, slightly fascinated.

He smiled, his smooth lips pulling outwards to show genuine delight. 'I've read many articles about you,' he said.

'You have?'

He held out his hand to shake hers, but she was carrying too large a box to reciprocate. 'Oh, of course, I'm sorry,' he said, withdrawing his hand and chuckling. 'You don't want to lose your jam now, not when you're so close to delivery.' She noted his neatly trimmed nails and caught the scent of starch from his shirt. 'I gather you're the most famous jam queen in this area, perhaps the whole country. I had to check out the competition.'

There was something in the way he said this that flattered her, rather than antagonised or baited her.

'Well,' she said, then failed to conjure any more words. The line in front of her moved and she shuffled forward.

'Are you busy after this?' he continued.

She was positive she heard at least one stifled gasp from a woman nearby. 'There's a cafe not far from here. Perhaps you'd like to share a pot of tea? I'd love to talk to you about jam making.'

She stared at him, completely and utterly caught off guard. It had been a terrible time recently, with the loss of Cora, Agatha's devastation and Valeria's own frustration and sadness that she couldn't be of comfort to her daughter; Agatha seemed intent on keeping her at arm's length. Most of the details had come to her via Myrtle, the woman Agatha had long ago chosen as her mother, pushing Valeria aside. It was all a great mess and some days she'd found herself weeping into a cup of tea, at home, alone.

The idea of a cup of tea now with a handsome, jam-making Englishman, even if he was a rival, was tempting. She was conscious of women watching her, waiting for her reply. Rupert held her gaze, a look of hopeful anticipation on his face.

'All right,' she said. 'Why not?'

•

Valeria cast her eyes to the ceiling for a moment before resigning herself to answering. 'I was in love with him once.'

'Once?' Aggie leant forward in her seat. This was the most interesting conversation she'd had with her mother in a long time. 'When? Is he . . . was he before Dad? A high school sweetheart or something?' She scanned her memories of conversations with her parents about their childhoods.

She remembered fragments about the introduction of television and the moon landing, the milk that came on trucks, the stinking, spider-infested outhouses, the strict teachers with a cane at the ready to beat kids into submission, and FJ Holdens. Nothing about former romances. As far as Aggie knew, Valeria and her father were each other's first loves. The idea that Valeria had a romantic history prior to marriage was, perhaps naively, new.

Her mother shook her head. 'It started two years ago, but ended a few months later. It was . . . intense . . . while it lasted.' She looked either cross or embarrassed about this.

'Two years?' Aggie felt her eyes pop. 'Why didn't you say something? Introduce us? Tell me about him, at least?'

Valeria sighed. 'It was a difficult time.' She held her daughter's gaze and waited for Aggie to catch up.

'Cora.' Aggie whispered her name.

'Yes.'

Aggie digested this. On the one hand, she understood why her mother wouldn't want to share happy news at a time like that. It was thoughtful, she supposed. But on the other, it made her feel downright crappy, as if her own misery had blocked something between them, something potentially wonderful for her mother. 'You didn't have to . . . you could have told me.'

'Yes, well, you weren't really talking to me about much of anything.' There was a sting in her tone, a bitterness.

What had her mother expected? Her daughter had just died. Her and Gideon's long, fraught, agonising, stressful journey through IVF had just ended in the worst possible way. True, she hadn't felt like talking. She'd all but stopped talking to Gideon too. And now she was ashamed, mortified that her inability to deal with the grief had destroyed her relationship with Gideon and driven a further wedge between herself and her mother. She swallowed the lump in her throat, having no idea where to even begin to unpack all the layers of all the things that lay between them.

Valeria rallied, continuing her story. 'We met at the show that year.' A small smile hovered on her lips, her eyes suddenly alight with the memory. 'He's a jam man.'

Aggie grinned. 'Really? They're as rare as hen's teeth.'

'Quite a good one, too.'

'But you won that year. I remember. It was your turn.' Aggie hadn't declared that year because she knew she'd be busy having a baby, or so she'd thought. As it turned out, she was busy cremating one instead.

'I did,' Valeria continued. 'His strawberry jam placed third, but he won the marmalade division.'

'Did he?' Aggie was impressed. 'Go on, what happened after that?'

Valeria's face closed again. 'As I said, with everything going on, I decided to keep it quiet, just between Rupert and I.'

Rupert. That was his name. It made Aggie smile, but she wasn't sure if it was because she liked the name or because it reminded her of the bear in the red sweater and yellow plaid pants from the children's books.

'He came to Adelaide because he has a self-managed superannuation fund and wanted to sink a portion of it into a vineyard. He chose Ladd's and came down to visit.'

'Oh, Gideon thinks that's a great vineyard. He always said he'd take a position there if one ever came up.'

'Yes, I think he's pleased with his investment.' She shifted in her seat. 'Well, he *was*, last we spoke about it. Things might have changed since then,' she said, obviously mulling over the time that had stretched between them. 'He comes from Queensland. Well, he comes from England, originally, south-west of London, and he moved to Brisbane with his wife and kids thirty years ago. He was a teacher, then a headmaster. One of his sons is still in Brisbane, the other is in north Queensland.'

'And his wife?'

'Died of a heart attack one day, without warning.'

'That's awful.'

'Yes,' Valeria agreed. Unspoken words hung heavily in the air between them – Valeria had just had a stroke and might have another any day now.

'But you know what it's like, losing a spouse.'

'Yes.' She gave a wry snort. 'When you're younger, people come with baggage in the form of exes and children. When you're older, it's their deceased spouses.'

Aggie let that thought sit for a moment before pressing her mother for more details. She wanted to know everything. 'What happened? Why did you split up?'

Valeria shook her head, dismayed. 'I'm not really sure. One day, he came to my house early in the morning. He looked rumpled and harried and said he was incredibly sorry but he had a family emergency and had to leave immediately. I asked him what had happened, but he said he couldn't explain and he would let me know as soon as he could.'

'But he didn't?'

'No.' She pressed her fingers to her forehead and smoothed the skin there.

Now Aggie was confused. The word *bastard* was on the tip of her tongue – how hard was it to pick up the phone? – but she tempered it, deciding to give him the benefit of the doubt. After all, there'd been a time in her life when she couldn't talk to anyone either.

The train's horn boomed, echoing out into the vast wilderness around them, and the locomotive began to creak and creep its way forward. Valeria seemed to snap to her senses, appearing uneasy with how much she'd divulged. 'You'd better go and find a hair dryer before dinner,' she said.

'Yes, I should.' Aggie rose slowly to a standing position, feeling both grateful her mother had shared so much and annoyed she had shut the door once more. 'Mum?'

'Mm?'

'Give him the chance to explain,' she said. 'You've nothing to lose.'

Valeria nodded, giving her a tight-lipped but grateful smile.

16

Myrtle checked her reflection in the carriage window as the train thundered onwards into the night. She wasn't looking too bad for her age, if she did say so herself. She shook her head slightly from side to side and watched her curls sway against her ears.

'So, who's on the top bunk?' Harry asked, breaking open a bread roll. He was sitting diagonally opposite her, on the aisle side, Dolce beside him, and Aggie to Myrtle's left.

'I am,' Myrtle said.

Harry chuckled.

'What are you laughing about?' she asked, in mock defensiveness.

'Not you, that's for sure. It was nothing but joy on your behalf. I wish my residents were as mobile.'

'Your residents?' Dolce asked, buttering her own bread roll.

'I work in an agedcare home.'

'Do you really? I bet you're everyone's favourite,' she said.

'Not everyone's,' he said, grimacing. 'There are some grumpy people in there.'

'Does that bother you?' Aggie asked.

His gaze leapt eagerly to Aggie's face; Myrtle could practically see the frisson between them. Well! This *was* interesting.

'Not generally. We all have our bad days.'

'That's a generous attitude,' Aggie said.

'Did you know Aggie's a jam queen?' Myrtle interjected.

Harry grinned. 'Really?'

'I don't have a crown and sash or anything,' Aggie rushed to assure him, colour rising in her cheeks. She gave Myrtle an exasperated look.

'She'll win this year, too,' Myrtle said proudly.

Harry was about to ask more about this when their waiter reappeared with their drinks – a martini for Dolce, a shandy for Myrtle, an orange juice and vodka for Aggie, and a Coke for Harry. After placing their drinks down, he took their dinner orders – one crocodile sausages, two fish, and a beef and ale pie. As soon as he left, Myrtle took the opportunity to grill Harry for information that she was certain Aggie would be dying to know but was too polite, or too afraid, to ask. 'So, Harry, are you married?'

'Nope.'

'Kids?'

His nose twitched, just slightly – *interesting* – then, 'Nope.'

'Girlfriend?'

He shook his head, smiling. She suspected he got a lot of these types of questions in the old folks' home, which made her squirm in her seat, slightly. She didn't like to think of herself as a senior person but she did like to use the privilege of lack of discretion if it suited her. Besides, she was doing this for Aggie. If there was a mutual attraction going on here, which seemed obvious to anyone with a pulse, it was for Aggie's good that she had as many facts as possible as early as possible. She'd already been through enough for one lifetime.

'Alcoholic?' she asked, in what she hoped was a more sensitive tone.

He laughed out loud at that. 'No.'

'But that is just a Coke, right?' she pressed.

'Correct.' He narrowed his eyes at her, as if deciding whether or not to elaborate, then shook his head slightly and continued. 'I went through some things a while back and my life went off the rails for a bit. One day, I decided it would be a good idea to stop drinking till I got my act together. That was about a year ago. To be honest, I've enjoyed being alcohol-free. It changes a lot of things.'

'Like what?' Myrtle asked, jumping at the chance to widen the doorway to Harry's mind a fraction more. Dolce was clearly interested too, and she turned awkwardly in her seat to see him better.

'Lots of things, simple things – like saving money, for one,' he said.

Myrtle raised her eyebrows and nodded, and Dolce grunted in agreement. They'd often bemoaned the cost of alcohol – their beloved cocktails, especially – and had even tried home-distilling spirits in Myrtle's laundry, with little success.

'But also . . .' He trailed off for a moment, trying to gather the right words. 'Big things too, like not being able to run away from how you're feeling or what you're thinking. It makes me face stuff full-on, no running away.'

Myrtle paused, assessing him. If she'd had a few questions drifting about before, now they were rushing to be asked. She wanted to hear the whole sorry tale that had brought him to this moment in life, that had left him battered – because she could see it now, the depth to his eyes that came with having gone through something difficult – but not being broken by it, and in fact it might have had that wonderfully rare effect of improving him as a person. *Post-traumatic growth*, that was what it was called. She'd read about it in a book.

'But how do you do that?' Aggie asked. 'How do you face the abyss and survive?'

Myrtle flicked her gaze to Dolce, slightly panicked. This wasn't the direction she'd been expecting this conversation to go in. She hadn't wanted to pry open a pit of grief for Aggie. Dolce raised one shoulder slightly, as helpless as Myrtle.

Harry took his time to answer Aggie's question, but then he cleared his throat and spoke carefully. 'I'd be a fool to suggest I had all the answers. And to be honest, some days are still rough. For me, I had to find something to focus on that was outside of me, outside of my life, and so I decided to do good. Just that. Do good. By doing good, I felt good, and so I kept doing good. At least I think that's what I'm doing with my residents. They definitely don't all love my bad jokes.' He smiled self-deprecatingly and it broke the tension just in time for their meals to arrive.

'Bon appétit,' Dolce said, cutting into a crocodile sausage.

'Remember when we were in Paris last, Dolce,' Myrtle said, hoping to bring the conversation around to something more cheerful and also to inspire Dolce to more travel.

'Mm, it must be, what, twelve years now?'

'At least.' Myrtle was about to remind Dolce about the night they had boarded the wrong train on the Metro but had fortuitously ended up somewhere near the Moulin Rouge, when Dolce abruptly changed the topic.

'Harry, what's it like inside the aged-care home?' she asked. 'Is it as bad as the media makes it out to be?'

Harry swallowed his mouthful of pie before answering. 'In what way?'

'The food, the abuse, the loneliness, the lack of privacy, the lack of care for things like contractures.'

Myrtle sat quite still, her knife and fork poised midair. Why was Dolce asking all these questions? Surely she wasn't thinking she was going to quit travelling and put herself into a facility? The two of them had a plan, a pact, one they had written down and both signed while drinking mai tais in Denpasar airport. Neither of them was going into a nursing home.

Harry took a sip of his drink while he thought. Myrtle's heart beat against her breast, waiting to hear what he had to say, desperately hoping he wasn't going to tell her it was a wonderful life. It wasn't. Clearly it wasn't, which was why a royal commission into aged care had taken place. Serious bruising of unknown origin and lack of treatment. Attempted suffocation. Beatings. Forgotten residents. This was precisely why the two of them had a plan.

'It's definitely not a perfect system,' Harry said, his brows knitting. 'I think it's one of the reasons I've stayed so long.'

'You feel as if you need to protect them,' Aggie said, and Myrtle could hear the admiration in her voice.

'A bit,' he admitted. 'That is, I can see we need good people on the inside, being advocates.'

'Is it changing?' Dolce pressed. 'Is it getting better?'

'Slowly. There has definitely been a shift to focus on more client-centred care: including residents in decision-making, giving them more autonomy over their lives, if possible.'

'Like what?' Myrtle asked.

'Like allowing them to choose what time they get up in the morning, rather than being woken up when the home says they should get up. It's something so simple, yet it gives them much more personal control.'

Dolce murmured appreciatively. 'You know, that *is* actually quite a big deal, to be able to exercise your right to honour your body's natural rhythms. I always hate it when we've been on a tour,' she said, motioning to Myrtle, 'and they tell you to bring your bags to the foyer in the morning and check-out before breakfast. I can't poop till I've had breakfast! Mucks me up for the rest of the day.'

Aggie laughed and Harry nodded in sympathy.

'Oh, I love you, Dolce,' Aggie said, mopping up sauce with a forkful of potato.

'Did you know,' Dolce continued, 'that the royal commission into banking received three hundred per cent more media coverage than the commission into aged care?'

'No,' Harry said, frowning. 'Shows you where society's priorities lie, doesn't it?'

'It's disheartening,' Aggie agreed.

Myrtle found herself mute, staring at Dolce as though she was just getting to know this woman, rather than having spent decades of friendship and adventuring with her. Had her personality changed? Was she succumbing to dementia? It would be a logical explanation for all of this. She seemed different, though not necessarily in decline.

'I'm not convinced much will change at all from that commission,' Dolce said.

'It has to, though, doesn't it?' Aggie added. 'We're an ageing population. Surely those of us who still can need to advocate for changes now if we want them to be there when it's our turn.'

'Well, in fact,' Dolce said, pointing her knife in the air to punctuate her thought. 'Dementia rates have actually fallen. People think dementia is rising but it's not.'

'What about the *tsunami of dementia* the media talks about?' Aggie said.

'The thing is that we're living longer, so there's more people in aged care, and so it looks like dementia rates are rising, but it's an illusion. Whatever we've been doing has been helping to slow the rate of new cases.'

'I didn't know that,' Harry said, casting his eyes to the golden ceiling of the train for a moment, as if applying this new information to his job.

'Maggie Beer has been such an advocate,' Aggie added. 'I've got her book *Maggie's Recipe for Life*. Mum does too. It's all about eating for brain health.'

Myrtle wanted to contribute to this conversation but was, frankly, stupefied. This was so unlike Dolce. Dolce was generally more likely to be joining yarn-bombing groups and watching videos of psychics on YouTube than researching dementia treatments and royal commissions. Maybe she was afraid? But, again, she didn't need to be because *they had a plan.*

Abruptly, Myrtle changed the topic. 'Harry, what option have you taken up for tomorrow in Alice Springs?'

Harry blinked, startled at her sudden departure from the dementia discussion. 'I'm going to Uluru,' he said, grinning.

'Oh wow,' Aggie murmured, placing her knife and fork together on her plate. 'That would be amazing.'

'Have you been to Uluru?' he asked her.

'Not yet. I'd love to go one day, though.'

'It's an expensive option.' He winced. 'But I just had to do it.'

'All that space,' she said, and smiled at him as if they were sharing a secret.

'Exactly.' He nodded. 'What are you doing?'

'I'm trekking with Holly to Simpsons Gap.'

He growled softly. 'I almost did that. It was difficult to pick between the two. I hope one day I get back out here to travel more, but if I only came once, I thought I'd truly regret not seeing the rock.'

Myrtle wondered if his little growl was one of being torn between two great tourist options or if it was in fact disappointment that he'd missed the chance to spend the day with Aggie. 'Dolce and I are going to the wildlife park,' she said, smiling across at Dolce. But Dolce gave her a hard look in return, which made Myrtle shrink inwardly. What on earth was going on with her?

'Mum's doing the tour around Alice Springs,' Aggie added. 'I think she might be going with the jam man.' She'd lowered her voice, despite the fact that her mother was seated a couple of rows back with the jam man himself and another couple their age.

'What have you found out about him?' Myrtle asked.

'Later,' Aggie said softly.

'You'll have to show me your photos of the trek after we get back,' Harry said, igniting a light of pure happiness in Aggie's eyes that made Myrtle's heart leap. Dolce had caught it too and smiled into her glass as she brought it to her lips. Myrtle considered them both for a moment . . . and made a plan. But unlike the plan she'd made with Dolce all those years ago, this plan didn't involve killing anyone.

17

Valeria and Rupert's dining companions – a couple who spent their lives cruising, and who were right now filling in time between voyages by travelling overland for once – had left, and so too had Aggie and the others at her table. Her daughter had given her a smile and a wave as they left, and the other three had beamed smiles in her direction. Thank goodness Rupert had his back to them and couldn't see their keen interest. She wasn't going to get up and walk past their table with Rupert on her heels, so she'd kept him here, waiting for them to leave.

Holly was still here but at the other end of the carriage. She'd been placed with a single traveller, a muscly woman Valeria guessed to be in her early fifties, with a shaved head and tattoos up her arms. She and Holly seemed to be hitting it off, given the laughter that exploded from that corner every now and then. Honestly, Holly could well do with showing some decorum. She was drunk, clearly.

Valeria sighed, forcing herself to let go of the annoyance she felt at Holly's current state, and picked up her glass. She and Rupert were on their second nightcap, shots of cloying dessert wine sticking in her throat and making her skin flush hot. The second round of diners was beginning to drift in and she knew she and Rupert should get up and vacate this spot, to at least move themselves to the lounge bar, but her legs had gone a little soft from the alcohol, and her knees were touching Rupert's and she didn't want to move them.

'Thank you,' Rupert said suddenly, leaning forward in his seat and stretching his fingers across the table between them. Instinctively she did the same, and their fingers interlocked. His touch shot a bolt of desire through her, landing with a thud abruptly below her navel.

'What for?' she whispered, focusing on his face now.

'For allowing me the chance to explain.'

Were they going to do this now? Have the conversation? She knew they had to have it, but the alcohol had made her thoughts fuzzy and she held the enticing notion that she'd like not to know anything at all, that she'd like to simply undo the top button of his shirt and lay small kisses on his collarbone.

She inhaled sharply and withdrew her fingers. 'I think I need to go back to my cabin,' she said, racing through her mind and tidying up her thoughts the way she might whisk through the lounge room and sweep away empty teacups and discarded blankets at the sound of a knock at the door.

Rupert's eyes widened. 'Yes, of course. I'll escort you.'

'Thank you.'

He held out his arm for her to steady herself as she slid awkwardly from the bench seat, her abdomen leading the centre of gravity till she was upright again, smoothing down her shirt – the fetching made-for-television shirt – as she gathered herself together. He led the way down the centre of the restaurant carriage, both of them treading carefully against the movement of the train. She gave

Holly a stern glare as they passed, but Holly was in the middle of sucking down another drink and merely waved at her in return.

Valeria and Rupert made their way through the lounge bar, many guests gathered around with full glasses and loud, laughing voices. Then, as they passed through to the next section, Rupert reached for her good hand, ostensibly to steady her while she traversed the moving parts beneath their feet, but also a convenient moment to initiate more touch. She found she didn't mind. He led the way down the straight hall of the twin rooms, then into her own carriage. The doors of her daughter's room were folded shut, and she wondered if Agatha was inside or whether she had disappeared somewhere with Harry. The idea that Agatha might have sneaked off somewhere with that young man was sharply irritating. She must speak to her as soon as possible about Harry. More specifically, she must speak to her about Gideon and her last chance to use those embryos. She would be a fool not to take the opportunity.

'They've made up the bed,' Rupert said, opening her door and folding it back on itself. Like magic, a steward had been in while they were dining and converted her small room into a bedroom. The narrow bed, having been released from its hiding spot against the wall, extended the length of the room, meaning there was nowhere for them to sit and talk. She found this instantly relieving. She wasn't good at the talking thing; she never had been. One only had to look at the state of her relationship with Agatha to see the evidence of that. If she and Agatha could simply have stuck to making jam together, in silence, their whole story might have been a different one. She suspected that if she and Rupert were to have any chance at all, she might be better to take talking out of the relationship.

'It looks good, doesn't it?' he said, pressing his hand into the mattress and testing its firmness.

'It does,' she agreed. The linen was all white and the doona plump, exactly as you'd expect to find in a lovely hotel.

They stared at the bed for a moment in silence, an awkward pause lingering in the air. No wonder she had got on well with Bertie. He was economical with words at the best of times, and on the days he taught at university he tended to use up his quota in the lecture theatre. They'd never needed to say much. When they'd had the sheep, they could work together in silence, keeping the sheep calm. It was precisely their lack of conversation that had saved them when they, too, had struggled to conceive again after Agatha. Secondary infertility – such a confounding condition. If no one talked, no one could blame the other. No one could talk about potential *what ifs* to drive the other crazy. No one could suggest they separate.

'Would you like to come to my cabin?' Rupert asked now, a hesitant catch in his words. 'They might not yet have made up my bed, and we could sit and talk.'

He was a chatter, this one.

She affected her most casual demeanour. 'We have plenty of time ahead of us. It's been a big day. I think I might call it a night, if that's okay.'

He blinked, taking her rejection stoically. 'Of course.'

'But tomorrow. We can talk then,' she added, gritting her teeth.

'Tomorrow.' He lifted the back of her hand to his lips and kissed it gently, then left her room, closing the doors behind him.

•

Aggie lay awake in her narrow bed. She'd been drifting in and out of sleep for some time, and the display on her phone told her it was now two o'clock in the morning. The bed was only as wide as her pillow, which meant she had to wake up each time she wanted to roll over. The doona was surprisingly warm, even though she could feel the cold from outside the train pressing in against the double window. She sat up and raised the blind to see if the view outside was really a desert sky full of stars, just as Harry had been hoping for. There they were, shining points in the black velvet dome, the curve of the earth obvious as the celestial bodies wrapped themselves around the globe, with no city or light pollution to stop her seeing them. She wondered if Harry was also awake, also gazing at the sky. She pressed her hand to the glass and let the chill seep into her flesh for a few moments, relishing the absolute *differentness* of this moment compared to her life in Angaston.

She flopped back down against her pillow. She'd brought earplugs with her, for which she was intensely grateful, though the noise of the train was still pronounced. Her concertina door rattled in its tracks. The train roared like a dragon hurtling through the desert. The cups and saucers in the tearoom clattered and crashed about as though a baby rhinoceros was having a party in there.

The rocking of the train, on the other hand, was soothing. She found she quite enjoyed it, as though the tense nerves in her body were being loosened and released. Despite her lack of sleep, she felt a level of peace she hadn't felt in some time. With her phone completely out of range, no television or computer to distract her, nowhere to go other than the bathroom, she could do nothing but simply surrender to the moment.

Listening to Harry talk over dinner about facing the abyss and not being able to run away had stirred up more memories of Cora, of her death, and of what it had done to her and Gideon. If Cora hadn't died, would they have survived as a couple, made it for the long haul? What if they'd never gone through IVF at all, had simply accepted that their version of forever wasn't going to include a baby? Would they have been okay then? She paused then, holding her breath, unable to stop the next thought that came to the foreground.

What if they *did* try, just one more time?

What if they went through with the final round of IVF, and gave the last of their embryos the chance to become new life in their arms? They still might not get a baby at the end, but if they did . . . well, they could work it out then, couldn't they? Perhaps they could co-parent if they didn't want to try to make a go of it as a couple. Would that be so bad? Probably half the kids in Australia were being raised by single parents or co-parents.

It was possible.

But it was also possible the most unbearable thing could happen . . . again.

•

She'd been in labour for more than a day.

'I told her so often she couldn't come out yet,' Aggie gasped, between torturous contractions. 'That she had to wait until she was fully grown. She'll be so confused.'

If she'd had enough time to sob between contractions she would have. But the waves of pain crashed onto her at such lightning speed that it took her breath away.

Gideon kissed her hand and closed his eyes, sleep deprivation and shock catching up with him. His skin was grey.

'But it's time to come out now,' she whispered to her baby inside her, her voice cracking as yet another contraction hit.

In her mind, she spoke to herself, focusing, repeating words of encouragement in an endless mantra.

You are her mother. This is the last and bravest thing you can do for her, to help her finish the journey you started together. Bring her into the world, Aggie – only you can do that.

After thirty-seven hours, in a tsunami of pain, Cora Clair Hermann-Johnson came into the world. But instead of the pain ending there, it only got worse as Aggie's heart ripped into a zillion pieces.

Her daughter was here . . . but soon she would be leaving forever.

The midwife lay Cora's small body upon Aggie's chest and wrapped her tiny, postage-stamp-sized hand around her mother's finger.

How could Aggie ever let her go?

•

Aggie wiped tears from her face and shook her head in the dark, gazing up at the stars. It was foolish to contemplate another round of IVF when that memory was strong enough to slay her at any moment.

A horizontal slash of bright red pierced the night sky outside her window, splitting the blackness in two. She smiled despite the weight of a largely sleepless night dragging at her eyes. She watched the lightening sky for a while, pulling the blanket up to her chin, sitting cross-legged on the bed, the cold air outside pushing doggedly at the windows.

Cora's ghost drifted around her in the quiet of the new day, but it was a comforting feeling, knowing she was close.

Then her mind turned to Holly, wondering about her and the woman in the dining car last night. Holly's eyes had been locked onto hers. She'd been enthralled by the woman's words, maybe by the woman herself. Holly had changed and, somehow, Aggie had been left out of the revolution, her daughter willing to talk more openly with a stranger than with her own mother.

*

As the train neared Alice Springs, Aggie's phone buzzed with notifications. She spent some time reading emails that had come into the Strawberry Sonnet inbox: inquiries about future functions, supplier newsletters, and unsolicited advertising material. She sent a text message to Savannah, asking her to let her know as soon as possible if there were any updates about the signage.

Then she began an email to Gideon.

I know we weren't going to talk about this till I got back. Funny thing about being in a microcosm on a train – time stretches and warps, the rest of the world falls away. It's like stepping into an intense bubble where you can dive straight to the depths of what's important in life. People talk about things they wouldn't normally talk about. Share things they wouldn't normally share. I've only been away a few days and yet it feels so much longer. I've had a few conversations that have made me think. I don't have an answer yet, but

Here, she paused. She was going to write that she definitely didn't want to use the embryos . . . but found she couldn't do it. More than any of the other choices to rule out, that was too final. She wasn't ready to say it – or even to type it – yet.

I do know I don't want to donate the embryos to science. I can't entirely say why. The only reason IVF was even an option for us was because scientists did research. We benefited from someone else's generosity of embryo donation to science. Yet it doesn't feel right, for me. I'm sorry. I hope that's okay.

She pressed send and then once again sat on her bed, watching the sky turn orange, then a tinge of blue creeping in, bleeding together like watercolours, until she knew she needed to get up and start the day. Today was her mum's birthday and she'd organised for everyone to meet in Myrtle and Dolce's cabin straight after breakfast for a jammy high tea. She wanted to check in with the restaurant steward to make sure the scones would be ready on time.

Outside in the brightly lit hallway, she padded in her Ghan slippers along the hall to the bathroom, all the other doors in her carriage tightly closed. She felt oddly alone in the world, just her and the clanking, rattling train hurtling through space. But upon her return, Harry's door popped open.

'Oh, morning,' she said, her voice low so as not to disturb others still sleeping around them. She suspected her mother, always an early riser, would be awake inside her cabin.

'Morning,' he said, and gave her an effortless smile. His hair was tousled and he wore long green pants with a cotton drawstring and a well-loved, soft T-shirt that hung loosely – and rather sexily – on his toned body. He had stubble, which, for some reason, made her smile.

'How'd you sleep?' she asked.

He grimaced. 'Patchy. Those beds are definitely not made for someone my height. I feel as if I need a round of yoga to stretch myself out again.' Illustrating his point, he raised his hands above his head to extend his spine, his fingers easily reaching the ceiling.

'It was pretty loud, too, wasn't it? I've got some spare earplugs if you'd like them.'

'I'll take you up on that, thanks.'

'I'll dig them out of my suitcase while you're in the bathroom and have them for you when you get back.'

Harry headed down the hall and Aggie squatted down in her paisley pyjama bottoms and pulled her suitcase out from under the bed. She ended up on her knees, her backside hanging out into the hallway while she hunted around in her clothes and toiletries to find the spare pair of earplugs, which were floating around with a woollen scarf and gloves. She pulled those out too, knowing she'd need them this morning when they arrived in Alice Springs.

'Excuse me.'

She startled and craned her neck to see a tall gentleman in long slacks and a pullover trying to look anywhere but at the top of her bum cheeks, which she could feel were now exposed. 'Oh god, sorry.' She quickly jumped to her feet, pulling up her pyjama bottoms, and the obviously embarrassed man continued on his way, passing Harry as he went.

'Don't stop on my account,' Harry ribbed.

She put a cool hand to her warm cheek for a moment. 'Here, these should help.' She passed him the packet of earplugs and, to her heart-stopping shock, he wrapped his hand around hers and held onto it.

'Have breakfast with me,' he said, evenly, confidently. 'There aren't set times so we can go whenever we're ready.' He peered at the closed doors of her mother's and Holly's cabins. 'Before any of the others are even up.'

She swooned – actually swooned, black pinpoints bursting in her eyes, though it must have been for a millisecond because she was still standing upright, still holding his hand.

She nodded her agreement, speechless.

18

Aggie arrived at the lounge bar wearing what she hoped was a good outfit for hiking to Simpsons Gap – jeans, farm boots (left over from her days wandering vineyards with Gideon), a T-shirt and a cotton jacket, which she could take off and tie around her waist as the day moved from two degrees in the morning to twenty later this afternoon. Her hair was scraped into a low ponytail, and her make-up was minimal, just some tinted sunscreen and kohl to line her eyes. Harry was already there, staring out the window at the desert zooming by. He stood as soon as he saw her. He had the best smile, one that reached all the way to his eyes and somehow further than that.

'Let's go,' he said.

'I just need to check with Christie about a morning tea plan.' She met Christie at the bar and the woman assured her all the plans for the jammy high tea were still in place. She flicked her eyes between Aggie and Harry, the slight tilt of her head suggesting she registered a change of status in their relationship, and led them inside to the dining carriage. They both ordered coffee, fruit, yoghurt and the barramundi eggs Benedict.

'It's mesmerising,' Aggie said, nodding to the view outside. 'The red of the earth is such a rich colour.'

'So much space,' he said, smiling.

'Has it met your expectations?'

'Yeah, I love it.'

Silence drifted easily between them for a few moments while they soaked in the landscape. Then Aggie saw something moving in the distance. It was dark and tall, with long legs, and at first she thought it was a person. 'Look.' She pointed. 'Is that . . . an emu?'

Harry followed her gaze. 'It is too.'

It was walking through the low, scrubby bushes that stretched to the horizon. 'How on earth do they survive out here? What do they even eat? Where do they drink?'

'No idea. I've never seen a wild emu before,' he said.

'Neither have I. Isn't that crazy? We have some of the most distinctive animals in the world in this country and most of us would never have seen a fraction of them in their natural state.'

As the Ghan thundered onwards, the emu drifted out of view just as their coffees, fruit and yoghurt arrived.

'No strawberries,' she said, motioning to the plate of sliced apple, pineapple, pear and rockmelon.

'Do you still appreciate strawberries after working with them so much?' he asked, then speared two slices of fruit with his fork and bit into them.

'Absolutely. I've always loved strawberries. There used to be a strawberry field next to the house I'm living in now. I'm just renting but I've been there for more than twenty years.'

'It must be a good home.'

'It is. I've got great landlords, and they've made improvements over the years. It's the house I moved into after I moved out of

Myrtle's place, and it's as though the house and I have grown up together. I raised my daughter there, and Banjo too,' she added, sadly.

'Who's Banjo?'

'My dog.' She sighed. 'He lives with my ex, Gideon.' Of course, Gideon had lived in the house too, and she'd been pregnant with Cora there as well. Now that she thought about it, the house had been shrouded in sadness more than joy for the past two years at least.

Harry chewed thoughtfully, and she wondered if he was debating whether or not to ask her about Gideon. It would be a good time to lay out all the cards, for both of them. He clearly had some baggage of his own. It was on the tip of her tongue to ask him, but then she realised she had no wish to drag any of her pain up right now.

'Let's talk about other things, happy things,' she said, then gulped down some coffee. Her suggestion seemed to cheer him.

'All right, then. Tell me what's on your bucket list,' he said.

'Ooh, good question. It's been a while since I reviewed it.'

'Mine's on my fridge,' he said, as he took his plate of barramundi eggs Benedict from the waiter. 'Thanks, mate.'

She received her plate too and the waiter moved away. 'You'd better go first then. It will give me a minute to drag mine out and dust it off.'

'I want to see Uluru,' he said, 'so I can tick that one off today.'

'That's on mine too, but I'll have to come back another time for that.'

'I want to learn to scuba dive, I want to visit Japan . . .'

'Oh, I'd love to see the cherry blossoms,' she said. 'I'm adding that to my list, thanks.'

'I'd like to walk the Camino de Santiago. I know, that's on lots of people's lists.'

'Doesn't mean you can't have it too.'

'I want to busk with my guitar under a palm tree at Hawaii's Waikiki beach after a morning swim,' he said, his face lighting up.

'Nice! What do you play?'

'Singer-songwriter stuff, mostly.'

'That's my favourite kind of music. But I can't play anything, sadly. I wish I could.'

'You've still got time,' he said. 'It's a fun thing to do. You can add it to your bucket list.'

'Okay, done. What else have you got?'

'Hmm . . . what else . . .' He paused and half-closed his eyes, almost wincing.

'That one,' she said. 'What is it?'

'It's embarrassing.'

'Excellent,' she said, definitely interested to hear this. 'That means it's a good one. Come on, tell me.'

For a second, he looked as though he might back out of confessing, then he straightened his shoulders and took command of himself. 'Okay, I'm man enough to say it.' He took a breath and let it out. 'I want to go to Disneyland.'

She could have whimpered for how cute he was in that moment, needing to work up the courage to say that out loud. 'That's adorable.'

He shook his head slightly, as though trying to rid himself of the last threads of shame.

'Tell me why you want to go,' she encouraged him.

'I grew up in foster homes,' he said, his knife and fork suspended over his food. 'A lot of my childhood was not so fun.'

'I'm sorry.' She couldn't imagine what he'd been through. She and Valeria might have a strained relationship but by comparison with many kids, she'd had a safe, stable and even joyful time of it – until she got pregnant, anyway.

'It's okay. It's just one of those things, you know, those crazy dreams you have as a kid, those places you go to in your head to escape stuff.' His mouth set then, she guessed with memories of the things he had to escape. 'Anyway, I'd like to go there for Little Harry.'

That was it, she thought – the hard, grinding pain she'd seen in the lines around his eyes yesterday in the kitchenette. Years of struggling to survive.

She felt alarmingly close to emotion and had to sternly pull herself together. 'It's brilliant. An inspired choice. Totally worthy bucket list item.'

'Okay, your turn,' he said, obviously keen to move the conversation away from him.

'Hmm . . . well, I don't like being in the ocean so much, so no scuba diving for me.'

'Fair enough.'

'I'd love to go on holiday with Holly, maybe through Scotland and Ireland. Maybe a horse-riding adventure on hairy, rugged horses through the marshes and hills, staying in stone castles or something.'

'Great one,' Harry said.

'Other than that, and Uluru, and the cherry blossoms in Japan . . . I don't know, maybe an African safari to see elephants and giraffes and lions.'

'Yes! I'm taking that one, adding it to mine too,' he said, pointing his knife to finalise the deal.

'Let's see, what else . . .' She was rummaging through her mind to find exotic and inspiring foodie adventures to add to her list when the restaurant doors opened and Myrtle and Dolce came into the carriage. 'Look out, trouble's here,' she said, waving to them, and checking the time on her phone, keeping track of when she would need to go and set up in the cabin. Myrtle approached their table first. She and Dolce were in long, soft trousers and billowing long-sleeved shirts with brightly coloured patterns. Dolce's short hair was a little flattened on one side where she'd been sleeping, but she was looking around eagerly at the various breakfast plates in front of other passengers, examining the options she might order for herself.

'Good morning, Harry,' Myrtle greeted him.

'Morning, Myrtle, did you sleep well?' he asked.

'Like a log,' she said.

'That's great,' Aggie said.

'I have news,' Myrtle said, putting her hand on Aggie's shoulder.

'What's that?'

'You're not trekking to Simpsons Gap today.'

'What do you mean?' Aggie looked over towards Dolce, who widened her eyes and gave her an apologetic look.

'I've changed your itinerary, and you'll be joining Harry on the flight over Uluru instead.'

'Wait, no. I'm trekking with Holly.'

Myrtle shook her head. 'I've already spoken to her and she was just as keen as I am to have you go to Uluru instead.'

Aggie felt winded. She'd been looking forward to spending the day with Holly, and the last thing she wanted was for Holly to feel she'd been abandoned. 'But she's—'

'Holly is perfectly fine and perfectly happy. Look, Aggie, the ticket is non-refundable, and it cost a lot, so don't you dare think of cancelling it. You can thank me by way of a bottle of vodka when we get back home.'

Aggie covered her face with her hands, mortified. 'I can't believe you did this,' she mumbled, afraid to remove her hands and see Harry's likely equally horrified face.

'Premium vodka will do just fine, thank you,' Myrtle said.

Aggie felt her great-aunt move away from the table and split her fingers to peek at Harry's face. He looked bemused but not unhappy. She dropped her hands. 'I'm so, so sorry.'

He laughed. 'Don't be.'

'Meddling Myrtle – she'd try to make a love match for the Pope.'

'Well, I think she's just made this particular bucket list trip a whole lot better.' He smiled at her and shrugged. 'What can you do?'

'Nothing,' she said, sighing. 'Nothing at all.'

After breakfast, she hurried to find Holly before they had to go to their jammy tea and found her in her cabin, inexplicably drawing on the inside of her forearm with a pen.

'What are you doing?' Aggie asked.

Holly shrugged, continuing to draw layered triangles, copying from an image on her phone screen. 'Just trying out this symbol to see if I like it.'

'What symbol?'

'It's supposed to be a protection symbol of some sort.'

Aggie stared at the image on Holly's phone. At first it looked like three separate triangles, but looking more closely she could see that the lines were a continuum of one shape. 'Why do you need a protection symbol?'

Holly sighed and put her pen down, forcing a neutral expression onto her face. 'It's not a big deal,' she said. 'Really. I was just thinking about a tattoo and thought I'd trial it first.'

'A tattoo?' Aggie was shocked. Holly had never seemed like the tattoo type, despite it being a popular trend these days.

Holly got to her feet, laughing. 'Yes, a tattoo.'

Aggie remembered the woman at Holly's table last night, the one with the many tattoos up her arm and the shaved head.

She was about to launch into a maternal interrogation on this new interest of Holly's but her daughter spoke first.

'I'm glad Myrtle's sending you to Uluru,' Holly said, abruptly changing the topic.

'You are? That's what I came to talk to you about, because I don't have to go. I've been looking forward to spending the day with you, and just because Myrtle says I have to do something doesn't mean—'

'No, really. I want you to go.'

'But . . . what about our mother–daughter day?' Aggie asked, saddened that Holly could be so quick to let it go.

'Honestly, I don't feel much like socialising today. A day of walking in silence in the outback will do me good.'

Holly was wearing a thin red neckerchief and Aggie had to curb the strong urge to reach out and pull it away, checking that the skin of her neck was okay beneath the cloth.

'But . . . I can help. You can talk to me,' Aggie said, her hand on her chest. 'That's what mums are for.'

Let me fix this, Holly, please.

Holly smiled, though her eyes were sad. 'You can't, Mum. Anyway, I'd rather be alone.'

Aggie sucked in a sharp breath, pained by her daughter's words, and Holly pushed past her into the hallway, beckoning Aggie to follow.

'Come on, it's time for tea.'

Aggie waited a beat, reeling from the rejection and the strange feeling that she'd walked in on Holly in the midst of something like an act of self-harm, then pulled herself together so she could be a good daughter and go and make a fuss of her mother on her big day.

19

Valeria was still lying on top of her bed, fully clothed, staring out the train window, when there was a gentle knock at the door.

'Mum, are you awake?'

'Yes,' she said, her voice sounding scratchy, as if weak from lack of use. She cleared her throat and gathered more air into her lungs. 'Come in. The door is unlocked.' She sat up, swinging her legs over the edge of the bed. The concertina doors folded back and Agatha's smiling face appeared.

'Happy birthday!' she cheered.

'Thank you,' Valeria said, feeling embarrassed to have been caught out still supine at this hour. She checked her watch. Goodness, it was nearly eight.

'It's time to go to Myrtle and Dolce's room,' Agatha said, and squashed herself into what little space was left in the cabin and hugged her. She smelt of coffee and hollandaise sauce, if Valeria wasn't mistaken. 'I know it's early for morning tea,' she said, laughing, 'but we need to get your spoiling in early. Have you had breakfast?'

Valeria patted her daughter on the shoulder. 'No, I wasn't feeling very hungry.' That was true. 'I had a cup of tea from the tearoom but then found myself lying back to watch the landscape.'

'That's probably a good thing. You'll have room for surprise birthday treats now,' Agatha said, holding out her arm with a flourish. Valeria followed her from the room, feeling awkward. She didn't much like surprises. It didn't give her enough time to prepare the correct response.

Myrtle, Dolce and Holly cried out 'Happy birthday!' as soon as Valeria stepped inside the double cabin. She was taken aback. There was a small silver tea trolley pressed up against the back wall, under the window. It held a basket of fragrant scones, with dishes of whipped cream and little pots of jam with silver spoons.

'Oh my goodness,' she said, taking in the champagne buckets holding open bottles and a tray of glasses.

'Welcome to your seventieth birthday jammy high tea,' Agatha said, grinning, obviously pleased with herself.

'This is incredible,' Valeria said, also noting the pink and white streamers that hung around the room and from the bunk beds, which hadn't yet been tucked away for the day.

'Here,' Myrtle said, pouring a drink and handing the champagne flute to her.

'Thank you.' Valeria moved further into the room, which was so cramped it really only had the space for her to take an extra couple of steps towards the silver tray.

'I made the mulberry jam,' Dolce said proudly. Her jar had a sweet paper doily on top.

'I still don't know how you have the patience for mulberries,' Myrtle said. 'All those stems to cut off.'

'Not many people do, which probably explains how many ribbons I've won over the years in the marginal categories. It doesn't have the respect that strawberry jam has.'

'Rubbish,' Myrtle scoffed. 'You win because it's good jam. It's simply a bonus that it's unique as well. It's always been one of the things I love about you, your ability to be part of the crowd yet still run your own race.'

Dolce tipped her head towards Myrtle in thanks.

'I made the brandied apricot jam,' Myrtle said.

'I made the strawberry jam,' Agatha added.

'I did not make jam,' Holly said, 'but I did hang the streamers and I'm the tea runner. Give me your orders, everyone, and I'll go fetch the teas and bring them back.'

'That's lovely, Holly, thank you,' Valeria said. 'Milky for me, please.'

'Wait, let's do gifts first,' Agatha said.

Valeria felt herself stiffen. It was all so awkward, being the centre of attention on an expensive trip that had been triggered by her ministroke. It made her feel guilty, and thankful, and frightened that this might be the one last great thing that happened to her before a huge stroke. If this were a movie, it would be the moment where everything was unbearably wonderful and in the next scene someone would be killed in a car accident.

She clutched at her throat.

'Mum? Are you okay?'

'Yes, of course.' She forced a smile.

'Here, sit down,' Myrtle instructed, and Valeria did so gratefully. Her aunt lay a gift in her lap.

'I don't need any presents,' Valeria said, dismissively, and then felt churlish for saying it because she knew deep down she'd still rather like one. She opened Myrtle's gift to find a pair of fluffy pink slippers with a bouquet of feathery pompoms and diamantés at the toe, and a Ghan-branded scarf stuffed inside as a memento of their trip. She was relieved it was something small. It was uncomfortable enough that Myrtle had paid for this trip. Sometimes, her aunt did know her well. 'Thank you, that's very kind. And of course you've already given me your true gift.' She gestured around the room. 'This trip. Thank you, again. It's more than anyone could ask for.'

'Yes, thank you' came Agatha's and Holly's voices too.

Myrtle waved them all away. 'My pleasure. We're having a ball, aren't we, Dolce?'

'We are,' Dolce agreed.

'This one's from me,' Holly said, passing her a lightweight gift wrapped in the same mauve paper. Valeria opened it to find a matching bathrobe to go with the slippers. 'So now you have the complete set,' Holly said.

'I love it, thank you,' Valeria said, beaming at Holly. 'I'm just so glad you're here in Australia and able to come on this trip with us.'

'I second that,' Agatha said, squeezing Holly's hand, then handed over her present to Valeria. It was large, square and heavy.

'Goodness, what's this?'

'Open it,' Agatha encouraged her.

Valeria undid the sparkly golden ribbon and then the paper, taking care not to rip it. She liked to repurpose wrapping paper and ribbons whenever she could.

There was a photo album inside. She opened it carefully to discover a bunch of long-forgotten photographs, some black-and-white, some the muted colours of film photographs from the 1970s and 1980s. They were all photographs of Agatha and Valeria and Bertie.

'Where did you get these?' she asked, bewildered.

'I found a couple of boxes of them stored in my old room at your place,' Agatha said, and shrugged. 'I thought it might be nice to organise them for you.'

Valeria turned a page and stared at a black-and-white image of herself holding Agatha on her hip out under a tree. It was from Agatha's first birthday, and her chubby-cheeked daughter was clutching a blankie in one fist, the other arm slung around her mother's neck, gazing up into Valeria's face with total love and devotion. It was clear that Valeria was her daughter's whole world.

She felt a sob attempting to erupt from deep inside her chest, and snapped the photo album shut. 'Thank you,' she said, thickly, clutching the album to her chest. 'It's beautiful. I'll have a good look through it when I have more time.'

Agatha nodded, her own eyes misty with emotion as well, which made Valeria look away quickly.

'Here's my gift,' Dolce said, shuffling over. She handed Valeria a long rectangular present. Beneath the wrapping, Valeria found a worn velvet jewellery box. The lid creaked and jerked on its aged hinges as she opened it. Inside was a long silver bracelet, the heavy, chunky kind from decades earlier, studded with sapphires.

'Oh, Dolce! I can't take this.'

'Of course you can,' Dolce said. 'I'm not wearing it anymore and my kids and grandkids don't wear things like that. It's too old-fashioned for them but it suits you. The colour matches your eyes.'

'I promise I'll look after it well and I will wear it. It's beautiful. Is it from the forties?'

'It is indeed. I think it might have even been my mother's, but I can't quite remember now.'

'This is very special. I'm honoured, thank you. Thank you all. I don't really know what to say.'

'We all just want you to have a wonderful birthday,' Agatha said.

Valeria felt foolishly sentimental. Her travel companions – her family – had truly made her feel cherished, and it was such an unusual and unexpected experience. It made her hopeful for the future, hopeful that some of the cracks in her relationships might actually have a chance to heal, just like her fractured wrist. Maybe she could be put back together with these people the way she should be, a part of the whole, not the piece that couldn't find its place. 'All right, Holly, I think I need that tea now.'

'On it,' Holly said, jumping to her feet, taking everyone's orders and heading to the tearoom. Valeria gulped her bubbly.

'We're not far from Alice Springs now,' Agatha said. 'Can I get you a plate of scones?'

'Lovely, thank you. And you and Holly should have a good feed before you go hiking,' she said.

Agatha took a breath. 'Actually, my plans have changed.'

'What do you mean?'

'I'm sending her on the flight over Uluru,' Myrtle said, her chin lifted, a sure sign she was expecting Valeria to protest.

'Well . . . that's quite a gift,' Valeria said, confused. She felt the warmth and connection to her family of only moments ago, the unusual sense of being the important one, slipping away. Myrtle had just given an expensive flight to Agatha, for what reason she wasn't sure.

'Yes,' Myrtle said. 'That lovely young Harry is going and I thought it would be in Aggie's best interests to join him.'

And there she was – Meddling Myrtle.

Holly returned with cups wobbling in saucers and Valeria put on a good show, she thought, of drinking and eating and saying all the right things. Then it was time to go back to her room to prepare for the day. Holly stayed behind to clean up, while Agatha followed her back to their cabins, carrying all her gifts. At the entrance to her room, Valeria reached out and took Agatha's elbow, causing her daughter to look at her in surprise.

'You can't do this, Agatha.'

'What?'

'Go on that flight. Don't you see? Myrtle is meddling, as she always does.'

She paused, knowing this conversation was heading into explosive territory, if the fight she'd had with Agatha several months ago was anything to go by. They had stopped speaking after that, and if she'd not had a stroke and broken her wrist they still might not be speaking. Still, this was too important to let go.

'She's trying to set you up with that man – that very *young* man – when what she should be doing, if she had half a brain and half a heart, is helping you reconcile with Gideon.'

Agatha opened her mouth, then closed it again. Several emotions skittered over her face till she took a long breath and slowly exhaled.

'Please, listen to me,' Valeria continued, still clutching her arm. 'The last thing I want to do is bring up disagreements that will make this trip unpleasant.'

Agatha's face hardened then – recalling their fight, she assumed.

'Those embryos are your last chance to have another baby. Please, *focus*. Talk to Gideon. Work it out. Flying around the countryside with a younger man might be fun but it will not get you to the place you want to be.'

'And where's that?' Agatha asked, her tone cool.

'To motherhood. To marriage. To family. To the life you dreamt of. To the goal – the one you worked and suffered so long for. For your baby.'

Tears brightened her daughter's eyes but she blinked them quickly away.

'You see? You still want it. You've been through hell, you both have. I get it. I really do.' She gave Agatha a meaningful look to remind her that she knew this pain. She too had wanted another baby. She too had been infertile. She knew the toll it took on a marriage. The toll it took on a woman – the constant push and pull of emotions, the despair with every monthly period, the endless questioning and the repeated hollowing out till you felt there was nothing left.

'But you are strong, Agatha. You can do it. One more time. That's it. Then you'll know for sure. You'll truly be done, one way or another. And you just might yet get your happily ever after.'

Agatha placed the bundle of birthday gifts on her bed, then straightened. 'I'd better get ready. We're nearly in Alice.' She left, and Valeria eased herself down onto the bed, praying her daughter would see sense.

•

When the Ghan came to a halt at Alice Springs station, the conductor's voice came over the loudspeaker, instructing them to ensure they were wearing their official lanyards before disembarking, then to look for their designated bus, which would be identified by destination. Their motley crew, which Harry had now joined, gathered outside their carriages to wish each other well for the day, and Myrtle found she was well pleased with herself for pushing Aggie and Harry together. They stood closely side by side and she felt a triumphant smile spread across her face. Valeria, on the other hand, was shooting daggers at both Aggie and Myrtle.

Holly hugged Aggie. 'You're going to have a fabulous time. Take loads of photos!'

'Are you sure about this?' Aggie asked, holding Holly's arm, clearly uncomfortable about leaving her.

Holly waved her away. 'Absolutely. I want to trek and I want you to have a good time.' She motioned with her eyes, most unsubtly, towards Harry. With that, she left for her bus, while Aggie watched her go, wrinkling her nose with concern. She'd get over that soon enough, Myrtle was certain.

The jam man approached cautiously, well-dressed in slacks and a sensible cardigan, his white hair neatly brushed, and Valeria smiled warmly at him before taking her moment to introduce them all. 'Everyone, I'd like you to meet Rupert,' she said.

'Good morning,' he said, in a smooth English accent. Myrtle found herself smiling again. There was something quite lovely and steady about his presence and she genuinely hoped things worked out well for him and Valeria.

'Rupert, this is my daughter, Agatha.'

'Lovely to meet you, Rupert,' Aggie said.

'Hello,' he replied, and shook Aggie's hand.

'And this is my aunt, Myrtle,' Valeria said, through tightened lips.

'Good morning to you,' Myrtle said, taking in his straight back and clean shoes. He seemed just the type for Valeria.

'And this is Dolce,' Valeria said. Judging by the way her feet were shifting, she was keen to get away.

'Dolce, lovely to meet you too,' he said, completing the introductions.

'Have a wonderful day,' Myrtle said. 'We look forward to seeing you tonight for your birthday dinner under the stars.'

'I'm looking forward to it,' Rupert said, his eyes on Valeria, who whisked him away to the bus that was heading into town.

'Right, then, we'll be off too, won't we, Dolce?' she said, turning to her friend, who nodded. Both she and Dolce had their sticks with them for some support while walking around the wildlife park, and Myrtle now tapped hers on the ground definitively. 'Goodbye, everyone. I can't wait to hear all about your adventures tonight.'

Myrtle and Dolce set off at a moderate pace towards their bus. They'd not long been settled when Dolce said, 'I hope you've done the right thing there with Aggie and Harry.'

Myrtle started. 'Whatever do you mean?'

Dolce smacked her lips together a few times, as if trying to decipher the taste of something in her mouth. 'Did you stop to think how horribly wrong it could all go if Aggie really does have feelings for him?'

'I don't think there's much question of their mutual attraction.'

'Agreed.'

'Then what are you saying?' The bus rumbled to life, the vibration rising through their sensible walking shoes and into the wobbly flesh at their knees.

'She has embryos to consider,' Dolce said, as if Myrtle was dense.

'The embryos have nothing to do with her love life.'

'How can you say that? What if she does decide to use them?'

Dolce may as well have slapped her for the shock the words gave her. '*Use* them? How?'

'We don't know what's in her heart, and we don't know what's in Gideon's heart either.'

A flash of anger shot through Myrtle, as if a mutiny had sprung up around her. 'You sound like Valeria.'

Dolce shrugged. 'Well, Valeria *is* her mother.'

Myrtle gasped at the insinuation – that *she* was not Aggie's mother and should stop trying to act as if she were.

Oh, that was too far, Dolce. Too far.

Just because Dolce had decided it wasn't worth the risk to live life anymore – as if *that* was even possible – it didn't mean she had to shut down everyone else's attempts to embrace new opportunities.

Truly angry now, she dragged a packet of butterscotch lollies from her handbag and thrust one at Dolce. 'Here, eat one.' Then she shoved one into her own gob. They both needed to occupy their mouths before one of them said something from which they might not recover.

20

If Aggie had thought that travelling through the desert on the train was amazing, she had no words to describe seeing Uluru as they flew in to Ayers Rock Airport. It rose high from the flat ground around it, like a giant beating heart in the centre of the country.

On the ground, the size of it alone was impressive enough. 'Taller than the Eiffel Tower,' their Anangu guide told them. 'And almost ten kilometres in circumference.'

The thing of it was, she realised, that to get the full rock into a photo frame, one had to be so very far away from it. Photos from that distance couldn't do it justice because there was nothing to give its scale. It was only when you were too close to get it all into frame that you could start to see the abundance of tall trees around its base, the greenery of the shrubs and grasses, or the shade cast onto the walking track below by the treetops high above. You certainly could feel its power – there was no other word for it.

'Uluru is like an iceberg,' their guide continued. 'Most of it is underground.'

Aggie turned to Harry with wide eyes. 'I had no idea.'

'Me either,' he said, looking up at the steep escarpment in front of them, at the multitude of folds and tucks and curves of the monolith, worn smooth over millennia.

Their group stopped at the entrance to a cave and their guide pointed out ancient drawings on the wall. 'This one was like a classroom,' he said, 'the place to teach the children.' At the next cave, he pointed out the blackened smoke stains on the roof, from where people had sheltered there. 'This one was like a sick bay, or hospital.'

She and Harry had been sticking closely together and it was easy to be here, completely present, her daughter's rebuff put aside for now, and her mother's provocative words easily forgotten in favour of the ease and joy she felt in Harry's company. More than once she'd felt the urge to reach out and take his hand. Each time, she'd shoved her hands into the pockets of her jeans to stop herself.

They were given some time to wander along the tracks around the rock, and she and Harry broke away from the crowd to step back and take in a wider view. There were so many direction changes in the rock wall that it was impossible to see the length of it while this close up. Harry squatted down, placing his palm onto the red soil. He grabbed a handful and smiled.

'What is it?' she asked.

'It's silky smooth. Nothing like I expected.'

She hunched down near him and did the same. 'It's beautiful. Would it sound crazy to say I have a really strong urge to rub it all over myself?'

'Not to me.'

She smoothed it over the back of her left hand, watching her skin change colour, watching the fine particles sink into the lines and crevices of her flesh. 'It's like that ultra-fine clay you get in face masks.'

'Haven't tried one,' Harry said, arching an eyebrow and grinning at her.

He rubbed earth between his hands and it bloomed around him in a powdery red mist.

It was the sexiest thing, watching him crouching on the desert soil, a bright blue sky above them, the vibrant, enormous rock at his back, falling in love with this ancient land.

She swallowed hard.

In that moment, they were the only two people in the world. Perhaps feeling the weight of her gaze – or her longing – his eyes snapped up to meet hers. She saw his chest rise with a deeply drawn breath and she imagined running her earth-covered fingers through his hair, pulling his face upwards and laying her lips on his.

But then she regained her senses and took a step backwards, breaking their trance. 'We'd better catch up,' she croaked, nodding to the group.

He blinked, as though emerging from sleep, and straightened. His hands were still red and he brushed them on the hips and thighs of his cargo pants, smiled at her and reached for her hand. 'Come on,' he said. 'Let's go.'

She accepted his hand as if it was the most natural thing to do. She could feel the silky earth between their fingers as they intertwined, and they rejoined the group on the way to the waterhole. All she could hear were their footfalls, soft in soft dirt, and her heart, loud in her ears, and she couldn't remember the last time she'd felt this happy.

At the conclusion of the walking tour, the group was driven to viewing platforms a short distance away, where the Ghan stewards had set out tables with starched white cloths, ice buckets holding bottles of wine, and platters of sandwiches and rolls to choose from. An Indigenous entertainer, in jeans and boots and a wide-brimmed hat, played a ukulele and sang 'Somewhere Over the Rainbow'.

'I love this version,' Aggie said.

'It's almost impossible to feel anything but happy when listening to a ukulele,' Harry mused.

'I think you're right.' She swayed along to the music while they heaped their plates with food. Then, grabbing drinks, they eased into chairs under the trees nearby. 'I'm starving,' she said, and bit into a roll with gusto.

'Why does food always taste better when you're outdoors?' Harry asked, between mouthfuls.

'Oh, I know the answer to this,' she said.

'Really? I thought it was a rhetorical question.'

'It's called sonic seasoning,' she said, feeling quite chuffed that she had this bit of trivia up her sleeve. 'It basically means that sounds can be used to enhance an eating experience, or make it worse. Research has shown, for example, that if you are eating fish and chips and the restaurant plays a soundtrack of the seaside, you'll rate your food higher. An ice cream company even tried creating the perfect soundtrack that would improve your taste experience of their products, and put QR codes onto the packaging so you could scan it and listen while you ate.'

'That's amazing,' he said.

'Higher frequencies also make things taste sweeter, while lower frequencies make bitter things more bitter.'

'Huh. Genius,' he said, clinking his glass to hers.

The man playing the ukulele announced he was taking a break, and cheers and applause rang through the air. Then a Ghan steward began walking around, offering the instrument to guests, asking if they played and if they'd like to do so now.

'Oh, Harry, look.' She pointed to the steward. 'It's your bucket list item come to life.'

He gave her a bemused look. 'Ah, that's not a guitar and this is definitely not Waikiki.'

'True,' she agreed, undeterred. 'But surely if you can play the guitar you can play a ukulele, can't you? Isn't it kind of a small version of a guitar?'

He snorted. 'No. Totally different. I have mucked around with a mate's uke and he taught me a few chords but I wouldn't say I'm proficient.' But there was something in the way he was narrowing his eyes at the steward that inspired her next words.

'But you can play *something*, can't you? I can tell.'

'How can you tell?'

'Just a feeling.' She was pleased to have him confirm that she was reading him correctly.

'I literally know how to play one song on a ukulele.'

'Perfect.' She jumped to her feet. 'Play that.'

'What are you doing?'

'I'm helping you tick off not just one but two bucket list items today.'

He looked momentarily alarmed, then said, 'What about the fact that this isn't a beach?'

'You heard the guide. All of Uluru and this desert used to be under the ocean. Surely by definition that makes it a beach.'

He put his plate on the ground beside him and stretched out his legs. 'You're a hard woman to resist.'

She took that as agreement and turned on her heel to head to the steward, who broke into a smile, relieved to have someone take up the offer, and waved him over. Harry shook his head, grimacing slightly but clearly resigned to his fate, and got to his feet, joining her near the microphone.

'Here you go,' the steward said, and handed over the instrument.

Harry cleared his throat. 'Thanks.'

Aggie's cheeks ached from smiling. She had the urge to kiss him on the cheek for good luck, but she didn't want to create an awkward moment in front of the tour group. Instead, she took a seat nearby and beamed her encouragement at Harry, who now looked nervous.

'Hi, everyone,' he said into the microphone. Harry took a few moments to test the strings and adjust the tuning knobs, plucked a few chords, then flicked his head back, fronting up to the microphone. Aggie pulled out her phone and snapped a photo of him.

'This song is by British group McFly and it's called "Love is Easy".' He stared straight at Aggie as he said it and she glowed from her toes to the roots of her hair. He struck up a jaunty, upbeat tune, the tone of his voice happy and confident, and Aggie felt like a teenager with a cool boyfriend – a non-pregnant, non-breastfeeding, non-ostracised teenager. The notes of the uke were bright and engaging, and people started tapping their toes or clapping along. Harry cut quite the figure, the little instrument cradled in his long, tanned arms, the sun making his dusty hair glow and Uluru in the background making him look like a rock star. Well, a folk star, perhaps. She took more photos of him. He looked nothing short of magnificent and she planned to text the images to him later so he had them as memories to look back on.

He was relaxing into the song now, moving his body with the groove, breaking into the chorus confidently. When he sang of love being easy he looked right at her, and her hands flew to her cheeks as she laughed, remembering the long-forgotten magic of a spark igniting between two people.

A white-haired couple got up to dance, and then another joined them. She snapped photos of them too, while a few people around her had picked up on the chorus and were singing along. Harry had them eating out of his hand. He broke into a whistle for a moment and a young female steward – clearly smitten by this performance – whooped and shimmied.

All too soon, he strummed the final chord and a wave of whistles and cheers washed over him. Harry was beaming with pride and Aggie cheered and cheered until he handed the ukulele to the smitten steward and walked back to her.

'You were amazing.' She clasped his arms. 'You're a superstar, look.' She gestured to the happy crowd.

He shook his head, disbelieving. 'I can't believe I did that.'

'You *killed* that, is what you did.' Without thinking about it, she threw her arms around him and hugged him, the way footballers might hug each other after scoring a goal, and he wasted no time in squeezing her back, even lifting her off the ground for a few moments before placing her back down.

He straightened his shirt. 'Thank you for making that happen,' he said.

She stepped back, straightening her shirt too, a little flushed from the feel of his body pressed against hers. 'Any time.'

'Encore, encore!' came the shouts from the crowd.

Harry waved at them but shook his head. 'Thanks, guys, but I think I'll quit while I'm ahead.'

A Ghan steward stepped up to the mic to announce that it was time to finish the meal and head back to the bus. 'We'll take a short drive back to Ayers Rock Airport,' she said, 'then we'll get you onto your fixed-wing aircraft and back up into the sky, this time to fly over Uluru and Kata Tjuta too to see the outback from a totally different perspective.'

'Just when I thought the day couldn't get any better,' Harry said, and reached for her hand.

She slipped her hand into his, delighting in how good it felt there. She had to agree – this was already a day she'd remember forever.

21

Valeria and Rupert spent the morning pottering around Alice Springs on what Valeria would term 'the oldies tour'. They started up at Anzac Hill, which served as both a war memorial site and also a fabulous lookout point, its elevation providing an abundant vista of the town below. The wind was fierce, which gave them the perfect opportunity to stand shoulder to shoulder to conserve warmth, their coated arms wrapped around their own bodies. They then visited the Royal Flying Doctor Service headquarters, where they watched a short film in a small movie theatre before ordering cake and tea in the adjoining cafe.

It was here, over a shared piece of butterscotch and banana cake and a pot of Earl Grey tea, that Rupert pulled a gift from the pocket of his tweed jacket.

'I got you a little something for your birthday,' he said, sliding the small box across the table. It was a velvet jewellery box.

'Rupert, you shouldn't have.'

He waved her away with a bemused smile. 'Open it.'

She felt her body flush at the idea of him not only remembering her birthday but choosing a gift for her and bringing it along. She could hazard a guess at what might be inside – earrings were the obvious choice, given the size of the box – but she reminded herself to look happy and grateful no matter what it was. It was always the thought that counted. Still, she had butterflies in her belly, hoping it was something wonderful, hoping it was a sign that they were in sync, that he knew her well, that it was evidence of their compatibility.

The box opened smoothly – a new box, not an antique like Dolce's, though both were lovely in their own way. Inside, lying on soft white material, was a key ring with a 1951 Australian penny set into it.

'Oh my goodness,' she said lifting it out to look at it. 'I can't remember the last time I saw one of these.' The image was of a kangaroo in full flight, with a star to the left of its feet and the year 1951 to the right. It was framed by the words *Australian Penny*. She turned it over to see King George's young, handsome head in profile, his hair neatly parted. 'Incredible,' she said, amazed to have such a thing in her hand, trying to recall the last thing she'd bought with a penny but retrieving no memory. As a teenager, she and so many others her age had been quick to discard the old copper coins in favour of the new decimal currency. Now she was delighted to see one.

'I love it,' she said, reaching over and placing her hand on his. Then she felt panic clutch at her throat. 'I do hope it didn't cost you the earth.'

Rupert chuckled and patted her hand. 'I'm not sure whether to assure you that they're not worth as much as you think, or let you think I spent lavishly on you.'

'I hope it's the former because it is the thought that counts and this is a beautiful gift, truly.'

'I'm glad.'

Valeria kept staring at the penny, touching it, tracing the raised surface with her fingertip. 'I could buy two cobber lollies for a penny,' she said, grinning, suddenly feeling younger than she had in ages.

'I believe cobbers were discontinued due to the number of dental accidents those little treats created,' he said.

'Oh dear,' she said with a smile, remembering the sweet but deadly hard caramel beneath the chocolate coating. She held the penny key ring to her chest. 'Thank you for this. I'll treasure it.'

Rupert lifted the teapot and refilled her cup. His face turned serious.

'What is it?' she asked. 'What are you thinking about?'

The corner of his mouth twitched and he lifted his teacup, sipping thoughtfully. 'I'd really like to explain my absence for the past couple of years,' he said, resting his fork on the plate. He'd barely touched his half of the cake, which she now considered might suggest nervousness.

She felt the joy of the past few moments drain away, wishing he hadn't mentioned this. It would have been lovely to spend her day in a bubble of denial, simply enjoying his presence once more. But now he'd broached the subject, she couldn't ignore it. Sighing inwardly, she swallowed her mouthful of tea and replaced her delicate yellow teacup on its saucer. 'All right.'

They were tucked into a corner of the room. Other travellers, also sporting Ghan lanyards, sat in clusters throughout the cafe, with their morning tea treats in various states of consumption. She didn't fear anyone overhearing. Besides which, all of her own family were elsewhere today, so it was likely as private a moment as she was going to get while on this tour.

Rupert leant forward, placing his elbows on the table. His energy seemed to fall away, his eyes betraying his distress, and she had the awful fear he was about to tell her he was dying.

She reached out and put her hand on his wrist. 'I'm listening,' she said, wanting to show him he had her full attention. He gave her a small nod of appreciation. Then he cleared his throat before beginning his story.

'You may remember that when I left I told you I had a family emergency I needed to deal with.'

'I do.' She lowered her hand and laid it in her lap.

'My eldest son, Peter, tried to kill himself.'

Valeria gasped. 'I'm so sorry. That's terrible.'

'It was. Very much. He was in hospital when I left the Barossa and was still there when I got to him.' He paused, working his jaw, whether to hold back emotion or to find the right words Valeria wasn't sure. 'I regret to say that I was many things, that I felt many things, and one of those was shame.' He paused for several moments, toying with his fork, while she waited, allowing him the time he needed. 'It's a terrible thing to feel shame about your child. An unnatural thing. A cruel thing.'

Valeria lifted her chin, his words biting, for she also knew this to be true.

'I didn't contact you because I didn't know what to say or how to say it. What did it say about me as a father? I felt shame over his actions but at the same time it was really me I felt ashamed of, because if I had done the job I was supposed to do, if I had been—' Again he paused, chewing words. 'If I had been a good father then it would never have come to that.'

'That's not true,' she said. 'It's absolutely not true.'

He took a breath and let it fall out heavily, jerkily. 'We don't know that.'

After a lengthy pause, she said, 'I know the shame of feeling ashamed of your child. It's an insidious feeling, a lot like gas that creeps under doorways and through cracks and crannies and has flooded the whole house before you know it.'

He watched her, his eyes questioning.

'My daughter was pregnant at sixteen. I didn't take it well. I was . . . humiliated, embarrassed, mortified and deeply ashamed. What had I done wrong? How could it have happened? What was everyone saying about us as a family, how were they judging us? Were they using us as a warning example to their own daughters about the evils of . . . sex and unmarried relations?' She shuddered, still able to feel it all as though it was last week, not nearly thirty years ago. The effort to hold her head up high in church on Sundays. The effort it took to look people in the eye and smile and answer their queries about Agatha's health and how she was going to finish school. 'But now the deepest shame I live with is that my reaction pushed her away. I pushed her into the arms of Myrtle, and that is where she has stayed.' She sniffed, not with tears, but with the forced effort of accepting the truth.

Rupert reached over and laid his hand on hers and she entwined her fingers with his. After a moment, he spoke. 'So now you know why I left so suddenly and why I couldn't bring myself to call you. I was mute with disgust.'

She felt for him, she really did, but she knew there was more. 'Yes, I can understand why you left and why you felt you couldn't speak of it. But that doesn't explain why it's taken two whole years to hear from you again.' She looked him straight in the eye. 'There is more, isn't there?'

He gave a rueful smile. 'There is. You see . . .'

'Actually, stop.' She held up her hand and forced a smile onto her face. The day had started so beautifully with the jammy high tea, and then her bubble of happiness had been popped by Myrtle's meddling. Then Rupert had spent the morning by her side and given her a lovely gift and she'd felt happy again. The last thing she wanted was to have her bubble burst yet again. Surely one close-to-perfect day wasn't too much to ask for her seventieth. 'I've had a lovely morning, and we have a long day ahead of us. Please, let's just enjoy ourselves.'

Rupert shifted, uneasily. 'Are you sure? I—'

'I'm sure. We have plenty of time. Look where we are. We're in the middle of Australia. We should make the most of it.'

He pressed his lips together briefly, then took her hand. 'Your birthday wish is my command.'

•

After Dolce and Myrtle had finished watching the huge raptors circling in the open-air nature theatre, they had made their way to the desert rivers section of the wildlife park. They were now watching two emus attempting to swim in a shallow pool, floundering about on their sides, their enormous long legs kicking through the water, half rolling to submerge themselves, spinning around in circles.

'How's that, Dolce? Just a couple of old birds like us. That's probably what we looked like last summer, splashing around in your great-grandkids' paddling pool at that barbecue at your daughter's place.'

Dolce grunted, a small smile on her lips, and took out her phone to take a video.

Myrtle waited till she'd finished. She laughed at the absurd sight of the two huge feathered creatures enjoying themselves. 'What on earth makes them think swimming is a good idea?'

'Maybe they wanted to do something different for once,' Dolce snapped, putting her phone away. The harsh sun shone down on them both, casting shade onto their faces beneath their sun visors.

'What's got into you lately?'

'What do you mean?' Dolce huffed, turning on her walking stick as if to move away.

'Stop,' Myrtle said, poking her friend with her own stick.

Dolce swatted at it with her free hand, then rounded on her. 'Don't poke me.'

'Then talk to me. Why were you so interested in Harry's job?'

Dolce looked startled, either by Myrtle's question or the sudden way one of the emus propelled itself to its feet and shook itself like a large dog, spraying water droplets onto them. Its friend was still in the water, lying on its side, wearing an expression Myrtle likened to the lazy friend waiting for the other one to bring a fresh cocktail to the pool.

'I was making conversation,' Dolce said.

'No, you weren't. You wanted to know lots of information, specific things, about aged care. And what about all the details you had about dementia and newspaper coverage of the royal commission?'

'Do you think I can't read, can't think for myself?' Dolce's chin jutted defensively.

'Don't be daft, of course not. But it's not like you.' Myrtle deliberately pulled herself up and adopted a more measured tone. A few other tourists were casting glances in their direction, eavesdropping on the two old ladies squabbling like seagulls in public. 'I'm worried about you.'

'Rubbish,' she growled.

'I'm serious, Dolce.' Myrtle heard the wobble in her voice. 'Are you dying?'

'What?' Dolce looked at her as if she was crazy.

'I can't think why you would want to stop travelling like this with me.'

'Maybe because you can be a pain in the arse.'

Myrtle ignored that and ploughed on. 'Are you thinking you'll end up in a nursing home? Is that it? Because we have a *plan*, remember? One we literally signed in Denpasar. Or do you . . . have you . . . are you having trouble remembering it? Is that why you've been researching dementia rates, because you feel you have dementia? I will uphold my end of the bargain. I would never let you go to an aged-care home against your wishes, but you need to tell me what's going on.' She could feel real tears threatening to spill and blinked rapidly. 'Please, let me help you.'

But Dolce did not look relieved or pleased or grateful. She looked irritated, frankly, wrestling with herself as though not wanting to speak the words on the tip of her tongue.

Myrtle gave her a reminder to speak, a small nudge to her left leg with the end of her stick.

'All right, all right,' Dolce hissed, looking around, searching for the right words to say. 'No, I'm not dying.'

'Thank Johnny Walker for that,' Myrtle said, which made Dolce snort with laughter, though a little reluctantly.

'And I don't think I've got dementia.'

'Then what is it? What is the real reason you won't travel anymore? I know what you said but I don't believe you. I've known you too long. What is it really?'

Dolce sighed. 'Promise me you won't laugh.'

Myrtle felt her head rear back, offended. 'Why would I laugh?'

Dolce huffed, annoyed. 'It doesn't matter. Look, the real reason I can't travel anymore is because next year I will be a full-time student at the University of South Australia in Adelaide. I won't have the time or the money to travel, because I'm going to become a uni student for the first time in my life. I'm going to complete a three-year Bachelor of Social Science in ageing and disability. I plan to work in aged care, serving my peers. What could be more empowering for those residents than to have one of their own in there advocating for them? I've already been accepted and I don't want to hear a word from you that is anything other than supportive.' She stamped the rubber tip of her stick on the ground, her eyes flashing.

Myrtle stared at her friend of more years than she could quickly add up in her head and simply nodded her understanding. Dolce's shoulders lowered, her usually mild-mannered voice returned and she said, 'Now, it must be wine o'clock, surely. Let's see if we can find ourselves a drink to celebrate my good news.' She turned and walked away, leaving Myrtle standing, a little unsteady on her feet, wondering what had surprised her more – the fact that Dolce was going to university or the fact that she hadn't included Myrtle in the decision-making at all.

22

Aggie and Harry sat in the back row of the small light-wing aircraft, waiting for take-off. Her thigh was pressed along his and she didn't know if the butterflies in her gut were from the impending ascent or the feel of his body against hers.

He held his left hand out in front of him, fingers splayed, studying his forearm and hand. 'I don't know where I come from,' he said. His tone wasn't bitter or morose but more like a sudden realisation. He dropped his hand onto his thigh and stared out at the desert. 'I have no idea about my own history.'

'Do you need to know?'

He considered this for a moment, then said, 'I guess not. But I barely know my biological mother and I don't know anything about my biological dad. Sometimes I think it would be nice to know more about my family tree, to know my roots.'

'I can appreciate that. My family is heavily of German stock. Well, Prussian, originally, like so many people in the Barossa, but you never really know. I've read articles about those ancestry websites and the terrible shocks people get when they receive their results. For some, it drastically changes their lives, and their relationships with their relatives.'

'Hmm. Maybe I'm better off not knowing,' he said, lightly. 'I seem to have done okay so far.'

'More than okay, I'd say,' she said, her face close to his in the small craft.

The plane's engine started and they put their headsets on as instructed, the pilot's voice now coming to them through the earpieces. The plane taxied on the runway and then accelerated. As it left the ground, Aggie's belly dived and she reached for Harry's hand. He clutched it in return and they beamed at each other as the earth fell away and they flew up into the blue sky. The aircraft rose and fell over air pockets, and Aggie was grateful to have Harry beside her. This was the smallest plane she'd ever been on and the turbulence was much more pronounced than in a large plane. She keenly felt the absence of ground beneath her feet, a sensation that was both scary and exhilarating. She felt like a bird, soaring free on currents.

From four thousand feet above Uluru, they gazed down at its beauty once more. From this altitude, it reminded Aggie of an island rising out of a flat, mottled sea. It was huge compared to the tiny threads of tarmac roads that surrounded it. Once again, she felt as though she'd slipped out of time and out of the ordinary world, now free of everything that had been weighing her down.

She had no idea how long they spent gazing down at Uluru, but all too soon they were winging their way to Kata Tjuta. The grouping of thirty-six red, dome-shaped sedimentary rocks was even larger than Uluru, and reminded Aggie of an ancient fortress or city. It was grand and imposing and, approaching from the air, she could see many layers ascending across the land towards the peaks. She could see gullies of green, where water must sometimes flow, and frothy edges that must be lines of trees. She could see caves and imagined people sheltering there, gathering there, celebrating and feasting. She took scores of photos on her phone, leaning across Harry at times to get the angle she wanted. They kept making faces at each other, of amazement and joy and incredulity. She was alive with wonder. Then they were flying away again, heading back to the airport, and if her face looked anything like Harry's, she was certain she was incandescent with joy.

•

The Alice Springs Telegraph Station lay four kilometres out of town and comprised more than half-a-dozen colonial stone buildings with new iron rooftops, serving as a museum and heritage centre for the history of Alice Springs. When Valeria got off her bus, along with the others, including Rupert – and Harry, to her annoyance – the sun was dipping towards the horizon and the air was already stiffly cold. She was dreading the falling temperature as night progressed, though her spirits were buoyed by the feel of Rupert's warm hand in hers.

They entered the grounds of the station to a sea of largely occupied round tables and chairs, all with skirts of white drapery, fanning out around a stage, which was positioned in front of a commanding sandstone-coloured building. Three musicians, all middle-aged men in country attire, played guitars and sang. Braziers were alight around the room, red flames jumping about in the biting wind.

Holly squealed and pointed, and they all followed her outstretched arm to see a contraption of metal stairs and a platform positioned at the side of a fence, and two straw-coloured camels with double saddles on their backs on the other. A couple was alighting from the first camel, clearly delighted, and another couple then climbed cautiously aboard. The cameleer led the animal around the yard, its plate-sized feet landing rhythmically on the ground.

'Who's coming?' Holly said, already moving towards the camels. She was dressed much as they all were, which was to say in practically everything they owned. As far as Valeria could see, everyone was wearing jeans, boots, socks, jumpers, coats, beanies and scarves. She'd heard stories about the desert in winter but was still unprepared for its vehemence. Still, it was exhilarating in its own way.

'Shall we?' Rupert asked Valeria, holding out his arm for her to take.

'Oh, no, I don't think so,' she said, her hand at her throat. 'They're so big.'

'Come on,' he encouraged her. 'I'm sure they're perfectly safe. We might never get another chance,' he said, cocking his head at her, an inviting glint in his eye.

She was about to refuse again but then remembered that it was her seventieth birthday and it was true that this opportunity would never appear again. Besides, it would be a nice distraction from the nagging questions she had about Rupert's son. It was her fault she'd asked him to say no more. That was her modus operandi, after all – the fewer words spoken, the less divulged, the less trouble you could cause. It was better to live in ignorance.

She pushed the uneasiness away. 'All right, let's do it.'

Aggie turned to look at Holly and they exchanged surprised expressions. This was a side of Valeria that neither of them had ever seen, and Valeria had to admit she liked shaking them up. Their group stood and then watched as first Holly lithely flung her leg over her camel and swayed off around the little circuit, and then Rupert cautiously climbed onto the next camel, followed by Valeria in front. She was shaking. The beast was huge, the saddle formidable. It was daunting, so soon after a fall and a fracture. She hadn't realised how much she'd repressed the fear and shock from that day until she was faced with this tall, strong beast that could kill her in an instant if it so chose.

As if to demonstrate this, the camel opened its mouth and emitted a tremendous, bawling roar. Valeria squealed and clung to the metal bar of the saddle in front of her as the handler led the camel away. Thank goodness they hadn't had to mount at ground level and be propelled into the air as the camel rose on its long legs. She peeked down and Agatha, Harry, Myrtle and Dolce all waved and took photos, and her fear began to ease with the rhythm of the camel's footfalls.

'Marvellous,' Rupert cheered from behind her, and laid a hand on her waist, making her blush. The setting sun was almost at the horizon, the sky in ribbons of white and pale pink, her breath misting out around her in the chilly air. Just as she started to embrace the ride and enjoy it, it all came to an end. She climbed off shakily onto the platform once more, grinning as Rupert did the same. He held her arm to assist her down the metal stairs.

'Anyone want to come for a walk?' Agatha suggested.

'Not for me, thanks,' Myrtle said. 'I think I might find us a table to sit at.'

'Me too,' Dolce said. 'My pins are done in for the day.' She moved off, close to Myrtle's side, yet somehow distant, Valeria noted.

'Do they look like they've had a tiff?' Agatha asked.

'I thought that too,' Holly said, wrinkling her nose. 'I don't think I've ever seen them out of sorts with each other.'

The remainder of their group set off towards the stone buildings at the rear of the dining tables. 'What was the best thing about Simpsons Gap?' Agatha asked Holly.

'It's incredible, in much the same way the gorge was. Lots of rocks and water and greenery, which all sounds quite ordinary, but there's something about it. Ancient, yes, but also kind of . . . I don't know.'

'Other-worldly?' Harry suggested.

'Definitely,' Holly agreed. 'The instagrammers were there too. We all had to keep moving out of the way so their film crew could set up the perfect shot of her half naked with a few flowing, blousy natural-fibre drapes on her body while she reclined against a ginormous egg-shaped rock and her new husband kissed her feet in perfect sunlight.'

'How frustrating,' Valeria sympathised.

Holly shrugged. 'Nah, they were all right. I envy their job. Seems pretty cushy.'

'Anyone want a drink?' Harry asked as they approached a row of wine buckets.

'Hell yes!' Holly said, reaching for two glasses of white, one of which she downed in one go, the other she held onto to take with her. 'Better already,' she said.

'What do you mean?' Valeria asked. 'You just said you had a great day.' Holly wasn't a big drinker, from memory, though she could have developed some sort of habit while she was overseas. She did seem to be excessively enthusiastic about wine every time it was near.

In response, Holly just shrugged and threw back a mouthful of her second glass. Valeria turned to Agatha, who was also watching Holly with an expression of concern.

The rest of them took a glass of wine too, aside from Harry, who took a lemonade. It irked Valeria to notice her approval of his lack of alcohol consumption. His sobriety was irrelevant. He had no place in Agatha's life, certainly not while those embryos were out there, and realistically not ever.

They stopped briefly to watch an old-fashioned blacksmith at work, though as far as Valeria was concerned the benefit of that was mostly to stand as close as possible to his red-hot coals. As the sun began to bleed into the horizon and the shadows lengthened and darkened across the green grass near the waterway, Holly – now two glasses of wine down – took Agatha's phone from her and instructed her and Harry stand together under a towering gum tree, its trunk and branches smooth and ghostly white behind them.

Agatha cast an uncertain look towards Valeria – which vindicated Valeria's belief that deep down Agatha must know that this was a foolish endeavour – but then Harry wrapped his arm around her and squeezed her to him, and they pulled a series of ridiculous faces until she was laughing so much that Holly made lots of sentimental noises about how good they looked together and took countless photos. Valeria had to look away.

'Come on,' Agatha said, breaking away. 'I think I can smell dinner cooking.'

'Smells great,' Harry said, sniffing the air.

They found the round table that Myrtle and Dolce had commandeered for them and took their places. 'Can I get anyone a drink?' Harry asked. He got a long list of requests, promising he'd remember them all, and left to fetch them.

'Agatha, I hear you took the flight over Uluru, is that right?' Rupert asked her.

'I did. It was amazing. Thank you, Myrtle,' she said looking across the table at her great-aunt.

'I'm happy it went well,' Myrtle said, though Valeria thought she didn't look especially so. Myrtle slid her eyes to the side to peer at Dolce, who responded with a begrudging nod, which wasn't their usual style at all. She wondered what was going on with them.

Harry returned with the drinks and Agatha tapped her glass with a fork, which everyone heeded, turning her way. She raised her glass and smiled at Valeria. 'To Mum – wishing you a very happy seventieth birthday, with many more to come.'

Valeria felt her cheeks grow warm, even beneath the icy wind, and nodded her thanks.

'To Grandma!'

'To Valeria!'

All glasses were raised and sipped and Valeria once again felt grateful to be here in this place with her family, and Rupert too.

'Thank you,' she said. 'I've truly had a wonderful day.'

A selection of small savoury tarts with flaky pastry arrived for entrees, and Valeria had just cut into hers when she noticed terse words and gestures passing between Myrtle and Dolce.

'What's going on with you two?' she asked, a glass of wine having loosened her restraint. She tried to affect a tone of gentle ribbing, but the stony faces that returned her gaze made her flinch. An awkward silence followed as all eyes turned to them.

'Well, tell them,' Myrtle snapped.

Dolce lifted her eyes to the dark sky above, the candlelight from the table flickering on her face. It was an expression of weariness, as though she and Myrtle had been discussing this matter at length and she was sick and tired of it. But after a moment she spoke.

'I am going to university in Adelaide next year as a full-time student.'

'What?' Agatha exclaimed, her mouth ajar with excitement. 'What are you studying?'

Holly laid her hand on her chest and her eyes filled with tears, shiny in the reflected lights. 'Dolce, that's amazing.'

Valeria was stiff. Had she heard Dolce correctly? She was going to university, at her age?

'I'm enrolled in a Bachelor of Social Science, majoring in ageing and disability,' Dolce said, jutting her chin forward as though prepared for an onslaught of shocked questions or perhaps arguments to deter her.

'Congratulations, Dolce,' Harry said, lifting his lemonade. 'That's wonderful.'

Valeria felt her lips tighten with frustration. Harry had known Dolce for a total of two days. He didn't know anything about her. Her heart thumped with frustration. This was ludicrous. Dolce was an old woman. She was eighty-two, for goodness sake. There was no way she was physically or mentally strong enough to complete a bachelor's degree. This was utter madness. This was a total waste of taxpayer money; she was taking a place in that course that a young person should be taking, and she might actually die before she finished it.

Yet all around her, people were smiling and toasting her. Even Rupert was gazing at her warmly and cheering her on.

'You are exactly what the aged-care system needs,' Harry continued, enthusiastically. 'We need diversity of perspectives, and we could certainly do with the view of someone who has a personal, vested interest in the system. This is fabulous,' he gushed. Beside him, Agatha was nodding and murmuring in agreement.

'Let me know if I can help in any way at all,' Holly said, then got to her feet and went to Dolce, wrapping her arms around her from behind and jiggling her from side to side – a little too roughly, Valeria thought.

'Thank you, dear,' Dolce said, patting the forearm at her chest.

'Where will you stay? What did your kids say? When does term start?'

The group fired questions at Dolce while Myrtle sat silently, listening. She looked up at that moment and caught Valeria's gaze, widening her eyes.

Isn't this crazy?

Valeria nodded. It was, though she suspected Myrtle's objections lay squarely in the inconvenience of losing her travel partner to this insanity.

The main courses arrived – barbecue dinner of steak and vegetables – more wine was poured, and the conversation continued. Harry had a lot to say, given that he worked in aged-care homes. He was unequivocally supportive, and well he could be, given he would never see them again after this trip. Holly kept offering more toasts to Dolce, and Valeria had lost track of how many glasses of wine her granddaughter had consumed now. Beside her, Rupert sat quietly, hiding his own little secret. A stone of resentment solidified in Valeria's gut. This night was supposed to be about her and they couldn't even manage that.

After the whole crowd of Ghan patrons had collected their desserts and taken them to their tables, the floodlights cut out without warning, pitching the station into total darkness. Before anyone could panic, the deep, penetrating tones of a didgeridoo cut through the air, making Valeria's skin break out in goosebumps that had nothing to do with the cold. It was a tremendous relief to not have to look at the people around the table any longer and not to have to listen to the misguided love and support they were showering on Dolce.

In the darkness, the sound of the instrument was dramatic and encompassing and Valeria let it wash over her, taking her mind away from all this. Above them, the sky was as dark as a panther's pelt, scintillating with more stars than she'd ever seen. After a few minutes of traditional didgeridoo sounds, the player switched to the opening bars of the theme song of *The Pink Panther*, instantly recognisable, catching everyone by surprise and eliciting a ripple of laughter across the tables. Beside her, Rupert chuckled too and leant into Valeria's side to share the joke with her, and she felt the knots of angst in her belly loosening.

The music ended, and man began to speak through a microphone, his location unidentifiable in the dark but his warmth and humour palpable. He shared an informative and entertaining mixture of comedy and astronomy, encompassing Indigenous stories and meanings for the constellations that held everyone silent, captivated by his words.

When the astronomy lesson came to a close, the performer received a huge round of applause and the floodlights snapped on. Valeria looked around the table and her eyes fell on Agatha, leaning into Harry's body, his arm around her pulling her tight, her left hand on his chest, her right slipped under the warmth of his jacket. He gazed down at her and smiled and she looked up at him, utterly smitten. He whispered something in her ear, she nodded, and they rose from their chairs, walking off into the dark, her hand in his.

Valeria stared at them, panic flooding her veins. She could feel her pulse under her jaw. She had to do something, anything. She had to stop this before it was too late. She rose from the table, her mobile phone in hand, and walked off into the dark in the opposite direction. She needed to call Gideon. Maybe *he* could stop this nonsense.

23

Their breaths cast clouds of mist as they walked. Aggie followed Harry as they wove through the tables, heading towards the spot where the camels had been earlier.

'I haven't laughed that much in ages,' he said, squeezing her hand tighter.

'Me neither.' She was still grinning, her cheeks aching.

'I wonder what else he can play on the didg. Maybe he could play "Agadoo".'

'Imagine that.'

They stopped at the fence and leant against it, Harry humming 'Agadoo'.

'Wait, I've got the song on my phone,' she said, pulling it from her pocket.

'Seriously?'

'Of course. You never know when you need to break out into "Agadoo".' She found the track and pressed play, resting the phone on the top of a fence post, and started shimmying her shoulders as the tune began. Harry grabbed her hand and spun her around, and when the chorus started they pulled out their best moves, pointing fingers to the sky to the *do-do-do* beat, then hands in front like stop signs at the mention of pineapples, then clutched hands to wave from side to side. Aggie was laughing so much she was wobbly on her feet.

When the verse came, Harry reached for both her hands and they jigged till Aggie noticed something in the song she'd never heard before.

'Oh my god,' she said, stopping. 'Did you hear that?'

Harry halted. 'Did they just say Waikiki?'

'And ukulele!' she said, and reached for her phone to skip back and replay that section.

They stood together, listening, then burst out laughing. 'Do it again,' he said. They listened, transfixed. The lyrics most definitely did talk about Waikiki and the wonderful instrument Harry had been playing that afternoon.

'I can't believe it,' Aggie said. 'It's as if it was written just for us.'

'Just for us, for this day,' Harry said. He grabbed her hand again and they kept dancing wildly to the utterly bonkers song. He swung her out, then pulled her back in and she landed against his chest. She looked up at him while the song carried on, filled with happiness. She didn't know who moved first but in a split second they were kissing, his hands on her upper back, pulling her close, her arms wound round his neck. The feel of him against her, his arms beneath her palms, one of his legs nudging between her knees . . . the desert, the sky, the wine, the mad song . . .

It was all so perfect.

And then her bloody phone rang, cutting the song short.

She jerked in surprise. 'Oh, crap,' she muttered.

Harry groaned in disappointment but let her go so she could answer it.

'So sorry, I need to take this. It's my assistant, Savannah. I don't know why she's calling at this time of night.' She held the glowing, ringing phone in her hand, not wanting to answer it at all.

'All good,' he said, waving her on, resting his hands on his hips and taking a deep breath.

'Savannah, hi.' She turned away from Harry; he was far too distracting to have in her view.

'Aggie, I'm so sorry,' Savannah said, her voice sharp with stress.

'Why? What's happened?' She braced herself for bad news while telling herself it probably wasn't as bad as she was imagining.

'The guy from yesterday said he couldn't come back today to deal with the sign. I couldn't get hold of you—'

'Sorry, I've been in a plane and in the desert, the reception is patchy.' She was pierced with guilt. She'd been having such a fantastic day that she'd forgotten all about the shop dramas for a while.

'—and I wanted to help.' Here, her assistant paused and Aggie waited, one hand covering her abdomen, preparing for a blow. She was staring into the darkness, the pale outline of the Macdonnell Ranges faintly in view.

'What happened?' Aggie asked, a finger of dread tracing down her spine.

'I got up on the ladder myself.'

'In the pouring rain?'

'Yes,' Savannah squeaked. 'I only wanted to look, to see how hard it could be to get the sign down, and . . . I had a drill in my hand and it was raining so hard, and the ladder was slippery. I fell.'

'Are you all right?'

'I'm okay. I hit my head and had to go to hospital for a scan, that's why I'm calling so late. Anyway, I'm fine.'

'Oh my gosh, Savannah. That's a relief.'

'I've got a bit of a banged-up knee, but that's okay . . . it's the guttering that's the problem.'

'The guttering?'

'I grabbed hold of it when I slipped and it came down with me. All of it. I'm so sorry. I'll work to pay for it, I promise,' Savannah pleaded, clearly distressed.

Aggie spun around to see where Harry was but couldn't spot him. 'Hang on, go back a bit. What's happening now, with the gutter gone?'

Savannah whimpered. 'There's a ton of water pouring off the roof and crashing onto the footpath, like a waterfall.'

Aggie sucked in air sharply through her teeth.

'No one can get in the door with it coming down like that,' Savannah said, her voice steady and sober now that she'd got past the worst part of her story. 'What should I do?'

'What's the weather forecast saying?'

'Rain,' Savannah moaned. 'Endless rain, for days.'

'Damn.'

'I'm so sorry.'

'I know,' she said, through gritted teeth. She wasn't sure what to say to Savannah in this moment. She knew she'd been trying to help, but now everything was a lot worse than a thousand-dollar fine. Aggie quelled the rising panic in her throat. 'Leave it with me. I need some time to think.'

'Okay. What should I do tomorrow, with the shop?'

'You'll have to close it,' she said, rubbing her forehead. 'If no one can get in the door it's no good, plus it will be a safety hazard for sure. I'll try to come up with something and get back to you.'

She ended the call and looked around, peering into the darkness. 'Harry?'

He took a moment to reappear out of a deep shadow cast by a towering gum.

She smiled. 'Thanks for waiting, though I wished I hadn't answered it, honestly, it's . . . What's wrong?' She'd caught sight of his face, which was no longer open and smiling but pinched and guarded.

'I need to go back to the train,' he said. 'There's a bus going soon and they're calling for people to board.'

She stepped towards him. 'I'll come with you—'

'No.'

She stopped as if she'd hit a wall.

'I shouldn't have kissed you,' he said.

'What do you mean?'

'I'm not supposed to be kissing anyone.'

'What?' She felt her lips pull into a disbelieving smile.

'As well as deciding to stop drinking, I also decided to stop kissing or . . . anything else.'

Her mind raced to catch up. No kissing? He was thirty-five years old. Was he saying he was going to become a monk or something? 'Are you saying you're celibate?'

'No. Yes. I don't know.'

She felt a little offended then. 'Because kissing doesn't mean . . . I wasn't throwing myself at you for sex . . . we were just dancing.'

'Sex probably isn't the problem here, in all honesty.'

'I don't understand.'

'It's me. I've been working hard to be in control of my life, my emotions, my thoughts. And you . . . you are amazing and you've kind of captured my heart.'

She swallowed, wanting so much to tell him she felt the same way, but equally frozen by this rejection.

He smiled at her, then quickly smothered it and kicked the dirt. 'I need to go. But you should know I've had the best day I can ever remember having.'

She scoffed then, annoyed. 'How can that possibly be a bad thing?'

He rubbed his hand across his face, as if trying to wipe away this uncomfortable conversation. 'I've got to go.'

He left her standing in the desert alone, the deep cold running down her spine, chilling her to the core.

24

Aggie headed to breakfast alone the next morning with a notebook and pen, needing to sit down and work through her options for Strawberry Sonnet. She resisted the urge to turn to Myrtle for help. Until only this week, when settlement for the sale had gone through, Myrtle had been the owner of the building and would have had some sort of hand in repairs of this nature, even if only in approving what sort of guttering was going to be used to replace the old. But now the shop was Aggie's alone; therefore, this problem was too. This was what it meant to be independent. She could fix this. She had to.

She met the restaurant manager at the bar. 'Only me this morning,' she said, smiling brightly. 'Getting a head start on the others.'

'You're in luck,' Christie said, beckoning for Aggie to follow her.

'Oh, why's that?' Aggie asked as the embossed doors slid smoothly open and they stepped back in time upon entering the graceful dining carriage.

'Because Harry's here alone too,' Christie said, stopping at Harry's table and flicking open a starched white napkin from the plate opposite him, motioning for her to sit.

'Oh . . .' Aggie began, but then shut her mouth. She wasn't a rude person and it would have been exceptionally rude to say outright that she didn't want to sit here. Likewise, Harry's facial features worked to keep up with this unexpected development.

Aggie sat gingerly.

'Thanks,' Harry said to Christie, a little weakly.

'Coffee?' Christie asked.

'Yes, please,' Aggie said, and the woman left them to it.

Aggie let her gaze wander around the carriage, not quite ready to look at Harry. There were only two other tables with seated guests, and their low voices and tinkling cutlery mingled with the rhythmic rattling of the wheels in a symphony of sorts. The train was even louder since departing Alice Springs, as they were now making their way along the oldest tracks on the line.

'Are you writing something?' Harry said.

She turned to look at him, in jeans and a pale-blue long-sleeved shirt. His eyes lacked the lightness and joy they'd held yesterday. Today, an invisible weight hung around his shoulders and he slumped in his seat.

Aggie glanced down at her notebook. 'A few dramas going on back in the Barossa with my cafe. I need to sort some stuff out.'

'Can I help?'

'Not unless you can you pop over to Angaston and repair the guttering on my cafe's roof in the pouring rain, and remove a large business sign that's going to cost me a thousand dollars if it's not gone by the end of today.'

'Damn,' he said. 'I knew I should have packed my teleportation kit.'

She held up her phone. 'No signal *and* no teleportation kit.'

'Where's Spock when you need him?' Harry looked around the carriage as if Spock might be hiding somewhere. She snorted gently with amusement, not quite ready to let her guard down entirely. What the hell had happened last night? They'd had the best day, the best night, the best dance, the best kiss, and then . . . he totally shut her out. She was embarrassed, confused and more than a little ticked off. He owed her an explanation.

Christie returned with her coffee and took their orders for breakfast. Outside the window, the view had changed again. Now that they were in South Australia, the desert was no longer red with olive-green shrubs. It was ochre yellow and grey, cracked, pebbly and largely devoid of vegetation. It reminded Aggie of images she'd seen of the surface of the moon. Every now and then she saw a filthy sheep or two heading towards a small depression in the earth, which she guessed held an inch of muddy water. A thin strand of barbed wire extending into nothingness. Perhaps a lone kangaroo. A black cow that could have belonged to someone hundreds of kilometres away, or was perhaps entirely feral. The leafless skeletons of dried shrubs.

'I can't understand how anything survives out there,' she said.

A lengthy silence followed as she waited for Harry to explain himself. The smell of bacon accompanied Christie's delivery of Harry's breakfast muffin. The fruit toast on Aggie's plate was warm, the scent of cinnamon comforting. Aggie picked up a triangle of the bread and took a bite just as Harry began to speak.

'I was a muppet last night.'

Aggie swallowed quickly. 'No argument here,' she said, her tone mild.

Harry furrowed his brow. He appeared to be trying to conjure the right words to say next.

'Are you married?' she asked.

'Myrtle already asked me that and the answer was, and still is, no.'

'Are you gay?'

'No.'

'Are you joining the priesthood? Becoming a monk?'

He laughed gently. 'No. I did spend some time on a retreat in a Buddhist community, learning to meditate, but no plans to make it a full-time lifestyle.'

'Are you saving yourself for marriage? Do you have a disease or illness I should know about?' She was counting off potential issues on her fingers, and he was shaking his head and smiling at her.

'No,' he said, 'none of those.'

'Did I have bad breath?' she asked, only half joking.

'No. You tasted like wine and chocolate cake and . . . stardust.'

'Stardust?' she said, unable to keep from smiling. After their magical night under the Milky Way, it felt like an apt description of their kiss, one sprinkled with cosmic glitter. But then she ruined the moment. 'I'm going to revert to my original theory of you being a poet.'

'Wait,' he said, leaning forward onto his elbows. He still hadn't touched his food. 'You had theories about me?'

She shifted in her seat, uncomfortable she'd been caught out. 'Yeah, okay. When I first went through your Instagram photos, there was something very . . .' She searched for the right word. 'They were quite *raw*, I guess. I thought maybe you were a poet, a recovering alcoholic, a melodramatic millennial or an annoying life coach.'

She bit her lip, wishing she hadn't confessed anything. It sounded horribly judgemental and mean when she said it out loud, and she wondered why on earth she'd let the words escape. Probably it was because he'd hurt her and now a part of her wanted to hurt him back. From the look on his face, she'd managed to, at least a little.

'And you got all that from my Instagram account?'

She swallowed. 'Sorry.' She *was* sorry. She'd taken his beautiful stardust compliment and turned it against him.

'Huh.' He was watching her now, and she had the nasty feeling he was reassessing her and everything they'd shared the day before, erasing it in his mind and replacing it with something that was tainted. It made her feel panicky, like she wanted to reach out and pluck her words out of the air, to turn back time to when it had been the two of them dancing and laughing to 'Agadoo' in the darkness, two people free of all responsibilities and dramas and past hurts.

Still, despite being sorry for the words she'd spoken, she was also defensive. She wasn't the one who had ruined the magic of last night. He'd walked away from her with no explanation. She'd been jilted – he'd left her standing alone, literally out in the cold. He'd run away, not her.

But equally, she was horrified she'd let herself get swept away in a fantasy so quickly. She'd only known the man for a matter of days. Yes, their connection was undeniably strong but it was ridiculous to get caught up in a whirlwind romance on a holiday, especially when they lived thousands of kilometres away from each other. This wasn't the real world; it was a bubble. They both needed to calm down and remember that all of this, no matter how big it had all felt, was an illusion.

'Do you know what?' she said, suddenly. 'I'd really like to catch up with you later today.'

'Okay,' he said, interested but a little wary.

She picked up her notebook and pen. 'Right now I need to sort something out to save my business.'

'Yeah, of course,' he said, encouraging her.

'I'm sorry we got off track here.'

'Same.'

'I had a great day yesterday,' she said, holding his gaze.

He swallowed. 'Yeah, me too.'

'If you want to be friends, that's great. Everyone needs more friends, right?' she said, more brightly than she felt.

'Definitely.'

She stood, swilled the last of her coffee then picked up her fruit toast with her free hand to take with her. 'I've got to go. Catch you later?'

'Sure thing.'

Back in her cabin, her bed had been folded away and her day seat was ready for her to make herself comfortable and brainstorm solutions to her current business woes. There was the loss of income while the shop was shut from the water gushing over the front door, there was the sign to remove by end of today and there was new guttering to install – all of them sizeable problems. She stared at the list for moment, wondering where to start.

Signing those papers for the cafe had felt as if she was finally flying Myrtle's nest, moving forward into a whole new phase of independence, that she was taking control of her destiny. The last thing she wanted was to let Myrtle down. She owed her a lot.

•

Aggie was two months pregnant before she took a test. She'd suspected it for weeks but kept hoping it would go away. After all, she and Mal had only done it twice. The first time was awful and she only did it again to see if she'd done something wrong that could be corrected. But no, it was still awful. She'd been working up the courage to break it off with Mal in a way that didn't hurt his feelings when he left a note in her locker saying *You are dumped*.

She'd spent weeks avoiding his gaze, her face burning with humiliation, imagining what he'd told his mates, wondering what their smirks at her really meant. Had he told them she was a dud? That she was ugly or fat? Something worse?

But *she* hadn't told a soul.

She stopped doing homework. She couldn't concentrate in class. She stopped eating, briefly hoping that would make it go away. Her palms sweated and her pulse pounded in her ears and she ran to the toilet ten times a day, hoping for blood. But it never came. She knew she needed a pregnancy test, but where could she get one in such a tiny town without being seen? She was paralysed with fear and mortification.

One Saturday afternoon, Myrtle arrived at their home, carrying a box of quinces she'd picked up at the markets. 'Quince paste for all!' she called, bumping open the front door with her hip and manoeuvring the box down the hallway.

'Lovely,' Valeria said, smiling at the yellow fruit as she took the box. 'I love quince season. Thanks for getting these for me. I really was needed at the ladies' auxiliary this morning. It's getting harder and harder to get people to volunteer for church working bees.'

'Imagine,' Myrtle said, dryly, and winked at Aggie, who was lying on the couch watching *Born Free* and blubbing her eyes out.

'Don't mind her,' Valeria said, waving a hand in Aggie's direction. 'She's always been a soft touch for animals.'

Myrtle narrowed her eyes behind her red cat's-eye spectacles and tilted her head at Aggie, and Aggie had the sudden, awful feeling that Myrtle could see right through her – that she absolutely *knew* the terrible truth of Aggie's situation.

'Valeria,' she called. 'Why don't you get started on those quinces? I'm hoping I might borrow Aggie for a couple of hours. I've still got a ton of pears to preserve and could really use the help. What do you say, Aggie? Could you spare some time?' Myrtle nodded at her, leaving Aggie in no doubt that she was going with her.

'Sure,' Aggie squeaked, and dragged herself up from the couch. The moment she was in Myrtle's van she burst into tears. Myrtle clunked the van into gear, laid a hand on Aggie's shoulder and said, 'It's all right. Everything's going to be all right.'

Aggie waited at Myrtle's house while her great-aunt drove to a chemist in another town. She returned with the test and a chocolate cake, opened the test with Aggie and went through the instructions with her. And when the test was done and the two pink lines appeared, Myrtle let Aggie cry and made her tea and cut her a piece of cake. When Aggie had calmed a little, Myrtle laid out her options.

'You have choices here, Aggie. You can have the baby and keep it. You can have the baby and hand it over for adoption. Or you can have an abortion.'

Aggie's mouth dropped open. 'An abortion?'

Myrtle nodded. 'Yes, an abortion.'

'But they told us at school that it's illegal. And also that we'd go to hell.'

Myrtle took a deep, steadying breath, keeping Aggie in her gaze. 'It is technically illegal, that's true. But there are ways to get it done, and I can help you.'

Aggie gulped, and picked at the corner of her piece of cake.

'I can take you away on a short trip, if you like, and we can go somewhere where no one knows us. I can pay for it and ensure you are safe. You are my highest priority here, not ridiculous laws created and enforced by men, and certainly not anything said by an outdated and increasingly irrelevant church.'

Aggie swallowed, allowing the tiniest ray of hope to pierce her darkened world.

'You'd be amazed how many women have abortions and you simply never hear of them. It is one of the greatest feminist challenges of our time, and I can't believe in 1992, the last decade of the twentieth century, we're *still* having to have these conversations in secret.' She swilled her tea noisily. 'I wish my sister had had access to safe abortions. It would have saved her sanity and certainly her life.'

The sister she was referring to was Valeria's mother, the grandmother Aggie had never met, who'd died in childbirth in her late forties.

Myrtle pulled herself together. 'Anyway, this is about you and what you want. It's *all* about you, Aggie. All of it. It's not about Mal, it's not about your parents. This is the moment where you get to decide solely and entirely for yourself what is right for *you*. You and only you can know that. Whatever you decide, I'm here for you.'

It only took her a further three days to decide what to do, and despite Myrtle's suggestion that she could support Aggie while she delivered the news to her parents, Aggie declined. She'd stopped crying by this time, a strange sense of stillness descending over her. Her new course was set. It wouldn't be easy but she could do it. She could bring this child into the world. Lots of young mothers around the world did exactly the same thing, and often in much worse circumstances. She wasn't alone. She had her parents, her best friend, and she had Myrtle. She would have to leave school, she knew that, but Myrtle was still teaching and was well connected, and would set up distance education for Aggie to complete her senior years.

Valeria was still making quince paste, not yet convinced that she'd created the best batch for her entry into this year's Royal Show. The house smelt of that unique quince fragrance – part floral, part pear, part apple – trays of jars of scarlet preserve sat on the bench, cooling, as Valeria began another batch, peeling the hard, knobbly yellow fruit while Pavarotti played on the stereo.

'Mum,' Aggie said, entering the room. Her arms hugged her body. Her dad was still in Adelaide, not due home till dinnertime.

'Mm?' Valeria continued to peel and chop, humming along to the tenor's song.

'I have something to tell you,' Aggie said.

'What's that?'

Her mother still wasn't looking at her – still thought this was an ordinary day and whatever Aggie was about to say was about something no more consequential than losing her lunchbox or tearing a hole in her school uniform.

'I'm pregnant.'

Valeria stopped chopping, the knife poised above half a quince, and looked at Aggie so sharply it made her feel as though she'd been slapped. 'What did you say?'

'I'm pregnant,' she repeated, her heart hammering in her chest.

'How?' Valeria demanded, looking Aggie up and down.

'Well . . . with . . . Mal,' Aggie said, weakly, her courage bleeding away.

'When?' Valeria demanded, her voice shrill now.

'At . . . a party . . .' Aggie lost her words.

Her mother dropped the knife and covered her mouth with one hand and her heart with the other, as though she was having a heart attack and needed to vomit all at the same time. 'I don't believe this. I don't believe this.' She shook her head and spun around, looking for a chair. Aggie rushed to pull one over for her and her mother sat down.

'How pregnant are you?'

Aggie swallowed painfully. 'Two months.'

'Two months! Oh, this is awful, this is awful. You stupid, stupid girl!

Aggie gasped and jumped backwards. 'Well . . . it wasn't just me, you know . . .'

'And this boy . . . are you even together? What does he say about this? Who are his parents? Where do they live? What are they going to do about this? How long has all this been going on behind my back?' She was bright red in the face now, furious, mortified.

'We're not together,' Aggie squeaked.

This was apparently the worst thing Aggie could have said. Valeria inhaled a noisy, disgusted intake of breath. 'So . . . so you're a . . . you just *sleep around*, do you?'

'What? No! This was just an accident.' Aggie retreated from Valeria's alternately deflating and writhing body.

'An accident?! This is no accident! You foolish, dreadful girl.'

'Mum!' Aggie wished very, very much that she'd allowed Myrtle to be here with her now.

'Oh, we'll be the talk of the town.' Valeria was on her feet now, a hand to her forehead, pacing in circles. Her quince paste was boiling on the stove and Aggie knew it would burn but didn't dare say anything. 'What will people say? How will I ever show my face again?' She glared at Aggie, as though her daughter had ruined Valeria's life too. 'How will you finish school? How will you pay for this baby? Do you expect your father and me to pay?'

'Mum, I haven't really had a chance to figure everything out yet . . .'

'Trust me, Agatha, that is blindingly obvious,' Valeria said through gritted teeth.

Aggie began to cry, wanting her mother to hold her and tell her it would all be okay. She'd expected her to be upset but not this level of rage, this hatred.

'Go to your room,' Valeria ordered. 'I can't look at you.'

*

That night, her mother came into Aggie's room, her father a step behind. Aggie sat up in bed, waiting for them to speak. Her father gave her a small, sad nod, but left Valeria to do the talking.

'Your father and I have spoken about your situation,' she said. 'We agree that the best thing for you to do is to find your own place to live.'

'What?'

'Having a baby is an adult thing to do. We feel this is the best way we can help you to embrace your new role as an adult as quickly as possible, to give you the time you'll need to set yourself up and learn to manage adult responsibilities now, before the baby arrives.'

'I don't understand.' Aggie wasn't sure she was still breathing.

'Having a newborn baby is not the time to be trying to sort out rental agreements, share-house arrangements, government services, electricity bills and household management skills. You need to be well and truly on your feet before you give birth. Your one and only job now is to prepare for the baby. You can have two weeks to get yourself organised, then you'll have to leave.'

'But why can't I stay here? This is my home. I want to be with you and Dad.'

'It's out of the question.'

There was a stiff silence in the room while her mother glared at her and her father shuffled his feet uneasily. They left in silence, and Aggie cried all night.

Myrtle arrived the next morning to see how the conversation had gone. Within seconds of her arrival, she and Valeria were yelling at each other. Aggie listened from her bedroom, her ear pressed to the door.

'You're throwing her *out*?' Myrtle's voice was incredulous.

'No, I'm helping her to grow up, immediately.'

'Rubbish. You're ashamed to have her here, aren't you? You're worried about what your ladies' auxiliary will say, what the pastor will say. You're more worried about yourself than Aggie, who needs our support!'

'Don't you dare tell me how to be a mother, especially when you're not one yourself.'

There was a moment's silence, then Myrtle challenged Aggie's father. 'And what are you doing about this, Bertie? Are you just going to stand by while Valeria kicks your daughter out onto the street?'

Bertie mumbled something Aggie couldn't hear.

'You're as bad as she is,' Myrtle spat. 'Where is she? Aggie?' she called.

'Don't you get involved. This is nothing to do with you,' Valeria snapped.

But Myrtle's determined footsteps were approaching Aggie's door. Aggie jumped back just in time for Myrtle to fling it open. 'Come here,' she said, beckoning Aggie into her arms. Aggie collapsed into her chest, gratefully, sobs rising in her throat. Of all the things she'd imagined might happen, being thrown out of home wasn't one of them. 'Get your things,' Myrtle said. 'You're coming home with me.'

25

The Ghan rolled to a gentle stop at a siding in the middle of the desert and Aggie peered out the window. There was nothing there except a short white sign on two posts announcing their location. *Manguri*. Aggie collected her bag and coat and stepped out into the hallway at precisely the same time as Holly did, carrying a woollen beanie in her hand.

Aggie froze.

Holly froze.

Aggie's mouth unhinged as she took in the sight of her daughter.

Holly flinched, rubbing her hand quickly over her head. 'It's just a rough job. A first draft. I'll do it properly when I get back home and get hold of some clippers, or get to a hairdresser.' She shrugged, obviously feeling slightly tender about this drunken decision, yet defiant.

Aggie carefully closed her mouth and nodded, taking in the rough, uneven close haircut Holly had given herself sometime during the night, clearly with a pair of scissors. Nail scissors, perhaps. There were patches that were nearly bald, the pale skin peeking through, and parts that were spiky and unfinished. It looked hideous, her gorgeous sleek curls gone and this . . . well, a mangy dog's coat was what it resembled. She carefully calmed herself. Freaking out was not going to help.

'I like it,' she said, and smiled.

Holly looked at her warily.

'Really. It's fresh and contemporary and . . . brave.' She patted Holly on the shoulder before continuing down the passageway. 'You've got a great-shaped head.'

'Thanks,' Holly said, uncertainly, and Aggie gratefully stepped into the vestibule to be blasted by cold winds.

After disembarking, the passengers boarded several buses, all headed to Coober Pedy via the Breakaways. Every member of Aggie's travel group, now including Rupert, who seemed to be a fixture at Valeria's side, and Harry, who'd been hovering uncertainly nearby but was encouraged into the group by Myrtle, boarded the same bus. Holly had, quite wisely, kept the green woollen beanie on her head, and Aggie was grateful for a little more time before Valeria discovered what was underneath. The bus was pleasantly warm as they climbed in and made their way down the aisle. Aggie's phone was clutched tightly in her hand and she checked it regularly, waiting for reception to kick in so she could start making calls about Strawberry Sonnet.

Holly plopped into the seat next to Aggie and exhaled heavily. 'Apparently Coober Pedy was only one degree overnight.' Her mood had flattened dramatically since her high spirits of last night, though it wasn't clear if that was the hangover or daylight regrets about the haircut.

'I'm not sure how people live in the desert,' Aggie said, gazing out at the vast emptiness in all directions around them. 'Boiling in summer, freezing in winter . . .'

'I guess that's why most of them live underground,' Holly said, sliding on her sunglasses.

'Feeling under the weather?' Aggie ribbed, gently.

Holly grunted and Aggie waited a few beats to see if anything further would come. When it didn't, she broached the topic most on her mind. 'I overheard you say to Myrtle last night that you were inspired to stay in Australia and become a tour guide?' She attempted to strike a tone of interest rather than desperate hope, but failed.

Holly was silent, staring straight ahead. Aggie wondered if she'd closed her eyes behind her sunglasses.

'Holly?'

'I should go back to the States,' she said wearily.

'Why? What's over there for you?'

She lifted a shoulder in an noncommittal shrug. 'My career.'

Not her father, Aggie noted, with some relief. She didn't like to feel second best to a man who'd had nothing much to do with Holly until she was in her twenties, and even then hadn't stuck around to nurture a relationship after the novelty of the first few months had worn off.

'But you could teach here.'

To her surprise, Holly lifted a finger and wiped away a solitary tear from under her shades.

'What is it?' Aggie clutched Holly's forearm between her hands. 'What's happened, sweetheart? Talk to me.'

But Holly just shook her head and forced a smile. 'Nothing. I've just been a bit blue, that's all.'

'Do you think you might be depressed? Have you spoken to someone – a doctor or psychologist?'

Holly shook her head.

'What about Nala? Are you two on good terms?'

'We're fine.'

Aggie wasn't convinced by this, having heard them on the phone. A new thought entered her mind, something unexpected. 'Are you . . .? You and Nala, are you together? As a couple?'

Holly turned to her swiftly, suddenly smiling, clearly amused. 'No.'

'I don't want to offend you or anything, but I can't remember you ever talking about anyone special . . .'

'Why would I be offended?'

'I . . . well . . . no reason, I guess.' As close as Aggie was to Holly, both in age and in emotional connection, she did at times feel the distance of a world that had become considerably more tolerant than she'd had the benefit of in her teens and twenties. 'So you're not gay?'

'No,' Holly said mildly. 'Kissed a girl once, though.'

'When?'

'A few years back. In a club. Dancing.'

'But you didn't like it?' Aggie ventured.

'It was okay, but not for me.'

'You seemed to be really interested in the woman at dinner the other night, the woman with the shaved head and tattoos.'

Holly shifted uncomfortably. 'She was interesting.'

Apparently interesting enough to inspire Holly to consider tattoos and a shaved head. 'What was so interesting about her?'

'She nearly died in a fire. A fire lit by her boyfriend, who was trying to kill her,' Holly said, soberly. 'She's a survivor. She said once she got through the post-traumatic stress, she actually got braver. Less fearful.' Holly's eyebrows lifted above the rims of her sunglasses. 'She's a motivational speaker now. There are so many interesting people in the world, aren't there?'

Aggie swallowed, trying to imagine how having your boyfriend try to kill you would forever change the way you saw the world. 'She does sound amazing.'

They rode in silence for a few moments, the rumble of the bus rocking them gently, and Aggie sensed that Holly would be drifting off to sleep soon, thanks to her hangover.

'What's so appealing about teaching in the States, anyway?' Aggie asked, hoping to get inside Holly's mind while she was drifting off. 'The pay is no better than Australia and the conditions are worse, not to mention the very real risk of—'

'Stop,' Holly said, holding up her hand. Apparently, she wasn't as close to sleep as Aggie thought. 'I don't want to talk about it.'

Aggie flinched at the steel in her daughter's voice. 'I'm just trying to understand.'

'Don't.'

Aggie felt the word pierce her heart. She nodded and peered out the window, the vibe between them tense with Holly's rebuke.

They rode in silence for over half an hour and Holly did, as predicted, fall asleep. Aggie gazed at her, easily accessing the maternal pleasure of watching her daughter slumber. She resisted reaching out and running the back of her hand down the side of Holly's face and turned to watch the endless sky outside the window instead.

A while later, her phone lit up in her hand as reception kicked in once more. Savannah. 'Morning. How are you? How's your head?'

'Good, yeah, all good,' Savannah said, though her voice was flat. 'But I've just come into the shop. I wanted to check on it to see if anything had changed overnight . . .'

'And?'

'There's water coming into the shop. It looks like it's come down through the wall beneath where the guttering is missing, and it's spreading across the floor.'

'What?!'

'It's coming in around the windows too. I guess it's because it's running straight down the side of the building. What should I do?'

Aggie was sitting on the edge of her seat now, trapped against the window by Holly's sleeping form, trapped inside a bus in the middle of the freaking desert.

'Can you get towels or something to try to contain it to one area?' It would be creeping across the parquetry flooring, doing who knows what amount of damage. 'Sandbags?' But even as she said the word, she knew they didn't have sandbags and she didn't know anyone who did.

'Right, yeah . . .' Savannah said, sounding distracted, as though looking around the cafe for a secret stash of sandbags.

'Do your best. I'll get back to you soon.'

With her heart pounding, imagining her newly acquired and beautiful cafe being destroyed by the second, she searched online for a supply of sandbags in the Barossa and located some for sale on Gumtree forty-five minutes away from Angaston. Then she posted a job on Airtasker, seeking someone to pick them up and take them to the cafe immediately. Miraculously, she'd managed to allocate the job by the time she'd finished texting Savannah to give her an update. It would still be an hour before the sandbags got to the cafe, but she felt marginally relieved knowing they were on the way.

What next, what next . . .?

Insurance! She would contact the insurance company. They would have dealt with water damage before, and would surely have advice about how to prevent the problem from getting worse. She shook Holly.

'Hols.'

'Huh?' Holly blinked herself awake, taking a shaky, startled breath. 'What's wrong?' She looked around, getting her bearings, then dragged her gaze back to Aggie. 'What's happened?'

'I need to get out, sorry. I need to see Myrtle,' she said, motioning that she needed to get into the aisle.

'Oh, okay.' Holly stood to allow Aggie to squeeze across. 'What's wrong?'

'I'll explain later.' She was in the aisle and moving towards the back of the bus, where Dolce was gazing out the window and Myrtle was watching Aggie coming towards her, her expression confused. In the seat directly across from Myrtle sat Valeria and Rupert. Aggie cursed under her breath, wishing her mother didn't have to witness this.

Aggie squatted down next to Myrtle's seat so as not to announce her issues to the whole of the bus. 'The shop's flooding,' she said bluntly.

Myrtle frowned. 'Flooding?'

'Yes.' Aggie quickly filled her in on Savannah's attempts to remove the sign yesterday ending in the guttering coming down and now water running into the shop. 'I've got sandbags on the way but we need to call the insurance company. They'll know what to do to prevent further damage until they can assess the claim.'

Dolce turned to listen in.

Myrtle's eyes widened and then her chin wobbled. 'Oh.'

'What?'

'Well, the insurance . . .'

Aggie's heart gave a painful lurch and Dolce closed her eyes for a moment, as though sensing what was coming.

Behind Aggie, Valeria spoke. 'What's happened?'

'I only recently signed the paperwork,' Aggie squeaked. 'Surely there's a process, a handover, like when you're buying a house and you're both supposed to have insurance at the same time while it settles.'

'*Did* you take out insurance?' Myrtle asked, a catch in her voice.

'I . . . It only just happened.' She could hear herself getting breathless now. 'But you still have yours, right? You didn't cancel it straightaway, did you? *Did* you?'

'I think I . . .' Myrtle stopped and swallowed, with some effort. 'You see, I forgot to pay the renewal. And then you were buying the shop and I thought, oh well, it'll be yours soon, and I meant to talk to you about it but I just . . . forgot.'

'Forgot?' Aggie's voice was high and thin.

'What's happening?' Valeria hissed. 'What's this about insurance? Is it the shop?'

'I'm so sorry,' Myrtle said, her hand to her throat.

'There's no insurance?' Aggie said.

Myrtle didn't speak.

Aggie sank to the floor of the bus in her woollen tights and navy dress, and held her head in her hands. Strawberry Sonnet was flooding and there was no insurance. What on earth could she do now?

•

'I don't understand,' Valeria said, inching further into the aisle. Her daughter was sitting on the floor of the bus. 'What's happened to the shop?'

'There's been some rain,' Myrtle began to say, but she stopped, her face drawn and white. Before she could continue, Aggie pulled herself to her feet and shook her head.

'I need to call the SES,' she said, then hurried back down the aisle to where she'd been sitting with Holly, swaying from side to side slightly with movement of the bus.

'What is going on?' Valeria demanded.

'The shop is flooding,' Myrtle said. 'The gutters have come down and now water is cascading down the walls, and it's started running inside.'

Valeria cast her gaze to Dolce, who was shaking her head worriedly. 'But why is there no insurance?' Beside her, she knew Rupert was listening in – he could hardly avoid it – but was refraining from interjecting. His thigh was a warm, reliable presence against hers.

Myrtle's shoulders rose and her jaw set. Defensiveness took over her features. 'I have sold the shop to Aggie,' she said.

'What?' Valeria was caught off guard by this news, and yet it also seemed like such a Myrtle thing to do, cashing in her assets to fund her extravagant lifestyle. But why had no one told her this? Who else knew? Was she the only one in the dark? Looking at Dolce, it was clear this wasn't news to her. Valeria's mind raced. Agatha didn't have enough money to buy the shop, so she must have taken out a loan. But Valeria knew for sure that the IVF bills had wiped her and Gideon clean of savings, and there was no way Agatha would have had time to recover. 'Has Agatha used her business as equity against the building?' A flooding event like this would put her business under terrible strain, but to lose it to the bank would be much worse.

Myrtle closed her eyes for a moment before sighing. 'No. I offered my house as equity.'

'Your house?'

'Yes.'

'But why?' She was utterly bewildered. Not that she ever liked to think of anyone dying, but Myrtle was aged and it was Valeria who was set to inherit her net worth. She had no idea what this entanglement would mean for her when Myrtle did pass away. Would Valeria then be responsible for the shop loan? Might she even end up in debt, if the markets swung the wrong way or if an extraordinary event – such as the shop being destroyed by flooding with no insurance – rendered it worthless but with a loan still to be repaid?

Myrtle seemed resigned to delivering the truth now. 'I have changed my will, Valeria. Aggie is now the sole beneficiary of my estate. When I die, my house will pass to her. She will finally be free of renting and will own her own home, and any money that remains from the sale of the shop will also go to her, so she should be in a position then to pay off a significant portion of the loan, if not all of it. It made perfect sense. It will set her up for life.'

Valeria's hand balled into a fist and she pressed it to her chest, winded. She opened and closed her mouth a couple of times like a startled fish flung onto the shore. She had no idea where to start with the magnitude and complexity of this secret deal that had just been laid out in front of her. She didn't know if she was more upset with Myrtle or Agatha . . . or herself for being made such a fool of.

•

Aggie stood at the wooden railing on the edge of the viewing site at the tour group's first stop, the Breakaways. After spending the rest of the drive wanting to claw her way out of the bus and hire a car to get back to Adelaide (which would take more than ten hours) or charter a plane to fly back there (which would cost money she didn't have), she'd realised she'd simply have to let go of any idea of spiriting herself back to the Barossa to solve this crisis. The SES would do their best. Savannah would update her. There was nothing else she could do but be here. She'd be back in the Barossa tomorrow and could face the full horror of it then.

Rolling out below her, and as far as the eye could see, were bare hills and mountains in the most breathtaking colours ranging from black to rusty red, iron red, white and ochre yellow. Some of the hills rose high, with fluffy-looking peaks like the humps of camels.

'Mind if I join you?' Harry asked, the smile audible in his voice as he approached.

She shook her head to show she didn't mind and he stood near her, his hands shoved deep into the pockets of his jacket, just as hers were. The icy wind was blasting them. Her hair was flying out behind her horizontally, occasionally whipping her face. She wished she had a band to secure it.

'I think you're right about space,' she said, nodding out towards the landscape. 'It does give you perspective.' She sighed heavily.

'I agree,' he said. 'Which is why I have decided that I was a total lunatic to walk away from you last night.'

She turned to stare at him, waiting.

'I fell in love with my foster sister and it blew my life up,' he said simply.

Aggie gave an involuntary whimper of sympathy. 'That sounds messy.'

He laughed, but it was empty. 'You could say that.'

'How old were you?'

'I lived with her and her mother on and off. When I was seventeen I left to go working all over the place – in cafes, mostly, a bit of labouring, some gardening. Transient stuff. Over the next ten years, I would go back to visit them for holidays and special events, but I was never a fully-fledged part of their family, you know?' He shrugged. 'I'm not really sure how you'd define it, but since I had no real family of my own, they were . . . important.

'Kayla is two years older than me, and there was never anything romantic between us when we were young. I was an annoying kid who shared her house some of the time. But we were friends, for sure.' He shook his head. 'She used to read me Harry Potter books, knowing that I would find comfort in the story of another Harry who had an awful family but who had magical powers.' He said this with the weight of a precious memory. 'Anyway, fast-forward a lot of years, Kayla had a baby – Charlotte – when she was twenty-nine. The guy took off after a few years and I had some work in the area, so I decided to hang around and help out. I became an important figure in Charlotte's life.' His face puckered with pain. 'I love that kid. I probably fell in love with Charlotte first, really,' he said. 'She was such a cheeky three-year-old.' He shook his head slowly, a corner of his mouth tugging upwards with some precious memory. 'I wanted so badly to protect her.' He paused. 'But then something changed and I fell in love with Kayla too; at least, I thought I did. In hindsight, I wonder if I just fell in love with the idea of having a proper family, of truly belonging somewhere. I imagined the three of us building a life together. I kept it to myself for about a year, not wanting to destroy what we had, but eventually I cracked and told her how I felt on my thirty-second birthday, right after Charlotte helped me blow out the candles.'

He stopped talking and squinted into the glaring blue sky. Aggie followed his gaze, watching some sort of raptor as it hovered on a strong current for a few moments before plunging straight down to the desert floor and snapping up something in its beak.

'I'm guessing it didn't go well,' Aggie said after a spell.

He shook his head. 'She said some terrible things and later apologised, but it was too late. Everything changed. I lost all three of them. I felt as if I'd lost my best friend, the little girl I would have loved as my own, the only mother figure I'd ever known, and my dreams of finally being normal and . . . loved, wanted . . . all at once. I moved interstate and drank too much and let everything spiral out of control for a while. Eventually, I decided to give up alcohol, start meditating every day, learn to surf, and find a job that had meaning. It's helped. Things are better.'

She remained silent for a few breaths, the only sound that of the wind snapping through her hair. Then she said, 'For what it's worth, I think you were brave. It's hard to go after what you want most in the world, knowing you could lose it all in the process.'

'You're right. It is. Which is why there is one more thing on my bucket list – one that's not practical but takes the most courage.'

She waited, intrigued.

'You know those sayings, like *Dance like no one's watching, Sing as if no one can hear you . . .*'

She blinked. 'Yeah, I do. I have them on a fridge magnet.'

'Well, there's one that says *Love like you've never been hurt.*'

She joined him for the last few words, speaking them at the same time. 'I know it.' She looked out at the big blue sky again. 'But the pain adds up over time and we get scared to risk our hearts again.' She turned back to face him and he studied her face, his eyes searching hers.

'You sound like you know something about that.'

'Oh yeah. Years of failed IVF with my ex, Gideon, and . . .' Here her words were snatched away on a blast of wind and she fought to keep her hair out of her face.

Harry unwound the fir-green scarf from his neck and laid it around hers, catching her hair and holding it out of her face in the most tender of gestures.

'I lost a baby two years ago,' she said, pushing the words out. 'We named her Cora. She was stillborn at seven months.'

Harry drew in a weighted breath. 'I'm so sorry.'

'It blew up my life too.'

'What happened with Gideon?'

'We didn't make it.'

He waited a moment, then said, 'And now?'

She opened her eyes wide in disbelief. 'And now my daughter is acting exceptionally oddly and my shop in Angaston is flooding and my livelihood is probably going down the toilet.' She snorted, verging on laughter, the kind that occurs when everything has gone wrong and there is nothing left to do but succumb to the hysteria.

'Shit,' he said. He looked around, as if for something that could help. 'Will you be okay?'

She shrugged. 'I honestly have no idea. But I do know I've been through worse. Nothing will ever be as bad as losing Cora.' She swallowed hard. 'I need a drink,' she said abruptly, shaking off the heaviness of an unexpected wave of grief. She eyed the bottles of wine that had been set up on tables near the buses, then flinched, her hand flying to her cheek. 'Sorry. That's so insensitive after what you've just told me.'

'It's all right, really. I'm okay now.' He gave her a reassuring smile. 'I've made peace with it.'

They began to walk towards the drinks table. 'Still, is it difficult, though, when wine turns up everywhere we go?'

He tilted his head from side to side, assessing this. 'I wouldn't say it's difficult, but I'll admit a small part of me is throwing a tiny tantrum that I'm committed to being alcohol-free on what is a once-in-a-lifetime holiday and every time I turn around someone is offering me a drink.'

'Or a ukulele,' she said, grinning.

'That bit was pretty cool.'

'*Love like you've never been hurt*. I'm adding it to my list too.'

'The hardest one of all.'

'Definitely.'

'But I'm game if you are,' he said, holding out his fist.

She bumped her fist to his. 'Deal.'

Almost at once, the blasting cold air had shaken off all the debris, Harry's smile was the sun, and she felt the most optimistic she'd been all morning.

26

Valeria stared at the bowl of marinated baby octopus in front of her – specifically, at the suckers on their legs. She had been a sucker too. She had believed Myrtle had organised this trip to celebrate her seventieth birthday, to celebrate her. Yet somehow the whole event had been hijacked into becoming a celebratory tour for the indomitable business duo of Myrtle and Agatha, and into some sort of matchmaking event for Agatha and the young man. They were seated on the other side of the table and Harry was staring at Agatha with gooey eyes. Valeria *tsk*ed loudly, but it was drowned out by the chatter around her. Thank goodness they would be back in the Barossa tomorrow afternoon and she could wave goodbye to them all.

Well, maybe not all of them. She tilted her head to watch Rupert, seated to her left, talking with a purple-haired lady in a black shawl opposite him. The older woman had been sucking on green and black olives and dropping the pits into her glass of white wine. It was the oddest, most displeasing thing and Valeria longed to ask her why on earth she was doing it. But she bit her tongue, knowing anything she said right now would come out razor sharp.

If you can't say anything nice, Valeria, don't say anything at all. That was her mother's voice hissing into her ear, while her fingers pinched Valeria's bicep painfully.

Valeria sucked in a breath and reached for her water, taking a large gulp. She was feeling a touch claustrophobic, seated as she was in the middle of the very long row of connected tables in a rectangular room that had been tunnelled under the ground. The walls, floor and roof showed a mixture of white and red earth, like a strawberry swirl, almost pretty. The surfaces were rough, the texture formed by mechanical chisel marks. She was perched on a fold-up chair behind the white-cloth-covered table and dreaded the moment when she'd have to wedge herself out. The woman with the olive pits had already rubbed against the wall as she'd wiggled in to take her seat and covered one side of her shawl with powdery white clay. Valeria kept staring up at the ceiling above her. What was holding it up? She could see no reinforcements of any kind. Were they going to end up on the nightly news – a freak tunnel collapse many metres underground in Coober Pedy?

Looking around, she saw that no one else seemed to be feeling perturbed. Barking chatter and laughter were inflated by the glasses of wine the waiters kept refilling and the novelty of dining underground. The only light came from lamps on the walls. She closed her eyes to block out the image of the walls collapsing and all those lights going out, plunging them into blackness. Only this morning the bus driver had delivered a commentary on the perils of mining and of the many people who'd fallen into the wide, deep holes left beind. The mines that had collapsed. Those who'd been spared death only to live on with a missing limb, or paraplegia, or brain damage from the dynamite fumes.

The efficient waiters whisked away small plates of half-eaten octopus and chewed olive pits and replaced them with skewers of marinated lamb and chicken. Myrtle and Dolce had separated from the rest of them and joined the tables in the next tunnel over. Valeria assumed they'd done that specifically to avoid Valeria and more discussion of the skulduggery that had gone on about the shop. She did, of course, have sympathy about the flooding that was apparently happening in Strawberry Sonnet right at this moment, but it was barbed with a certain unattractive urge to tell Agatha that if she was going to leave a teenager in charge of her business then she had to expect that things would go wrong.

Valeria took a bite of her lamb and chewed slowly, then took a sip of red wine and washed it down before giving up. She didn't have an appetite.

'Salad?' Rupert asked, offering a plate of greens.

'No, thank you,' she said.

'Bread?' He exchanged the plate for the bowl of carbs.

'No, thank you.'

He gave her a concerned look. 'Are you okay?'

'Yes, fine,' she assured him, though she could hear the strain in her voice and knew he wasn't convinced.

'Is it because of what Myrtle did with the will?'

Rupert had overheard the conversation on the bus but had refrained from pressing her for more information. It was unfortunate that Myrtle's revelation had happened on a bus full of people. Fortunately, the engine noise would have restricted how far the words could carry to perfect strangers, who didn't need to hear their dirty laundry being aired in public.

'It's not . . .' she began, then sighed. 'It's such a Myrtle thing to do!' she sniped.

'How so?' he asked calmly, seeming genuinely interested, and she had the uncomfortable sense of what it might have been like to be a student in his school who'd come to the principal to complain about another student, only to have him encourage her to turn her criticism inwards to consider exactly how she too might be culpable in the situation. She didn't enjoy the feeling and straightened her shoulders.

'She's always trying to one-up me,' she said, disliking the whine in her voice. It sounded so juvenile. Yet it was true. She slid her gaze across to Agatha to make sure she wasn't listening in. But no, she was busy talking with Harry and Holly, smiling, even looking as though she was having a good time. Valeria found it distinctly odd to see Harry seated next to Holly. Shouldn't Harry be more interested in Holly, who was closer to his age and could give him a child, than Agatha? She also noted, with displeasure, that Holly had chosen guzzling wine over eating the meal in front of her. And why was she wearing that hideous green beanie at the dining table? It was rude.

Agatha was either oblivious to this or was ignoring it, too busy falling in love with Harry. What was *wrong* with her? Her business was right at this very moment being destroyed. Did she have so little agency in her life that she simply trusted Myrtle would save her? Again? And why wasn't she hopping mad with Myrtle? Myrtle had been so busy celebrating her own success that she'd not even done a proper handover with Agatha. It was a disaster. If either of them had come to her, had informed her of their plans, had included her, she would have brought up the subject of insurance. She was good with details, good at worrying about the small things that mattered – or, in this case, one very large thing.

Suddenly, Holly threw back her glass of wine and missed her mouth, spilling it onto her denim jacket.

'Bugger,' Holly said, wiping wine from her chin.

'Language, Holly,' Valeria said, then quickly snatched up her napkin and passed it across the table.

Holly flicked an eyebrow, dismissive. 'Sorry.'

She wasn't sorry, though, that was clear. 'You're drunk,' Valeria said, and the steel in her tone was not lost on Holly, whose face fell.

'Excuse me for being on holiday,' Holly said, sulkily.

Harry's eyes moved between Holly and Valeria but he said nothing, which was wise. He could clearly read a room, could sense trouble coming.

'What's wrong?' That was Agatha, her mother's instinct having picked up on the friction, rushing to her daughter's defence. Mothers always did that, rushed in to fix everything, when what they really needed to do was let their child make a mistake, fix it themselves and learn from it. It was what she'd tried to do with Agatha – to let her grow through the experience of teenage pregnancy, rather than having someone solve it all for her. And look where it had left them. She was so dependent on Myrtle she hadn't even insured the property she'd just bought. This was why everyone went on about building resilience in children these days. None of today's young people had it, and this was why. Helicopter parenting. Concierge parenting. Bulldozer parenting.

'It's fine, Agatha,' Valeria said. 'Holly's just had too much to drink.'

Agatha sighed in an infuriatingly dismissive way.

For fear of combusting like an explosive in a mine shaft, Valeria pushed back her chair. It took her much longer to get to her feet in the cramped space than she would have liked, which spiked her fury further.

She pointed a trembling finger at Agatha. 'You would do wise to know who's on your side.' She delivered her words heavily.

The smile on Agatha's face faltered. 'What?'

'You always run to Myrtle. Now look where it's landed you.'

She turned and left, but not before she saw the disbelieving shake of Agatha's head, and the wincing twitch in Rupert's eyes.

She moved as fast as she could, murmuring *sorry* and *excuse me* over and over, forcing a waiter to walk backwards so she could exit the room.

•

Aggie, still flustered after the uncomfortable end to their lunch, lurched up the tunnel to ground level once more, just as her phone rang.

Gideon.

'Hi.' She moved away from Harry and the buses, where Ghan guests were lining up to board the rumbling vehicles.

'Hi.' There was a tension in his voice that made her shoulders rise.

She squinted into the stark winter sunshine. Up here the light bounced off the endless hard surfaces of the dusty ground, rusted machinery and corrugated iron. She continued to move further away from the noise of the buses' engines.

'How are things going?' Gideon asked. 'Where are you now?'

'We're in Coober Pedy. We just had lunch in an underground restaurant.'

He made an appreciative noise. 'How was it?'

'Not as scary as it could have been,' she said, omitting her mother's fractiousness. She stopped walking, wondering why Gideon was phoning, keeping an eye on her assigned bus and the rate at which the passengers were climbing aboard. She didn't have much time left to join them. 'What's happening?'

'Your mother called me.'

'*What?*'

'Last night. She wants us to use the embryos.'

She sucked in a deep breath. 'I can't believe her.' She couldn't work out which words wanted to come out of her mouth first – that her mother had no right to interfere, or that the thought of using the embryos was complicated at best and terrifying at worst. She was charged with fury. 'How dare she? I'm so sorry, Gideon, it wasn't her place to say anything to you.'

He cleared his throat. 'I just thought you should know that she's running a campaign,' he said, wryly.

'Isn't she always?'

He chuckled. 'She can't help herself.' He waited a beat and she thought he might be about to say goodbye but then he cleared his throat and went on. 'Putting Valeria's interference aside, I do agree that we need to talk properly about our options. Her words got me thinking and I . . . I just needed to hear your voice.'

She bent down and picked up a small grey stone, toying with it to calm herself and allow Gideon's words to sink in. She wanted to tell him she couldn't do this now, but she also knew he was suffering as much as she was. She'd caused Gideon significant pain, and blamed herself entirely for the breakdown of their relationship. She'd run away from him. The least she could do now was listen.

'I think we should pay the renewal,' he said.

The stone halted in her fingers. 'Really?' The word squeaked from her throat. 'Why?'

Gideon sighed heavily. 'It buys us more time to think.'

On the face of it, this was a reasonable idea, one she'd certainly had herself, but it was still problematic. 'I've considered that too. It seems like a good solution, an easy one to make that doesn't close any doors and doesn't force us to make a choice we might regret later.'

'But?'

'But we'll still have to make a choice eventually,' she said, sadly. On top of that, she was forty-five years old. If he was in any way in favour of implanting the embryos, they really didn't have time to waste. She didn't allow herself to think too far down that track, though; the idea of them trying another round of implantation was too much to face full-on in this moment. 'All renewing would do is string out this difficult decision even longer.' She could hear Gideon scratching his whiskers. He was a deep-thinking man, one who didn't like to be rushed. She'd learnt that any time she'd needed to talk to him about something significant – like making a big financial decision, or getting a puppy – she'd need to give him advance warning, let him know what she was thinking, and then they could talk about it in a few days' time. That gave him time to mull it over, and usually he came up with a better response than hers, having thought through the details.

Now he grunted, and she knew him well enough to know that he was acknowledging her point but was not quite ready to give up on the idea of renewal yet.

Years' worth of memories washed over her. Gideon surprising her with bright yellow gerberas to ease the misery and anxiety of yet another cycle of IVF. Him making her a big dish of potato bake because potatoes were the only thing she could stomach, permanently queasy from the medication. Of their carefree days before IVF, taking a sunny holiday in Noosa, buying trays of mangoes from the farmers' markets and blending them into daiquiris in their rented apartment. Of the day they picked up Banjo, soft and floppy and wriggling in their arms, his delightful puppy breath as he lay sleeping between them in their bed.

How had their relationship gone so horribly wrong? If they'd only been content to have Banjo as their fur baby; if they'd only let go after two rounds of IVF; if they'd only had a plan before they began, an agreed moment for when to call it quits; if only Cora hadn't died.

So many *ifs*. So many different time lines they could be living right now, still together.

'I'm not ruling it out,' she said, returning to the present. They were down to only three options: renew, destroy . . . or implant. Of the three choices, renewal was the most appealing. 'I'm so sorry, Gideon, but I have to go. The bus is fully loaded and they're waiting for me.'

'Okay,' he said, his voice weighed down with the difficulty of it all. 'Sorry, I shouldn't have brought it up now.'

'No, it's okay. I understand.'

Holly was out of the bus now, looking for her. She spotted Aggie and waved frantically at her. Aggie held up her pointer finger. *One more minute.*

'I just need a bit more time,' she said. 'Is that okay?'

'Of course, Ags. Anything for you. Let's speak again soon,' he said, his words kind but brisk, not wanting to intrude any further on her holiday, a holiday he wasn't a part of.

'Thank you.' They felt like entirely inadequate words in this moment, yet she felt them in every cell of her body. She was flooded with gratitude for Gideon, for everything they'd shared, and for the obvious care and respect they still had for each other. He was a good man. She ended the call and headed back to the vibrating bus, climbing the steps on slightly shaky legs.

27

Myrtle eased herself from the bus, squinting in the bright light that shone directly in her eyes.

'You all right?' Dolce asked, joining her on the ground with an *oomph*.

'Yes, fine.' They moved slowly away from the vehicle, allowing others to disembark, and Myrtle held a hand above her face, shielding it while she surveyed the vista.

From the outside, the Church of Saint Elijah didn't look like much. Like so many dwellings in Coober Pedy, the entrance to the Serbian Orthodox church had been cut into the side of a hill. A row of several arched doorways and windows sat in the flattened facade, and a half-dozen metal air-vent pipes poked skyward through the 'roof', which was several levels of terraced earth rising higher and higher towards a large *Welcome* sign, finishing with a tall cross at the peak.

The Ghan stewards ushered the travellers towards the front door, where the church caretaker greeted them and directed them down to the belly of the building below. Myrtle and Dolce lingered to one side, waiting for their companions to arrive, and soon they were all there except for one.

'Where's Holly?' Dolce asked, peering around.

'Still on the bus,' Aggie said, her features grim.

Dolce stretched her neck to see better above the heads of those around her, trying to get a glimpse of Holly through the bus window.

Valeria shook her head and grunted a noise of exasperation. 'Honestly, I didn't say anything that wasn't true.'

'What are you talking about?' Myrtle asked.

'I merely pointed out that Holly was drunk . . . again.'

'You just can't help but interfere, can you?' Aggie challenged Valeria, her arms crossed defensively.

'What are you accusing me of now?'

'Gideon.'

Valeria's face hardened. 'I make no apologies for that. That man has been through enough.'

Aggie gasped. She dropped her arms, setting her shoulders as if for battle, but then, catching sight of Harry, quickly swallowed whatever she had been about to say.

'Excuse me, I need to make a call.' She strode away, staring at the phone in her hand, leaving Harry gazing after her, his brow wrinkled, his feet shuffling as though trying to decide whether to follow her or not.

Myrtle rubbed at her forehead, where a headache had suddenly sprung up, and shot Valeria a dark look. Anyone with eyes could see that Holly was struggling with something. Public shaming wasn't going to be any help. As for Aggie, Myrtle was sure that whatever Valeria had done with Gideon would only backfire.

'We're ready when you are,' came a steward's cheery voice, as she waved them over.

'Thank you,' Valeria said, giving her a curt nod.

Myrtle noticed that Harry and Rupert had inched away from the rest of their group and were heading to the doorway to begin the tour. A wise move. 'Well, I wasn't with you at lunch,' Myrtle said. 'Perhaps I could go and have a word with her.' She rather fancied herself a calming influence. She had once talked a student down from the roof of the sports shed, when he'd been threatening to jump in front of the whole school. She suspected the poor boy wouldn't have died jumping from that height, but would have certainly broken many bones, perhaps even leaving himself paralysed. Upon her retirement, she'd half considered volunteering her time as a hostage negotiator.

Valeria rolled her eyes. 'Saving the day again, are you?'

'I beg your pardon?' Myrtle was shocked by Valeria's tone. 'What are you talking about?'

'What am I—' Valeria looked briefly as though she might combust, then spun in a circle on the spot and returned to glare at Myrtle, standing a little too close. Myrtle resisted the urge to take a step back from her. 'You honestly don't even know, do you?'

'Know what?' Myrtle could feel the waves of anger emanating from Valeria's body but was struggling to work out exactly what she had done wrong.

'How you ruin everything.'

Myrtle was quiet, considering which things in the context of *everything* she was supposed to have ruined. She glanced at Aggie, who was standing several yards away, stabbing at her phone. The poor love. A fresh argument with Valeria was the last thing she needed right now, with the state of the shop back at home. Guilt pierced the pride Myrtle had felt just a moment ago at her ability to calm a situation. She'd done badly by Aggie and that pained her deeply.

'Are you talking about the shop?' she asked Valeria, and stepped back slightly. She deserved Valeria's wrath for that. Aggie's too, though Aggie had so far not directed any her way. She'd still be in shock, still in problem-solving mode. Her anger would come later, most likely.

'Why didn't you tell me about the will?' Valeria said, her nostrils flaring, betrayal written all over her face. 'Why didn't you tell me about the shop?'

'It was all my doing,' Myrtle rushed to assure her, distracted now by pain in her hip. She leant more heavily on her stick, feeling a strong desire to sit down, preferably with a cup of tea and a biscuit. 'Don't blame Aggie. I did what I thought was right. Of course I was going to tell you about it.'

'When?' Valeria demanded.

'Soon,' Myrtle said, her voice losing its resolve.

Valeria scoffed and turned around, walked a few steps towards the entrance to the church – to the obvious relief of the waiting Ghan steward – but then turned again to hurry back. The steward's face fell in response and she shifted from one foot to another, glancing at her watch.

'The only reason you would have kept this secret is because you don't trust me. You thought I'd be angry, or try to talk Agatha out of it, or . . . I don't know. Perhaps because you think I'm greedy and would fight for the money, or that I'm unworthy and didn't deserve it. You tell me. Why didn't I deserve to know? Why do it all in secret behind my back?'

'I . . .' Myrtle scrabbled for something soothing to say.

'You know what? I don't care.' Valeria turned and left, this time not stopping when she reached the steward, disappearing into the dark tunnel inside the church.

'Wait!' Myrtle called. 'I just wanted you to have a good birthday.' But it was too late. The words were snatched away on the breeze.

•

Aggie had her back to the bus. She'd stealthily picked up Holly's phone with the intention of finding the phone number she needed. She knew her daughter's passcode – her birthday – and googled the time difference between here and California. She needed to help Holly, and if Holly wasn't going to talk to her then she'd have to find the answers herself. It was about 9 pm in California. She had no desire to speak to Mal, but she was getting desperate. Holly had said her father had checked in with her recently, which suggested he might know something helpful. It was the only lead she had.

The wind rushed through her open jacket and she shivered while navigating away from the web browser and into the address book, searching for *Mal* or *Dad*. But just as she was about to hit dial on the call, a WhatsApp notification popped up across the top of the screen. It was from Nala.

> If I was u I'd get out of Cali
> and out of this school. Save ur
> health, stay where u are. This
> is bigger than u. Wish I was an
> oz citizen too. ☹

Aggie froze, staring at the message. She read it and re-read it, committing it to memory. What did Nala mean? She wrestled with her conscience, desperate to open the message and read the entire conversation chain, to finally know what was going on, but it was a huge invasion of privacy. Locating Mal's phone number was one thing but reading Holly's messages was something else. Still, if her daughter was in trouble – and her behaviour seemed very much to suggest she was – wasn't it her duty to do everything she could to help, even if her daughter was an adult?

'Mum?' Holly's voice made Aggie jump.

She spun around. 'Holly!' She shoved the phone behind her back.

Holly's eyes narrowed. 'Why have you got my phone?'

'I don't.'

Holly rolled her eyes. 'I thought I'd lost it. I've been crawling around on the floor of the bus looking for it.' She rubbed at the beanie on her head, as though the wool might be itching her.

'It was an accident.'

'An accident?' Holly half laughed and half scoffed, both cranky and amused. 'Like the time you accidentally blew up condoms instead of balloons at my twelfth birthday party?'

'That's not how it happened at all,' Aggie retorted, indignant now.

'No? My friends weren't playing balloon volleyball with inflated condoms?'

'Well, no. It was only one condom. But it wasn't *supposed* to be that way. Don't you remember?' She was waving her hands around now, clearly displaying the stolen phone. 'I had two birthday cards for you, one to be opened at the party and one for private. I accidentally mixed them up and you opened the one with the condom in front of everyone. That's all.'

Despite clearly trying not to laugh, Holly was losing the battle. 'You told them all it was a balloon in the shape of a cow's udder.'

'I've never been great at thinking on my feet, that's true.'

'What kind of udder has only one teat?'

'It's important to show diversity.'

Holly growled in a mixture of humour and frustration, pressing her hands over her eyes.

'Look, my mother didn't tell me anything about sex,' Aggie said. 'I was never going to do that to you. I always wanted you to have all the information, whatever you wanted to know – good, bad and ugly.'

'You got me the pill when I was sixteen.'

'That was for your acne,' Aggie said, lifting her chin. It *wasn't* for acne, but Holly didn't need to know that at the time. 'Besides, I didn't make you take it. I was just giving you the choice. That was all I ever offered – choices, information, support.'

'I know.' Holly sighed and held out her hand for the phone.

Aggie dropped it into her palm and confessed. 'I was trying to call your father.'

'*What?*' Holly stamped her foot, just as she'd done as a child when she couldn't find the words to express herself.

'I'm worried about you,' Aggie said. 'If you won't tell me what's going on then I'm going to keep trying to help you in any way I can.'

Holly's jaw muscles twitched with unspoken counterarguments.

'I didn't get to make the call. But a message from Nala did pop up while I was looking at the screen.'

Holly stopped breathing.

'I had no intention of reading your messages, but it appeared right in front of my eyes. I couldn't miss it.'

Holly waited.

'Why does Nala say you should get out of California and out of the school?'

'I have no idea,' Holly said, flatly.

'You know I can tell when you're lying, right?'

'*How* do you know?'

'I'm not going to tell you that,' Aggie said. 'Then you'll know how to avoid me knowing. Mothers need to have some super-powers.'

'It's nothing,' Holly said, her shoulders drooping. 'She's just being dramatic.' She walked away towards the bus.

'Wait!' Aggie called, and hurried to catch up with her. 'Are you sure you won't come down to see the church?'

Holly paused at the open door of the empty bus, considered the church and shook her head. 'No.' She climbed the steps, leaving Aggie behind. 'I don't want to be trapped underground.'

•

Valeria and Rupert wandered through the cool underground church. She donated a gold coin and lit a candle, but found no words to say a prayer for anything specific. The main chapel was rectangular in shape, with light fixtures on the wall that added a warm glow. The vaulted earthen ceiling had many arches, and images of saints were carved into the stone behind the austere wooden pulpit. Valeria appreciated the bare nature of it, and the obvious love and devotion that had gone into its creation. She approved of its lack of showiness or grandeur. All in all, it was a small but striking piece of architecture, if you could call it that. Did it still count as architecture if you dug a building out of the ground rather than building a structure on top of it?

'What a lovely church,' Rupert said, attempting to coax conversation.

'Yes, lovely,' she agreed. She was willing her brain to come up with further dialogue when the guests around them fell quiet. At the head of the chapel, the church's caretaker began to chant. The language was unknown to Valeria, the words without meaning, but the *sound*. It reverberated around the whole church and pinned everyone into stillness. His voice moved up and down the octaves, slowing, pausing, then booming from his chest – a rich, soul-stirring sound. Valeria felt her eyes mist with tears as the power of it filled her very soul. She felt her anger fall away like old leaves dropping from winter branches in the face of this magnificent singing.

She gazed at her surroundings, wondering how many life-changing events had occurred in this small space – baptisms, funerals and weddings. Her mind recalled the words of a minister at a wedding she'd attended recently in Adelaide.

'Marriage is an institution that should only be entered into willingly, lovingly and with a clear head and heart,' he'd said.

She still wished Agatha had had the chance to wed Malcolm when she was pregnant with Holly. Valeria and Bertie had suggested it, of course, but their daughter had been determined.

'Mum,' Agatha had protested, stroppily, 'I'm too young to get married.'

'Yes, and you're too young to have a baby as well, but that hasn't stopped you,' Valeria had countered.

Oh, everyone went on about how difficult the early years of motherhood were – the exhaustion, the sleeplessness, the breast-feeding woes, the lack of personal space and time. But in so many ways, those days were easier. Her daughter had loved her then. Valeria had been Agatha's moon and sun and stars. Her daughter had believed what she'd had to say, unquestioning. It was later that her child had caused her to lie awake all night for entirely different reasons. It was later that she'd seen all the faults of her mothering in front of her face. Agatha had become a mirror for all her failures.

Valeria rubbed at the cast on her broken wrist, unable to scratch the skin beneath it but trying anyway. At least bones could be mended. She wasn't so sure about hearts.

28

Aggie sat with Harry towards the back of the bus, with Holly occupying a double seat to herself directly across the aisle. She was scrunched up like a little girl, leaning against the window.

Although Aggie was certain her voice wouldn't be heard above the bus's engine, she angled her body away from the aisle, towards Harry, leaning against him to talk quietly in his ear. Despite the message from Nala, Valeria's interference and her conversation with Gideon, not to mention the worry over what was going on back in the Barossa, she acknowledged how pleasant it felt to press her weight into Harry's body.

'Holly's hiding something from me,' she confided, noticing the musky scent of Harry's skin mere centimetres from her lips. 'I accidentally saw a message on her phone from a friend in California,' she said, then repeated the words she had committed to memory.

Harry shook his head slightly. 'What do you think it means?'

'I have no idea.'

'*Get out of this school . . . save your health*. That's odd.'

'Sounds like poisoning or something, right?'

Harry pulled back sharply to look at her, his mouth slightly ajar. 'Like, environmental toxins?'

'Who knows? All I know is that she's been acting very strangely since she's been back, and now her best friend is telling her to get out. That sounds serious.'

'She did seem a bit – I don't know – *disconnected* at lunch,' he said.

'Yes, she did. And while I'm not happy that my mother decided to call her out on her alcohol consumption, I can see where she's coming from. Holly was never a big drinker and she's been hitting the bottle hard since she's been back, and even more so on the train.'

Harry scratched the side of his face. 'That's what I did when everything fell apart,' he said.

Aggie rubbed her eyes with her fists, frustrated and suddenly weary. They rode in silence a little way, till Aggie realised she was still leaning into him and wondered if she should pull away. She was just convincing herself to do so when Harry took her hand. She threaded her fingers through his, then gazed up into his eyes. He was smiling at her.

'What are you smiling about?' she asked, intrigued.

'Ah, it's nothing, really.'

'Tell me.'

'It was a random memory, from back when I was feeling really bad. I'd moved to Byron on my own. I'd been practising meditation each morning, the way the monks had taught me – simple stuff, I'm not a master or anything. But it was Byron Bay, you know, so there's incense and crystals and prayer flags everywhere.' He gave her a self-deprecating look. 'Anyway, I'd bought myself a meditation cushion and I would light an incense stick each morning and sit on my cushion and count my breaths.'

'Sounds peaceful.'

'It was. But this one morning I was having a really bad time of it. I was super low. I'd been dumped by a wave and had a black eye. The old surfers had heaped shit on me and told me to go back to the paddling pool. I didn't have a job. I'd run out of coffee. Everything had gone wrong and I couldn't see how any of it would ever get better.' He swallowed then, as though it was difficult to recall just how low he'd been. 'So anyway, I was thumping around the house and didn't want to meditate at all, but I remembered my teacher from the retreat telling me the quality of meditation wasn't the goal: the primary goal was simply to turn up at the cushion. So I did. I put on my big boy pants and went to get the incense.'

He paused, smiling.

'And?' she prompted.

'The packet was empty.'

'What did you do?'

'I was determined not to let that shitty day get the better of me. There *had* to be another incense stick. I rummaged through all the drawers, tipping stuff on the floor, desperate to conquer this one small thing.' He held his thumb and forefinger a few millimetres apart for emphasis. 'I kept going, and I found one. Yes!' He mimed a little fist pump, but she knew there was more coming.

'I stuck it in the incense holder, totally triumphant, struck a match and lit it.' Here he paused for dramatic effect.

'And?'

'It wasn't an incense stick.'

'What was it? Oh, no . . . it wasn't a weed stick or something, was it?'

'No, but that probably would have been useful in the moment.' He snorted with laughter.

'What was it?'

'It was a sparkler. I lit it and it burst into a display of mini fireworks right there in my living room.'

Aggie laughed. 'That's brilliant.'

'It was. I was having the worst day I'd had in a long time and then, boom, just like that, there was a party in my house. I burst out laughing, and then I laughed till I cried. It was a perfect reminder that no feeling lasts forever. Everything changes. There is always light around the corner.'

Aggie blinked furiously at the sudden rush of tears to her eyes. 'It's true.'

'Holly will be okay,' he said, and gave her hand a gentle squeeze. 'She's got you, and you will never give up on her. She's one lucky woman.' He reached out and touched her cheek with his knuckle. 'You'll also be okay too, just so you know. No matter what happens with the cafe.'

•

Myrtle was bone-tired, and she was wishing dinner would hurry up so their room could be converted into sleeping quarters while she downed a few stiff drinks in the bar.

'Today's been a bit of a disappointing last day of the trip,' Dolce said, using the toe of one shoe to scratch methodically at the opposite calf.

Myrtle huffed, restless. 'What a wretched thing to happen to the cafe, and such terrible timing for Valeria to find out about the will.'

'Look how dry my skin is, Myrtle,' Dolce said, hoicking up her trouser leg to survey the cracked, discoloured skin. 'Grease me up, would you?'

Glad of the distraction, Myrtle rummaged in her luggage for her deluxe Ligurian honey body lotion, purchased at Kangaroo

Island, and brought it to the couch. Dolce manoeuvred herself to the side to lift her leg for attention.

A weighty silence settled between them as Myrtle rubbed lotion into her friend's skin. Her mind was preoccupied: guilt-ridden about the insurance debacle, grumpy with Valeria's determination to always see the worst in someone's intentions, concerned that Holly would be heading back to America so soon given the state she was in, hopeful that Aggie and Harry might continue to see each other after this trip, desperate to know that she hadn't ruined her relationship with Aggie by letting her down with the cafe, and sad that this was the last night she might ever spend on an adventure with Dolce.

'What are you going to do now?' Dolce asked meaningfully.

'About which part?'

'Good point,' Dolce said, and raised what was left of her eyebrows. 'How about Aggie, first?'

'Whatever I have to do, like always. I won't leave her in the lurch.'

'Maybe she'd like to be left there.'

'What do you mean?'

'Did you notice she didn't tell you about the flooding issue until it got really bad? Seems to me she wanted to figure it out herself. She only came to you because she needed to know about the insurance. I'd say she's been doing a good job of handling it on her own till now.'

Myrtle stopped rubbing in lotion and stared at Dolce.

'Does it hurt?' Dolce persisted. 'Knowing that Aggie is deliberately crafting a life out of your shadow?'

Myrtle scoffed, defensive. 'Don't be ridiculous.' She checked her watch. 'It's dinnertime. We should go.'

But Dolce didn't move. 'Are you upset that I've done the same? That I organised a new life for myself at university and didn't include you?'

'Yes, frankly, I am. What's wrong with that? I thought we were friends. More than that – sisters, really.' Despite herself, she felt her lower lip tremble. 'What is so awful about me that you felt you couldn't confide in me?'

Dolce removed her leg from Myrtle's lap and shook it so the hem of her pants fell straight. 'You're not awful.'

'Then why?'

Dolce scratched her head and puckered her lips, thinking. When she was younger, this gesture had been cute. It had given her little cupid's-bow lips that were hard for anyone to ignore. 'I thought you'd laugh at me.'

'Why would I laugh at you?'

'Likely the same reasons I expect my children to laugh at me when I tell them,' she said, dryly. 'Because I'm old, I've never studied before, I forget things, I'm not particularly mobile, or maybe because I'm likely not that far from needing an aged-care home myself.'

'I told you that will never happen.'

'I've changed my mind,' Dolce said, calmly.

'What do you mean?'

'I'm not afraid anymore. I'm not afraid of the end.'

'Neither am I,' Myrtle snapped. 'I only want the chance to have it happen on my terms.'

'I won't kill you,' Dolce said now.

'You promised me you would.' Myrtle heard her voice rising. 'We signed our names to it. How could you go back on that?'

Dolce's expression was firm. 'People change, Myrtle. Even at our age. I don't want to pull the pin on my life, I want to live it. More than that, I want to help others, right up to the end. Going to university is one way I can do that. Academic study will also help keep my brain active. Being social, doing new things, continually challenging myself . . . all of these help stave off dementia. There are people out there who need us. Our peers, our friends, our relatives. It's the war of our times and I'm not going down without a fight.'

'And you think I am?' Myrtle pulled herself from the couch to stand as straight as her spine would allow.

'I think you might have got . . . stuck.'

'Stuck? You're the one who wants to stop travelling and stay in the one spot.'

Dolce sighed. 'Help me up, would you? I'm hungry.'

'You're always hungry,' Myrtle grumbled, but pulled on Dolce's arm nonetheless.

'I'm greedy now too, am I?' Dolce's tone was frustratingly mild. 'Watch it, not too fast, the old pins aren't what they used to be.' She encouraged herself on as she straightened her knees, then Myrtle let go of her arm.

'You're so frustrating.'

'Some things never change,' Dolce agreed. 'That might be one of them. Come on, you'll feel better after a feed and a mojito or three.'

Myrtle followed Dolce down the narrow hallway. The train rocked sharply and they both staggered to the side to lean on the wall for support. She turned Dolce's words over in her mind. Stuck? How was she stuck? She'd sold her commercial building and given up her own house as guarantee. She'd organised this trip, and if Dolce wasn't deserting her she'd be organising another. These didn't seem like the actions of someone who was stuck.

Maybe Dolce was losing her marbles after all.

•

'We'll be in Adelaide tomorrow,' Rupert said, swirling the red wine in his glass, staring out at the blackness as the train whizzed through the desert once more.

'We will,' Valeria agreed, weary from the emotion of the day. She couldn't stop thinking about Aggie and Holly and Myrtle and the things she'd said. Guilt crept like an oil slick in the pit of her belly. Her sauvignon blanc was not sitting well. This was not how she'd hoped their trip would end.

At that moment, Dolce entered the bar carriage, followed by Myrtle. Dolce gave her a pleasant smile and nod but Myrtle did not. Her aunt's mouth was set in a grim line, further agitating Valeria's gut. They passed by, heading for a table on the other side of the carriage.

'Given that . . . before we . . . well, we haven't actually finished talking about my . . . son,' Rupert said.

Valeria blinked, forcing her mind to sift through a thousand moments and back to the conversation she and Rupert had started yesterday in Alice Springs. How could that only be yesterday? It felt like a lifetime ago. It was astounding the way time stretched on this journey. So many days back in Angaston flew by and she felt she'd achieved nothing at all. Yet here on this trip, she'd sunk wholly into every moment, her total immersion in each experience warping time into something else entirely.

Now, however, she wished she could warp it some more. She honestly didn't want to hear whatever it was that Rupert had to say.

'Yes, of course,' she said instead, knowing it was the polite thing to do. What she would rather have said was, *Please, let's just live in ignorant bliss.* 'I'm all ears.'

Rupert gulped a mouthful of wine and licked his lips. He stared into his glass for a moment, as though needing to let his words settle. 'You see, the reason Peter wanted to die was because he was carrying a tremendously large secret, something he felt he couldn't share with anyone.'

Valeria tilted her head, like a bird trying to focus on a flicker of movement.

Rupert swallowed audibly. 'The woman you saw in the photo on Facebook . . .'

'Oh yes?' She felt her shoulders and chin rise defensively, waiting for the blow.

'That woman is Peter. Her name is now Lorrel.'

Valeria stared at him. Her brain seemed to be stuck in low gear. 'I'm sorry, what?'

'Lorrel is my daughter, whom I once called Peter.'

She frowned, digging around in her memories for stories or articles she'd read about such things. 'Are you saying he's . . . trans, something? He has decided to live as a woman?' She shifted in her seat, feeling out of her depth.

'Yes and no. He—' Rupert caught his mistake, holding up a finger. 'Sorry, sometimes I still get it wrong. *She* is transgender. Lorrel has always known she was a woman but the body she was born with didn't reflect that to the rest of the world. She has been undergoing gender affirmation processes to correct that.'

'I don't understand.'

Rupert gave a half-laugh. 'I appreciate that, believe me. It's taken me quite some time to get my head around it myself. But Lorrel is my child and I love her dearly. I have seen the transformative effect of her unburdening herself of this secret. I couldn't be anything other than supportive. After decades of despair and depression, and an attempt on her life, she has received psychiatric assessments and treatment, and has been undergoing medical and surgical interventions to allow her to live openly as a woman.'

Valeria stared at Rupert. 'Oh.' It was the only thing she could say.

'I know this is a shock.'

'Yes,' she murmured. A shock? She couldn't begin to process this revelation. What did Rupert expect her to say? She cleared her throat, summoning her voice. 'How do you feel about this?' She'd read somewhere that this was a good phrase to use when lost for words. It opened up the conversation and allowed the other person to speak freely, which is what she needed right now, because she certainly didn't know what to say.

'I still have good days and not-so-good days,' he said, rubbing the side of his smooth cheek. 'I'd like to say that I am a modern man who understands all these things, but all I can do is believe what Lorrel says and support her as best I can. Hers is not an easy path, but I want her to be happy.'

She suddenly understood. He was asking her to be okay about this. He was laying down his need. If they were to have a relationship, she would need to be welcoming and supportive of his child.

There was a long moment of silence in which she fiddled with the large, round, pink earrings in her lobes, another Maggie-inspired choice. They were striking against the rest of her outfit – black pants and a black cowl-neck shirt – a lovely pop of colour to match the hint of blush she'd applied to her cheeks. She'd been feeling so low after today's events that she'd taken the age-old approach of dressing up to try to lift one's spirits. Now here she sat, presenting her best self, but it was only on the exterior. The version of herself that Rupert wanted was nowhere to be found inside her. She was inadequate in so many ways.

'I'm sorry,' she said, dropping her hand from her earring. 'I don't think I can help you in the way you want. As people seem keen to remind me, my judgement of others can be a source of great pain, and yet . . . and yet, I cannot seem to stop it.' She swallowed down any further words. She never said the right thing. She would only make this worse.

His face drew back from hers, while his brows furrowed so low over his eyes that they turned into small slits. She reached over and squeezed his hand, then left, returning to her cabin.

29

It was nearing 8 pm when they finished dinner, and Aggie, Harry and Holly moved back through the doors to settle in the bar carriage for a while longer, talking through the events of the day.

'Sorry, Harry,' Holly said, gesturing to the mineral water in front of him.

'Why?' he said good-naturedly. The three of them were seated at one of the U-shaped benches near the bar. A few other groups of passengers were scattered about but most people seemed to have retired to their rooms for the last night on the train. Aggie hadn't seen her mother at all and assumed she was with Rupert.

'Oh, I don't know,' Holly said, waving a hand. 'I just feel bad drinking rum when all you have is . . . that.' Holly might have felt bad about drinking, perhaps even self-conscious after Valeria had brought it to everyone's attention, but it wasn't stopping her from doing so now.

Harry laughed easily, carefree. Aggie noticed that when he laughed, the lobes of his ears moved up and down. It was adorable.

'I'm all good, Hols,' he said, and Aggie loved the way he called her *Hols*, like they'd been mates for ages, because that was how it felt.

'What do you think you'll find at the cafe when we get home tomorrow?' Holly asked Aggie.

Aggie shook her head. 'I haven't got a clue.'

'Maybe it's not as bad as you think,' Harry said. They talked about this for a while, and then moved on to their favourite moments from the trip, until Holly yawned loudly. 'I'm so tired,' she said. 'I should go to bed, but I feel like I need another drink.'

Aggie exchanged a concerned look with Harry.

'Trust me, you'll sleep better if you go now,' Harry said gently, and after staring at him for a moment, considering this, Holly nodded, got to her feet and left, swaying slightly as she made her way through the carriage.

'Thanks,' Aggie said, grateful for his ability to get through to Holly in such a calm and caring way.

'We all get a bit lost sometimes,' he said. He paused, and Aggie wondered about him. She knew almost nothing of his youth yet. *Yet.* The word made her excited. *Yet* meant there was so much more to come.

'I'd be pretty scared right now, if I was her, feeling that bad.'

'That doesn't make me feel better,' she said.

'No, I suppose not. Just remember, she's got you.'

'You're a gorgeous soul,' Aggie said, and hugged him.

When she released him, she found him gazing into her eyes, his face serious, taking her in. 'You're beautiful.'

It was difficult not to look away – his attention was so intense – but she dared not move. 'You're not bad yourself,' she croaked.

'I promise,' he said, his voice low and husky, 'that if you allow me to kiss you again I absolutely will not leave.' He had been inching closer to her as he spoke, until she could feel the warmth of his body through her clothes.

'Okay,' she breathed.

He took her hand in his and brought it to his chest. She placed the palm there, her fingertips resting in the slight dip below his collarbone, his hand still covering hers. His eyes roamed over her face, her lips, and down her neck. She shivered as he gently lowered the silk of her flowing kimono-style wrap shirt away from her neck, then dipped his head to place his warm lips below her ear, kissing his way down to her shoulder, turning her blood to warm treacle. His lips continued across her neck, back up to her jaw and then, finally, met her own. His mouth covered hers and she was more than happy to reciprocate. She leant her body into his, her eyes closed, with no thought for anyone else in the quiet carriage – just the two of them, their bodies rocking slightly into each other with the movement of the train.

He rested his forehead against hers. 'Is it just me . . .' he said, whispering only to her, 'or do you feel this too . . . this bond between us?'

'It's not just you.'

He waited a beat, still holding her. 'What are we going to do about it?' he asked, with a certain grit in his voice that made her twist the material of his shirt between her fingers. She wanted him, badly. She didn't think she'd ever felt such an instant attraction to anyone. Not just an attraction, but an inexplicable congruence, and she'd certainly never felt this degree of physical pull towards a man, ever. She didn't know an awful lot about Harry and yet she felt she knew him, on some sort of deep, soul level.

He'd started nibbling his way down the side of her neck again and it was all she could do to stop herself from letting out a growl of desire.

'The shower,' she whispered.

He stopped and brought his lips to her ear, his breath hot, a smile in his sexy, lusty voice. 'Did you just proposition me?'

'Uh-huh.'

He stood up swiftly from the table, smiling at her, and held out his hand. 'Let's go.'

He led the way, reaching behind him so their fingers could stay intertwined as they lurched through the shuddering carriages in single file. One carriage, two carriages. She prayed not to run into any of her family members, but every cabin they passed had its door closed. They entered their own carriage, went all the way to the end and made a sharp right into the bathroom, the only place on the train with enough space for the kind of entanglement she was hoping for.

Harry spun around, grinning, and locked the door. She was already pulling her chiffon scarf from her neck and shucking off her shoes. The light in here was bright, not ideal, but she couldn't care less. Harry pinned her against the wall, kissing her, then stopped, looking her in the eye. 'Are you sure you want to do this?'

'No question.' She pulled him to her. Their clothes were off in moments, their hands a frenzy of exploration. She shivered with delight at the sound of his belt buckle jangling as it was flung free of his jeans. By the time their naked bodies were pressed together, moving to the shower as one, she was ready. He flicked on the tap and she yelped as cold water hit her back.

'Sorry.' He spun her away from the stream, turning the tap for more hot water.

'It's fine,' she panted, taking his nipple between her teeth. It was his turn to yelp, then splutter with a delighted yowl. Warm water poured over her head and face and down her body. His tongue was on her nipple and she tried to grip the slippery tiles for purchase. His hand between her legs had her gasping for air.

Harry paused, his breath ragged, gazing around the shower for options.

She was small enough for him to pick up, of that she was sure, but she wanted more control than that. Looking around the room, she spied her silk wrap shirt where it had been discarded, snatched it up and spread it across the shower floor.

'That'll do,' she gasped.

He wasted no time, sliding onto the silk material and pulling her down on top of him. She took him in and knew she was about four seconds away from ecstasy.

'Oh god,' she said, feeling the delicious tightness growing and growing, wanting to stop to wait for him to catch up but knowing it was futile. She was there at her peak and he urged her on, pulling her closer to him as they came together.

She laughed with the sheer joy of it.

Afterwards, they sat on the floor of the shower, their naked bodies entwined, the warm water running down their limbs. She nestled beside him, resting her head on his shoulder, their fingers threaded together.

'Well, that was a first,' she said.

'Which part?' he asked croakily, his other arm wrapped around her, his fingers tracing lines up and down her arm. 'The shower or the train?'

'Both.'

'It's a pity we don't have any candles,' he said, then let out a deep sigh of contentment.

'Or sparklers.'

He snorted.

'I know we should get up so we don't use all the water on the train, but I don't think I can move.'

'Me either.'

She groaned, her energy spent. 'We'd better move, though. We don't want a steward knocking on the door and dragging us out.'

'I suppose.'

Reluctantly, and rather clumsily, they pulled themselves up from the floor, had a final rinse, and stepped out.

'Damn,' Harry said, looking around.

'We didn't bring our towels . . . and my shirt is saturated,' she said, then laughed.

'Maybe we could dry ourselves under the hand dryer,' Harry said, waving his hands under the blower till it whirred into action. They did the best they could, placing small parts of themselves under the dryer, till they were at least not saturated. Still damp, they collected their discarded clothes and got dressed, Aggie forgoing the silk shirt and wearing the singlet that had been underneath it. Harry stuck his head out the door first, looking both ways, then waved for her to follow him, both of them sniggering as they hurried, hand in hand, towards their cabins. She dropped her wet shirt in her room and grabbed a warmer long-sleeved shirt to slip over her head, then Harry pulled her into his room. They could barely fit in there together with the bed made up but they sat on it, their backs to the walls at each end of the bed, their toes touching in the middle. They grinned at each other, the window between them.

'I definitely didn't expect that when I woke up this morning,' he said.

'Me either,' she said, raising an eyebrow, amused at her own recklessness. Then her face fell. 'I know it's too late now,' she said, her lips twisting, 'but I guess we should have found a condom.' She suddenly felt stupid, like the sixteen-year-old who got knocked up in the back of her boyfriend's dad's car. 'Not that I can get pregnant anymore,' she said, shrugging. 'We know that.'

'I get yearly health checks done,' Harry said. 'I'm clean, if that makes you feel better.'

'It does, thanks. Same here. There isn't a test I haven't had in order to rule out everything under the sun.' Her nose twitched.

She knew she needed to say those things but wished she didn't have to, wished they lived in a fantasy world where you could act on animal instincts and didn't have to consider consequences.

He leant forward and took her hand. 'So we're all good here.'

She smiled. 'We're more than good.' She couldn't remember the last time she'd had sex simply for the pure joy of it. She'd forgotten how great it could be. He'd woken a part of her she'd thought was long gone. 'Thank you,' she said.

He laughed out loud. 'Shit, you don't need to thank me. It was my pleasure, I assure you.'

She blushed, all that ecstasy still humming in her bones. He must have read her thoughts because he gave her a cheeky, suggestive smile, that faint dimple reminding her of his youth. She pushed that thought away – their age difference was the last thing she wanted to think about now. In fact, she didn't want to think about anything at all.

'How do you feel?' she said. 'You know, about your vow not to do what we just did.'

He grinned. 'Absolutely no regrets. I feel like I can trust myself again – with you, anyway.'

She allowed the happiness that statement inspired to sink in. Harry trusted himself because of *her.*

'What are you doing when you get to Adelaide?' she asked, suddenly alarmed at the idea of him disappearing. 'Are you doing more travel, or heading straight back to Byron?'

He tilted his head to the side, the effortless joy that had possessed him only a moment ago disappearing from his face. 'I'm booked onto a flight to Sydney tomorrow afternoon, then another to Ballina airport, then a bus back to Byron.'

'Oh.' She nodded, trying to affect an expression of casual indifference, of understanding that this was never going to be a long-term thing, but suspected she was failing.

They held their silence, as though each was afraid to speak, and she stared out the window into the dark, craning her neck to see up to the stars above. She wanted to ask him to change his flight. To stay with her. But even as she felt the words forming, she knew it would be hopeless. Aside from the fact that she'd be running around trying to sort out her cafe's disaster from the moment she hit the ground, what would happen if he did change his flight? He'd stay for a bit and then go back to Byron and the outcome would be the same. He had a life to go back to and so did she. As real as this felt between them, there was no way it had a future.

'Come here,' he said, holding out his hand. She placed hers into his and he tugged her towards him. He shuffled down the bed and she lay on top of him while he wrapped his arms around her. She pushed all thoughts of the future away, instead savouring the feel of her body on his, of his arms holding her tightly. She lay there, listening to his heartbeat, till she fell asleep, the two of them rocking gently together into the night.

30

Aggie awoke in her own cabin, having reluctantly left Harry sometime during the night when it was clear they couldn't stay huddled together like sardines layered in a can. They'd kissed indulgently, not wanting to let go, and she couldn't remember when she'd last felt so excited about anything. She dismissed all her previous worries about what would happen next. She would ask him to stay. Who knew what would happen? She'd certainly never know if she didn't take the chance. Yes, the timing was awful, with everything she'd have to deal with when she got back to Angaston, but you never got to choose the perfect moment for anything in life.

She opened the blinds and was greeted by rain pummelling the acres of green farmland surrounding the train, watery channels filling furrows between rows of sodden crops. The sight was a sharp reminder of what had been going on in the valley while she'd been away, and something solidified in her belly. She reached for her phone in the tiny cupboard next to her and saw there was a voicemail from Gideon, left in the early hours of the morning.

'Ags, the whole of the valley is flooding. Roads are cut, highways closed, flash flooding in the street. They're calling it a disaster zone. The vineyard is flooding too. It's pretty bad. Call me, as soon as you can.'

She immediately went to her web browser to access the news. Rivers had broken their banks. Huge trees had toppled, taking powerlines with them. Water evacuations by boat and helicopter had taken place in Nuriootpa, Tanunda and Gawler. Angaston hadn't yet been hit by the rising river waters, but the danger wasn't far from home.

She called Savannah.

'Where are you?' her assistant asked.

'A few hours out of Adelaide, I think. Are you okay? Are you flooded?'

'Our house is okay but we can't get out of Angaston. I haven't been down to see the shop today. The Airtasker guy dropped off the sandbags yesterday but I'm not sure how much good they will have done. The SES didn't turn up because they were too busy rescuing people.'

'Is everyone okay? Have they . . . lost anyone?' Images of floods around Australia zoomed through her head: of mothers and children stranded on top of cars as rescue dinghies motored out to help them, of people being hauled out of the water and into the sky by helicopters.

'I don't think so,' Savannah said, then quietly shushed her grizzling baby.

Aggie exhaled shakily. 'That's a relief.'

'I don't know what's happening to the cafe, though. Sorry. I just . . . there was nothing more I could do. It could be filling with water, I don't know.'

Aggie closed her eyes. It was true. Her gorgeous little shop for which she'd worked so hard, for which she'd recently obtained a significant loan, and which had no insurance, could be being swept away at this very moment.

'I'll just have to deal with it when I get there. Don't worry about it. There's nothing you can do. You just take care of yourself and that gorgeous baby, okay?'

'Okay,' Savannah said, sounding uncertain.

Her assistant would know, just as Aggie did, that if Strawberry Sonnet was washing away or being irreparably damaged, there'd be no job for Savannah at the end of this. That fact hurt Aggie more than she could bear. She'd prided herself on providing a lifeline for young mothers. Now something as foolish as forgetting about insurance might have ruined everything.

She sat with her phone in her hands, staring out at the driving rain splattering her window. She could hear voices in the hallway, people talking in heightened tones about the flooding. Phones tinged and beeped.

'Good morning, ladies and gentlemen.' The sombre male voice came through the speakers in every cabin. 'If you're just waking up, you might not have heard the news of the widespread flooding in the Barossa Valley, Adelaide Hills and Clare Valley. For those guests who have booked connecting tours through these areas, our stewards will be coming to speak to you this morning before we disembark to discuss alternative arrangements . . .'

Aggie tuned out the rest and stared out her window, a ball of dread growing in her gut. As soon as the announcements had ended, she called Gideon, hoping he might have seen her shop, but it went through to his voicemail. A quiet knock at the door interrupted her thoughts.

'Hello?'

'Hey, it's me.' Harry's voice cheered her, despite everything she'd just learnt. She could practically feel his hands on her body. She was smiling when she opened the doors.

He grinned at her for a moment, then cleared his throat and steadied his tone. 'I just heard the announcement.'

She took a deep breath, reality settling heavily on her chest. 'It's a bit of a shock.'

'How's your shop?'

'No idea. I'm trying to get hold of . . .' She was about to say *Gideon* but stopped herself. '. . . someone who can tell me what's happening.'

She paused, taking in his jeans and long-sleeved pink shirt. She loved a pink shirt on a man. 'You look great,' she said quietly, with a flirty raise of her brows.

'So do you.' He reached out and lifted a lock of hair resting against her neck, brushing it gently behind her shoulder. She closed her eyes under his touch and lay her hand on his arm, feeling his warm skin, his strong muscles just below the surface. She didn't want him to leave her.

'Would you stay?' she asked, gazing into his teal eyes, the eyes that had bewitched her from the start.

'Stay?'

She swallowed, hard. 'With me. In the Barossa. For a bit. I know it's awful, terrible, shitty timing . . .' She let out a mirthless laugh. 'Not exactly the tourist destination of choice right now. And I could quite likely be in for a bit of a nervous breakdown when I see my store,' she joked. 'But I feel as if we have something here, and it shouldn't end now.'

'Yes,' he said, rubbing his thumb in spine-tingling circles along her collarbone.

'Y-you will?'

He didn't hesitate. 'Yes.'

'Really? Cause I know that means changing flights and . . .'

'I don't care,' he said, his voice low and husky. He lowered his lips to hers and she let herself sink into the kiss, let everything outside the train fall away. Here, with his arms sliding around her waist, all was well.

•

Valeria bristled at the sight of Harry following Agatha into the bar as they made their way to the U-shaped bench where Valeria, Holly, Myrtle and Dolce already sat, waiting to be escorted into the dining carriage. She felt sickly, the result of a night full of regret for the way she'd left things with Rupert. She hadn't seen him this morning and assumed she wouldn't again. But she couldn't change who she was, not now, at seventy years of age.

Agatha slid onto the bench, and Harry, with all the confidence of someone who believed he had a rightful place at this table, sat next to her. Valeria sipped her orange juice, which was bitter, just how she liked it, while keeping an eye on the door, not expecting Rupert to come in, but keeping watch nonetheless.

'Where's Rupert this morning?' Dolce asked, as though reading her thoughts.

'He won't be joining us,' she said, trying to keep her tone light but failing.

'Why not?' Myrtle asked, in her annoyingly direct way.

It was all Valeria could do not to *tsk* at her. 'I don't care to discuss it.'

A heavy silence fell over the group and Valeria refused to meet any of their gazes. It was absolutely none of their business, and if she were to share it with them she would have to confess. Confess that she was a prideful, stubborn old fool who'd rather lose her last chance at love than bend her beliefs about what was right and wrong. Instead, she deflected them.

'Holly, why are you still wearing that awful beanie?'

Holly lifted her head from her hand where she'd been leaning on the table.

'Leave her alone, Mum,' Agatha implored her.

'Why? It's not good manners to wear hats at the table.'

'It's not a hat, it's a beanie,' Myrtle countered.

Suddenly Valeria was suspicious. She narrowed her eyes at Holly. 'Holly, what's under your beanie?'

The mood at the table became stiff as all eyes turned to Holly. In return, she swallowed, then slid the woollen covering from her head.

Valeria gasped and sat up as straight as she could on the squishy bench seat. 'What have you done to your hair?'

Holly raised her chin. 'I gave myself a haircut. Deal with it.'

'Holly,' Agatha admonished, quietly.

'*That* is not a haircut. That is a rebellion,' Valeria hissed. 'What on earth has got into you? You look dreadful.'

Agatha intervened. 'Leave her alone. It's her hair. She can do what she likes with it.'

'You look like a cancer patient,' Valeria continued. 'Or a street urchin. Or a thug from a girl gang.'

'Mum!' Agatha said, and slapped her hand on the table. 'Stop it.'

Valeria could feel her heart pounding in her chest, and briefly wondered if this was an acceptable level of blood pressure for a stroke victim to accommodate. But she was affronted by the state of Holly's hair, by Agatha's insistence on standing up for her daughter no matter what, and by Agatha's determination to lead Harry on.

Myrtle and Dolce shuffled uncomfortably in their seats, and Dolce patted Holly's hand in support. Valeria turned her steely judgement on her own daughter, lowering her voice but not so much that it couldn't be heard by those around the table.

'Agatha, have you spoken to Gideon yet?'

Agatha flicked an uneasy glance in Harry's direction. 'Not now, Mum.' Harry sat back from the table, watchful now, and Valeria felt the prick of victory. Agatha rushed to explain. 'I was trying to get hold of him to see if he could check my cafe and see what sort of damage there was.'

Harry nodded as though he understood, but something had darkened his eyes. Now was the moment Valeria could save Agatha from making a huge mistake. There was no future with that man sitting beside her. Agatha had very little time remaining to see her dreams come true.

'I wasn't talking about the cafe,' Valeria said.

'I know,' Agatha replied, her voice brittle with warning. 'It doesn't matter right now.'

Valeria ploughed on. 'Have you two made a final decision about the embryos?' she said, smiling encouragingly at her daughter.

Agatha froze and glared at Valeria so sharply it made her flinch, further spiking her blood pressure. 'There's enough going on with the flooding, don't you think?' Agatha delivered each word with weight.

'Of course,' Valeria said. 'But if you're going to implant those embryos, surely every moment counts?'

Holly gasped. Dolce shook her head in outrage. Myrtle, Valeria was certain, stamped her foot on the floor.

Harry gazed at Agatha with a look of complete shock and surprise.

She *knew* it. Agatha hadn't even told him about the embryos. What a foolish thing to do, to string this young man along when there was clearly no future there. It was far better he knew now. She'd just done them both a favour.

'Don't worry about that,' Agatha quickly rushed to reassure Harry. 'I'll tell you about it later.'

But Valeria could see Harry's shoulders sagging. Her work here was done. It might cause Agatha temporary sadness – and she was sorry about that, whatever her daughter might think – but now she'd be free of distractions and would realise that her last chance for a baby was right now, with Gideon.

'Actually,' Harry said, sliding out from the seat, 'I'm not that hungry.' He gazed at the women around the table. 'Excuse me.'

'Wait.' Agatha stood and followed him.

As soon as they had gone, Myrtle broke the silence. 'That was entirely uncalled for,' she said, fixing Valeria with a hard, disgusted glare. 'What right do you have to ruin her chance at happiness?'

A quick look around the table told Valeria all she needed to know. Holly – with her hair that resembled a lawn vandalised by bandicoots – was staring at Valeria with pure contempt. Myrtle looked as if she wanted to eviscerate her. Dolce's expression was one of . . . pity. She was alone, she realised. Completely alone.

'Excuse me,' she said, and left the room.

•

Aggie hurried after Harry through the carriages. He was understandably confused and shaken, and it hurt her, in her chest, in her gut, in her throat. In such a short time, he'd come to mean so much to her. They stopped when they reached the doors to their cabins.

'Please, can we talk?' she said, nodding towards her cabin.

'Okay.'

She pushed the door open. Her bed had been folded away and they sat on the facing bench seats on either side of the window.

'Please, let me explain. My mother was way out of line to say what she did back there,' Aggie said, grinding her teeth over the words. Outside the window, it was still raining, low dark clouds heralding no relief from the flooding any time soon. 'She is fixated on me having another baby and can't seem to let it go.'

'You have embryos?' he said, cutting to the chase.

She pressed her lips together for a moment, not wanting to let any words out at all, wanting to wind back the clock to last night, when their breaths had united.

'Yes. They are left over from the rounds of IVF Gideon and I went through.'

'But didn't you say that you two have been done for some time now?'

She nodded. 'More than a year. We've only started talking again recently, because of the embryos.'

'So why is this an issue right now?'

'Because the clinic where they are stored sent a letter to both of us, saying we have to make a decision about what to do with them.'

'What are the options?' Harry asked, his shoulders relaxing a little, trying to stay open.

'We can donate them to science, donate them to another couple trying to conceive, pay a renewal fee so that they will continue to be stored, destroy them . . . or use them.'

He raised an eyebrow at that last option, questioning.

Aggie squirmed in her seat. She really didn't want to be having this conversation. She wanted to continue existing in the bubble world of the Ghan. 'We ruled out donating them to science or to another couple. Gideon suggested renewing the storage, but I don't think that's the best idea as it would only prolong the decision we need to make.'

'So that leaves you with either destroying them or using them,' he clarified.

'Yes.'

After a lengthy pause he said, 'Do you want another baby?'

Aggie opened her mouth to assure him she didn't. But somehow her mother's voice had wormed its way into her brain. Valeria was right about one thing – this was absolutely her last chance for a baby. She closed her mouth, wrestling with the notion until she said, 'I don't *think* so.'

He took in a slow breath. 'Okay. So, if you did use the embryos and try for another baby, would that mean you and Gideon would be back together? Or would you be a solo parent?'

'I . . .' Words abandoned her. She and Gideon were over. She'd rebuilt her life without him. The thought of being with him again was, well, *weird*. But then, they were both undoubtedly different people now. What if all the time apart had healed them in a way they couldn't heal when they'd been together, grieving before each other's eyes? Was her mother right? Could this actually be the moment they would come together, united, stronger, their relationship blooming once more with a baby to complete their family?

But before she could finish that thought, she was struck through with fear. She *couldn't* lose another baby.

People liked to believe the human spirit was unbreakable, but that simply wasn't true. It could crack, it could shatter, it could well and truly break and never be put back together. She had Holly. Holly was enough for her.

Was that selfish, though? Gideon didn't have a child. Should she do this for him, give him the thing he wanted so badly? He'd invested years of hope with her and had been nothing but supportive, and still he didn't have a child. On the other hand, Gideon could find a younger woman and still get his baby. Aggie wasn't his only option to have that life. Running out of time wasn't a problem for him.

She still didn't know if he wanted to implant the embryos. He hadn't said he did. But then, he hadn't said he didn't. If he did want to use them, could that mean he actually hoped they would get back together? Then what if they did get back together, went through IVF again and still didn't have a baby? Would they endure that pain only to break up again?

'Aggie?' Harry prompted.

'Oh, sorry. What was the question?'

'Would you get back together with Gideon to have a baby?' he said directly.

She answered with the truth. 'I don't know.'

His body flinched and she knew she'd lost him.

'I'm so sorry, Harry. This is all so unexpected, and such dreadful timing. I honestly thought that chapter of my life was closed for good until this came out of the blue.'

She reached forward and took his hands in hers. She wanted to beg him to stay with her, to take some time to see what they had together, but she knew it wasn't fair. How could she ask someone she'd known for such a short time to compete with the years of history, a daughter, embryos and another potential baby she had in common with Gideon? Harry lived in Byron Bay. He was ten years younger than her. He didn't need this kind of drama from a middle-aged woman. He could find a woman twenty years younger than Aggie and start a family with her, if that was what he wanted.

After a moment, Harry withdrew his hands, and she felt the cool air hit her skin like a slap. He cleared his throat. 'I think, given the circumstances – everything you have to sort out with your shop, and these big decisions you need to make with Gideon – that I should jump on the plane and head back to Byron today.'

She nodded, her eyes burning furiously. 'I understand,' she croaked.

He moved to the edge of his seat, reached out with his hand and cupped her cheek. 'I think I might love you, Aggie.'

'What?'

'What I feel for you is the deepest, most pure light I've ever felt, and it spreads through every part of me. I want you. With a baby or without a baby, I just want you.'

She let his words linger in the air for a moment, breathing them in. 'Really?'

'Yes. But it can't be with Gideon too.'

His gorgeous eyes searched hers and she swallowed the painful lump in her throat. He *was* a poet. A rare breed of human who'd had his heart broken endlessly and yet still managed to wear it firmly on the outside of his body, knowing it could be smashed again and again. It was the bravest way to live, and she envied his resilience.

She wanted to tell him she thought she loved him too, but knew if she opened her mouth she would collapse into ugly, self-pitying sobs that were completely unacceptable in this moment. Instead she nodded furiously at him, her hand on her heart, tears falling down her face.

He dropped his hand to his knee and sighed heavily, then stood and left her cabin, taking two steps across the hall and into his own room, closing the door behind him.

Aggie pulled closed the door to her own cabin. She would stay here until she heard him leave the train, then wait a little longer still. She couldn't see him on the platform and say goodbye there. It would be too awful. She'd let him go on his way, free to wander the world, and she would get on with dealing with her business and her embryos. Harry was a shooting star, impossible to catch, blindingly bright and exhilarating while it lasted.

Long after the train had pulled into Adelaide station, her mother knocked on Aggie's door, calling her name.

'Agatha, we need to get off the train.'

But Aggie was curled up on her seat, leaning against the window, watching the rain slide down the glass, blurring the world.

'Agatha?' Valeria called, sternly now.

'Go away,' Aggie said. 'I don't want to see you.'

31

Myrtle sat in the passenger seat of the minibus, with Dolce, Aggie, Holly and Valeria dispersed behind her. With so much room, they'd each taken seats away from one another, Aggie deliberately positioning herself as far away from Valeria as possible. The mood in the vehicle was stiff and silent, and Myrtle had no enthusiasm to try to fix it.

She reached into her handbag for a salted caramel and unwrapped it slowly. The taxi had crawled through traffic to the city's outer limits. Now on the highway headed towards the Barossa, they were still only moving at a modest pace. Roadblocks were in place due to the flooding, and from time to time the traffic was forced to halt, then continue single file as water spilled over the road. Tow trucks sat haphazardly on the shoulder, orange lights spinning on their roofs. The taxi's windscreen wipers whooshed and thumped, whooshed and thumped.

Myrtle sucked on the lolly, rolling it around her mouth. So this was how it ended, her and Dolce. A lifetime of adventures over and done with. Not with a cocktail and an overdose of medication, but sitting in an uncomfortable maxi taxi with the radio reporting on a natural disaster and Dolce setting off on a whole new career and adventure – without Myrtle. She'd never seen it coming. Her vision of the future had been swept away in a landslide.

And what now for dear Aggie? What lay ahead for her now that Valeria had ruined any chance there was for her and Harry? Oh, how she wanted to shake Valeria. The selfishness of her! She wouldn't blame Aggie if she never spoke to her mother again.

Then again, Aggie might not ever want to speak to her again, either. She cursed her foolish mistake with the insurance, which might be the end of Aggie's shop, business and livelihood all at once. Something as simple as a lapsed payment could leave decades of careful relationship-building damaged for life.

As they approached Angaston, the taxi took a left turn along a potholed road, following a detour. The nearby children's playground looked like a swamp. She felt herself inch forward in her seat, desperate for the first glimpse of the main street and whatever was left of Strawberry Sonnet.

•

'Stop here, I need to get out,' Aggie called urgently to the driver.

'Now?' Valeria asked, as Aggie climbed past her seat towards the sliding door. 'Can't it wait?'

'No, it can't,' Aggie growled.

The driver pulled over as far to the side of the road as he could but he was hampered by the river of dirty water gushing along the gutter. It was the same on both sides of Murray Street, the water gathering speed as it tumbled down the hills.

'I'll come too,' Holly said.

'Us too,' Myrtle said.

'No, wait here. I'll only be a second.' She didn't want the oldies getting wet or falling in the street. She pulled back the taxi's sliding door and stepped out carefully, Holly behind her. Leaves, sticks and empty chip packets bobbed and swirled in the current. Fat raindrops hit Aggie's, but she didn't care.

They ran across the road to the cafe. Water sluiced down the red roof tiles and tumbled over the gutterless edge, just as Savannah had described. Aggie held her hand above her eyes to see through the pouring rain, and fumbled in the pocket of her jeans for her keys, while Holly hopped from one foot to the other, trying in vain to avoid being drenched. The terracotta planters at the front of the shop were fast-flowing water features.

The bottom of the black-painted door was swollen, and water oozed out from inside the shop. She swallowed, bracing herself for what she'd find on the other side. She shouldered open the heavy, waterlogged door and a small wave made its escape, soaking her boots, Holly skipping out of its way just in time. It was dim inside. Holly reached for the switch.

'Don't,' Aggie warned. 'We might be electrocuted.'

The small row of sandbags had prevented excess water from running into the rest of the building, which was something. She stepped over them to get a better look at the damage.

The entire facade of her shop was saturated, window frames bulging and cracking, a ruined door, framed sonnets stained by water, the parquetry floor damaged and uneven. The ceiling, too, had cracked and water dripped freely into the shop, droplets landing with regular percussion. A fallen strawberry flower floated past her foot, untethered.

She put a hand to her belly and forced herself to take a deep breath. Holly came to stand beside her, placing her arm around her shoulders.

'It could be worse,' Holly said, but it was an empty statement.

Aggie was no builder but she could see there was many thousands of dollars of damage here. It would take a skill level well beyond anything she possessed in order to repair it. She'd learnt to do a few things over the years – minor plastering, painting, changing washers in taps, replacing doorknobs and staining wood – but nothing that would make a dent in damage of this scale, even if she could find the world's best DIY videos on YouTube. Add to that the loss of income while repairs were done, and of course the council's fine, and it was clear she was in financial trouble.

She moved further into the cafe. The water extended into the belly of the shop, though it was not as deep on this side of the sandbags. Still, it had damaged chair legs and the bottom of the wooden counter. Water had also seeped up the ends of her prize-winner's ribbons in dull, dark stains.

She turned to look back towards the entrance to her shop and watched sheets of water falling down the windows, like tears from a bottomless tank of sadness. If she hadn't felt so completely hollowed out, she might have sat on the floor and joined in. She couldn't see how she could possibly recover from this.

If there was one silver lining to cling to, it was that Aggie's house was safe from flooding, as were most in Angaston. She'd received text messages from Myrtle, Dolce and Valeria to say the same, and for that she was glad, but she wasn't yet ready to accept that everything she'd worked for, for so long, was gone.

As was Harry.

'Everything will be okay, Mum,' Holly said, making Aggie a pot of pekoe tea and a plate of marmalade toast.

'How?' Aggie said.

'I don't know yet, but it will be. I'm sure of it.' She didn't sound sure, though. She sounded worried and distracted by thoughts of the flight she was soon to be on.

Aggie gave her an exhausted but appreciative smile, thanked her for the tea and toast and took herself to bed, leaving her bag still packed. She needed to numb herself for a while and chose to disappear into a Netflix binge session of a compelling new Australian mystery and was only a few episodes in when she drifted off to sleep.

She awoke some time later to her phone ringing, the vibrations travelling through the mattress.

'Hi, Ags. I wanted to get back to you earlier but it's been crazy here.' Gideon sighed heavily, weariness unmistakable in his voice.

'It's fine,' she said, rubbing her eyes and pulling herself up to lean against a pillow. 'Is everything okay?'

'Mostly. The vineyard's awfully wet. A ton of water's gone through, but hopefully it will recede quickly enough not to damage the vines. Otherwise we're in for a bad season. I've been over at Ernie's property next door, helping him shift the sheep to higher ground.'

'Are they okay?'

'I think he's lost a few.'

'That's horrible.'

'Yeah.' He waited a beat. 'So you're home now?'

'Yes.'

'Have you seen the shop?' he asked, hesitation in his words.

She swallowed and blinked away sudden tears. 'Yes.'

'I got the four-wheel drive through the water this afternoon and drove past it. I know it doesn't look good – I'm sorry.'

'Thanks,' she squeaked.

'Oh, Ags,' he said, softly, responding to the pain in her voice. 'Can I come over?'

'Okay.'

'Be there soon.'

*

When Aggie opened the door to Gideon, she had to bite her lip hard to stop herself from bursting into tears. He was such a man of the earth, stable and grounded – a sturdy place in this time of unrest. His skin, brown, with a permanent undertone of gentle sunburn, was so familiar. The many lines around his eyes spoke of wisdom and experience. His grey-streaked hair was wavier than usual, the rain accentuating the curls as they lifted and spun in the wind outside.

'Hey,' he soothed her, shrugging out of his wet jacket and hanging it on a coat hook before stepping forward to hug her. 'It'll be okay.'

She inhaled the aroma of his damp wool sweater, feeling his soft salt-and-pepper whiskers against her cheek, and welcomed the sense of calm they brought. 'Come in,' she said, releasing him.

She led the way through to the kitchen and clicked on the kettle to boil. 'Tea?' she asked, as an afterthought. It was such an automatic thing to make tea for Gideon.

He smiled, taking a seat at the little kitchen table, moving her metal rooster sculpture to the side. 'Thanks.'

'Holly's sleeping, but I'll wake her before you go. I'm sure she'd love to see you. She's due to fly back on Monday.' She was still hoping to change Holly's mind before then, but she didn't have the energy to get into all of that with Gideon right now.

'It will be great to see her. She hasn't been home in years,' he said, gazing down the hallway towards her room. Gideon had entered their lives just as Holly had started university and they had always got on well. Holly had been old enough that Gideon was never in the position of having to parent her, so they could just be friends and housemates when she was home during the holidays. She was busy building her new life and Gideon and Aggie were busy building theirs. It was the golden age before it all spun out of control.

'I bet you're sad she's leaving.'

'More than you know,' she said. Taking a shaky breath, she popped a bag of green tea into the big stoneware mug – *Gideon's* mug – then leant against the sink with her arms folded.

'How was your trip?' he asked, leaning back, one arm resting over the back of the chair, a trademark pose.

How was her trip? She scanned through her mind for something to say that wouldn't make her weep about Harry. 'It was amazing,' she said, as innocuously as possible. 'A once-in-a-lifetime experience. Right through the centre of the country, from top to bottom. Incredible.'

'Did Valeria have a good birthday?'

Aggie felt her face harden at her mother's name. 'Yes, she did.'

But Gideon knew her too well, could read the subtext in her tone. He half smiled. 'You and she had a fight?'

'You could say that.' Behind her, the kettle rumbled loudly.

'About?'

'A few things.'

'Just a few?'

'You know how she is.'

'I do.' The kettle behind her clicked off and she turned around to pour water into his mug, jiggled the bag exactly five times – how Gideon liked it – then tossed it into the metal compost bin on the sink. She delivered the steaming mug to him and sat on the other side of the table. 'Thanks,' he said, reaching for it.

She watched steam twist and curl, rising in wisps from the surface of the tea. 'Just before we left for the trip, I bought the cafe from Myrtle,' she said.

Gideon raised his eyes to hers, surprised. 'Really?'

She felt the need to explain the financial situation, given how much they'd both spent on years of IVF treatments. 'Myrtle put her house up as a guarantee to the bank, and also changed her will so that her house will go to me when she . . . dies,' she said, the reality of that inevitable day catching in her throat.

Gideon blew on his tea, thinking, the frown line between his brows deepening. 'That was generous of her.'

'It was,' she agreed. 'But it made my mother angry.'

'Because she won't get the house?'

'No, because we didn't tell her about it.'

'Then why did you tell her while you were on holiday together?'

That was a reasonable question. Why poke the sleeping bear when you knew it would wake up and take a swipe at you? 'Because of the flooding. Because, as it turns out, the matter of building insurance fell through the cracks in the handover from Myrtle to me, which means that at this moment it is uninsured.'

'Seriously?'

'Yep.'

He grunted, then tapped his knuckle on the table for a few seconds, trying to solve the problem but coming up short. 'This is not good.'

Rain drummed on the roof in a heavy burst. She suddenly wondered if the Royal Adelaide Show would still be going ahead. The deadline to drop off her jam entries was in three days' time, on Tuesday.

'Are you furious with Myrtle?' he said, and took a sip of his tea.

Aggie cast her gaze to the ceiling, considering this. 'Yes . . . and no. It's as much my fault as it is hers. I think I've lost everything.'

'That's not true.' He reached over and squeezed her hand. 'You'll come back from this, I'm sure of it. You're the strongest person I know.'

She took a deep breath and held it for a moment. Was that true? She didn't feel strong. She felt all kinds of wobbly and raw. When she looked at Harry, she saw strength – a person who'd been through so much yet still held light in his eyes and heart, who still believed in a good world and a brighter future. She'd felt that way once but had lost it, and had only recently begun to believe she could find it again.

When she looked at Gideon, she saw a man still bruised but healing, like her. Did that make them strong people, just for continuing to show up in the world?

Gideon caught her watching him and put his mug down on the table. 'What?'

She swallowed the bubble of nerves that had risen from her stomach to her throat. 'Mum thinks I'm mad not to implant the embryos. She says you're a good man and this is our last chance.'

He scratched at the shorter whiskers on his neck. 'Yeah, she made a strong case for that when she called me.'

Aggie rolled her eyes at the audacity of her mother calling Gideon to beg him to commit to implanting the embryos. 'She's out of control,' she muttered.

A long silence stretched between them, and a thousand and one feelings and thoughts swirled through Aggie. She could see now that all the time she'd spent thinking about the options for the embryos while she was on the train had been a practice run. Here now, with Gideon sitting across from her, the very physical presence of him – the sound of his voice, the feel of him as he'd hugged her, his genuine care and concern for her, his belief in her strength and ability to bounce back – could change everything. Her mouth was suddenly dry and she lunged across the table for his mug of tea, taking a noisy gulp.

'Sorry,' she said, handing it back.

He snorted gently, amused, and tentatively reached across to touch his fingertips to hers. 'I've been thinking about it. I've thought of nothing else, to be truthful, and I think she's right.'

Aggie locked eyes with him, and the world tilted on its axis.

32

Valeria pulled the wet washing from the front loader and fed it into the dryer next to it, her arm much stronger now and able to be of use, though she was nevertheless keen to have the cast off next week. She added another load to the washing machine. She couldn't stand to leave bags unpacked after a trip, whereas Agatha would probably take days to unpack hers. She shut the door of the machine and pressed the start button, irritated with herself for thinking so critically of her daughter. It was a habit, she conceded – an unpleasant, unhelpful one.

She pressed her hands against the laundry bench and rested her weight there. Was it really so bad to have standards? Wasn't it a good thing to be constantly seeking excellence, for her daughter and everything else in her life? That was what competitive jam making was all about, something Agatha surely understood, which was why she did it too and why she was successful at it. Valeria had taught her daughter to make jam, so surely she had passed on those values too.

As the heat from the dryer began to warm her legs, she cast her mind back to a day when her daughter was probably around ten years old. Agatha was sitting in the kitchen, watching her gingerbread biscuits bake in the oven, the heat radiating into the room, while outside winter cold had set in, the trees bowing in the wind and tossing branches to the ground.

Valeria had her bottled jams lined up on the wooden benchtop and was comparing the information she had written on sticky notes that were placed on top of each with regard to the visual appearance of the contents. She was attempting to decide which jams from which batches were the ones to enter in the show. Every batch came out a little differently, and once they were bottled it wasn't as easy to assess them. But the jam had to be bottled immediately, and once the lid was on she couldn't open it again to test. She only had her notes to go on.

'Hmm,' she murmured, pulling out a jar and bringing it to the front of the line. 'This one, I think.' She pulled out another. Bending down so the jars were at eye level, she studied them. The one on the left was slightly darker in colour, which wasn't necessarily a problem, but the strawberry seeds had clumped in a few spots, and an uneven distribution would go against her. She consulted the notes she'd written. *Really good jam, rich flavour, perfect amount of lemon*. She clicked her tongue and compared it to the jar on the right, which had a lovelier visual appearance, but for which her notes said, *Good jam, but maybe not a champion?*

'What's the matter?' Agatha asked, swivelling sideways in her chair and swinging a leg about.

'Sit up straight, sweetheart,' Valeria said automatically.

Agatha did as she was told but rolled her eyes slightly.

'No eyerolls,' she reminded her daughter. It was becoming a habit, one she didn't want to see continue. Agatha sucked on her cheeks instead.

'This jam,' Valeria said, pointing to the one on her left, 'tastes the best but isn't as pretty as this one,' she said, pointing to the other.

Agatha screwed up her nose. 'Why does it matter what it looks like? You only eat it and it gets all mixed up in your belly.' She pushed her long hair out of her face, irritated by it.

'A perfect jam needs to be perfect in every way – how it looks, how it tastes, it can't be too firm or too runny, it can't be overcooked or burnt, the jar must pop perfectly when it's opened, the label must be positioned exactly, the poured quantity must be within millimetres of the required distance from the top, there should be no splatter of jam, it should smell fresh and fruity, it should not be too sweet or too sour, and it absolutely must not have any jam setter in it.'

Agatha widened her eyes. 'Who cares about all that?'

'We do,' Valeria said, gravely. 'Because we value standards and excellence. The competition assessment criteria are there to uphold a respect for quality that is so lacking these days. These competitions are the eye in the storm in a decaying society.'

'Huh?'

'If we don't strive to be the best, if we let everything go, if we *don't care*, then where does it stop?'

Agatha stared at her blankly, pulling up her knees so that her feet were resting on the chair, and wrapping her arms around her legs.

'You must always do your best,' Valeria said, and she saw this as one of her greatest teaching moments. Through the power of jam competitions, she could teach her daughter to never give up, to constantly strive for better, to lose *and* win gracefully, to keep going no matter how stiff the competition or how high the odds to win, to respect authority, to follow the rules.

'They should teach this at school,' she said, absent-mindedly.

'What?'

'How to make jam,' Valeria said, returning to her notes. 'There are so many life lessons in jam making.'

Her thoughts returned to the present, and she wondered how long it would be before she and Agatha spoke again. Another three months, like last time, after their fight? Gideon had been the cause of that argument too. She'd seen Gideon out while grocery shopping and her heart had ached for the man, with his trolley for one. Valeria had left the store and marched straight into Strawberry Sonnet, begging Agatha to give him another chance.

'Death is not a reason to break up with someone,' she'd told her.

Agatha, who had been stoning peaches in the kitchen to make peach, raspberry and champagne jam, froze, knife in midair. Lively chatter filtered in from the dining area of the cafe, where patrons ate and drank and laughed.

'What are you talking about?' she said, her nostrils flaring.

'You and Gideon. You seem to have forgotten that you were actually a wonderful couple. He is a good and kind man who stood by you for years. You loved each other. Things went badly, I know.'

'Badly? Our baby *died*.'

'Of course, of course,' Valeria said, spreading her fingers, placating. 'All couples would struggle after that.'

Agatha closed her eyes for a moment, clearly trying to calm herself. 'You think I'm selfish,' she said. 'Don't you? You think I'm weak, that I gave in, that I was only thinking of myself.'

'Well, I . . . I know it's not that simple, of course. I just think you might have lost sight of what is important. You and Gideon had something. You're in the middle of your life, Agatha, and I don't think you realise that men like Gideon don't just come along every day. Women tend to be forgotten by the rest of the world as they age. Gideon might be it for you, your last chance.'

Agatha slammed the knife down on the bench, making Valeria jump.

'Agatha!'

Her daughter spun in a slow circle and then spoke through clenched teeth. 'How dare you?'

'All I'm saying is that everyone you know is going to die one day,' she said, her tone reasonable. 'You can't cut people out of your life every time you lose someone. Grief is something you have to bear. You have to find a way to work through it or around it, but you cannot simply give up.'

'Our separation is hardly unique,' Agatha said, hands on hips. 'Many couples break up after losing a child.' Her eyes glistened.

'That doesn't mean you have to be one of them. Many couples also make it through. Don't let Gideon get away. He's single now, but he won't be forever. Give it another try, please.'

'Get over myself, is that what you're saying?' she said, her eyes flashing.

Valeria felt a rush of fury. She wanted to shake Agatha. 'Yes, that's what I'm saying. Your generation is so quick to throw things away – the first generation in history to be smothered with disposable items rather than having to learn to take care of things. You think you can throw away relationships and pick up another but it's not always true. I'm saying, in your generation's terminology, that you need to build a bridge and get over it.'

Agatha sucked in a long, slow breath. 'Get out,' she said, her voice barely audible. She picked up the knife, pointed it to the door, then continued cutting peaches, ignoring Valeria completely. After a moment, Valeria left the room.

She knew Agatha was upset with her for ruining her chances with Harry, but now the path was clear for her and Gideon to finally reunite. She *would* thank her, one day.

In the lounge room, she found her mobile phone on the heavy wooden coffee table in front of the sofa. She had the volume set high so she'd be sure to hear if a message or call came through from Rupert. Although she had not heard anything, she checked anyway. She felt . . . aggrieved. Rupert's farewell to her at the station this morning had left a tight pinching in her throat.

'I understand that you feel unable to accept my daughter at this time,' he said. 'But I can't say I'm not disappointed.'

She'd remained silent, the correct words to say nowhere to be found.

'Goodbye, Valeria. I enjoyed our time together on the Ghan. I will always remember that.' Then he'd dipped his head at her in farewell and walked away. He didn't look back.

Now she fidgeted with the mobile phone in her hand, wondering if she should call him. He was still around, having booked a month-long stay. She could tell him that while she'd never understand how someone could do what his son had done – to change what God had given him, what nature had dictated – she could be polite, she could simply not speak of her feelings about the matter, she could avoid it at all costs. That was a perfectly valid way to deal with differences of opinion and belief, in her experience. It was the reason for the adage to never speak of politics or religion. She would just *pretend* she didn't know anything about Lorrel's past. She could pretend Lorrel had always been the way she was. Was that really so bad? If she couldn't say anything nice, as her mother had warned her, then she wouldn't say anything at all. It was sage advice that had worked wonderfully for many generations.

She located Rupert's name on her phone and was about to call him when she stopped herself. What on earth made her think that at her age, having lived alone for more than twenty years, stubborn and set in her ways, she would ever manage to navigate a new relationship now? What made her think that love was ever a likely prospect in her twilight years? She placed the phone back down on the coffee table. It was a foolish thing to hope for.

•

Aggie woke on Sunday morning with a single-minded focus. She could do nothing about her shop while the rain continued to fall, and she had still made no decision about the embryos, but she could do one thing. By hook or by crook she was going to find out what was going on with Holly.

The house was quiet, Holly still asleep, and the early morning light was soft in Aggie's room. She pulled herself up in bed, tucking pillows behind her back, and opened her laptop. Nala had clearly said there was something wrong at the school and that Holly should get out and not go back. She began searching for environmental scandals in Californian schools, but nothing came up other than 'college admission scandals'.

She closed that search and instead entered the name of the school where Holly taught. If it was really something as dangerous as Nala was suggesting then it would surely have made the news. She pressed enter and the search results loaded, one after the other, with articles about Holly's school. With her heart firmly wedged in her throat, she read the first one.

And then the second.

And then the third.

She checked the dates of the articles again, just to make sure she had this right, then her hands began to tremble. *This* was what had happened to Holly.

Holly didn't get out of bed for hours, which was a good thing because it gave Aggie time to calm down and plan what she wanted to say. For the first hour, her emotions ran the full gamut, from fury and the hysterical need to shake Holly awake and order her to stay in the Barossa while she eviscerated the perpetrators on the other side of the world, through to crying every time she imagined what Holly had been through, to relief that at least she knew now why her daughter had been behaving as she had. It all made perfect sense. She even allowed hope to spring that surely this meant Holly would choose to stay in Australia now. It was the obvious thing to do. But she was running out of time, the hours counting down now till Holly's departure. She had to handle this right.

When Holly rose at half-past ten, Aggie made her a cup of coffee and asked her to sit on the couch.

'Sounds serious,' Holly quipped, settling herself and running her hand over what was left of her hair, as if unconsciously seeking her curls, still surprised when her fingers found nothing to wind through.

'It is,' Aggie said.

Holly's eyes narrowed. 'Is it about the shop?'

'No, not at all. I wanted to show you something.'

Holly gulped down her coffee while Aggie fetched her laptop and returned with one of the articles open on the screen. She sat beside Holly on the couch and spun the laptop towards her. 'I found this online this morning.'

Holly squinted at the screen as she began to read, then her face fell, the colour draining from her cheeks. Her fingers went white around the handle of the coffee cup.

Aggie closed the laptop and placed it on the table beside the sofa. 'Is this true?'

Holly took in a shuddering breath and nodded.

'Tell me,' Aggie said. 'Tell me what happened.'

33

It was the second-last day of the school year and Holly felt light, with the California sun shining brightly over the expanse of green lawn outside her second-floor classroom, the well-tended flowerbeds showing off bright bursts of pink, yellow and white blooms. With all exams complete, her freshman English class was in high spirits and she'd given them a poetry slam competition to keep them occupied for the last couple of lessons of the year before summer break. It had been a raucous session, with much laughter, cheering, whistling and stamping. The deputy principal had walked past and cast a disapproving glance through the glass window in the door, but Holly had merely waved at her and called the next student to present his poem.

The bell rang, shrill and off-key, signalling the end of the class, and she and the kids applauded. Chairs scraped back across the floor and gangly teenage boys punched each other on the arm and loped out of the room. Several of the girls pulled out their cell phones and began elbowing their friends to share the latest news.

Holly waited for them to exit, then picked up her laptop bag and slung it over her shoulder, waiting for Gracie.

'Have you got any summer plans?' she asked the girl.

Gracie smiled, slipping her backpack onto her shoulders, leaving her hands free to use the crutches she needed to move around the school grounds. 'Mom and I are going to redecorate my room.'

Holly walked next to her. The hallway was full of students, moving like a river to their next classes, and Holly and Gracie stepped carefully into the flow. Metal locker doors clanged open and shut above the noise of the chatter. 'That sounds lovely. Have you decided on a theme?'

'Not yet,' Gracie said, pausing for a moment to push her glasses up her nose. 'I was thinking all black with diamantés to make a space theme. I'd love to be an astronaut. But Mom says I can't have black walls.'

'It must be peaceful to sleep in space,' Holly said.

'What about you?' Gracie asked. 'What are you doing?'

'Basically, as little as possible,' Holly said. 'There's a riverboat involved and . . .'

A sudden bang interrupted Holly's words and she stopped walking, confused, looking around. Others did the same. A second bang, closer this time, and time slowed. Through the throng of students she could see him, a huge man, a black ski mask, with an enormous automatic rifle in his hand, walking towards them.

Students scattered in all directions, some falling to the ground. Holly's ears were full of screaming and the deafening shots that rang out down the hallway, the sound bouncing off the hard surfaces of walls, floor and lockers, echoing till there was nothing but the sound. Time had stopped. The gunman used his rifle to shove a boy – Tyler, sophomore, basketball player, huge family – against a locker before shooting him in the chest. Blood spurted out in an arc. Tyler crumpled to the ground, hands flailing, grasping at emptiness.

Holly must have grabbed Gracie, because suddenly she found she was dragging the girl with her. The grey crutches fell from the girl's hands and tripped a purple-haired girl who was running away from the gunman.

He was shouting.

'On your knees! On your knees!'

The lights were extinguished, the hallway now dim, and the repeated, high-pitched shrill of the fire alarm began.

Breep. Breep. Breep.

Classroom doors slammed shut and blinds came down. Above the alarm, she could hear furniture scraping across the floors, students and teachers barricading doors. Up ahead, she caught sight of Nala's tight dark curls on the top of her head as she herded students into an open classroom.

'Nala.' She whispered her friend's name and wondered if she'd ever see her again.

Holly was at the stairwell now, still pulling Gracie beside her, half dragging her. 'This way!' She hiss-whispered it over and over, beckoning students down the stairwell, the green *Exit* sign taunting her with the safety it offered.

'Quickly. Hurry. Leave it. Come on now. Let's go.'

Under her arm, Gracie had begun to cry.

The gunman was still shooting . . . and the shots were getting closer.

Breep. Breep. Breep.

The students had gone quiet now, their lockdown training kicking in. A bizarre orderliness had broken through the initial panic. She wasn't sure where the students had dispersed to but the hallway was emptying. Hope spiked. They could do this.

One foot in front of the other.

Don't think about the bullets at your back.

Focus.

Focus.

She started down the stairs herself, Gracie still under her arm. She could hear the girl's teeth chattering as they stumbled. Some sort of smoke had filled the air. It filled her airways. At the landing, she turned to the left to continue down the second flight but instead found herself facing a number of students coming back up the stairs.

'There's a second shooter,' a girl said.

'Another two,' the boy beside her corrected. They pointed down the stairs, their eyes filled with terror.

Breep. Breep. Breep.

Holly's stomach plummeted. She could no longer feel her legs. She was nothing but roaring blood. Liquefied. There was a gunman above them and another two below. She, Gracie and the three students huddled together, backed into the corner of a landing in the stairwell with nowhere to run. One of the girls began to recite the Lord's Prayer. The smell of urine reached Holly's nostrils and she realised Gracie had wet herself.

In the hallway above, bright lights flashed through the smoky dimness with every shot. Then she heard a girl's voice, pleading.

'Let me in! Please, please, let me in!' she screamed, banging on a classroom door. It was coming from the direction in which Holly had seen Nala run. 'He's going to kill me,' the girl sobbed. 'Please, please, save me!' She was crying. Hysterical. Running from room to room now, banging on every door she could, and every door remained shut to her plea.

Holly placed her arms around the students on the landing, as far as she could reach, pulling them together, and they slid silently to the floor.

'Play dead,' she whispered. 'Don't move a muscle.'

They did as they were told, lying down at awkward angles, their bodies touching. The boy had half fallen on Holly's foot and sharp pain shot through her ankle but she dared not move. She willed her heart to slow down so she could control her breathing. She had to look like she was dead. No moving. Shallow breathing. Closed eyes.

Breep. Breep. Breep.

A scream. A round of bullets. The sound of a body falling to the floor. The pleading girl's voice was silenced. No more banging on doors.

Then he was in the stairwell.

Heavy boots descending, calmly, relentlessly.

Hunting them, one by one.

She was going to die here on this landing, right now, with her students in her arms.

•

Aggie took hold of Holly's shaking hands. 'I can't believe they did this to you.'

Holly inhaled a ragged breath.

'It was all fake?' Aggie asked, still unable to comprehend it.

'It was just an act,' Holly said, her voice conveying her disbelief, her sense of betrayal, her anger, her trauma.

'Why? Why did they do this?'

'Drills. We practise them regularly. Now they do active shooter drills too.'

'But . . . recruiting the drama students to act as victims and play dead?'

Holly nodded.

'Using fake blood? A gun with blank cartridges?'

'Yes. The more realistic the better, apparently. In some schools they've had students strapped to fake bombs, or lined up teachers, execution style, to be shot with rubber bullets. They say it's the only way for us to truly prepare for the real thing.'

'Oh, Holly. It *was* real to you. Your mind and body went through the same trauma as if that man had had real bullets, and as if those kids really were dying.' Aggie took a deep breath. 'Why didn't you tell me?'

Holly shook her head repeatedly, her eyes wide. 'How could I tell you when this scenario has always been your worst fear for me?'

Aggie got to her feet, pacing. Holly was right – her worry about school shootings was never far away, intensified every time one hit the news in Australia.

'You'd already lost one child,' Holly said.

Aggie ceased pacing and closed her eyes. It was true. After Cora's death, her desperation to get Holly home again had sometimes paralysed her. But she needed to be the parent here, the calming influence. 'I know this is hard for you to talk about, but I want you to know I'm here to help.'

'You can't,' Holly squeaked, scrubbing at her forehead now as though trying to erase the memories. 'Now I've been through that, I *do* know exactly what it will be like. The drills are supposed to empower us but all I feel is broken and terrified.' She wiped at the tears sliding down her face.

'Then why would you—' Aggie forced herself to stop, to not tell Holly she was insane to even consider returning to the school. Her daughter was an independent thinker and wouldn't tolerate being told what to do. With a concerted effort, though, she willed herself to find a place of reason. 'I can't even imagine what you went through. It must have been terrifying.'

Holly gulped noisily, looking up to the ceiling, avoiding Aggie's gaze.

'Have you had any counselling or seen a doctor?'

Holly shook her head. 'I just needed to get out of there and come home.'

'Is this why you didn't want to come into the underground church in Coober Pedy?'

Holly nodded. 'I'd been really anxious in the underground restaurant just before that. I felt trapped there, and it triggered flashbacks of being trapped on that landing, of having no way out.'

Aggie took the coffee cup from Holly and placed it on the table, then took her daughter's hand in her own. 'I'm sorry, Holly. I had no idea what you were going through.' She waited a beat, conjuring the best words she could find. 'I can understand why you didn't tell me. But if there's anything I've learnt from losing Cora, and having my life break apart, it's that we must keep talking to each other. No matter how difficult or impossible it feels.'

Holly looked at her with tear-filled eyes and nodded.

Aggie took a deep breath. 'You are a smart woman and I know you will make the decision that's right for you. I also know that you have a huge heart. I suspect, and correct me if I'm wrong, that the reason you feel you have to go back to the school is for your students. Is that right?'

Holly burst into tears. 'I held those students in my arms. Gracie has palsy and can't move quickly. I covered her body with mine. Do you know how many kids pulled out their phones to message their parents and say goodbye? Can you imagine being a parent and getting that message?' She looked at Aggie, aghast.

'No, I can't,' Aggie said.

'As bad as it is for me to go back there, I'm an adult. How much worse will it be for them? How frightened must they be? If they turn up on their first day of school and I'm not there . . .' She shook her head. 'How can I do that to them?'

Aggie held Holly, rocking her gently, then she spoke again. 'You are an exceptional teacher, Holly. But you have to help yourself before you can help anyone else. You have to put on your own oxygen mask before helping the kids.' Aggie could feel the dampness of Holly's tears on her shoulder.

'The truth is you can't stop the bullets. What you went through was a drill. How long will it be before you're doing it for real? You can't beat the system, Nala is right about that. It's too big for you to handle on your own.'

'But I'm the one they look to for guidance and protection. If I abandon them now, I'll be failing them.' She hung her head.

Aggie inhaled slowly, knowing that whatever she said next could make or break this conversation, could be the words that decided Holly's fate. 'Only you can make this decision. I know that if you take the time today to find some peace and tap into your inner wisdom, you'll know what to do. I will support you, whatever you decide. Please, just remember that your physical and mental health are important, that you don't have to get on that plane tomorrow if you don't want to, and . . .' Aggie took a shaky breath, 'I need you, too.'

Aggie barely managed to stop herself from telling Holly that she was certain she would never survive the loss of another daughter. Instead, she hugged Holly hard, then walked away on trembling legs, hoping with all she had that Holly would never go back there.

34

Myrtle's pink Mini puttered into Aggie's driveway early on Monday morning. She knew Aggie would be up, always an early riser, and especially today, when Holly was due to return to the States. The rain had stopped, though the sky was still bleak and the air cold and damp. Myrtle shuffled out of the driver's seat and closed the door, then walked to the house, leaning heavily on her stick. The front door swung open before she could knock. Aggie stood there in a zebra-print pyjama set, with a loose, pale pink cardigan over the top.

'Are you okay?' she asked, frowning at Myrtle. 'Come in, you look like you need a cuppa.'

'Thanks,' Myrtle said, trying for a jocular tone but hearing it fall flat, sliding into gratitude. She *would* like a cuppa.

Aggie moved towards the kitchen, her chocolate-brown slippers padding gently on the wooden floor. Inside, the house was warm, but not too warm, several oil heaters positioned through the home keeping the temperature comfortable.

'Why are you out and about so early?' Aggie asked, filling the kettle and setting it on to boil. 'Not that you're not welcome, you just look . . .' She trailed off, studying Myrtle's face. 'Has something happened?'

Myrtle let her heavy navy coat fall from her shoulders before laying it over the back of a chair. 'I wanted to come and say goodbye to Holly, of course.'

Aggie's eyes darted to the hallway. 'Her plane leaves this afternoon and I still don't know if she'll be getting on it.'

'Why, what's changed?'

'Long story. I'll fill you in later but she'll be happy you've come to see her off. She loves you so much,' Aggie said.

'I wouldn't miss saying goodbye, but I came for another reason. I haven't slept,' she admitted, blinking heavily.

'What, all night?'

'Most of it,' Myrtle admitted, lowering herself into the chair.

'Not sure I got much either. Coffee?'

'Double shot, thanks.'

Aggie turned off the kettle and went about filling the coffee basket and setting the espresso to drip through to the cups below.

'Is that the jam?' Myrtle asked, spying jars of preserves sitting on the shelf above the stove. 'This year's entries?'

Aggie looked up at them, as though she'd forgotten they were there. 'Yes. Strawberry, raspberry, mandarin marmalade, and peach, raspberry and champagne jam. They were made with a lot of love and a variety of musical accompaniments. I just hope I still get to enter. I haven't heard anything about the show being cancelled, but I'm not sure if the floodwaters will recede in time for me to drop off the jars tomorrow.' She took the cups from the coffee machine, poured milk into her own and delivered Myrtle's black.

'Thank you.'

Aggie took the seat opposite her great-aunt. 'So what's with all the sleeplessness? Did you miss the rocking of the train? I keep having moments where I'm sure I'm still on board. Like when you get off a boat but still feel as if you're at sea.'

'Yes, me too, but that wasn't it.' She blew on her coffee and sipped carefully. 'It was the shop keeping me up.'

Aggie winced.

Myrtle's eyes filled with tears. 'I'm so sorry, Aggie.' She reached across the table and clasped hold of Aggie's hand. 'I'm so sorry.'

'Shh, it's okay,' Aggie said, and her generosity of spirit only made Myrtle more emotional. She had to swallow hard to force back a wave of sentiment. 'It's as much my fault as yours,' Aggie said, shrugging in a resigned way. 'It was an accident,' she said, and sighed heavily. She let go of Myrtle's hand and reached for her coffee cup instead, holding it to her chest as though needing its warmth.

'An accident?' Myrtle repeated, incredulous. 'Dear girl, that may be true, but it is still unforgivable. I was supposed to be making your life better and instead I've . . . I've . . .' She couldn't even finish that. Had she ruined Aggie's future? It was quite possible that her business may not recover from this. 'I want you to know that I fully intend to pay for all the repairs,' she went on, lifting her chin now, determined. 'I won't abandon you.'

Aggie was shaking her head. 'No. It's too much and it's not fair.'

'Don't be daft. I will give you the money and you will take it. You have to salvage your business.'

'No, I won't accept it.'

'What is wrong with you? You don't have the money to fix this. You must at the very least take half, as I am at least half responsible.' Myrtle pulled out her tone of seniority.

Aggie fixed her eyes on Myrtle. 'No, I will not.'

Myrtle thumped the table. '*Why* not?

'Because you have been rescuing me since I was sixteen years old,' Aggie said, shaking her head slowly at her. 'You gave me and my daughter a home, a family to be a part of, a car, with a baby capsule already installed, cheap rent, childcare, a location and seed money when I decided to start my own business, a guarantee on a business loan, and you even changed your will to leave me your house. Myrtle, you've done enough.'

'Nonsense. This is what family does.' She felt her lip quiver. 'You couldn't possibly be more of a daughter to me.'

Aggie blinked back tears. 'I know.' She smiled at Myrtle and took her hand in both of her own, squeezing reassuringly. 'And you are my bonus mother and always will be.'

Myrtle nodded over the lump in her throat.

'But I need to stand on my own two feet. I need to show myself, my mother, Holly and the world that I can do this.'

Myrtle huffed then and rolled her eyes slightly. 'I've no idea where you get this stubbornness from.'

'I'm sure you've got some idea,' Aggie said, dryly, releasing Myrtle's hand once more. 'I cannot take your money.'

'But this is what love in action looks like,' Myrtle countered.

'Are you sure you and my mother come from the same family tree?'

Myrtle thought back to Valeria's mother, Dorothy – Myrtle's harried, dull-eyed sister. In every memory of her as an adult, there was a small baby or child somewhere nearby, pulling at her clothes, crying in her arms, needing something from her, and in not one memory could Myrtle ever remember Dorothy bestowing affection on Valeria.

'Your mother came from a different era. She did her best with you with what capacity she had.'

'But you were from that era too,' Aggie countered.

'But I got all the opportunities Valeria never did. Mine was an unusual life for the times. I studied. I built a career. I had independence, always.'

Aggie shrugged, not entirely convinced by this little speech, and fair enough. Valeria had been openly ashamed of Aggie's pregnancy. She'd asked Aggie to leave under the pretence of helping her grow up, of accepting her new role as a responsible adult, but it had been clear to see that she simply didn't want to absorb the shame into her life. She wanted distance from it. She wanted to make an example of her disapproval. The wounds she'd left on Aggie ran deep and would possibly never heal.

'All of that aside,' Myrtle said, 'I have the ability to help you with the cafe. There is no shame in accepting help.' Aggie's face still seemed resolutely set, so Myrtle tried once more. 'You may not want to accept my money because you want to show your mother that you can stand on your own two feet. But you have employees, young mothers who need secure jobs. If you want to help *them*, and their children, you'll need to get that shop back up and running as soon as possible.'

Aggie rubbed her forehead and exhaled. 'I know,' she said, a little petulantly. 'But I still want to do it on my own terms. I'll have to find a way.'

Myrtle nodded, knowing when to shut her mouth. She sipped her coffee and let the silence stretch.

'But thank you,' Aggie said. 'I'm grateful to you for all you've done and all you are still doing. I just wish you didn't have to bail me out,' she admitted, reluctantly. 'I would like for once to be someone who doesn't need rescuing.'

'Oh, Aggie, darling. Humans are the most messed-up animals on the planet. We all need rescuing. Even your mother.'

Aggie snapped her gaze to meet Myrtle's, as though this thought might never have occurred to her before.

'Please, take my offer and save yourself from your own stubbornness, then pay it forward if it makes you feel better.'

'How?'

'Oh, I don't know. Perhaps you could find a way to save Valeria from herself.'

Aggie huffed.

'What about Harry?' Myrtle asked, feeling stronger now, glad she'd come to sort this out this morning.

Aggie put a hand to her heart and gazed out the window at the rain that had begun to fall once more. 'He loves me,' she whispered, as though she didn't dare say it aloud.

Myrtle beamed. 'Of course he does – look at you.'

Aggie dropped her hand and turned back to Myrtle, laughing. 'Yeah, because I'm such a catch right now. My life's a shambles.'

Myrtle shook her head. 'Harry sees past all that. He sees into your heart. Why wouldn't he love you?'

Aggie's face sobered and her eyes drifted around the room as if trying to find an answer to that.

'Can I offer a piece of advice?'

'Since when do you ask first before offering advice?'

'Well, we can all change, even at my age,' Myrtle said, thinking of Dolce.

'Go on, then,' Aggie said, beckoning the words with a wave of her hand. 'Give it to me.'

'It's not your job to decide whether or not Harry should love you. That's up to him. If he says he loves you, then it's your job to believe him . . . and then decide if you love him too.'

•

Aggie and Myrtle had been talking for nearly an hour when Holly emerged. Her hair was a mess, her eyes red-rimmed with dark shadows beneath them. She wore pyjamas and was holding her phone to her chest.

Aggie looked up and locked eyes with her daughter. 'Well?' she said, unable to force herself to walk through pleasantries first.

Across the table, Myrtle considererd the two of them. 'What's going on?'

'I've been up all night,' Holly said.

'There's a bit of that going around,' Myrtle said.

'Have you talked to Nala?' Aggie asked, hoping Nala would have managed to talk sense into Holly.

Holly nodded. 'Yes. And she tracked down Gracie, the student I told you about, the one I dragged down the stairwell.'

'Gracious, Holly, why are you dragging students down stairwells?' Myrtle asked, bewildered.

Aggie waved a hand at her, shushing her. 'And?'

'Nala wanted to check in on her, and she told Gracie I was thinking about not coming back.'

'And?'

'Gracie told me not to come back, that she couldn't live with herself if I came back for her and it happened again . . . or worse.'

'If *what* happened?' Myrtle said, clearly annoyed now.

'She told Nala to tell me that the right thing to do was to stay in Australia and help kids here, and that she and her parents had decided to try home schooling. They're moving on.' Holly shrugged and let out a noise that was half a sob and half a laugh. 'So I'm thinking that maybe I should too,' she said. Her face split into a slightly stunned but tentative grin.

'How do you feel?'

'Mostly, I'm relieved.'

Aggie stood and grabbed her in a bear hug. 'Me too.'

35

It had stopped raining. It felt as though Holly's decision to stay had changed the direction of fate, and Aggie shouldered open Strawberry Sonnet's door buoyed with renewed strength. She stepped into the cafe and shoved the swollen door closed behind her with her hip. Now she felt ready to tackle the shop. The first thing that had to be fixed was the guttering. She sat at the long table with her phone and a notepad and called thirteen numbers to find a handyman who could come and fix it today.

'It won't be matching, *noo*,' he said, in a thick Scottish accent. 'A different colour but it'll do the job, is that all right?'

'It can be rainbow unicorn sparkles as far as I'm concerned, as long as it holds water,' she assured him.

She was mopping the floor when Savannah heaved open the door around lunchtime, her baby on her hip. The infant wore a pink jacket and a bonnet on her still largely hairless head, and her chunky legs were wrapped around Savannah's waist.

'Hello,' Aggie called, resting her mop against the end of the table. Puffing slightly, she went to greet them. 'Hello, gorgeous girl,' she crooned, offering her hand to the baby, who clutched it strongly in her fat fingers and grinned behind the dummy in her mouth.

Savannah looked around, her face twisted with regret. 'What can I do to help?'

Aggie assessed the shop. 'Well, the good news is I found someone to come and put up some guttering today, so that will stop any more water coming down the walls.'

'Great,' Savannah said, sounding relieved. 'I'm so sorry, Aggie. This is all my fault.'

Aggie wrapped both Savannah and the baby in a hug. 'No, it's not. You were trying to help. It was an accident. Accidents happen every day to good people, with no rhyme or reason.' She released them and Savannah nodded, though she didn't seem convinced.

'The insurance will cover it, won't it?' her assistant asked, desperate for consolation.

Aggie took a deep breath. What good would it do to tell Savannah the truth and burden her with more guilt? Besides, it was Aggie and Myrtle's fault there was no insurance. She gave Savannah a fortifying smile. 'Everything will be absolutely fine,' she said.

Savannah nodded but still looked anxious, and Aggie was fairly certain she was concerned about her income, and who could blame her. The brief optimism Aggie had enjoyed earlier popped like a gigantic balloon. It hurt to have to deliver this news, but it was only fair to let Savannah know as soon as possible.

'Listen, repairs for this kind of damage usually take a long time to sort out,' she began. The young woman lifted her chin, anticipating what was coming. 'I'm sorry to say that I won't have any work for you in the foreseeable future.' She paused, allowing Savannah a moment to process this. 'It might be a good idea to contact Centrelink today and see if they can help you with extra payments or finding a new job as quickly as possible.'

'Oh . . . okay,' Savannah said, and cast a worried glance at her daughter.

'I'm going to get this place up and running as fast as I can. If you're still looking for work when the cafe's back in action, there'll be a job here for you. In the meantime, if you need anything, I want you to know you can ask me, okay?'

'Okay.' Savannah smiled and hugged Aggie gratefully, though Aggie knew she wouldn't ask for help. Like Aggie, she wanted to prove to the world that she could make it on her own. Even so, Aggie knew that young mums benefited from having someone nearby, watching from the wings, ready to assist if they were needed.

The Scotsman was up on a ladder fixing the gutters when Gideon arrived around lunchtime, carrying a brown paper bag that emitted an amazing aroma.

'Is that . . . Indian?' she asked, sniffing the air and putting down her phone.

Gideon smiled. 'Lamb biryani, yellow dhal, pappadums, garlic cheese naan, and raita.'

'I hadn't even realised I was hungry till just now. You're a gem.'

'I figured you'd be here today. Things are under control at the vineyard and I thought I might be able to help.'

'Oh, stop, you had me at "biryani",' she said, making gooey eyes at the bag of food. 'I'll get some plates.' When she returned, Gideon was seated, pulling lids from containers, and her belly flipped, but not from hunger. She still hadn't given him an answer about the embryos, and she knew, as much as he would genuinely want to help her right now, he was here hoping for her decision.

He looked up as she approached the table. 'What have you been doing this morning so far?'

'Oh, man. Let me fill you in on Holly first.' She told him everything and he listened while he served the food.

Like her, he was horrified at what they'd put her through. 'I'm so glad she decided to stay,' he said, exhaling with relief.

'You and me both,' she said, suddenly feeling fragile, now the shock was wearing off.

After a moment's silence, Gideon tilted his head towards the entrance to the shop, where noisy bangs and metallic thumps abounded. 'What's happening there?'

'That's Gerard, the handyman, installing fluorescent-pink guttering. Don't worry, it's temporary,' she rushed to assure him. 'When you arrived, I was looking online for a door. I asked him if he might be able to hang a new one for me today.'

'What did he say?'

'He said, "Well, I'm no carpenter, but I 'ave a few skills if you're desperate."'

Gideon shook his head at her appalling Scottish accent. 'What did you say?'

'I said I was very, very desperate,' she said, demonstrating with her hands clasped together, pleading. 'But then he looked at the door and said that it needed a new architrave as well. And then we looked at the walls, and they need new plaster sheeting, and the windows need new architraves, and he said it was all too much.' She sighed, reaching for the plate that Gideon had heaped with food, finally able to eat now she'd finished talking.

'So what are you going to do?' he asked, following suit and loading his fork with biryani.

Aggie took a mouthful of the food and closed her eyes with pleasure. It was warm and spicy and utterly perfect for this weather. 'That is so good,' she muttered, then rested her fork on the plate. 'Well, since I can't even lock the front door right now, he suggested I get some wood and nail it shut, and use the back door in the kitchen instead until I can get the front door replaced. If I drive over to Gawler this afternoon and pick up some wood, he'll board it up for me.'

Gideon reached down beside him and rustled the paper bag again. 'Maybe this will help.' He lifted up a bottle of red wine, one bearing his vineyard's label. One she knew he'd made. One she knew was really good.

'It most certainly would,' she said, and hopped up to fetch wineglasses from the kitchen. She returned to the table and Gideon poured a glass for each of them, and if it weren't for the scraping and squeaking of metal on metal outside, and the fact they were sitting in shadow because she was too afraid to turn on the electricity, this could almost have been romantic. She took a large gulp, enjoying feeling the warmth slide down her throat, enjoying being taken care of. Remembering the many, many ways Gideon had taken care of her over the years.

Their shared love of food had always been one of their love languages. As she spent her days preparing food in the cafe, she rarely ever felt like cooking dinner. But Gideon had happily cooked for her almost every night. He loved experimenting with cuisines from all over the world and could usually perfect a dish after just a couple of attempts. He knew exactly how she liked her coffee, that coconut made her feel sick, and precisely which white fish she liked and which ones were 'too fishy'. He knew she loved getting the first quinces of the season – just like her mother – and would bring her a box the moment he saw them appear at the farmers' market.

But he showed her love in more ways than that, of course. He noticed when the head of her electric toothbrush needed changing and did it for her, most of the time without her even knowing he'd done it. If it was bitterly cold or raining, he took Banjo out for a walk, or put the bins out or went to the postbox so she didn't have to.

He showed her love by responding with patience and kindness to the savage hormonal mood swings that came with IVF. When she needed a day in bed to hide from the world, he brought her tea and crumpets and let her be, let her sob her heart out alone, just as she wanted to, and never tried to make her speak the unutterable thoughts of despair that ran through her mind. He was a good, good man. She'd loved him and he'd loved her. But it hadn't been enough to save them.

'What happened to us?' she asked now, twirling the wineglass stem in her fingers.

The deeply weathered lines around Gideon's eyes deepened. He looked at her for a long moment. 'We got lost at sea,' he said, his voice slightly gravelly. 'Then we got marooned on separate islands, with no raft to paddle back to each other, and there we stayed.'

Aggie felt a lump of emotion rise in her throat. 'And where are we now?'

Gideon swirled his wine in his glass and held it to his nose, inhaling the aroma, thinking. 'Maybe we have finally been reunited.'

Was that true? She glanced up at *Sonnet 116* in its frame on the wall, water-stained but still hanging. Shakespeare had written that love *looks on tempests and is never shaken*. But she and Gideon *had* been shaken, and they had got lost. Was it possible that this was their moment to get it right this time? To be not shaken but see the storm through to the end?

'The idea of another round . . .' she began.

'It scares me too.'

'What if we get shipwrecked again?' she whispered.

'But what if we make it to the other side, safe and sound?'

Back at home that evening, tucked up on her couch with one of Dolce's soft crocheted blankets over her legs, Aggie found herself opening Instagram and searching for Harry's profile, partly as a way of avoiding what she knew she really needed to do tonight. The idea of seeing Harry's face was a far more enjoyable option. On the coffee table at her side she had a warm cup of her very own creation of hot chocolate laced with Baileys Irish Cream and muddled with raspberry jam. It was like drinking a chocolate-coated raspberry marshmallow.

She smiled the moment she saw his profile picture, different now from when she'd first seen it. It was no longer just of half his face, but a full image from his shoulders up, smiling – beaming, really. It was one she'd snapped of him at Uluru as he played the ukulele and sang that gorgeous song. The song he'd sung to her while she'd cheered him on. The song he'd sung on the best day she could ever remember having – and that included many great days with Gideon.

She remembered staring at him as he hunched in the red dirt, running his fingers through it. The way the sight of him had made the whole world fall away. Remembered him reaching for her hand. Their long and effortless conversations about dreams and courage. Dancing and singing with him that night under the stars. Laughing till her cheeks ached. His mouth on hers. That last night on the train. She reached for the drink beside her, swallowing a large mouthful.

He'd posted several photos from the trip too, including one Holly had taken of them both, huddled together for warmth under the gum tree at Telegraph Station after their day in the desert. They radiated happiness. His caption read, *Life is full of the greatest days.*

'It is,' she said out loud to her phone, out loud to him. She wanted to write a comment to tell him how much she'd loved that day, about how much she wished things were different right now, about how much she wished he'd come back with her. That she wanted to while away hours talking with him about how simultaneously difficult and wonderful it was just to be alive in this world.

Harry had been through so much in his life that he'd matured well beyond his years, and he had turned his pain into action, facing the darkness instead of running from it, converting it into kindness, towards himself and others. He was amazing. She wanted to tell him how much she *missed* him. In such a short time, he'd imprinted on her, or she'd imprinted on him, one or the other. Maybe they'd imprinted on each other.

But she didn't know how to put any of that into words. Everything seemed too small for the magnitude of her feelings and thoughts. In the end, she simply liked his photo and closed the app. She couldn't be distracted when she had such a pressing task in front of her. She needed to make one of the biggest decisions of her life.

She reached for her hot chocolate and its sweetness comforted her as she researched, yet again, the options for dealing with the embryos. She read other women's experiences of making the decision, their accounts of the outcomes of those decisions and all the feelings that went with them – guilt, grief, regret, hope, relief, the breakdown of relationships and the renewal of ones previously written off. She wasn't alone in this. She was not the only woman to be in this situation. Although reading these women's accounts didn't give her the answer to her own predicament, it did make her feel less alone.

36

Jam delivery day arrived with a burst of blue sky. The roads to the showgrounds were clear, though washed-up debris, fallen trees, flooded fields and large potholes spoke of the battering the valley had received. Valeria had more than an hour to think on the drive into the city and most of it was spent debating the value of entering her many preserves, which were currently sitting upright in a wicker basket on the passenger seat. There were enough to ensure she'd be in the running for the purple championship ribbon. Occasionally, she lifted her left hand from the steering wheel and reached over and touched them, fondly.

Her mind was in knots. Why would she go ahead and enter her preserves this year when it was, in theory, Agatha's turn to enter, and when her relationship with her daughter was at an obvious low? Was it simply because she was stubborn?

There was that word again – *stubborn*. She was about to argue aloud to the jam jars that she was not stubborn, merely consistent. But before she could get the words out she realised that she *wasn't* being consistent because entering her jam this year, openly ignoring that Agatha had declared entry first, was worse than stubborn; it was selfish.

And yet she still wanted to enter, perhaps especially so now that both Agatha and Rupert had walked away from her. She wanted to win this competition. She would happily hand over the prize money to Agatha, who clearly needed it, with all the repairs she'd have to do. But the chance to cook with Maggie Beer was too much to give up. It was too much for anyone to ask of Valeria. Blinking back tears that threatened to obscure her view through the windscreen, she had the quite horrible thought that she had ruined everything and that this jam sitting beside her was the only thing she had left.

•

Aggie manoeuvred her car around a large eucalyptus branch that covered half the road, as a cheery volunteer in a high-vis vest waved her on while holding up a stop sign to the oncoming traffic. The Barossa Valley volunteer army was out in force, goodwill and community spirit taking the form of a fence-repair squadron, out and about restoring stock fences that had been taken down by floodwaters, a team of female drovers on horseback, rounding up wandering sheep, cattle and horses, and a collective of volunteer wildlife carers rescuing wallabies, wombats and echidnas from rooftops and treetops. Farmers with chainsaws traversed the valley cutting away fallen trees to clear streets and driveways. Community halls were full of donated goods and food staples, waiting to be distributed.

Aggie drove carefully, waving to volunteers as she passed, proud to be part of such a generous community. Beside her, Myrtle held the box of Aggie's jams on her lap.

'Have you spoken to Harry yet?' she asked, suddenly.

'Not yet.'

'I like Harry,' chimed in Holly from the back seat. 'Are you sure you can't figure things out with him?'

Aggie didn't answer, instead accelerating along the highway as the path was once again clear. They drove on in silence for a few moments, Aggie's mood lifting the closer they got to the cookery pavilion. She was happy to be here with two of her favourite people in the world, though she had to confess she was nervous. While she did want to win, the reality was that the prize money would be a drop in the ocean compared to what she would need to get the cafe up and running again, and the television spot with Maggie Beer would probably be useless if she had no business that could benefit from the exposure. But in spite of that, she still wanted to win because it was something familiar, something she was good at, and a beacon of hope – a sign that she could rise again. She felt as nervous and excited as she'd been the very first time she'd entered her jam in an adult division.

Lost in her reverie, imagining the winning ribbons, Aggie was jolted back to reality by the sound of Myrtle's voice. 'Sorry, what?'

'I said I thought I saw Gideon's ute parked outside the cafe yesterday,' Myrtle repeated.

Aggie shook her head. She couldn't get anything past Myrtle. 'Yes, it was.' Her passengers remained silent, waiting for her to continue, so at last she forced herself to take a breath and explain. 'Gideon wants to use the embryos for one last IVF cycle.' She was surprised how good it felt to get that weight off her chest and share it.

'What?' Holly squeaked from the back seat. 'When did this happen?'

'Yesterday, over lunch. He brought me Indian food.'

'And?' Myrtle prompted.

'The dhal was amazing,' Aggie said.

'Stop it,' Myrtle chastised her. 'What about the embryos?'

'It's complicated,' Aggie said, the greatest understatement of her life. Silence yawned in the car as the others waited for her to go on. She tried to speak but found herself empty of words.

At last, Myrtle began again. 'You do remember that he left you, don't you?'

Aggie frowned, trying to decipher this. 'What do you mean? We broke up because we couldn't go on, because I was too consumed with grief and couldn't function anymore, because I withdrew from him until he didn't have a choice.'

Myrtle shook her head. 'That's not true. He had a choice, and he chose to bail.'

'But I . . .' Aggie was truly confused. She'd always blamed herself, believed that she'd pushed him away. Sometimes she even remembered telling him to leave, but now, with a clearer head than she'd had a year ago, she wondered if that was even true or if it was something she'd convinced herself had happened.

In her mind, Gideon had been a hero left with no choice but to walk away in order to save himself. Was it possible she had that wrong, that she'd imagined the ending to dampen the reality of what had really happened? It was an uncomfortable notion, yet something about it shifted the lens of remembrance a few degrees till it actually began to look different in her memory.

Holly broke the silence. 'I know there must be a thousand different reasons that would make this a complicated decision,' she said, carefully. 'But can I ask a question?'

'Of course,' Aggie said, pushing away the disquieting reconfiguring of her history with Gideon.

Holly inched forward on her seat so she was closer to Aggie's and Myrtle's shoulders. Aggie cast her a quick, inquiring glance in the rear-view mirror. Holly had been to the hairdresser early this morning and had her hair tidied into an even all-over crop so that now she looked pretty cool, Aggie thought. Like a musician or an artist.

'Is Harry one of the reasons it's complicated?' Holly asked.

Myrtle clapped her hands together. 'Oh, please say yes.' Holly mock-slapped her lightly on the shoulder. 'What? I'm only saying what we all want to hear.'

'Fair point,' Holly agreed.

Aggie didn't even know where to begin to answer that. Harry's Instagram image of the two of them, arms wrapped around each other at Telegraph Station, flashed in her mind. Even now, with some time and distance between them, with all of her available emotional energy being channelled into saving her shop and wrestling with the idea of another round of IVF, there was still a flame of hope when she thought about Harry. But it was all impossible, wasn't it? The man was on the other side of the country. He was ten years younger than her. They had a bond, of that she was sure. But was that enough? Enough to upend your life? Enough on which to base an enormous decision such as whether or not to try *just one last time* for a baby?

'I . . .' She began but then trailed off.

'Yes?' Myrtle prompted.

'I don't know what to say,' Aggie admitted. Beside her, Myrtle turned to look at Holly. Aggie watched in the rear-view mirror as Holly met Myrtle's gaze, then turned her eyes to meet Aggie's, giving her a small encouraging smile. Aggie concentrated as they passed a couple of escaped cows grazing on the side of the road.

Myrtle resettled herself, facing forward once more, and spoke. 'Let me put it this way, then. If you hadn't met Harry, if you didn't know he existed, if he was nowhere on your radar, would you be trying again with Gideon?'

Aggie gave Myrtle a quick sideways glance, then looked back at the road. She hadn't actually considered it like that. Her emotional landscape seemed to shift into focus as she imagined removing Harry from the equation. She knew she had feelings for him, but she hadn't fully realised just how much room he had been occupying in her heart.

'The problem is,' she began, stumbling over the words, 'I'm not sure I know how to trust myself anymore.'

'Well, that *is* a pickle of a doozy,' Myrtle agreed, and patted Aggie's knee in support. The three of them were quiet for the rest of the drive, Aggie afraid to open her mouth in case she spoke the words that scared her the most.

She wanted a chance with Harry. Moreover, she might not trust herself, but she knew she could trust him.

37

The cookery pavilion was heaving with contestants. This was the largest group of entrants Valeria had ever seen. For a moment, she was surprised by this, as she'd been expecting the disruption of the flooding to have prevented some people from entering, but then she found herself smiling. Cookery competitors were made of steel. Looming high on a vertical banner behind the officials' table was the biggest motivating force of all: Maggie Beer's smiling face beaming down on them all. Her grey hair was a mark of her experience, the large, colourful beads hanging around her neck a sign of her perfect taste. These contestants were like moths drawn to her vibrant, glowing flame. Valeria felt a flutter of nerves in her belly and clutched her basket tighter still. She'd won the purple championship ribbon before, but none had ever meant so much as this one would.

She joined the long, slow-moving line of show hopefuls inching their way towards the officials' table. She craned her neck to see if she recognised anyone and immediately caught sight of

Margaret Beetle with a box under her left arm, a handbag hanging from her shoulder and a walking stick in her right hand. She was chatting and peering at others' jars. There were obviously a number of first-time entrants about, young women dressed in heels and full hair and make-up, as if they thought they might be caught on camera for some sort of footage that might be used later in Maggie's show. The idea made Valeria take in a sharp breath and appraise the competition nervously. Perhaps they were right. Perhaps that was exactly what would happen. She'd seen episodes of *The Voice*. They always showed all those deluded singers milling about at auditions.

She raised a hand and patted her hair self-consciously. Naturally, she looked respectable. She wouldn't have left the house any other way. But if there were cameras about, that was another matter. She peered around surreptitiously. The last thing she needed was to be seen trying to be seen, or trying *not* to be seen. She allowed herself ten full seconds of this ridiculous behaviour before she forced her eyes back to the front, just in time to see him walking in her direction.

'Rupert?' She spoke the word in surprise. Of course she'd known he'd registered for the competition, and today was the delivery day, but he'd been about to walk straight past her on his way to the back of the queue.

He looked down at her hand on his elbow. She took it away, not having remembered deciding to reach out and catch him.

'Valeria,' he said, and the coldness in his tone pierced her heart.

She pressed her fingers to her lips for a moment, then rallied, forcing herself to smile, her tone ebullient. 'How lovely to see you. Did you get through the roads okay?' She immediately regretted such a banal comment. Obviously he'd got through the roads okay or he wouldn't be here.

He didn't respond straightaway, and in that moment she took in his appearance. He wore a pressed business suit, his white hair brilliant in the sunshine above the smoky grey fabric.

'I stayed in the city last night,' he said, his eyes lacking their usual warmth and affection. 'I'm cutting short my stay in the Barossa and heading back to Queensland this afternoon.' He lifted his Ghan-branded canvas tote a fraction. 'But I had the preserves here with me so I thought I might as well deliver them.'

Valeria felt her heart rate kick up a notch. 'So you won't be here on Friday to see if you've won,' she said. She didn't want him to leave, and she most certainly didn't want him to leave because of her. All the time they'd spent together on the Ghan, she'd been preoccupied: with Agatha, with Myrtle, with her anxieties and her determination to make Rupert *work* for her affection. But why should he have to work for it? And then, the moment he asked *her* to work for *his* affection, she couldn't do the one thing he needed – accept his daughter.

Why couldn't she simply give him her support, accept that life was messy and he was here now in front of her, wanting a relationship, and that *she* was the one ruining it all, not him. Why couldn't she simply say what she wanted to say? *Please don't go. Stay with me. We'll work it out.* There – she'd said it in her head. *Now just say it out loud, Valeria, for goodness sake!* But the words lodged thickly in her throat, like she'd tried to swallow cardboard, which would now budge neither up nor down, instead holding fast, choking her slowly.

Rupert was staring at her, waiting for her to speak, his beautiful, sad eyes imploring her to give him something, anything, to go on with.

'Well,' he said at last, his voice croaky. 'If I do win, I'm sure they'll post me the ribbons. Good luck with your entry, Valeria.' He nodded and continued on his way to the back of the line.

'You too,' she whispered, watching his shoulders slump as he left. Then she hit herself on the forehead, an open-handed slap. 'You stupid old fool.'

•

Aggie directed Myrtle and Holly to the nearby cafe to order them all some lunch while she popped over to the cookery pavilion to submit her entries. Her palms were sweating, just a little. No matter how many times she had done this, she always felt nervous. She loved the process of entering competitions – the focus, the constant challenge to improve or overcome challenges. Some years, she'd been forced to work with less-than-ideal fruit, when a jam queen knew you should only ever use the best fruit. Quite an irony, really, given that jam was likely invented as a way to make use of and preserve substandard fruit. One year she'd been relying on a sugar thermometer but had dropped it, and it smashed. She'd had to rely on her instincts alone to know if the jam was set or not. Another year, she'd had to decide if it was worth submitting the absolutely perfect jam she'd made months ago, but which had been sitting on the shelf for a fraction too long, resulting in the colour fading, which she knew would cause it to lose marks, or to start again with a new batch. No two batches were ever the same. The strengths and weaknesses were different each time. One was the perfect colour but didn't taste fruity enough. One had the perfect sugar–lemon balance, but the seeds had arranged themselves awkwardly in the jar. One seemed perfect except for jam splashes at the rim, and in a fierce contest a single lost point could be the difference between first and second place. A jam competition was a living thing. She could control many variables but never all of them, and that was what made it exciting.

She paused, searching for the end of the line. Goodness, it was long and had swayed out to the left, beginning to curl around itself. Perhaps she should message Holly and tell her and Myrtle not to wait for her for lunch. She stepped up to take her place at the same time as Rupert did.

'Rupert, hi,' she said, giving him a big smile. 'It's lovely to see you.'

'Morning, Aggie,' he said, offering a smile that didn't quite reach his eyes.

'Dropping off your jam?' she asked.

He gazed down at the Ghan bag. 'Ah, yes. I'm leaving for Queensland this afternoon, so I was hoping to make a flying dash here, but . . .' He gazed at the long line ahead.

'I thought you were here for a few weeks,' she said, puzzled. 'Is something wrong?'

'Er . . .' He mumbled over a few words before saying, 'No, no, everything's fine, but I think maybe I should skip the jam. I really don't have time to wait.'

'I'm happy to drop it in for you,' she said, holding out her hand. 'It's no problem, so long as you've got all the paperwork ready to go.'

'Yes, it's all here,' he said.

Aggie studied him. He looked pale, the lines on his face deeper. His cheeks, usually rosy, looked slack. Aggie gazed around. 'Have you spoken to Mum recently?'

'Yes.'

'Does she know you're leaving?'

'She does.'

There was an awkward silence, Aggie's hand still hovering in space, waiting for his bag, Rupert looking down at the ground, seemingly unsure whether to pass it over or not. Aggie dropped her hand and said, gently, 'What's happened? Why are you leaving so soon?'

His chin quivered with unspoken thoughts, then he regained his composure and gave her a reassuring smile. 'It's been so lovely getting to know you and spend time with you on the Ghan. It's a trip I won't forget, that's for sure. Unfortunately, this is the end of the line for Valeria and me.' He passed her the bag of preserves. It was heavy, the glass bottles clunking together as she took it.

'Oh, I'm sorry to hear that,' she said.

'Thank you for delivering those for me. I do need to get going. I hope you manage to get your cafe back up on its feet as quickly as possible.' He placed a fatherly hand at her elbow, giving it a supportive squeeze, then turned on his heel and walked away with straight shoulders and his head held high.

She watched him walk, baffled by the conversation, wondering what could have happened between her mother and Rupert. They'd seemed so good together. Despite her anger at Valeria's deliberate sabotage of her and Harry, she did feel sympathetic to her mother's loss.

As she was contemplating this, the most surprising thing happened. She saw her mother exiting the pavilion, carrying a note of receipt for entries in her hand, the paper flapping in the breeze as she walked. Aggie stared at her as she strode away without a backwards glance. Despite this being Aggie's year to enter uncontested by either Valeria or Myrtle – a year that happened to have the highest stakes ever on offer – her mother had gone ahead and pitted herself against Aggie anyway. She watched her for as long as she could keep her in her sight, stupefied by what she was seeing. This was *not* the done thing. How could she do this to Aggie when she knew how badly she needed this win for her business? She wondered, briefly, if it was possible she had been adopted. Then her thoughts became more serious. She considered whether it had ever been worth trying to fix things between herself and her mother, or if their relationship was an entirely lost cause.

38

Aggie finished her early morning coffee with a final glance at Harry's face on the camera reel on her phone, then closed the app. She'd allowed herself precisely fifteen minutes to moon over Harry, and that time was up. She had to get on with sorting out her life, starting with the shop. Even though her pride was screaming at her that under no circumstances should she accept money from Myrtle, she couldn't ignore her great-aunt's advice. If she wanted to maintain her role as an employer of young women who needed a leg-up, then she couldn't waste any time getting the cafe back to working order. She texted Myrtle.

I've been thinking about your offer to help with the shop. I can't let my ego get in the way of being able to provide work for other people. I would like to accept your financial assistance with the repairs, but I insist we go halves in the costs, if you are willing to give me a loan for my half. I want it written out with an agreement on instalments for me to repay. No charity, all business. Okay? x

Myrtle, always an early riser, took only minutes to respond.

Of course, my girl. Whatever you need. X

Aggie smiled, and sent Myrtle a cute gif of Tigger hugging Eeyore, with a caption saying *You're the Best*, to which Myrtle replied with a gif of a woman in a red-and-orange work uniform saying *You are the only person in the entire world I'm not sick of*, which made Aggie laugh.

With the beginning of an action plan for the cafe in place, she messaged Holly next; she was still asleep, but Aggie knew she'd check her phone as soon as she woke up.

Just a reminder to book a doctor's appointment for a referral to a psychologist. Love you. x

Last was the biggest thing on her list: Gideon and the embryos. Inhaling deeply and working up her courage, she texted him.

Hey, I'm making jam drops today and I know how much you love them. Thought I'd bring some around and we could talk?

His reply was instant.

Come over whenever you like.

She turned her efforts then to the jam drops, baking being the one thing guaranteed to soothe her in this moment. With a high-pitched whir, the hand-beaters ploughed through butter and sugar, then egg and vanilla and flour, quickly resulting in a smooth, comforting dough. With her fingers coated in icing mixture, instead of flour, she rolled out small balls and placed them onto two baking trays, with a generous distance between each one to ensure they had enough space to spread out. She pressed her thumb into each ball, creating little doughy belly buttons, then spooned in her reddish-indigo blueberry and apple jam. It was Gideon's favourite. Her heart hammered, thinking of the conversation they needed to have, and a tremor ran all the way down to the spoon as she eased the jam into each biscuit.

She arrived at Gideon's place in time for morning tea. Since their separation, he'd been renting a two-bedroom brick home with carpet that needed replacing but with dozens of rose bushes lining the garden's perimeter, whose cheerful colours made up for the threadbare floor covering inside. Gideon's muddy workboots were on the landing and Banjo barked from behind the heavy front door as she approached.

'Banjo!' she called, 'It's me.'

The dog whined and scratched, eager to greet her.

Gideon opened the door and Banjo barrelled out. Aggie tucked her container of biscuits under her left arm and bent towards him, patting him as he twirled in circles, yipping and whining with excitement.

'Hi! Here, take these,' she said, grinning with delight and passing the container to Gideon. She bent over to hug Banjo properly while his tail whipped in circles. With some effort, she managed to get inside the house and fall onto the blue couch in the lounge room, whereupon Banjo leapt up beside her and threw himself into her lap, getting one perfectly aimed wet kiss on her lips.

'Argh!' she squealed, wiping her mouth, but laughing with joy. 'I've missed you too,' she said, managing to calm him enough that he lay on the couch with his shoulders and head in her lap, panting heavily from exertion. 'Good boy,' she said, stroking him slowly. 'I love you too.' She bent and kissed his furry head.

Gideon returned from the kitchen and smiled at them on the couch. 'I've put the kettle on.' Then he moved to the pot-belly stove and started building a pile of wood and paper, leaving her to continue her reunion with Banjo while he lit it. Gideon was a better fire-lighter than she'd ever been, and the pile of kindling and paper quickly burst to life. He closed the door to the stove while he waited for it to settle enough for a log.

'How are things at the vineyard?' she asked.

'Not too bad. The water has drained quickly. I think we might have lost a couple of rows but I'm hopeful for most of them – as long as the rain stays away for a while, anyway.'

'That's good.'

He sat on the armchair to her left and crossed his legs, resting an ankle on the opposite knee. He wore slippers, his ankles bare below his jeans.

She smiled at him. 'I've missed this guy so much,' she said, nodding at Banjo, who was lolling his tongue happily and panting slowly while she ran her fingers through his silky red hair.

'The feeling appears to be mutual.'

'Do you think . . . I know we decided it would be better for Banjo to live with you, because he loves being with you at the vineyard, but I've been wondering if we could organise shared care.'

Gideon's nose twitched. 'You mean co-parenting, like he's a child?'

She smiled. 'Yep. Just like that. Maybe he could come and stay with me some weekends.'

Gideon rubbed a hand across his unshaven face and didn't speak for several moments. She resisted the urge to plead her case, reminding herself that Gideon was a considered processor and that he'd need to examine this idea from many angles. He got up and added a log to the fire, taking his time to poke and rearrange the kindling, then straightened, hands on hips. He studied Banjo's obviously blissful expression in her lap. 'I suppose that would be okay.'

'Really?' She was so excited she almost squealed.

'He was always ours,' he said, reasonably. 'And he clearly misses you.'

Tears sprang in her eyes and she bent down to place her face against Banjo's cheek for a moment. 'Thank you,' she whispered, breathing in the scent of his shampooed coat.

Gideon cleared his throat. 'I'll make you a coffee.'

Upon his return, he placed a steaming mug on the table in front of her and a plate of the jam drops, telling Banjo a firm 'No' when the dog made eyes at it, then sat down in the armchair with his mug of green tea in one hand and a jam drop in the other.

'Mmm,' he murmured, appreciatively. 'My favourite.'

'I remembered,' she said.

She reached for her coffee while negotiating Banjo's weight, as he was clearly unwilling to remove himself from her lap, and took a sip. 'Good coffee, thanks.'

She swallowed another mouthful and then reminded herself why she was here, replacing the mug on the coffee table. 'We need to talk.'

'I'm guessing you don't want to go ahead with one more round of IVF,' he said, catching her by surprise.

'W— Why do you say that?'

He nodded towards Banjo. 'Because you wanted to sort out co-parenting for the dog. I assume that means we won't be together.' His bluntness winded her and relieved her in equal measure. She was glad he'd got straight to the point.

'Well, I . . . If we *did* do another round, the embryos might not take, and then we wouldn't be together anyway . . . would we?' she asked, suddenly confused.

'Would you like us to be together?'

'Would *you*? Gideon, I need to know how much of this is about me, and how much of it is about the idea of another baby.'

He took a moment to gather his words. 'It's true that the renewal is the reason we've come back into each other's lives. Since then it's been obvious to me that we still have a strong connection, but I admit it is difficult to separate the two things.'

'How can I know you won't run back to your island if we hit rough seas again?'

He gave the question real thought, then admitted, 'I guess you can't.'

She opened her mouth to speak, then closed it again and returned to stroking Banjo's ear, fixing her gaze on the dog. After a while, she took a deep breath and spoke. 'It's no use if I wade through all the options intellectually, because I can argue myself into and out of any scenario. I *can* imagine you and I together again, and I *can* imagine trying just one more time. That notion is *so close* to being right that it's very hard to ignore.'

She saw him swallow, digesting her words.

'But now is the time to trust myself.'

'What are you saying?'

'For a while there, I felt as if I owed you this, that I was the failure in our relationship—'

He shook his head, pained by the suggestion. 'That's not true.'

She continued, this time more gently. 'There was so much that was good about us that I felt that I should give it a go, for you. But I know that I can't go back there. I can't go back to being lost alone at sea.'

She waited for him to promise that he wouldn't leave her adrift, but he didn't, and she knew right then that she could never trust him with her heart again. He moved to the couch to sit beside her and took her hand in both of his, holding it tightly as she spoke.

'I might never know for sure what really happened at the end of our relationship, but I know that we didn't make it and I cannot go through that again.'

He pressed his forehead to hers and they sat there for a moment, letting the decision settle into their bones. She felt a tear slide down her face and he wiped it away with the back of his hand.

'Then we should let them go,' he said, quietly but decisively. 'If it's not right, it's not right. You've been through enough, more than anyone should ever have to bear.' He sliced his hand through the air in a gesture of finality. 'It's finished, and that's okay.' And then he cried too.

They didn't tell anyone about their decision. Gideon called the clinic and they both signed the consent form for the embryos to be destroyed at 11 am the next day.

Aggie returned to his place the next morning. They packed Banjo into Gideon's ute and the three of them took a ride up to the outdoor Barossa Sculpture Park, high on the slope of the lookout outside of Tanunda. They laid out a picnic blanket and sat on the grass. Huge stone and marble sculptures dotted the sides of the hill on which they sat, with the Barossa Valley stretching out below them, a grid of dark and light green farms and properties stretching to the mountain range in the distance. Banjo lay between them and gnawed on a chew toy. Gideon cracked open a bottle of sweet and fruity muscat and poured them each a plastic cupful of the pale wine. Aggie took it gratefully.

They were here to say goodbye to the embryos but, of course, memories of Cora were at the foreground of her mind too.

Of the bereavement photographer joining her and Gideon in the delivery room.

Of the midwife wrapping a soft pink bunny blanket around Cora's body and gently wiping her little face.

Of Cora lying on Aggie's chest and Gideon on the bed with them, his arms encircling them both, a tiny family of three for a brief moment in time.

Of Aggie singing 'Twinkle, Twinkle Little Star' to her daughter, forever asleep in her arms.

Of the midwife telling them that they could bath and dress Cora and keep her with them for as long as they needed, and all Aggie could think was *Forever – I need my daughter forever* – because how could she ever be ready to hand her over and watch her be taken away?

Now she checked her phone for the time.

It was a quarter-past eleven.

It was done.

She took a deep, shaky breath and held her cup aloft. 'To the babies – all of them that have accompanied us on this journey.'

'To you, and your bravery,' Gideon said, tapping her cup with his.

'To us, for trying our goddamn best,' she said, her throat constricting, her eyes spilling over again.

Gideon lay his arm around her shoulders, still holding his cup to hers. 'To happier days ahead, for both of us. I know they will come.'

Aggie nodded but couldn't speak. She gulped down her wine, knowing that by the time they got back in the car, her and Gideon's journey together would be over.

39

Aggie awoke to butterflies in her belly on Friday morning. It was show day, and she wanted to be one of the first through the gates to get to the cookery pavilion and see where the ribbons had been awarded. She switched on her phone and stretched under her warm doona while she waited for it to start up. Her phone vibrated with an incoming message and she stopped breathing when she saw his name.

Harry.

She tapped the notification to find it was in fact a video that he'd taken of himself, and she stabbed at the play button to hear what he had to say. He was shirtless, delightfully so, with slightly wet hair. He was standing in his kitchen, she assumed, given the small slice of background she could see – a window frame with a sprawling air plant cascading from a bottle, a kitchen tap, a section of a draining rack with stacked plates – and she took him in greedily as his joy-filled, engaging voice reached her ears.

'Hey, Aggie, how're you going? I've just been surfing, much to the disappointment of the old guys, who probably hoped I'd have given up by now.' He grinned and the fine lines on either side of his mouth made her heart twitch. She felt herself smiling back at him. 'Anyway, the craziest thing happened to me this morning,' he went on, shaking his head in disbelief. 'I was walking along the sand and passed another surfer wearing a Waikiki Beach T-shirt, and then I passed a fruit shop on the way back to my car and there was a big box of pineapples on the footpath.' He reached off screen and pulled a pineapple into view for a moment. 'And then I walked past a cafe, and they were grinding coffee.' He paused, his eyebrows raised meaningfully. 'You see where I'm going with this?'

She laughed and shouted to the screen, 'It's "Agadoo"!'

He hummed a snippet of the song and she clutched the phone so hard in her hand it made her finger cramp.

'Anyway,' he said, his gorgeous teal eyes staring straight into hers. 'I remembered that today is show day and I wanted to wish you luck.' He scratched the back of his tousled hair. 'And tell you I was thinking of you.' His voice softened. 'That's all.' With a final smile that made her insides glow, he ended the video.

She replayed it again, and again, and again.

'Did you call him?' Holly practically screeched.

'No, I didn't know what to say.'

Her daughter made a disgusted noise and slapped her arm.

'Ow! Watch it, I'm driving,' Aggie protested.

'Oh, Aggie,' Holly scolded, as though she were the parent and Aggie were the child. 'He clearly wants to be with you.'

'I think that's a long bow to draw from a short message about a pineapple,' Aggie scoffed. 'Harry's a compassionate guy. I bet he sends lots of messages to people he cares about.'

'You're only saying that because you don't want to get hurt. And I get it, but I'm telling you, it's not over for the two of you.'

Aggie didn't respond. She was too busy imaging how things could be.

Tickets in hand, Aggie and Holly moved slowly with the crowd through the iconic Ridley Memorial Gates on Goodwood Road. The towering grey masonry structure, with its rendered facade, iron fixtures and state and national flags waving in the breeze at its peak, bore a resemblance to castle battlements.

The gates had not been open long. Carnival music played from the showgrounds beyond, and from time to time they could hear the mechanical whoosh of a ride as it plunged its screaming patrons towards earth.

'You look great, by the way,' Holly said, eyeing Aggie's outfit approvingly. 'Definitely photo-ready.'

'Thanks,' Aggie said, gazing down at her skinny jeans disappearing into brown three-quarter-length boots, and adjusting the forest-green cardigan that hung loosely around her body, layered over a white tee. She had matched it with a long leather necklace with a pendant in the shape of a bird on the end. 'The bird's not too much?'

'Nope. You're totally chic.'

One year, Aggie had rocked up to the show in her casual jeans and an ill-fitting long-sleeved tee, with scraped-back hair and a puffer jacket, and a photographer had snapped her standing next to her winning jam. The photo that had gone out in the paper and online had made Aggie grimace. That wasn't the image she wanted associated with Strawberry Sonnet.

'Not very Maggie Beer of you,' her mother had observed dryly. Since then, she'd always made an effort to be ready for anything.

At last they were through the gates and Aggie picked up the pace, scooting past a clown who was hawking magic slime and bird whistles, and sidestepping a family with little children who were already overwhelmed and in tears. She was jittery with nerves and desperate to know if she'd won, or if her mother had, or if perhaps neither of them had won. The scent of hot, greasy food wafted through the air as she and Holly covered the short distance from the entrance to the cookery pavilion. Inside, rows and rows of brightly lit glass cabinets displayed cakes, loaves, biscuits, pikelets, pies and more. Aggie and Holly wove expertly through the aisles, familiar with the fastest route to avoid the crowds and reach the preserves.

Valeria was already there, staring up at a row of strawberry jams. Aggie was prepared to feel a lot of things when she saw her mother – anger, betrayal, hopelessness, even numbness. But her step faltered when Valeria turned to stare at her, her chin quivering, nostrils flaring. She placed her hands on either side of her face, as if wanting to hide from Aggie's gaze. 'Oh, Aggie, I'm so sorry.' To Aggie's shock, she sounded quite broken.

'What is it?' Aggie asked, moving closer to stare at the jams. Light bounced off the shiny surfaces of the green, red, blue and purple ribbons. The accompanying certificates named the winners and Aggie's eyes darted along them, seeking the results.

First place, first place, first place.

Valeria Hermann.

Aggie's gut sank.

'You got second place in all of them,' Valeria said, weakly, her face screwed up.

'Oh, well, that's good,' Aggie responded, though the words were empty.

'Congratulations, Grandma,' Holly said. Her tone was earnest, though laced with chagrin. 'Sorry, Mum.' She squeezed Aggie's arm.

'No, it's fine,' Aggie said. 'Congratulations, Mum, well done.' She said the words because she should, because it was right to congratulate the victor, but all she felt was her energy draining from her body. She knew her voice was quavering, betraying her disappointment. Strawberry Sonnet – her beautiful cafe – felt fatally wounded. That two thousand dollars could have meant a month's difference or more for its reopening, in having work for Savannah, in generating more income.

'I'm sorry,' Valeria said, her hands now clasped in front of her chest, beseeching. She shook her head. 'I know it wasn't my year, I know you needed to win. I shouldn't have entered. I thought it would make me happy. It was Maggie Beer! You know how I feel about her. But now it just feels . . .'

'Hollow?' Aggie suggested. She recognised that it was a mean thing to say, but she felt deeply betrayed by her mother, both for snatching away an opportunity for Strawberry Sonnet to get amazing publicity and for driving Harry to do the only sensible thing he could have done after Valeria's intervention and return to Byron Bay. She might never see him again, and his beautiful video from this morning only made her ache for him even more.

'I don't care about the money,' Valeria said, lurching towards Aggie now and snatching her hands in her own. Her eyes pleaded for mercy. 'You can have the two thousand dollars. I never wanted that. I only wanted to be with Maggie.'

'That's . . .' Aggie didn't quite know what to say. More competitors had arrived to look at the preserves, seeking out their names, pointing, sighing with disappointment that their names weren't on the certificates. They then began to make their way along the rows, trying to find their own entries by identifying their handwriting on the labels. A microphone screeched as it was turned on and a woman welcomed everyone to the cookery pavilion and began to run through the live judging events that were to take place that morning. It was impossible for Aggie to speak over the noise.

'Please, forgive me,' Valeria begged, and she released Aggie's hands, then seemed unsure what to do with her own. She settled on holding them to her chest while she chewed her bottom lip.

Aggie didn't know what to say, torn between acknowledging her mother's distress and protecting herself from the hurt she was feeling in this moment.

A young blonde woman arrived at the preserves display, alongside a tall, lanky man with a fancy camera slung across his body. 'Are you one of the winners?' she asked, looking between Valeria and Aggie and pointing to the glass cabinet with her pen.

Aggie and Valeria glanced at each other but neither spoke.

'She is,' Holly piped up, helpfully. 'This is Valeria Hermann.'

'Oh, you're Valeria,' the young woman said. 'I'm Cassandra. We've spoken via email before – I sent you some questions a few months ago for an article about the jam competition.' She thrust out her hand. 'It's nice to meet you.'

'Yes, you too,' Valeria said, straightening her shoulders, her voice limp and uninterested.

'Could I ask you a few questions?' Cassandra tapped her notebook.

'Of course,' Valeria said, adjusting her long, multicoloured necklace, the same as one Maggie had once worn on TV as a judge for *The Great Australian Bake Off*. Aggie knew Valeria had bought it for good luck, and she now gripped the flat resin beads in her fingers.

'We'll leave you to it,' Aggie said.

'No, wait,' Valeria said, reaching for her.

'It's fine, Mum, we'll talk later. Enjoy this.' She gestured towards Cassandra and the photographer.

'Oh, excuse me, are you Agatha Hermann?' Cassandra asked.

Aggie nodded once. 'I'm so sorry, I've got to go.' She held up a hand in farewell.

Holly looped their arms together as they headed for the nearest exit. 'Come on,' she said, 'let's go and find a big pile of hot food.'

They stepped out of the pavilion and into the bright sunlight. In the fresh air, Aggie found it a little easier to breathe and make sense of her complex emotions. 'It's not that I didn't win,' Aggie said, feeling the need to explain her sinking mood.

'I know it's not.'

'It's Mum, of course, and I'll have to sort out things with her later, but mostly it's the shop.' A cool wind slipped under Aggie's cardigan and she pulled it tighter around her body. 'It all feels so . . . hopeless.'

'I know.'

'As if this is the beginning of the end.' Aggie stopped and turned to face Holly. '*Is* this the beginning of the end?'

Holly studied her for a moment. She seemed on the verge of saying something before stopping herself. 'Maybe it is.'

'It feels like it is.'

'Maybe that's a good thing?' Holly said carefully.

Aggie stared at her daughter, at the corner of her mouth that was hinting at a smile. At the wise, knowing way she held her mother's gaze. Perhaps she was right.

She'd been hellbent on resurrecting Strawberry Sonnet, believing that she should, that she needed to, that she wanted to. But maybe this was actually one of those moments in life when the right thing was not to keep going in the same direction but to pivot instead, to take a look at what was behind her, in front of her, and all around. Out of the ashes came renewal. Nature taught that again and again. When everything changed overnight, new life, new ventures, new ways of living and working were always there, waiting to be found.

'What does your inner wisdom say?' Holly encouraged her, passing Aggie's words back to her.

Two teenage girls walked past carrying mountains of multi-coloured fairy floss, their cheeks rosy from the cold air, or perhaps some thrilling ride they'd just been on, and it reminded Aggie of the years she'd taken Holly to the show, spending every last dollar they had on rides and ice cream and show bags. 'Thank you for being my daughter,' she said. 'I don't know how I would have made it this far without you.'

'That's lovely, really, but please stop avoiding the question. What does your heart want? Right now? What do you want in your deepest, craziest, wildest dreams?' She threw her hands theatrically into the air, making Aggie laugh. 'Come on, give it to me.'

'All right.' Aggie took a breath and closed her eyes, looking within herself. When she opened them, she spoke the words that felt both the truest and the scariest. 'I don't want to reopen Strawberry Sonnet – at least, not the way it was.'

'Okay,' Holly said, sounding slightly surprised but also supportive.

'And I want to see Harry.'

Holly waited a beat then pounced, plucking Aggie's phone from her handbag.

'What are you doing?' Aggie asked in alarm. Holly knew the passcode to her phone and was busily entering it. 'Give it back.'

Holly snatched it away and Aggie lunged after her, wrapping her arms around Holly from the back while Holly clutched the phone to her chest.

'No, I won't give it back. I'm texting Harry.'

'Hols, stop,' Aggie said, half furious, half laughing. Their scuffle was starting to draw some attention now, and Aggie had to let go of Holly before they caused even more of a scene.

Holly held the phone up high in her hand. 'Either you tell him, or I will.' She fixed Aggie with her sternest look and raised her eyebrows. 'Well?'

'Give it to me, you dork,' Aggie said, still laughing.

'Not until you promise.'

'Okay, I promise,' Aggie said, holding out her hand and returning Holly's stern stare with a fiercer maternal one of her own.

'I'm serious, this is not a joke. Your happiness and entire possible future rests on you telling him the truth.'

Aggie rubbed her forehead. 'Okay,' she said, exasperated now.

'You absolutely promise?'

'Yes.'

Slowly, Holly held out the phone, her wary eyes watching Aggie as though she expected her to take the phone and sprint away to the other side of the showground, which she might have done if she were twenty years younger.

'Give it to me,' Aggie said, prising it from Holly's hand.

'I'm waiting,' Holly said, standing close enough to Aggie that she'd be able to tackle her and get it back if she needed to.

Aggie growled in frustration but opened a new message to Harry. With shaking fingers, she typed, *I want to see you again.* She sent it before she could think about it a second longer. 'Happy?'

Holly gave a tiny squeal and clapped with delight. 'Yes! Now come on. Celebrations of deep-fried potato spirals and buttery popcorn await.'

40

Myrtle opened the creaky old gate that led to Dolce's front path. 'I know how you feel,' she sympathised with the iron. She was feeling awfully creaky herself today. Still, the sight of Dolce's house made her smile every time. It was so very Dolce, painted lavender on the outside, with gathered lace curtains at the windows and bushes of lavender waving in the garden beds at the edges.

'Sherry?' Dolce asked, throwing open the door.

'Why not?' It was midday, after all.

Inside, the small home was toasty warm. Dolce had given up on pot-belly stoves years ago, as had Myrtle. It was simply too difficult to manage all that wood, and the bending and squatting to stoke the fire or clean it out. Both now opted for wall-mounted gas heaters.

Myrtle eased herself into the deep brocade one-seater and Dolce returned shortly with two small sherry glasses. They clinked them together and Dolce sat down heavily at the end of the two-seater lounge.

Myrtle took a sip and let the dry finish sit in her mouth for a moment before speaking. 'I've been thinking about what you said – that I've become stuck in my ways.'

'Oh?' Dolce said, as though she was wholly unsurprised that Myrtle had come over today to say exactly this. She wore a maternal air of one waiting for a wayward child to come and confess so as to be forgiven. 'And what have you decided?'

'That you are possibly correct,' Myrtle said, unable to bring herself to agree one hundred per cent. 'I thought that my adventuring lifestyle was keeping me open-minded and flexible.'

'I'm sure it has. You are one of the most open-minded people I know.'

'That's generous, thank you.' Myrtle took another sip, feeling the heat through her chest as the sherry slid down. 'But perhaps I have enjoyed being the leader,' she said in rush, before she could change her mind.

'Oh yes?' Dolce offered a gentle smirk.

'I have come to rely on the idea that I research and organise the trips, that I come up with the plans, that I lead and you . . .'

'Follow?'

Myrtle's face burnt with embarrassment. 'Perhaps.'

Dolce nodded slowly. 'You know, when we were younger, I probably needed you to be the leader. Your life was always so much more glamorous, so carefree. I needed you to provide my escape from the house and the children and whichever husband I was with at the time. I think I gave away a lot of my power. Being with you, it gave power back to me, even if I was benefiting from your charge.'

Myrtle took in Dolce's face, mottled and lined, and her hair, thin and white now, the one who'd been by her side for decades. They weren't married, they weren't lovers, but they were as close as she imagined any couple could be. Her eyes stung with tears.

'I don't know what I'm going to do without you while you're away.' She was afraid, she realised, scared of being left behind, of being . . . lonely. She wasn't afraid of being alone; she loved her own company. But Dolce's constant chatter, banter, humour and companionship ignited her.

'I will miss you too,' Dolce said, leaning forward to take Myrtle's papery, sun-spotted, veiny hand in hers. 'Hey, remember that time I flashed my boobs at you?' she said, a twinkle in her eye.

Myrtle snuffled a laugh. 'Ha. You forgot you'd taken your bra off.' Dolce cackled and Myrtle found herself wheezing in tandem. 'I nearly choked on the cracker I was eating. Imagine if you'd had to resuscitate me. Your floppy old girls would have smothered me.'

They continued to laugh and giggle till their eyes were wet with tears. When Dolce waved a hand up in surrender, they pulled themselves together.

Dolce resumed her serious tone. 'I need to go to university for myself as much as for our peers. I need to feel worthwhile and valued and of use to the world.'

Myrtle nodded. 'I know.'

'You could come with me,' Dolce suggested, and grinned again, her eyes gleaming with mischief.

'How?'

'You could enrol in a course too, maybe fine arts or media studies.'

Myrtle tried to imagine herself as a student at university, alongside Dolce. The two of them would make a dynamic duo.

'Or maybe you could just come and live in the city with me. You could bring me burgers and cocktails while I study all night,' Dolce said, her face alight with the idea. 'Or find the best source of weed on campus. There's bound to be plenty of it and the prescription stuff is far too expensive to be sustainable. We could be the most pain-free we've been in years.'

Myrtle scoffed. 'You want me to be your drug mule?'

'Why not? You say you crave adventure. I bet there's a whole world of adventure on campus that you and I have never dreamt of. We can take trips to Nimbin over the holidays, looking for the backdoor weed dealers.'

'I'll admit, I like the sound of that,' Myrtle agreed. 'Brownies are the way to go, I believe.'

'You could follow me for once,' Dolce said, putting her shoulders back proudly. 'I never got the chance to study when I was young. Let me lead this adventure. Come on, what do you say?'

Myrtle opened her mouth to tell Dolce it was a crazy idea, that she had no intention of spending three years or more studying for a degree she'd quite likely never get to use. Instead, she discovered she had the smallest flicker of interest. It *would* be an adventure. A marathon, in fact. Endurance would be required. It would be a test of mental and physical strength. Did she have it in her? If Dolce felt she could handle it, maybe Myrtle could too.

'I'll think about it,' she said, and clinked her glass against Dolce's.

'Here's to us being young again,' Dolce toasted, and downed her sherry in one.

•

Valeria arranged the bunch of brightly coloured gerberas and sunflowers in a vase on the kitchen bench. 'You really didn't have to do this,' she muttered, guilt eating away at her insides.

'Yes, I did,' Agatha said, sliding onto a kitchen stool, her car keys jangling on the marble benchtop as she did. 'You're the show champion and you're going to be on television with your hero. You should be proud. I'm happy for you.'

Valeria sneaked a peek at her daughter but couldn't see any sign that these well wishes were forced. Her daughter's generosity only served to deepen her guilt. 'I meant what I said this morning. I want you to have the money.'

Agatha waved a hand. 'No, it's yours.'

'I mean it. The last thing I wanted was to disadvantage you. To be honest . . .' She took a deep breath. 'I don't feel I deserve it. I want to talk to Maggie, or to her people, and ask them to have you on the show instead. You're the one with the business. I should never have entered. It was wrong of me.' She stared at Agatha, imploring her to understand. 'Please forgive me,' she said, so quietly she wasn't sure if the words were audible. 'I should never have entered. For a moment there I felt as if jam was the only thing I was ever good at, the only thing left in my life after Rupert walked away and . . . you did too.'

Agatha held her gaze for several seconds, though Valeria was unable to decipher what thoughts might be passing through her mind.

'I admit that I deserve your wrath. I don't know how to be with people. I was never very good at it. But please know, I only called Gideon because I genuinely wanted to help. I wanted to be able to fix something for you.'

Agatha's chin lifted and her features softened. 'That's funny,' she said at last. 'I wanted to do the same for Holly. I was desperate to help her because'—she peered up at Valeria's face—'because I love her so much, and I'd do anything for her.'

Valeria's heart heaved with relief. 'So you understand?'

Agatha waggled her head from side to side. 'I can see some similarities, yes.'

'I'm offering you a blanket apology for everything I have ever done wrong. I know it's a lot,' Valeria said. 'You are my only child. You truly mean the world to me.'

'I forgive you, if that's what you need to hear,' Aggie said.

Valeria nodded. 'Thank you.'

Agatha rubbed her forehead for a moment, then said, 'I owe you an apology too.'

'What? Why?'

'I thought I had to fix things between us but I can see now that was wrong. Everything that's happened lately has shown me how little control I have over anything, let alone over you and me. I've realised that it's not my job to fix us because we are not broken. We're a bit bent out of shape, perhaps, but that just adds character.'

Valeria considered this. Agatha might not be broken, but she wasn't so sure about herself.

'Holly has reminded me that the most important thing we can do is to keep talking. I've done poorly at that in the past but I want to change that. My job is simply to love you, and keep talking to you. To accept us just as we are.'

Valeria placed her hand at her throat, willing the tears to stay away.

'Is that okay?'

Valeria nodded quickly and blinked until her vision cleared once more.

'Good,' Agatha said. 'Now that we agree on that, there are a few other things I wanted to talk to you about.'

Agatha's tone was serious and Valeria braced herself for bad news. 'Is it the shop? What's happened?'

'The shop is part of it, yes. There's a lot of damage, as you know, and there's no insurance.'

Valeria bit back the words about Myrtle and the insurance that leapt to her throat. It wouldn't change anything, and she didn't want to risk this new-found understanding between them. Agatha loved Myrtle as a mother figure, and Valeria had finally accepted that would never change. Perhaps one day she might even see it as a blessing for Agatha, that two women loved her so much they fought over her.

'It's going to take a lot of money and, possibly even worse, time to get it back together. To be honest, I don't think I want to reopen Strawberry Sonnet as it was.'

Valeria heard herself gasp. 'But you just took on a loan to buy the building. What are you going to do with it? Are you going to try to sell it? You'd lose money for sure.'

Agatha's chin raised a fraction. 'Selling the building is one option, and yes, it would probably be at a loss, given the state it's in, but it might come down to choosing which is worse, a loss in the short term or one in the long term.' She jerked a shoulder, as though she didn't want to dwell on this any longer. 'I have some other ideas I'm working on.'

Valeria longed to ask her about them, to help her figure it out, but she could sense that her daughter wanted to do this on her own. She'd have to be content to watch from the sidelines, for now. She could feel her lips pursing tightly together, something they always seemed to do whenever Myrtle's presence could be felt hovering nearby. The shop was an Agatha–Myrtle deal.

Agatha tapped the benchtop to signal the end of that conversation for now and her face grew serious once more. 'I also came over to tell you that Gideon and I made a decision on the embryos.' She paused, waiting for a reaction. For Valeria's part, she fixed her face into an expression of interest, rather than hope for what she wanted them to have decided. She didn't have to wait long. 'We decided to let them go,' Agatha said, gently.

'Go?' Valeria sifted through the various options in her mind, trying to figure out where the embryos had gone.

'We decided not to renew the storage,' Agatha said, 'and we let them defrost.'

Valeria felt a wrench in her chest. 'What . . .?'

'They've been destroyed,' Agatha said, as matter-of-factly as she could, though Valeria detected a quaver in her voice. 'Gideon and I are also done. There won't be any more babies. Ever.'

Valeria looked to the gerberas on her benchtop and touched a crimson petal. They felt like funeral blooms now. She had so wanted the chance to be a grandmother again, the right way this time, whatever that meant. But she'd also wanted this for Agatha. Whatever Agatha thought of her, she did want her daughter to be happy, and she knew how much she'd wanted another baby. She blinked rapidly as tears sprang to her eyes. 'Okay,' she said, nodding. 'Thanks for letting me know.' She infused her tone with kindness and understanding, and realised they weren't actually that difficult to find.

She should have been a better mother to Agatha. She should have been warmer, more lenient, more forgiving. 'There's so much I'd do differently in my life if I could have my time again,' she said, and smiled sadly at Agatha. 'You were a great mum to Holly – you still are.'

Agatha stood up from her stool and came around the bench, taking Valeria in her arms. She squeezed her tightly. 'We all do the best we can with what we've got.'

Valeria nodded, pressing her chin into Agatha's shoulder. 'That's true.'

Agatha released her and held her by the elbows instead. 'And Myrtle and I should have told you about the shop straightaway. We should have trusted you. I'm sorry.'

Valeria pressed her hand to Agatha's cheek. 'Thank you. I forgive you, if that's what you need to hear,' she said, repeating her daughter's words and making them both smile.

'Hey, should we order Thai food?'

'Okay,' Valeria said, welcoming the extension of the visit. 'I'll pay.'

Agatha laughed. 'Today, I won't argue. Thanks.'

While Valeria fished through the kitchen drawer in her hunt for the relevant menu, Agatha said, 'I saw Rupert at the jam drop-off on Friday.'

Valeria's hand stilled.

'He didn't say a lot, but he did say he was heading back to Queensland and that he probably wouldn't be back.'

'Right.' Her heart beat rapidly in her chest.

'What happened between you two?' Agatha asked, concern in her voice. 'You seemed like such a good match.'

Valeria located the menu and shut the drawer with her hip, turning to face Agatha. 'It's . . . tricky,' she said.

Agatha smiled. 'Well, luckily for you, we have plenty of time for you to tell me all about it.' She reached out her hand for the menu. 'Are you having your usual?'

'Yes.'

'Me too. Give me a minute to order then we can have a nice long chat.'

Valeria stared at her daughter – this accomplished, mature woman who was a business owner, an employer, an amazing mother, a survivor of tremendous loss, a talented cook, and someone with a huge, loving heart. She couldn't have been more proud of her. Perhaps it was time to trust her, starting by sharing her own problems, divulging her shameful judgement with the notion that Agatha just might be able to help, that she might bear some wisdom that Valeria needed to hear.

'Okay,' she said. 'Let's do that.'

'Then tomorrow, I'll drive you to your appointment to get that cast off your arm, after which we can go out to afternoon tea to celebrate. Sound good?'

Valeria looked down at the cast on her arm, relieved that she would finally be free of the weight of it. 'That sounds wonderful.'

41

Can I FaceTime you?

Aggie rushed to the mirror in the bathroom and checked her reflection. She had mascara smudges under her eyes from the tears at her mother's place, and she used a face cloth to wipe away the marks. She ran a brush through her hair and applied some tinted lip gloss to her dry lips. Then she texted Harry back – *Sure thing* – as though she was completely chill about it all, as if she hadn't been checking her phone every ten minutes all day after texting him this morning at the showgrounds.

She positioned herself on the couch where she knew the soft lighting would flatter her, then chastised herself for being so ridiculous. The guy had seen her naked, under harsh bathroom lighting, and had still seemed to fancy her quite a lot. But her excitement was making her jittery. They'd been separated a week but it felt like an age. Without the Ghan holding them together, would there even be anything left between them? Was the bubble of bliss they'd found on the train all they'd ever have?

'Stop it,' she growled to herself.

The phone lit up in her hand.

'Hi,' she said as his face appeared on the screen. He was wearing the lovely pink long-sleeved shirt she'd seen him in on the Ghan and his eyes practically leapt through the screen to meet hers.

'Hi, yourself,' he said, his smile conveying his pleasure at seeing her. You look gorgeous.'

She laughed. 'You too.'

'I've been working all day, sorry. I wanted to call when I had enough time to speak to you properly.'

'It's fine, really.'

They sat in silence for a moment, grinning at each other, then he started. 'Did you win?'

'What? Oh, the jam. No, got a few seconds.'

'Ah, that's a shame.'

'It's okay. My mum won everything.'

'Good for her. She must be thrilled about meeting Maggie.'

'She is. I just had dinner with her.'

'How'd that go?'

'It was interesting, actually. We had a good talk and I think we're finally making progress. Also, she and Rupert broke up.'

He wrinkled his nose in sympathy.

'But I'm going to meddle,' she said, proudly. 'Be like Myrtle and fix things.'

He laughed. 'I think I'd like that on a T-shirt – *Be Like Myrtle*. It could become a meme. Her interference certainly worked for us.'

'It did,' she agreed, flushing with the memories of their kisses . . . and more.

'How's your shop?'

She blew out a breath. 'Not good.'

'Is it salvageable?'

'Probably, but not quickly and definitely not cheaply.' She ran her fingers through her hair, thinking. New ideas for the shop had started brewing.

'Sorry to hear that,' he said, pulling up a leg onto the couch and resting the arm that held his phone on it. 'I wish I could help,' he said, sounding genuinely remorseful.

'You know what?' she said, lifting the tone.

'What?'

'I'm okay with it. I'm taking it as a sign that I can start something new, go in a whole different direction. It's a fresh chapter.'

'What are you thinking?'

'You mean, detail? *Pft.* Yeah, I don't actually have much of that yet.' She waved a hand and laughed. She was so happy that they could still talk so easily, slight delays or distorted vision due to reception issues aside. There was still undeniably a vibe here, which both relieved and taunted her. She wanted to be closer to him.

'Sounds like my kind of plan,' he said.

'I loved your pineapple video.' She ached to reach through the phone and touch him.

He rubbed absently at his shoulder where her gaze had been lingering just a moment before. 'I've missed you.'

She swallowed. 'I've missed you too.'

He looked down, appearing to pick at fluff on his pants or the couch where he sat. 'How did you go with Gideon?' he asked, his forehead wrinkling.

'We agreed to destroy the embryos,' she said, hating the word *destroy* but using it as a way to convince herself that it really was over.

He looked at her intensely, and she tried to guess what he was feeling or thinking but couldn't read his expression properly. 'That must have been difficult.'

She nodded. 'It was. We took the dog up to a lookout and drank wine while it happened.'

His cheek twitched in a sympathetic wince 'So, what now?'

'We get on with our lives . . . separately,' she said, emphasising the last word.

A tense silence settled between them. She wondered if he was thinking anything like what she was thinking: a hundred different questions, which all boiled down to one thing.

Could they make this work between them?

Her nerves got the better of her and she broke the silence. 'I did ask for shared parenting of the dog, Banjo, and I'll soon get to have weekend visitations with him.'

That cheered Harry up. 'I hope to meet him one day.'

'I hope you do too,' she said, and meant it with every cell in her body. 'Also, Holly has decided to stay in Australia.'

'That's great news.'

His words were positive, and they were getting on well. Yet she still felt sad. She'd fantasised that the moment she told Harry things were over with Gideon and that the embryos were out of the picture, it would lift this huge obstacle between them – that they would somehow be free to run into each other's arms. But of course, they couldn't. He was in Byron Bay. It was a lengthy trip to get from Angaston to Byron and back again, not to mention expensive.

'I wish I could see you in person,' she said. 'If I wasn't so financially wrecked at the moment I'd get on a couple of planes and a bus and come and see you right now.'

'I know. It's the same for me. I spent all my savings on the Ghan – not that I regret that for a moment,' he rushed to assure her. 'I wouldn't have found you if I hadn't.'

'What are we going to do?'

He plucked up a hopeful smile. 'I'll start saving, okay? You've got a lot of commitments down there that make it hard for you to come up here and I don't have many ties here. I'm more mobile than you. I'm going to come and see you just as soon I can.'

'Really?'

'Really.' He reached out and touched the screen with his finger and she let her fingertip touch his. It was nowhere near sufficient, but for now it was all they had.

42

Aggie called a family meeting for Tuesday night at her place, once she had the plan straight in her head. She dressed in her best jeans and a soft cashmere knit for this gathering, making sure her home was tidy and her hair and make-up done. Serious business called for a serious presentation.

'Come in, come in.' Aggie beckoned Valeria, Myrtle and Dolce inside. 'I'm so glad you could make it.'

'Wouldn't miss it,' Myrtle said. 'I love a mystery.'

Their shoes clunked down the wooden hall and into the lounge room, where Holly was already seated. She got up to greet the guests, while Aggie poured them all a glass of wine. As soon as everyone was settled, Myrtle hurried her on. 'Don't keep us in suspense. Come on, tell us why we are here.'

Aggie took a deep breath. 'Okay. Let's do this.' She opened her laptop, clicked the mouse a few times, then turned the laptop around to show them the screen. On it was a logo of a jar of jam with a crown on top. 'This is just a basic mock-up to get you thinking,' she hurried to say. 'It's really the name I'm hoping you like.'

'The Jam Queens,' read Valeria.

Inquisitive eyes moved to Aggie's face. 'I don't want to open Strawberry Sonnet again,' she began. 'While the flooding is unfortunate and difficult, I think it's more than that. I think it's a sign.' She paused for effect. 'I think now is the right time to reinvent the business.'

'So you're going to call it The Jam Queens?' Myrtle prompted.

'No, *we* are going to call it The Jam Queens.'

'I don't understand,' Valeria said.

'We are a family of jam queens,' Aggie said, getting to her feet so she could pace and talk at the same time.

'I'm not a queen,' Holly interjected.

'You're an honorary queen,' Aggie replied. 'We are a family. We are a family of strong, talented women who happen to be kick-arse jam makers.'

'Hells yeah,' Dolce said, raising her glass, apparently practising the phrases of the youth in preparation for becoming a student.

'I would like us all to be in business together,' Aggie said, and she let that notion sink in. She pointed to Holly. 'This includes you too, Hols, if you want. I know you have your own career but I want you to know that you will always have a seat at the table in this business.'

'In what business, exactly?' Valeria asked, inching forward in her seat.

'Cafes are tricky propositions,' Aggie said. 'I've loved my years running the cafe, but the reality is they are expensive to operate, have high labour costs and occupy a lot of space in the building, space that could otherwise be repurposed for higher productivity.' She pressed the mouse again and a graphic appeared, listing multiple jam opportunities. Myrtle reached for her glasses.

'It's okay – I have handouts,' Aggie said, and passed around printed pages with concept ideas for The Jam Queens.

'I want us to make jam, of course. That is our specialty, after all, and between us we have a mountain of publicity and reputation behind us. We've got generations of local contacts throughout the valley, and I'm sure we can get our jams distributed through many outlets.'

'What about me?' Holly asked. 'What would I do, other than assist?'

Aggie smiled. 'Well, you seemed to be really interested in what the instagrammers on the Ghan were doing. I thought you might lead our social media and promotions team.'

Holly pummelled her feet on the floorboards in excitement. 'Yes! Absolutely yes!'

'But the jams are just the start. You'll see on the next few pages that I have outlined ideas for a cooking school. The Barossa is famous for its food, and many visitors come here to eat and drink their way through the valley. Interest in home cooking, kitchen gardens and preserving food has gone through the roof in the past couple of years. We can teach that, and Holly, that's where you would come in again, coordinating our teaching program.'

'I can't believe this,' Holly said, her face alight with more excitement than Aggie had seen on her in years. 'This is brilliant.'

Myrtle winked at Aggie. 'Sounds like a solid investment to me,' she said.

'But that's not all. Turn the page again and you'll see a range of baked goods we can produce with our jams, too – jam drops and biscuits, jam rolls, bars, shortbread and tarts, just to start with.'

'I love the sound of that,' Dolce said. 'I'm going to be too busy next year to work in the kitchen, but I am always looking for a good investment, and you, Aggie, are exactly that.'

'Thank you, Dolce, that means a lot. Also, you never know – lots of students need a part-time job. If you feel the need to supplement your income during the holidays, you can always come and teach in the cooking school too.'

'That's true,' Dolce said, eagerly.

'I'm in,' Holly said. 'Do you think we could start a range of homewares too?'

Aggie nodded and picked up her pen to write it down. 'Great idea.'

'I like the idea of aprons,' Dolce murmured, writing something on her handout.

'There's more,' Aggie said, thrilled with how excited they all were. 'We can start at markets and sell out of a pop-up store at the front of the cafe while the building is undergoing repairs, and we can offer home delivery and postal options too. We'll turn the building into a production house, utilising all that space, and we'll be able to employ more people and offer apprenticeships too, hopefully to people like Savannah, if she is still available then. We'll continue entering the show each year but we'll do it under our trade name and then every win will build on our brand.'

'Wait, what's this on the last page?' Holly asked, racing ahead. 'Oh, that is genius,' she said, laughing.

The others rustled to find the last page of the handout. 'Gin jam?' Myrtle blurted out. 'I'm in.'

'Jam wine?' Valeria queried. 'What is that?'

'That's wine that tastes like jam,' Aggie explained. 'And the wine jam . . .'

'Is wine-infused jam,' Myrtle finished. 'I love it.'

'Really?' Aggie asked.

'Absolutely.' She nodded. 'This is good, Aggie.' Myrtle's words gave Aggie confidence. Myrtle had been her guide for many years. There was no reason she couldn't still be part of her future. She didn't have to do it all alone. In fact, it would be crazy to try to do it that way when she had this incredible trust of brains and talent all around her.

'Obviously, we'll need a winemaker to do the jam wine range,' Aggie continued. Here she hesitated for a moment. 'I was thinking about asking Gideon if he wanted to do it,' she said, raising her shoulders. 'I could subcontract him, so there are clear boundaries around it and it's all business. I just thought it would be a nice thing to do, and it would be a show of respect for our future as friends. We'll always be connected by Cora. He'll never be out of my life. Do you think that would be okay?'

'I think it would be lovely,' Valeria said, giving Aggie an encouraging nod. The others showed their enthusiasm for having Gideon on the team too.

'Does he get a crown?' Holly asked, lightening the mood.

'Sure, and we'll get one for Banjo too,' Aggie said. She turned to her left. 'Mum? What do you think?'

Valeria shifted uneasily in her seat. 'I think these are all good ideas . . .'

Aggie's gut sank. 'But?'

'But . . . I don't know why you need me. I can see why you need Gideon, and I know Myrtle is your business partner. Dolce is an amazing baker and Holly's your daughter. But you've no need of me.'

Aggie took a step towards her. 'Yes, I have. You are my mother. I want this to be a family business, and you are part of this family.' She held her arm out to the whole circle. 'Not to mention, you *are* this year's jam queen. You have decades of experience and you are still the leading jam queen in the history books. Your precision and uncompromising standards are exactly what this business needs. Besides,' Aggie said with a smile, 'you would never let me or Myrtle forget about the boring things . . . like insurance.' She winked at Myrtle to let her know there were no hard feelings.

'That is true,' Valeria said, nodding.

'But aside from all that, I want to spend time with you.' Aggie knew that her mother was ageing, and no one knew how much longer they had on earth. Holly had just learnt that in a very real, terrifying way and had decided to change her life because of it. Valeria had had a stroke and could likely have another. Her mother needed to reassess her life, and so did Aggie. The way for the two of them to move forward was in partnership. She didn't say any of these things out loud but she suspected – hoped, at the very least – that her mother understood them. Instead, she summarised by saying, 'A girl always needs her mum. I don't think it's independence we should be striving for, but *inter*dependence. We need each other, simple as that.'

Valeria's face had gone very red and she wiped at her nose with her knuckle, sniffed loudly, and straightened her shoulders. 'Okay,' she said. 'If you really want me, I'll do it.'

'Truly?'

'Truly.'

Aggie turned in a circle, the way Banjo did when he was so excited he couldn't contain himself. She looked at everyone. 'So, we're doing this?'

Everyone looked at one another and nodded.

'We're doing it,' Myrtle said, raising her glass. 'A toast: to Aggie.'

'To Aggie,' everyone repeated, thrusting their glasses high.

'No, to The Jam Queens,' Aggie said.

'To The Jam Queens,' came the reply, followed by much whooping and hugging, a few tears, excited chatter, some note-writing, a lot of financial discussion, and a jubilant group FaceTime to Gideon, who jumped at the opportunity to collaborate. Aggie realised she was so happy she might float up through the ceiling and hover on a cloud. There was just one person missing from all this, and she would find a way to fix that. She had to.

43

Valeria chopped the figs that she'd procured in bulk several months ago when they were in season and had frozen to save for jam making later on. Now with a mission to develop iconic jams for The Jam Queens business, she was relishing the chance to play with this fruit, starting with making a batch of fig and vanilla jam. She was humming along to Dion singing 'The Wanderer', swinging her hips as she slit a vanilla pod in half, inhaling the aroma, when her phone vibrated on the bench, cutting the music. She laid down her knife, wiped her hands on a tea towel and picked up the phone. It wasn't a number she recognised but its area code indicated that it was coming from Queensland.

Could it be . . . Rupert? Her heart squeezed at the notion.

'Are you going to answer that?' Agatha called from the dining table, where she was working on a business plan on her laptop.

'Y-yes.' Valeria put the phone to her ear. 'Hello?'

'Is that Valeria?' a woman's voice asked. She sounded middle-aged, at a guess, and friendly enough, possibly trying too hard to get Valeria onside from the get-go. Oh, great. A telemarketer, then.

'Yes,' Valeria responded, already counting the seconds until she could tell that this woman she wasn't interested in whatever product she was selling, and ask her to please take her number off the register.

'Hi, Valeria. My name is Lorrel.'

Valeria frowned. That name sounded familiar.

'My dad is Rupert.'

Valeria froze. An invisible hand had reached into her throat and clamped her vocal cords into silence. After a pause, Lorrel continued. 'Your daughter, Aggie, contacted me a few weeks ago.'

Valeria frowned, glancing sideways at Aggie, who wasn't looking up at all, her eyes still firmly glued to the laptop screen.

'Hello? Are you still there?'

Valeria forced herself to speak through the shock. 'Yes.'

Lorrel sighed. 'Look, I've spoken to Dad. He hadn't told me much about you. Not because he doesn't have feelings for you,' she rushed to assure her. 'Quite the opposite, actually.' Lorrel's voice softened. 'I've never seen him so smitten.'

Valeria swallowed the lump in her throat.

'But Dad seems to think that things ended between the two of you because of me.' Lorrel's voice wavered on those last two words. Her pain was obvious. Valeria might have been many things, but she was not heartless. Lorrel's raw emotion flicked a switch in Valeria's mind. She felt dreadful. Utterly awful, to her surprise. Hearing how much her judgemental nature had hurt this living, breathing person on the other end of the line made her feel deeply ashamed.

'I'm sorry, Lorrel. I didn't handle it well when he told me about your . . . changes.'

To her surprise, Lorrel chuckled. 'I assure you, you're not the only one to have that reaction.'

Again, Valeria felt pained, both for the hint of sadness in Lorrel's voice and her own stabbing guilt. 'For what it's worth, I care deeply about your father, and I was very sad to lose him.'

Now Agatha looked up, catching the drift of the conversation.

'Then fight for him,' Lorrel said, the pitch of her voice rising. 'Tell him it was a mistake and you want another chance. Dad is loyal to his kids and he wouldn't want to do anything that would hurt me.' She paused.

'He thinks he's helping, but honestly, I need him to have a life of his own, too. His constant attention, while honourable – and it makes me love him like never before – is also suffocating.'

Here Valeria found herself laughing, imagining Rupert anxiously hovering around Lorrel.

'You'd be doing me a favour by giving him someone else to occupy his time. If he goes down to visit you, you wouldn't have to see me, if it upsets you,' she said. Her tone was reasonable, but Valeria could imagine the courage it must have taken Lorrel to say that. It snapped her mind to attention.

'Lorrel, I've been a fool,' she said. Agatha had now risen to her feet and was creeping closer to the kitchen bench. Valeria gave her a small smile before continuing. 'I thought holding onto my beliefs and principles was what made me a good person, but your kindness today has made me see the error of my ways. I'm an old-fashioned woman, and I'm not saying I will completely understand all of this immediately – my generation was different – but if you could be patient with me . . .' She inhaled, filling her chest with courage of her own. 'I'm willing to change . . . to *try*, at least.'

'I should have called you a week ago,' Lorrel said, her voice thickening with emotion. 'I was so afraid you'd hang up on me.'

'I'm sorry about that, I really am.'

'Phew!' Lorrel expelled a burst of air, much relieved. 'Thank you, Valeria. I really appreciate this.'

'No, Lorrel, thank you for giving me the chance to redeem myself.'

They ended the call with the agreement that Valeria would contact Rupert, and she wasted not a moment and composed a text, explaining to him that she had spoken to Lorrel, begging him for another chance. She returned the phone to the kitchen bench and turned to see Agatha's anxious face.

'Well?' she asked. 'Was that Lorrel? What happened?'

'It was Lorrel,' Valeria said, not quite believing it. 'And I have messaged Rupert to see if he might give me another chance.'

'Oh, Mum.' Agatha wrapped her arms around her mother's shoulders. 'Well done.'

By the time they'd made a cup of tea to talk it through properly, Rupert had replied.

Can I call you tonight at 8?

Yes please.

44

Harry called first thing in the morning, just as he'd done for weeks now, every day after he'd been surfing. From the second she opened her eyes each morning, the thought of him calling made her happy. Today she wanted to hear his cheerful voice even more.

'Happy birthday, Ags.'

'Thank you,' she said, wishing more than anything that she could be there with him. It was sunny here in Angaston, though not nearly as warm as in Byron Bay, and she envied his ability to throw himself into the ocean without freezing.

Myrtle had offered to give her the money to visit him, of course, but until now Aggie had refused, but with each day that ticked by, her conviction grew shakier. She needed to see him.

She dreamt of all the ways she might be able to get to him. She fantasised about surprising him in a hot air balloon, or riding a horse along the beach early one morning as he prepared to surf. She'd even gone as far as to search online to see what it would take to make either option happen in real life. She wondered if she could become an Uber driver and pick up passengers in order to pay for her to drive all the way to him. They spoke every day, often several times a day, but it wasn't the same. She needed to wrap her arms around him, to breathe in his oceany smell, to feel her skin on his.

'I so wish I was there,' he said, as if reading her mind. 'But I've put something in the mail for you. It should be winging its way to you soon.' He sounded as excited as a child. 'Can you call me when you get it? I want to be there when you see what it is.'

'Okay,' she agreed, wondering what it could be. 'How's your day looking?'

'The usual. Bingo with my residents, music therapy, a visit from the local kindy.'

She smiled. 'Sounds fun.'

'Fun? You haven't seen how Desma Castellanos plays bingo. We have to make sure all the crockery is out of reach. She smashes plates if she wins *and* if she loses. John Tannon tries to slip money to the kindy kids so they can place bets on horseraces for him. And Marina Faulkner has a black-market cigar trade going on that would make your toes curl.'

Later that day, Aggie and Holly were making yet another batch of mandarin marmalade, and the whole house was filled with the piercing scent of citrus oil. Aggie defied anyone to feel miserable in the presence of mandarin oil; it was the smell of a joyful childhood. It also helped that she and Holly had been listening to Alicia Keyes, Holly dancing and singing 'Girl on Fire' while stirring the pot, Aggie busting out moves while washing the jars to be sterilised.

Banjo was here too, lying in a corner of the kitchen on the new bed Aggie had bought him, and thumping his tail every now and then in appreciation of their hip wiggling and grooving.

This was his second weekend here and he had settled in easily, adapting smoothly to the new routine. Gideon had seemed sad at first to hand him over but this time it was easier for them both. Having Holly here had also helped to disperse any awkwardness between them, and Gideon had embraced the opportunity of contract work for The Jam Queens, coming up with several exciting wine and jam combinations.

'What time are we supposed to be at Myrtle's, again?' Aggie asked, leaning to peer at the clock on the wall.

'Five-thirty,' Holly said, lifting the spoon to assess the marmalade. She was a little rusty at jam making but was picking it up again quickly. Everyone in The Jam Queens collective had been working on product development and they'd agreed to gather at Myrtle's today for taste-testing.

'We might as well put all that food to good use,' Myrtle had said. 'Let's use it to celebrate Aggie's birthday.'

She'd had a great day so far. Holly had made her scrambled eggs and toast for breakfast, delivering it to her in bed the way she used to when she was a child. These days, though, the toast was not burnt and the coffee was not cold, making it much more appealing, though no more appreciated. Holly had wasted no time at all in leaping into her role at The Jam Queens, and as well as looking after their social media and planning workshop content, she'd taken on the role of project manager for the renovations of the cafe, for which Aggie was most grateful. She'd been tied to that building for so many years and was enjoying being free of needing to be there every day.

Once the marmalade had been bottled, it was time to head to Myrtle's place.

'Hi, all,' Holly called, pushing open Myrtle's front door with her hip. She was carrying a box full of goodies, including lavender and blueberry jam, mint jelly, lemon butter and the mandarin marmalade they'd just made, which was still warm. 'Wow!' she exclaimed, seeing Myrtle's oak dining table covered in baked goods and jars of pink gin jam.

'That gin jam looks incredible,' Aggie said to Valeria, lifting a jar to the light to study it. 'You and Gideon did a good job on that.'

'It was fun,' Valeria said. 'I am pleased that I still get to see Gideon. He feels like family.'

'He is,' Aggie assured her.

The house smelt invitingly of lasagne, and Aggie turned towards the kitchen, where she spied two trays of exactly that bubbling away under the oven light. Her belly rumbled appreciatively.

'Happy birthday,' Myrtle said, coming to hug her.

Aggie held her close. 'Thank you.'

Dolce followed Myrtle, and Aggie received their hugs and gifts joyfully. Holly popped open a bottle of champagne to a rousing cheer, then poured everyone half a flute each and they all drank a toast to Aggie. Aggie sipped her champagne gratefully, but when the merriment calmed she was struck by a dull ache between her ribs. She recognised it at once – she was longing for Harry.

Suddenly, she couldn't stand it anymore. 'Excuse me,' she said. 'I just need to make a call.'

She placed her glass on the table and hurried outside into the fading light, tucking her scarf into her top where the wind was sneaking in beneath her clothes. She pulled out her phone and called Harry.

'Hello?' He answered on the second ring and sounded surprised by her call.

'I can't wait to see you anymore,' she blurted.

He waited a beat, perhaps wondering where this outburst had come from, then said, 'I feel the same.' She was relieved to hear the warmth in his voice. 'Where are you?' he asked.

'Outside Myrtle's house. They're throwing me a birthday party, but I had to come out and speak to you, to hear your voice. And to let you know that I've come up with a plan.'

'Oh yeah, what's that?' He sounded amused already and he hadn't even heard it yet.

'I'm coming to see you.'

He chuckled, amused and delighted, and she could picture his beautiful smile. 'When?'

'As soon as I can. In fact, I can start walking right now. I'm heading up Myrtle's street. I'm on my way. I should be there in, I don't know, a few months or so? It will be our love story, the grandest of grand gestures.'

'Your plan is to walk all the way to Byron Bay? How far is that, anyway?'

'I actually know the answer to that,' she said, passing white picket fences and tumbling roses. 'I looked it up the other day when I was missing you.'

'Did you really?' He sounded touched.

'Yep. It's one thousand, eight hundred and seventy-four kilometres,' she said.

'That sounds like a long way.'

'Close to three million steps. I worked it out.'

He was silent for several moments, then said quietly, 'You would do that for me?'

'Yes, because I love you. Do you know what I love about you?'

'What?'

'I love that you're a bad surfer.'

He burst out laughing. 'Okay, that wasn't what I was expecting.'

'I love that you're a bad surfer and you do it anyway. I love that you fall off – all the time, by the sounds of it – but you keep getting up again. When the storms hit, when the waves smash you around, you don't bail. You keep showing up, again and again and again.'

She could feel herself tearing up, thinking of Harry and his calm resilience, his steady influence, his unwavering commitment to her. He'd known. He'd known from the beginning that they were meant to be together. 'As the song goes, I would walk five hundred miles for you.' She paused, leaning against a power pole, having charged up the hill a bit faster than she'd realised and now a little out of breath, which was disappointing given she'd only just left Myrtle's house. At this rate, it would be a long walk to Byron Bay indeed.

'You would really do that for me?'

'In a heartbeat.'

'Aggie, you don't have to walk three million steps, or five hundred . . . you can actually just walk five.'

'I don't understand.'

'Turn around.'

'Huh?'

'Turn around. Look back down the hill.'

Confused, she did as she was instructed, hauling herself off the power pole and looking around. Her eyes skimmed over parked cars, a roaming cat and a man watering his vegetables until her gaze collided with Harry's.

He was standing several metres downhill, his phone still jammed to his ear. 'Hi,' he said, breaking into an enormous grin. He was wearing a white T-shirt tucked into jeans, and behind him was a cluster of people – *her* people – Myrtle, Dolce, Valeria and Holly, huddled together, grinning like kids who'd pulled off an incredible feat.

'Harry?' She thought she might have been having a stroke. 'I just spoke to you this morning. You were in Byron Bay. You'd been surfing.' She pointed uselessly at her phone.

He was shaking his head, walking towards her, not taking his eyes off her for a second. 'No, I wasn't. I was here.'

'Here . . . at Myrtle's?'

'Yep.'

He was in front of her, placing his hands on her arms. 'Happy birthday. I did say I wanted to see your face when you opened your gift.'

Suddenly, her brain thawed. This was a surprise party, and *Harry* was the surprise. Her family had done this. She threw herself into his arms, squeezing him to her as hard as she could. 'You're real.'

'I am.'

She stepped back to look at him. 'And you look bloody amazing. Even better than I remember.' Behind him, her family laughed. 'You guys are so naughty,' she scolded them, making them laugh harder. But she didn't look at them for long. Instead, she ran a finger along Harry's smoothly shaved jaw, twisted his hair between her fingers, and tentatively put her hands on his hips, gazing up at him to silently seek permission to touch him. He grinned at her, his eyes alight with passion, and covered her hands with his, sliding them up to his chest where he caught them in his own.

'You're here,' she said, still struggling to believe it.

'Here to stay,' he said, his face growing serious.

'For the weekend?'

He shook his head and lifted his hand to her chin, leaning down slowly. She raised herself up onto her toes to meet his kiss, feeling her blood thunder in her ears.

'Here to stay,' he whispered against her lips, 'for as long as you'll have me.'

For a moment she froze, sure she was going to cry. But then a wave of pure happiness washed over her and she squealed with joy. He lifted her off her feet and twirled her around, and she pressed a dozen kisses all over him before he set her back down again.

'How did this happen?' she asked, still running her hands over him, still not able to believe he was real.

'Your mum,' he said.

'Mum?'

'It was a good thing she won first place in the jam competition. She organised all this.'

Aggie looked down towards her mum, who had her hands clasped together at her chest and was watching Aggie with obvious delight on her face. Aggie put her hand on her heart and mouthed *Thank you.* Valeria nodded and waved a hand at her daughter, knowing there would be plenty of time for Aggie to thank her later.

Aggie turned back to Harry. 'Are you sure about staying for as long as I want? You might have underestimated how long that is.'

'I hope not. I sold all my stuff except my guitar, cancelled my lease, quit my job. All I've got left is what I brought with me . . . and you.'

Aggie swallowed. 'I love you.' She lifted his hand to her lips and kissed his knuckles.

'I've loved you from the moment I saw you on the bus in Darwin,' he said.

'Me too.'

'So let's do this. You and me, walking through the world together.'

She nodded. 'I'm in.'

'Can we hug you now?' Holly called excitedly.

Aggie had nearly forgotten the others were there. 'Yes,' she laughed. 'Get over here.'

The four of them surrounded Aggie and Harry, and together they formed a crying, laughing, astounded huddle of jolly people in the last light of a spring evening in Angaston, attracting curious looks from Myrtle's neighbours. Aggie was forty-six and she couldn't have been happier. There was not a single thing out of place, not a single thing that needed to be fixed.

Epilogue

Three years later

Aggie and Harry lay in bed, facing each other, the little bundle between them. Aggie couldn't take her eyes off Francesca, couldn't turn away from the perfection of her tiny snub nose, her fair, feather-soft brows, or the way her chest rose and fell with each sleepy breath. If the baby hadn't been so well swaddled, Aggie would have loved to play with every little toe and marvel at every adorable translucent toenail.

'She's like an angel,' Harry said, running the tip of his forefinger gently over the curve of her head and the fine, dark hair.

'She *is* an angel,' Aggie said, 'and also our newest jam queen.'

Holly was at her home, sleeping. The birth had been long and difficult and loaded with postpartum complications, and every time Aggie saw her she was crying. With supreme maternal tactfulness, Aggie had coaxed her into accepting an afternoon of rest while her husband, Ishaan, was on site at his building development on the north side of Adelaide. Aggie had brought Francesca back to her house and hadn't moved since, content to while away the hours just staring at her granddaughter, pouring love into her, and tearing up at Harry's face when he looked at her. The man was besotted.

'I wish we could have done this together,' she said, reaching for his hand.

He entwined his fingers with hers and smiled. 'Yeah, I know the feeling. But it's the roads not travelled, right?'

'Yeah.'

'Maybe if we'd had a baby, we wouldn't have got this, though,' he said, cooing at Francesca. 'All my residents tell me being a grandparent is way more fun than being a parent.'

Aggie grinned. 'Is it weird, being a grandpa at thirty-eight?'

'I think it makes me rather cool.'

'Certainly distinguished.'

'Definitely blessed.'

She leant carefully over Francesca to kiss him. Three years ago, she could never have imagined her life would be so full, so rich.

Harry was finishing off a degree in physiotherapy and would be starting his own practice next year, specialising in ageing clients. He and Dolce had all sorts of plans together for future aged-care endeavours.

Dolce would take another year to finish her degree, something that had disappointed her at first until she'd accepted it simply as a minor detour in order to get to her destination. She had struggled with the pace of university requirements and Myrtle had gone to stay with her in Adelaide, supporting her, committed to making her dreams come true. She said she'd lived a lifetime of doing exactly what she wanted, when she wanted to do it. It was her turn to play the supporting role. They were both guest tutors for The Jam Queens cooking school, which was sold out most weekends. Aggie had worried Myrtle might miss her travels too much, but she seemed to have settled in to her new role as a Barossa Queen, as she liked to call herself, and was a well-known identity about town.

Right now, Valeria was in north Queensland with her husband. She and Rupert had married last year and now split their time between Angaston and Rupert's place in Cairns, where they could be near Lorrel, who was working full-time as a counsellor, and was also an advocate for the LGBTIQ+ community. She'd also recently started dating someone Rupert and Valeria were quite fond of. 'It's early days,' Valeria had said last week when Aggie spoke to her. 'But we're quietly hopeful.'

Valeria, Myrtle and Dolce had settled into a rotating system of contribution to The Jam Queens business, with Aggie and Holly holding it together full-time. The business had grown to a size where Aggie could employ eight extra people at any given time. Savannah had joined for a while before deciding to study accounting, looking for a job where she could work from home as a single parent, and it had cheered Aggie to see her move on to start a new chapter of life.

Last year, Gideon had flown over to Israel to see his ageing mother and had fallen in love with a winemaker twenty years his junior. Liora had followed him back here to the valley, and they'd married and were expecting their first baby next year. Gideon had continued to make contract wines for The Jam Queens, and his range was one of their bestsellers.

Banjo still visited every second weekend but had managed to make his way off his dog bed and up onto the end of Aggie and Harry's. As neither of them could refuse his pleading eyes, they'd invested in a king-sized bed to accommodate them all.

Aggie stopped kissing Harry and lay back down, her head on the pillow. He was staring at her, still holding his hand across Francesca's bunny blanket, his face suddenly serious.

'What is it?'

'I was just thinking . . .'

'What?'

'I was just thinking that I'd like to trade in my bucket list for just one thing.'

'What's that?'

'To marry you under the blossom trees in Japan.'

She blinked, wondering if she had heard him correctly.

'Aggie, will you marry me?' There was a tiny quiver in his bottom lip and she reached up to lay her fingers there.

'Yes.'

His nervous expression immediately evaporated. 'Really?'

She laughed. 'Yes. A thousand times yes.'

They kissed for the longest time. Then she bent down to whisper into the baby's sleeping ear. 'Francesca, your nana and poppa are getting married, and you and your mummy and daddy will come with us and we will scatter cherry blossoms through the air until the whole world shimmers in pink.'

•

Francesca stretched her little arms as far as the swaddle would allow, and worked her lips as though tasting something new. The sounds of the quietly spoken words floating over her reminded her of something, something that felt warm and peaceful.

Home.

She felt the arms of her mother and grandmother, and all of the family who'd whispered her name, holding her gently. She was connected to them all.

She sighed the breath of an angel who'd finally landed safely in the world.

Acknowledgements

Somehow, I've managed to convince my sister Amanda to come on research trips and adventures with me for nearly every book I've written. She is the best travel buddy, friend and companion I could hope for. In June 2019, we went on our first trip on the Ghan and something magical happened – we found our alter egos in Myrtle and Dolce. I look forward to decades of travel yet to come, especially now that I've foreseen how we will turn out in old age.

The journey on the Ghan was an incredible experience and I highly recommend it to anyone who's been considering it. Obviously, a lot of inspiration from that trip made its way into this book, but this is fiction and I have altered and invented people, details and events. Also, I feel certain the local council of the Barossa Valley would be more reasonable than Luke is in this book.

With each book, my friend Kate Smibert helps me brainstorm and listens to me read out sections of my work in progress over and over, always with wisdom and encouragement to offer. Kate, I don't know what I'd do without you.